The One Who Loves Me

JOAN EMBOLA

THE ONE WHO LOVES ME

SOVEREIGN LOVE. BOOK TWO

JOAN EMBOLA

Manuscript edited by Michaela Bush

Blurb edited by Abigayle Claire

Cover designed and illustrated by Elle Maxwell

For more information, contact;

www.joanembola.co.uk

ALSO BY JOAN EMBOLA

Fiction

The One Who Knows Me: Sovereign Love Book 1

Devotionals

Outpourings Of A Beloved Heart: A 30 Day Poetry Devotional About God's Love

To my Heavenly Father, the One who loves me

But God showed His great love for us by sending Christ to die for us while we were still sinners.

— ROMANS 5:8

NAME PRONUNCIATION GUIDE

Amarachukwu (A-ma-ra-chu-ku)- An Igbo name for girls which means "God's grace."

Ifeoma (E-for-ma)- An Igbo name for girls which means "a good, beautiful, fine thing."

Ikezie- (E-kay-zi-ay)- An Igbo name which means "to apportion (something) fairly or to create (someone) perfectly."

Oluwagbemiga (Oh-lu-wa-gbe-mi-ga)- A Yoruba name which means "the Lord lifts me up."

Aderinto (Ah-day-rin-tor)- A Yoruba name which means "the crown walks well."

Kemi (Keh-mi)- A Yoruba name usually short for Oluwakemi. It means "God pampers me."

Chidinma (Chi-din-ma)- An Igbo name which means "God is beautiful"

Seun (Shay-oon)- Short for Oluwaseun, a Yoruba name which means "Thank God."

Njideka (Nn-ji-day-ka)- An igbo name for girls which means "I have the best" or "the one I'm with/ holding is greater."

Nnamdi (Nn-nam-di)- An Igbo name for boys which means "my Father is alive" or "My God is alive."

Adekunle (Ah-day-kun-lay)- A Yoruba name which means "the king/crown/royalty filled the house."

Oluwafunmilayo (Oh-lu-wa-fu-mi-la-yor)- A Yoruba name which means "the Lord gave me an endorsement of joy."

Adebayo (Ah-day-ba-yor)- A Yoruba name which means "the crown meets joy" or "he came in a joyful time."

Etomi (Eh-toh-mi)- A Nigerian name of the Esan tribe (Edo state) which means "my own" or "my right."

Kojo (Koh-joh)- A Ghanaian name for a boy born on Monday. The name has an appellation and association to the power/ nature of peace.

Boluwatife (Boh-lu-wa-ti-feh)- A Yoruba name which means "as God pleases/wishes/wills."

Taiwo (Tai-woh)- A Yoruba name which means "the first twin to taste the world."

Kehinde (Keh-hin-day)- A Yoruba name which means "the second-born of twins."

Ekene (E-keh-neh)- An Igbo name which means "praise."

Feyi (Fay-yee)- Shortened form of the name Feyikemi which means "care for me."

Ayobola (A-yor-bor-la)- A Yoruba name which means "happiness and wealth."

Makinde (Ma-kin-day)- A Yoruba name which means "a warrior has arrived" or "to come with strength."

Nkechi (Nn-kay-chi)- It's shortened form of the Igbo name Nkechinyere which means "what God has given" or "gift of God."

Chinonye (Chi-non-yeh)- An Igbo name which means "God is with me."

Chibuzor (Chi-bu-zor)- An Igbo name which means "God first" or "God leads."

Dayo (Da-yor)- A shortened form for the Yoruba name Adedayo which means "the king/crown/royalty became joy."

1

AMARA

I'm going to let you in on a little secret: my best friend is getting engaged today and she has no idea. Let me say that again so you understand why I can't keep calm. Teeyana, my girl, my person, is about to be taken off the market and she's sitting next to me right now without the slightest clue.

It was only yesterday when Teeyana and I were fighting off bullies in high school and today she's getting engaged? Sometimes life feels so surreal that I live each day waiting for someone to pinch me back into reality. But no, this is not a dream. My girl is really getting engaged. *Eeeek!!!!*

Myself and Jayden, Teeyana's soon-to-be-fiancé, brainstormed and planned the whole engagement behind her back. I'm so proud of myself for keeping it a secret for three *whole* months, but boy, I'm tired of hiding things from Teeyana. She thinks this is just her college graduation party, but Jayden is going to pop the question any minute now.

Teeyana's family and closest friends are sitting on tables of five spread out across Teeyana's grandpa's backyard here in Atlanta. With a temperature of eighty degrees Fahrenheit, this sunny April afternoon will be perfect for taking photos—engagement photos, of course.

Clusters of purple balloons are floating on the side of each table with the words, 'Congratulations Teeyana' plastered on them. Teeyana's cake is a four tier mound of sugary goodness, much taller than the one I ordered for her eighteenth birthday, and a porcelain figurine of a smiling Teeyana is sitting on the top tier on a bed of purple roses.

Everyone is chattering and sipping on their drinks as soft music plays in the background. Nobody knows what's coming except me, Jayden, and Teeyana's parents. I ain't gonna lie though, I can't sit still. Excitement is welling up in my chest, butterflies are flying around in my belly, I'm pretty sure my heart is pounding at two hundred beats per minute, and—

Wait a minute. Am I sweating? Oh, come on, girl. I pick up a folded sheet of paper and fan under my arms. I'm wearing an off-shoulder turquoise dress, so I don't want to get a sweat patch in the engagement photos. That would *absolutely* not look cute.

"Amara, are you okay?" Teeyana's voice draws me back to earth, and I turn to look at her as she tucks a curly strand of her weave behind her ear. She's wearing a white one-shoulder dress which I helped her pick out and she looks *lit* in it.

"Girl, I'm fine." I nod and lean back in my seat. Jayden, who is sitting on the other side of Teeyana, gives me a knowing look and I smile. He nods and turns his head away before fixing the collars of his grey suit and white shirt.

I ball my hands into tight fists and place them under my thighs to curb my fidgets. *Girl, you've come so far. You can't ruin the surprise now.* I rock back and forth in my chair as Teeyana's dad, Trevor Sparks, clinks his glass to get everyone's attention. *Yaas, it's about to go down.*

"Thank you, everyone, for coming to celebrate with my beautiful daughter, Teeyana." Mr. Sparks begins. "I can't believe

I now have a daughter who is a college graduate. I'm getting old." The crowd bursts into laughter before Mr. Sparks continues. "It's time for the speeches, and I'd like to invite my father-in-law to do the honors and start us off." Mr. Sparks gestures to the table across from ours.

Everyone cheers and claps as Grandpa Thompson pushes himself up from his seat. He balances on his walking stick as Teeyana's mom, Jamila Sparks, helps her dad walk across the lawn to the central open space where Mr. Sparks is waiting.

Grandpa Thompson clears his throat, and the crowd quiets down. He adjusts his glasses and turns to focus on Teeyana. "I remember the day my daughter, Jamila, phoned myself and my wife to tell us we had become grandparents. It was the best news I received that day, and holding her in my arms for the first time was nothing short of a miracle.

"Teeyana, it has been a joyful experience watching you grow over the past twenty-two years and I believe that this is only the beginning of greater things for you. I want you to always remember that I love you so much, and..." his voice breaks and his bottom lip quivers. "I know your grandma would have been so proud of you too." He takes off his glasses and wipes the tears away from his eyes.

Teeyana walks up to Grandpa Thompson and wraps him up in a hug as everyone cheers again. After Grandpa Thompson returns to his seat, Mr. and Mrs. Sparks give their speeches, followed by Teeyana's aunt—Bella, who is Mrs. Sparks' younger sister. She's here with her husband and their two-year-old daughter, Letoya.

Letoya and Teeyana's younger brother, Danny, come in to give their own speeches. Danny is wearing a white shirt over black trousers with a black bow tie, while Letoya is wearing a burgundy puffy dress. They both hold on to the microphone and lean in. "Congratulations, Teeyana. We love you." They say in unison before giving Teeyana a hug and running back to their seats.

Mr. Sparks clears his throat again and says, "And now, for the moment we've all been waiting for, Teeyana, honey, we have a surprise for you."

I suppress a squeal and lean forward as Jayden rises from his seat and walks up to Teeyana. After loosening the blue tie around his neck, he takes her hand and clears his throat. "Tee, I love you." Jayden starts. "I'm so proud of everything God has helped you accomplish, and I love the woman you are becoming. I want to keep walking this purpose God has given us with you by my side, and I want to keep loving you every single day for the rest of my life. So..." Jayden reaches into his pocket and takes out a small black box before going down on one knee.

Teeyana's hands fly up to her chest as Jayden reveals the silver amethyst three-stone ring. The center stone is a deep purple color and judging from the tears running down Teeyana's cheeks now, I can tell the ring is still as beautiful as it was the day I helped Jayden pick it out.

"Teeyana Joy Sparks," Jayden continues. "Will you make me the happiest man on earth by agreeing to be my wife?"

"Yes!!!" Teeyana bends over and plants many kisses on his lips. Everyone in the crowd stands, clapping and cheering as Jayden slides the ring on Teeyana's finger. She turns around to look at me, and since I'm now unable to contain my excitement, I run up to her and wrap my arms around her in a tight hug.

"Bet you never thought your graduation party was going to be your engagement party, huh?" I wink at her and she pushes me with her hips.

"Amara, I can't believe you and Jay hid this away from me." She sniffles and dabs the tears sliding down her cheeks with a handkerchief.

I lean back and cross my arms against my chest. "The same

way you hid the fact that you were transitioning to your natural hair?" I laugh as the soft music starts playing again in the background.

"*Ugh*, you're so annoying." Teeyana pokes my shoulder.

"Ouch, I'm kidding, girl." I say before turning to Jayden. "Well done, lover boy. We did it." I give him a high five.

"Thanks, Amara. I would've never done this without your help." Jayden smiles before wrapping his arm around Teeyana's waist. "Amara was the brain behind this operation. I just followed her lead."

"Well, thank you. Thank you. I'll be here all week." I flip my braids to the side and pat my shoulders and we all laugh. "Seriously though, I'd do anything for this girl right here. She's my person." I grin at the couple, but only Teeyana gives me a knowing smile as I use the famous phrase from *Grey's Anatomy* —the medical drama I've been trying to convince her to watch for years.

An auburn-haired, green-eyed girl, wearing a black jumpsuit touches Teeyana's shoulder from behind, and she turns around. "Heather." Teeyana gasps and pulls the girl in for a hug. "I'm so glad you could make it."

Heather Osborne was Teeyana's dorm room mate in freshman year at St. John's university. Heather gave Teeyana a hard time at first, and they hated each other for most of the year. But since Teeyana shared the gospel with her, Heather has changed and I heard she even started going to anger management therapy. I ain't gonna lie, the girl still scares me a little.

"Hey, Amara. Hey, Jayden." Heather flashes a smile at me.

"Hi, Heather." I send her a small wave. "I'm so glad you're here with us." She flew in all the way from New York to be here. That was very nice of her.

"Thank you. Please excuse me while I get a drink. It's very warm today." Heather says before fanning herself.

"Alright, I'll catch up with you soon." Teeyana says and Heather turns around and walks toward the house.

"Oh, before I forget," I say when Teeyana turns to face me again. "I have one last surprise for you."

Teeyana frowns. "Seriously? What else have you been hiding?" Her gaze switches from me to Jayden.

I bite my bottom lip to build the suspense, but in the end, it all comes pouring out of me. "I passed my N-Clex exam yesterday. I'm officially a registered nurse."

"Oh my gosh, you did?" Teeyana squeals and pulls me in for another hug. "Congratulations. Jesus did it." She says, holding me at arm's length.

"*Yaas,* Jesus." I wave one arm above my head before doing a short praise break dance.

We laugh and Jayden gives me a side hug. "Congrats, Amara. I never doubted you. You always work so hard."

"Thanks, Jayden."

"What about jobs?" Teeyana asks. "Have you applied for any yet?"

I nod. "Yeah, I started applying last month. I'm praying I get a NICU one though."

"Oh, I'm sure you will." Teeyana squeezes my hand.

Jayden leans in and scratches his head. "Errrm... what's a NICU again?"

"Neonatal intensive care unit, babe." Teeyana responds on my behalf.

"Yeah, it's where they look after all the cute newborn babies who are premature or critically ill."

"I see." Jayden says before wrapping his arm around Teeyana and pulling her close.

"Okay, enough about me. You two go on and celebrate your engagement." I push them toward the crowd of people behind them. "I'll just wait here until it's time to take photos."

As I take a step back to study the newly engaged couple, I can't help but notice their broad smiles, the way Jayden holds Teeyana protectively, and the way Teeyana leans in to him—confirming that she feels safe in his arms.

It's hard to believe that I watched this romance blossom from friends to lovers. I was right there encouraging Teeyana when they faced their challenges, and I was also there to celebrate their victories with them. It's like watching two of my children grow into adults.

I swallow to fight off the surprising tears of joy leaking out of my eyes, but my desperate attempt is fruitless as the tears trickle down my cheeks, ruining the makeup I worked so hard to perfect this morning.

"Darn it, girl." I sniffle and take a tissue out of my bag before dabbing under my eyelids. And then it hits me—a feeling I've never felt before.

I want to share a love like this with a special someone too. I want someone to love me like Jayden loves Teeyana. There's only one problem though; there's no man, and there never has been one.

All I've had since high school are countless crushes; boys who never seem to notice me and who I've always admired from afar. But things are changing now. I'm no longer in high school or college. Soon, Mom will start asking whether there's a man in my life—especially when she finds out Teeyana is engaged.

"Don't worry, Adamma." Mom said to me last Christmas as she used her famous nickname for me. *"Your husband will come as soon as you finish nursing school and get a good job."* I don't know why she ever got the impression I was worried. I certainly never told her that.

Mom owns her own catering business, so she has catered to the weddings of the daughters of her friends in the Boston Igbo women's society. She used to drag me to a lot of these weddings, but she never mentioned marriage until last Christmas. Even then, I never thought twice about marriage until today —until now.

I love Teeyana and I'm happy she has found her dream man, but honestly, this engagement has only made me realize how behind I am in life. Ever since Teeyana and Jayden started dating in freshman year of college, they've worked perfectly well together; going on mission trips and helping others.

I wish I had the confidence to do things like that without letting all the mean words of my high school bullies hold me back. For something that happened years ago, I thought I would have gotten over it by now. But the truth is, those words still greet me every morning, they still make me question every decision I make, and they still have the same dreadful impact they had on me the first time they were screamed in my face in high school. *Amara, you'll never be good enough.*

2

RAYMOND

I f my father was still alive, I would've wished for him to see this day—the day I ask the woman I love to marry me. He would've been proud of the man I've become—a man who has vowed to commit to loving Kate the same way he loved my mother.

I'm sure the old man's heart would've been bursting with joy, and the evidence for this would've been the broad smile on his face, the sparkle in his eyes, and the infectious laughter radiating from his lips.

But even though I'm happy knowing that my father would shake my hand if he was here, I still wonder every day what he would've thought of Kate. Some days, I convince myself he would've welcomed her with open arms, the same way he welcomed every visitor who came to our family home in Nigeria. But other days, I can't help but imagine him having his reservations too, like my mother does.

I thought after three failed relationships, my mother would be happy that I found a woman to marry. I thought after a year of dating Kate, my mother would've finally warmed up to her and started seeing her as her daughter-in-law. But I thought wrong.

"*Oko mi, are you sure about this?*" my mother asked when I called her last week.

"*Mommy, of course I'm sure. I love Kate.*" I replied.

"*Hmm, of course you love her.*" She clicked her tongue. "*You have a soft heart like your father, but please think about this some more, my son. I just feel in my spirit that this girl is not the right one for you.*" She said, and my shoulders slumped.

I always imagined that when I told my mother I wanted to propose to the woman I love, she would scream for joy and start singing her favorite Yoruba songs. I imagined her dancing around the living room, the same way the mothers did in all the Nollywood movies I watched while growing up. I never imagined that she'd be trying to talk me out of it.

"Come on, Raymond. Focus." I mumble to myself as I stare at my reflection in the restaurant bathroom mirror, my bald haircut bringing out all the features of my face. Today is my twenty-ninth birthday and if Kate...I mean *when* Kate says yes to my proposal, I would be the one breaking into Yoruba songs and dancing around the restaurant. I've prayed about this, and I'm choosing to dismiss my mother's fears. I know Kate loves me and tonight will be the proof of that.

Opening the faucet, I wash my hands before drying them with a paper towel. Then I slap my cheek lightly, as if doing so will slap the doubts out of my head. "Everything will go as planned." I say as I adjust the sleeves of my navy blue blazer.

Slipping my hands into my pocket, my fingers brush against the velvet box which has the ring, and I let out a sigh of relief. I've done that at least fifteen times since I got here half an hour ago. Out of all the things that could go wrong tonight, losing the ring would be the worst. *At least I'd like to think so.*

My phone vibrates in my pocket and when I take it out, a

new message pops up on the screen. It's from Joe—my best friend. Last night, I practiced my mini-speech with him and he shared experiences on how not to propose, like not putting the ring in any kind of food, so the girl doesn't end up choking on it. Joe would know that because that's exactly what happened when he proposed to his wife Josephine.

Joe: Papa G. The hour has finally come. I hope you remember everything we talked about. I pray it goes well and I'll call you tonight.

Smiling, I swipe up and type a quick response.

Me: Thanks, my guy. I appreciate all your help. You will definitely get the gist tonight.

Slipping my phone back into my pocket, I rest both arms on the sink in front of me and close my eyes. Turkish music from the speakers above fills my ears, but I block it out of my thoughts and say a quiet prayer. "Lord, I commit this night into Your hands. Please take control."

Opening my eyes again, I fix the collar of my white shirt before stepping out of the bathroom and walking back to the table I reserved for Kate and I. The music is louder in the main sitting area and the lights dimmer to fit the mood. The clanking of plates and silverware is mixed with the chatter of guests scattered around the room.

A waiter walks past me carrying a colorful tray of meat, rice, and salads, the sight of the food making my mouth water. *This Turkish food better be as delicious as it looks.* I settle behind the table and roll one sleeve up to check my watch again; it's 7:05 pm. Kate and I planned to meet at seven pm, but she takes this "African timing" thing way too seriously and she's always late for events. I'm hoping she'll at least make my birthday dinner an exception and not turn up an hour late.

Twenty-five minutes pass, and I'm still sitting at the table alone, tapping the silverware, endlessly checking my watch, and glancing at the door so often that my neck starts cramps up. "Where is she?" I groan and let my head fall into my hands. She promised she won't be *too* late this time, and I gave her the benefit of the doubt. *So much for getting my hopes up.*

"Excuse me, sir?"

I snap my head up and the same waiter who walked past me earlier is standing in front of me.

"Are you ready to order?" He smiles as he pulls out his note-book and pen. This is the third time he's asked me since I got here. I don't blame him, though. Between my purposeless flipping through the menu pages, and endless bathroom breaks, I'm sure the guy is thinking I'm acting suspicious.

"Erm..." I clear my throat and straighten my back, preparing to give him the same awkward reply. "Sorry, I...uh...I'm still waiting for my girlfriend who should be here any—"

"Did someone say *girlfriend*?" A familiar voice from behind me takes me off guard and I turn around.

"And she's here." I push my chair back and stand up. "My girlfriend is here, so please come back after ten minutes and I'm sure we'll be ready to order then," I say to the waiter, who nods at us and walks away.

"Hey, babe." I lean in and kiss her cheek, inhaling her fruity scent.

"Hey, sugar. Did you miss me?" She winks at me before walking to the opposite side of the table. Her elegant black dress compliments her brown skin and her heels are so high, she looks like she's much taller than her five foot two self. Her black weave is laying bone straight on her head, and her edges are neatly laid—as always.

"Of course I missed you," I say, before pulling out a chair for her. "I think the waiter was getting impatient." I shoot a glance at the young man, who is now talking to a customer at the far end of the restaurant.

"Aww, I'm sorry about that." Kate places her bag on the floor as I take my seat opposite her. "My makeup just wasn't cooperating with me today. I couldn't get it right but in the end, I had to give up and get here."

I lean across the table and hold her hand. "Well, if it means anything, I think your makeup looks amazing."

Kate smiles and leans forward to hold my other hand. "Thanks, baby."

"Okay, let's have a look at this menu before the waiter comes back."

Kate giggles as we go through our menu and place our orders. She opts for the vegetarian special while I go for the roasted lamb meatballs cooked in tomato sauce with potatoes and served with Turkish bread. There's no way I'll come to a restaurant and eat only vegetables.

When the waiter walks away to the back of the restaurant, my heart rate, which has been cooperating so far, picks up speed again. Soon, I'll ask Kate to be my wife and it'll all be real.

"So." I smile at her. "How was work today?" I proceed with the first step of my plan, like Joe and I discussed. If I want Kate to be surprised, I have to play it calm and ask her normal questions. If not, she might join the waiter and start suspecting my actions.

"Oh, please." Kate's smile disappears, and she rolls her eyes. "Babe, we spend so much time in that hospital, and you know patients can be so annoying, so don't even get me started."

Hmm. That wasn't the answer I was expecting, but I can always scrap the plan. Kate and I met at the hospital a year ago. I had just completed my residency and started my fellowship program at the pediatric cardiology unit. She was the assigned physical therapist for one of the children I was caring for. We immediately got along and it was really hard not to fall in love with her. She's beautiful, she's a Christian, and she's very hard-working. I mean, what more could I possibly ask for?

"That's okay." I clear my throat. "We don't have to talk about work. How are you?"

Her smile returns. "I'm doing good, but I'm sure I'll feel so much better when I find out what you've planned." She squeezes my hands.

Oh? Planned? Does she know I'm going to propose to her?

"Last year's road trip for my birthday was amazing, so I can't wait to hear what you planned for us this year. Ooh, let me guess, are we going to Paris like we always said we would? Oooh, we could treat ourselves to a very relaxing spa day, you know. You and I both need to get rid of all the tension from work. And speaking of a spa, you won't believe what happened when Laura and I went to the spa the other day..."

As I half-listen to Kate ramble on about her experience at the spa, I run through my mini-speech in my head again. Joe and I had a plan, but if I don't propose soon, Kate might keep guessing until she ruins the surprise for herself.

"...so I had to ask him to call his manager because he was being rude to Laura and I." Kate slaps her palm lightly on the table, and brings my attention back to her. "In the end, the manager compensated us and told us our next visit to the spa will be free." She squeals.

"Wow, honey, that's great." I swallow to wet my dry mouth, silently praying she doesn't ask me to recount details of what she just said. "Well done for sticking up for yourself like that."

"Thanks, baby." She says before turning her head to the back of the restaurant. "Oh, where is the food? I'm starving."

Okay, this is it. I have nothing to lose. I can't wait any longer. "Kate?"

"Yes, babe?" She turns to face me again and sips on a glass of water.

I clear my throat, but as I open my mouth, the speech I've been practicing for weeks vanishes from my head. In its place are a jumble of words, which are no good, so I give up and freestyle. "You know I love you, right?"

Her smile broadens. "Of course, I know. You tell me every day, and I love you too." She brushes my cheek with her soft palms.

"The past year with you has been amazing and I'm so grateful God brought you into my life. I never want this to end. I want to continue growing and learning with you." I pause and exhale. "So, that's why..." I reach into my jacket pocket and pull out the black velvet box, before going down on one knee. Excited gasps and whispers swoosh across the whole restaurant as everyone's eyes focus on us.

"Erm, babe, what are you doing?" Kate says through gritted teeth as she forces a smile and looks around the restaurant.

"Kate, will you marry me?" I open the box to show her the rose gold diamond ring I picked out for her. But instead of the tears of joy, gasps and excited shrieks I see in movies and on social media, Kate's smile slowly fades until it's nonexistent.

"Erm...Raymond, I..." She rubs the back of her neck and avoids my gaze. "Are you sure about this?"

Raymond? She never calls me Raymond. The doubts creep up my chest again and my mother's words echo in my head, asking me the same question. Am I sure about this?

"Yes, honey, I am." I take out the ring and place the velvet box on the table, but when I try to reach for Kate's hand, she moves it away and my heart drops. "Kate, I want you to be my wife. Don't you...don't you want that too?"

"Oh, boy." Kate's dark gaze finally settles on me and she drops her hand. Fidgeting with the hem of her sleeve, she lowers her head and her voice. "Raymond, I...I can't marry you."

The words hit me like a bat, and for a second, it feels like all the air has been zapped out of my lungs.

"We're different people." She continues. "We want different things, you know?"

What? Where is all this coming from? "We're not supposed to want the same things. They say opposites attract, right? What matters is that we love each other, right?"

Kate remains silent, her forehead creasing, and her eyes clearly relaying a message I'm refusing to accept.

"Right?" I ask again, frustration erupting in my chest.

Her silence this time is loud and clear. I swallow the lump in my throat as my knee aches from the weight of the embarrassment pinning me down. *How can she do this to me?*

Kate takes the ring and places it safely in the hollow of my palm before folding my hand closed. "I'm sorry." She stands and picks up her bag, but before I can utter another word, she runs out of the restaurant without once looking at me again.

This wasn't how tonight was supposed to go. This is nothing like I thought it would be, and if my father was still alive, I certainly would not have wished for him to see or hear of this day.

3

RAYMOND

Y ou know how people say good guys never win? Well, I
didn't believe it until I came to America and saw it
with my own *koro-koro* eyes.

Seriously, what can a guy do to find true love in this country?
You give, and give, and keep giving, but the only thing you get
back is girls who use and dump you in the toilet like tissue
paper. They stand there and watch while you beg them to stay,
and they look you in the eye and flush you away, forgetting
about you like you never existed.

Chai, I have suffered. My mother warned me. She told me
there was something not right about Kate. She also warned me
about Angel, Kemi, and even Chidinma, but I didn't listen.
Instead, I ignored all the signs and ran after beauty. Now look
where it has landed me. *Who beauty epp, sef?*

I think it's time for me to stop jumping into relationships
blind-folded and seek God's face first. These heartbreaks need to
stop. Am I the only one who knows how to love someone?

My phone vibrates on my bedside table, forcing the
depressing thoughts out of my head. But when I lean in, Joe's
name flashes on my screen and I sigh.

I push my duvet cover away and swing my legs over the side of my bed, the soles of my feet warming as they hit the grey carpeted floor. I pick up the call and put it on speakerphone. "Hello?"

"*Aye,* Papa G. G for general. General in America. The one and only heart doctor. *How body, nau*?" Joe hails from the other end of the line. "Guy, I called you, like, a hundred times last night. How did it go?"

"Ah, *bros, body no fine o.* This life is too hard. I'm tired."

"Wait, what happened? Is Kate okay?" Joe asks and I make a kissing sound by sucking air between my teeth from behind pursed lips, a gesture which signifies how frustrated I am.

"Which Kate? You mean the same Kate who broke up with me last night?"

"*Issa lie*." Joe yells out. "She did what? Why?"

"*O boi,* I don't even know how to explain."

"Wait, wait, wait. Raymond, please get up and get ready. I'll be at your house in half an hour. You need to explain this to me before we go to church." Joe says.

"Guy, *abeg*. It's not a big deal. I'd rather forget about all this."

"Ah, forget *wetin*? Come and see this guy *o*. Your girlfriend rejected your proposal *and* dumped you on your birthday, and you're saying it's not a big deal?" Joe clicks his tongue and I can imagine him shaking his head too. "I'll drop Josephine and Chelsea off at church first, and then I'll be at your place in half an hour. Be ready *o*. I will not let you come and kill yourself in America because of a woman. You must talk about it by fire by force." With that, the phone line cuts off, and I throw myself on my bed again, spreading my arms wide.

I fix my gaze on the ticking clock hanging on the wall across from me. It's shaped like the Nigerian map and my mother gave it to me the day I left Nigeria. She said she wanted me to have things around my house which will remind me of home. I've been thinking about home since last night, and I wonder if I would've ever struggled this much to find a wife if I had stayed in Nigeria.

Boluwatife—the last of my younger cousins got married last month, and all my close friends from secondary school have families of their own now. My plan has always been to get married before turning thirty, but here I am at twenty-nine—with nothing to show for it apart from four failed relationships. *Lord, what am I doing wrong?*

I push myself up from the bed before walking to my window and sliding my grey curtains apart with both hands. The rays of sunlight hit my face and I exhale before taking in the view in front of me. The skyscrapers stand high above the smaller buildings and the straight roads stretch for miles on end, with clusters of bright green trees dotted all around. I smile at the blue sky and white clouds floating above me—clear indications that summer is around the corner.

Nostalgia pinches at my chest as memories of the bustling streets of Abuja swirl in my head. While growing up, motorcyclists, yellow taxis, and hawkers were the norm on the dusty streets for me. I remember how my mouth watered when the hawkers passed by with their sweet *agege* bread and *akara* as I walked to school every morning.

Here in America, all I crave in the morning is coffee—a terrible habit I picked up in medical school. *Sigh.* It's not my fault, though. How else was I supposed to survive all those all-nighters, and eight a.m. classes which helped me pass finals? My mother will definitely start preaching to me if she ever finds out about my caffeine addiction.

"Oko mi, don't you know this thing is not good for you?" She would say. *"How can you be a doctor for the heart and you are still doing this to yourself? Do you not know that coffee makes your heart beat faster?"* Her voice echoes in my head, and I smile to myself.

Oh, how I miss the old woman—my confidante, my prayer warrior, my dearest mother.

I know she'll start looking for a woman for me to marry when I tell her about Kate dumping me—that's if she hasn't already started. She has always had my back, but I won't let anyone choose my wife for me. Besides, Joe found his wife here in America, so I know there are women who love God here. I just need to trust God to lead me this time.

I sigh and walk away from the window, strolling past my T.V. before opening my bedroom door and entering my living room. Placing both hands on my hips, I shake my head as I look around my apartment, disappointed at the mess I made last night.

The bouquet of roses I bought for Kate is still lying on the floor next to the garbage can. I left the bouquet in my car and I was going to give it to her after dinner, but now I have no use for it. My well-polished shoes are on opposite ends of the room, and my blazer is barely hanging from the edge of my long grey couch.

I toss the bouquet into the garbage can and pick up my shoes before grabbing my blazer from the couch. As I swing the blazer over my shoulder, the black velvet box escapes from its pocket, falling to the floor.

Picking up the box, I open it to take one last look at the ring. "At this rate, I don't think I'll be needing you for a very long time, buddy." I close the box and put it back in my blazer pocket before heading to the kitchen. Turning on the kettle, I open the cupboard and pull out a mug from it which reads "Pediatric Cardiologist." It was one of the many gifts Uncle Seun gave me when I graduated from medical school.

Being my mother's younger brother, Uncle Seun shares the same caring attitude and common concern for me. He swore to my mother when he left Nigeria twenty-four years ago that he would repay her for helping him raise the money to come to America. Like he had promised, when he got his green card and married Aunty Lara, he invited me to come live with him and helped me through medical school.

Uncle Seun has been like a father to me, and it has made it easier to deal with the loss of my own father. But I can't lie, I still wish my father was here. I wish I could talk to him again, and soak in all the wise advice he would be giving me right now. But that wish is far from becoming the truth. I've had to accept that since I was fifteen years old. God has been faithful to me and honestly, I can't complain. Well, except for one thing; to start my own family. First, I need to find the right woman.

After drinking my coffee, I jump into the shower and let the lukewarm water trickle down my skin. The events of last night replay in my head again, but the anger in my heart slowly dissipates with the steam.

Lord, please show me where I've gone wrong the last four times. I need a change, Lord. Please show me the way.

Joe couldn't come to my place before church because he got caught up with "daddy duties," so we agreed to catch up after church. When service ended an hour ago, Joe let his wife, Josephine, take their three-year-old daughter, Chelsea, home and then he dragged me to the *Holy Granules* coffee shop across from church so he could fire questions at me.

"Wait, so you're telling me Kate said she doesn't think you two are compatible?" Joe rubs his moustache before leaning on the round table separating the two of us. Cars swoosh past us and the sound of chattering fills the air as old school gospel music radiates from the speakers inside the coffee shop.

"Yes *o*, my brother. That's what she said." I lean back and cross my arms against my chest. "She ran out of the restaurant and left me on one knee. I couldn't move from that spot and people in the restaurant started walking up to me and patting my shoulder. Guy, I've never been so embarrassed in my life."

"So it took her a whole year to realize you guys weren't compatible? *Wawu.*" Joe shakes his head. "Honestly, I feel for you, man. Didn't Chidinma say you weren't the right fit for her? And then Kemi said she fell out of love with you? And then Angel said there was no spark anymore?"

"Exactly. Thank God you were there when all this happened." I kiss my teeth before pulling my coffee mug closer. "I don't get it, man. Why do girls always lie to me? It's painful."

Joe shakes his head. "*Ashia* o, my brother. These girls have just been dribbling you around like a football."

I laugh at his football reference, my mind jumping back to my childhood days when I played street football with the other children in our compound in Abuja. "Dr. Taku, I believe they call it *soccer* in America and not football." I fake an American accent but can't contain my laughter when Joe rolls his eyes.

"*Abeg, who soccer epp*? It's football. They should come and fight me," Joe says, and I snort. It's so funny that Joe, who is Cameroonian, has slowly adopted all my Nigerian slang over the years and he now speaks Nigerian pidgin English too.

"You make a good point, though." I nod. "These girls have turned into Okocha, and Drogba, and, erm... what's that famous footballer from your country again?" I click my fingers at Joe.

"Samuel Eto'o."

"*Ehe*, Mr. Eto'o Fils from Cameroon. These girls have had a dribbling conference and they are now taking turns on me. Can you imagine the nonsense?"

Joe places his cup of tea down. "Maybe it's your shiny head that's confusing them."

"*Abi, o.* Can't you even see it's as smooth as a football?" I lean forward and touch my bald head as we both burst into laughter. Unlike Joe, who has his nicely trimmed, full head of hair and moustache, I started shaving my head and beard at the start of our first year of residency. I liked the bald haircut, so I've kept the look since then.

I can't even explain how much I treasure Joe's friendship. He's the only one who can turn a dire situation like mine into light-hearted humor. We met in medical school when I moved from Phoenix, Arizona to Atlanta, and we have endured sleepless nights together, passed finals together, survived residency training, and now Joe is doing his fellowship in surgery and I in pediatric cardiology at the same hospital.

Four years ago, Joe married his college sweetheart—Josephine, leaving me alone in the single men's club. But it's alright, *sha*. We still support each other through thick and thin. Joe has definitely been a great helper to me since I came into this country. In fact, I don't know how I would've survived those first few years of medical school if he had not shared some survival tips with me.

"Honestly, my guy, you need a break." Joe bites into his chocolate croissant. "You can't keep finding shallow girls like this. I wouldn't be surprised if they were only interested in you because you're a doctor." He muffles as he chews.

I bring my fork up to my mouth, putting a piece of pancake into it before sipping on my coffee. "Yes, I agree. That's why I've been praying to God not to let me get into another relationship until He gives me the go ahead."

"Hmm." Joe nods and wipes the corners of his mouth with a napkin as an ambulance passes by, blowing its sirens. "I'm joining in that prayer as well. In fact, we're all starting prayer and fasting tomorrow because I'm angered in my spirit."

I snort and place my cup down. "See your head. Are you the one who is looking for a wife? Please, I don't want to get into trouble with your madam *o*." I put my hands up and Joe laughs.

"On a more serious note, your time will come, my brother," Joe says. "You're a good guy, a gentleman, and you're patient to a fault. But above all, you love God. He sees the desires of your heart and He will lead you to the right woman. I'm sure of it. Please forget about all these *yeye* girls. Just make sure you're not following your feelings, but God's voice."

I blink back in surprise as Joe mentions the same thing I was pondering on earlier this morning. It's obvious I've always put my feelings first, and that has yielded no fruit. It's time for a change, and change is now.

"You're right, bro. I'm taking the next few months to seek God's face about this matter, and who knows, with the way God works, I might still find my wife before I turn thirty."

Joe raises his eyebrows. "Guy, that means you have exactly a year to find a woman and get to know her well enough to marry her."

I shrug. "God works wonders, does He not?"

"Yes, He does," Joe says, although he doesn't look convinced. He and Josephine courted for three years before they got married, so of course he'll be skeptical. "Please, don't rush this thing *o*. Marriage is not a rushing matter. Let's pray for God to work out His plan at His own time."

"Of course." I respond. "In fact, fasting and prayer starts tonight. *Oya,* finish this food, make we *dey go* before your madam queries me for keeping you out too long." We laugh and dig into the rest of our brunch.

4

AMARA

Man, *my feet are killing me.* I take off my heeled boots and place them carefully on the shoe stand next to my front door. After hanging my jacket in the hallway, I limp to the kitchen area of my studio apartment, my stomach growling with every movement.

Opening my freezer, I take out the ice cream tub, which has the jollof rice Mom cooked for me, and I place the tub on the kitchen counter to defrost.

Walking over to my couch at the center of the living room, I stretch myself out on it and drop my bag on my round center table. I let out a heavy sigh before crossing my legs and massaging my feet, the sweaty smell hitting my nose. *Eww, girl, you need a shower.* But first, I need to rest.

Leaning forward, I pick up the remote and press the power button to turn the TV on. *"Grey's Anatomy"* is playing and a flutter of excitement rushes through me. But I don't need this right now. I need to rest.

I can't believe three months ago, I had just passed my N-CLEX and now, after countless applications and interviews, I got my dream job at a NICU. After church today, I went to the hospital to sort out some paperwork and boy, nobody prepared me for all these never-ending pre-employment checks. *Adulting is a scam.*

I turn down the volume of the TV until I can barely hear anything, and then I lean back on the couch and shut my eyelids, praying the pounding headache goes away when I wake up. But before I can drift off, vibrating sounds fill the room and snap me out of my slumber.

"Go away." I wave a dismissive hand toward my bag on the table and cover my head with a throw pillow until the vibration stops. When I slip back into my daze, the vibrations start again. "Leave me alone, I need to rest." But my desperate pleas fall on deaf ears as the vibration continues.

I let out a loud groan and stretch my hand into my bag. When I take out my phone, the reason for the vibration becomes apparent—Mom is calling me on FaceTime. I frown and sit up. "When did she learn how to use FaceTime?"

Using my front view camera, I fix my African print head wrap, check my eyebrows are still on fleek, and also check I haven't smeared my mascara. *I'm not ready for Mom's critiques this evening.*

I move the phone back so my whole head fits into the camera frame and then I swipe right. "Mom, I'm trying to rest." I say when her face, or rather her body, appears on my screen.

She has placed her phone too close and too low and I can only see the bottom half of her face and her torso, as well as a small portion of Dad's arm on the right-hand side of the screen.

"Hey, Dad," I say, and he pokes his head into the frame and smiles at me. Everyone says I look like Dad, but I think I only got his warm smile and broad nose. Everything else, from the voluminous hair, to the big brown eyes, thick lips, wide hips, and short stature, I give Mom credit for.

"Hmm, *Adamma*, so you can only greet your father but you cannot greet me?" Mom asks, her voice already filled with irritation.

I sigh. *And here we go again.*

"Is it wrong for me to check on my daughter?" She continues, raising her voice this time.

Well, I won't have a problem if you don't call me when I'm trying to rest. "Sorry, Mom. I've been out all day today, so I'm tired, that's all." I rub my neck and balance my phone against a throw pillow so my parents can have a better view of me.

"*Eyaa.* Sorry, my dear. You have done well," Dad says, and I relax in my seat.

"Thanks, Dad. Mom, the phone is too close to your body." I snort. "Move it back so I can see Dad's face."

"*Ah, ah.* He's right here, *nau.*" Mom moves the phone around, dropping it a few times on the table before finally turning it landscape so they both fit in the frame. Mom is wearing a black t-shirt with a blue African print wrapper tied around her chest, and a satin scarf around her head.

Dad is wearing the white tank top he usually wears to lounge around in the living room when watching TV and he is chewing on fresh kola nuts. He always brings back kola nuts when they visit Nigeria. You would think it is the tastiest thing in the world when you watch him chew it, but my curious ten-year-old self tasted it when he offered it to me and I quickly learnt that was a mistake.

"So are you all set for tomorrow?" Dad asks before throwing another kola nut into his mouth. Goosebumps ravage my arm and I shiver as the bitter taste of the nuts comes to my mind.

"Yes, Dad. Tomorrow, I'll officially be working as a nurse." A grin stretches across my face.

"*Chai, Chukwu, daalu o.* Thank you, God." Mom raises her hands over her head and starts praying. "You carried my only child through this very hard nursing school in this America. You helped her finish this very hard degree in just four years. You made her pass all her exams and now you have brought her here, Lord. Please protect her."

"Amen." Dad and I reply in unison.

"Favor her as she starts her new job tomorrow. She will be the head and not the tail."

"Amen."

"She will walk left and right and never see shame."

"Amen."

"Lord, find her a good man to marry."

"Ame—" My eyes flick open and I stare at Mom as she continues praying her heart out. I sit up and shake my head, bracing myself for the talk that's about to come after her prayer.

"Amen." We shout out in unison as Mom tightens her wrapper around her chest, making me note she's wearing one of Dad's t-shirts. *Aww, aren't they cute?*

"Thank you, Mom. I'm exhausted. Let me rest, so I can get up and eat."

"No, wait, *Adamma*. We have something to discuss with you." Mom clears her throat.

She elbows Dad, who also leans forward and starts talking. "So, you know you are our only child and we want the best for you."

Uh oh. What are they going to lecture me about this time?

"We just wanted you to be careful when you go out there because not everyone means well for you. Be careful, especially with these boys who will start flocking around you now like pigeons."

I knew it. I knew this conversation was coming. But why is Dad doing the talking? Usually Mom's the one who talks about this kind of stuff.

"We know boys will soon start coming because you have

reached that season in your life. My only advice for you is that you should be careful. When they come, please choose wisely." Dad pulls on his ear. "Have you heard me?"

"Yes, *nna m*." I nod.

"And to add to that," Mom jumps in.

I would have been surprised if she had nothing to say.

"Remember that God is faithful. He has done it for your friend, Teeyana, and you have seen it with your own eyes. He can do it for you too. I didn't get married at an old age so my daughter too will not get married at an old age."

I roll my eyes. "Mom, I'm only twenty-two."

Mom twists her mouth and turns her palms so they are facing upward. "And so what? Are you not old enough to marry and be somebody's mother? At your age, did I not already have you?"

"*Biko, obi m*, times have changed." Dad steps in, holding Mom's hand to calm her down. "*Adamma*, please don't mind your mother."

Dad has always been my hero and the one who calms Mom's anxious rants. I can't thank him enough for bailing me out of this one.

"The purpose of this conversation is not to pressure you." Dad continues. "Don't let anyone ever pressure you to marry them. In fact, if you feel pressured, then that is a bad sign. No matter what you do, put God first and get His say on the matter. We will be here to guide you, but we will never choose for you."

Mom shakes her head. "But that doesn't mean you can bring any kind of person to this house o. I have already said a Yoruba boy is out of the question, but even with that, if I don't like him, then the marriage is not happening."

Seriously, why do African parents always have beef with at least one other tribe?

"*Obi m,* leave Yoruba boys out of this, *nau.*" Dad turns to Mom. "We are not quarrelling with our daughter, are we?"

"Of course not. I'm just speaking my mind." Mom leans back and crosses her arms. "She needs to know she has standards."

"Yes, we are saying the same thing." Dad nods and then turns back to me. "*Adamma,* God has been kind to your friend, Teeyana, and we thank God for her life, but never compare your journey to her own. I know you might start feeling somehow when the wedding preparations begin, but don't worry about it. God will direct you to your own man. Do you hear me?"

I nod. "Yes, *nna m*, I hear you. Thank you so much."

My parents have not had a serious conversation with me like this since they decided to move to the US. I was born in Nigeria and we all moved to Brooklyn when I was five years old. A young Nnamdi and Njideka were so excited to leave Nigeria and come to the US to start a new life with me.

Unfortunately, life in New York city wasn't as easy as they thought it would be. In the end, we had to move to Boston and Dad found a new job at the post office. Fortunately for us, Mom knows how to market herself, so she has had no problems finding new customers for her catering business.

I never liked the idea of changing high schools, making new friends, and adjusting to a new state, city, and neighborhood. The first few months in Boston were horrible; I was bullied, teased, and mocked by the meanest girl back then, called Olivia Hastings.

But when I look back at it today, I don't regret that my parents moved to Boston, and I don't regret going to Coverton High. My life would be a lot easier now if I wasn't bullied, but it was through those struggles that God helped me form the unbreakable bond I have with Teeyana. Those struggles helped me find a sister, and they drew me closer to God. The last few years have been tough; but I ain't gonna lie, nothing prepared me for this current season of my life.

I've always envied the love my parents share. Mom might be a handful to deal with sometimes, but Dad's calm demeanor complements her well. They have stayed together and loved each other for twenty-five years, and I think that's enough reason for me to listen to them.

5

AMARA

"Girl, have you been moisturizing it regularly?" I raise my eyebrows at Teeyana on my iPad screen.

"Yeah, I've been following the regime you suggested to the T, and the products you recommended are working." Teeyana runs her hands through her soft curly strands and brings her head close to the camera.

I pull my chair from underneath my dressing table and plop down on it before leaning close to the screen. "Yeah, your hair looks a lot healthier." I smile at her. It seems like it was only yesterday when I helped Teeyana do the "big chop." Now three years down the line, her stretched natural hair is comfortably grazing her shoulders and I can't be more proud.

"The next thing you need to do is get rid of those single strand knots. You need to buy hair shears and trim the dead ends." I take off my satin bonnet and reveal my flat twists.

"Yes, Ma'am." Teeyana nods. "Sorry if I'm bothering you with so many hair questions tonight. I just want to make sure my hair looks healthy for the wedding."

"*Pfft*, girl, you're not bothering me. I'm your hair coach, remember? I won't sit back and watch your hair go all musty, dusty, and crusty."

Teeyana laughs. "Yes, Ma'am. I'm so happy we get to plan this wedding together. Thank you for all you do for me."

"Aww, girl please, don't thank me. As your maid of honor, it is my duty to make sure your wedding is lit. In sixteen months, you'll finally become Mrs. Williams."

"Yes, I'm so excited." Teeyana squeals and then settles down as I unravel my flat twists. "So...how are you feeling about starting work tomorrow?" Her tone turns serious.

I drop my hands by my side and turn my head to get a better view of my curls in the mirror. "Honestly, girl, I'm nervous. Not because I'm going to be responsible for patients, but I'm scared about the workload. I hope I'll be able to balance it all and still have a social life."

"Aww, you'll be great. You are Amarachukwu Ifeoma Ikezie and you're going to grace that hospital with your black girl magic, crowned with *Frolita* and all."

I snort at her attempt to pronounce my full name. "You're getting better with the pronunciation, you know."

"Really?" Teeyana flips her hair. "I've been practicing." She pats herself on the shoulder. "But seriously though, you'll be a wonderful NICU nurse and I'm always here for you to socialize with."

I kiss my teeth. "That's what you think now, but wait until you get married. You won't have time for me, and all you'll be thinking about is Jayden."

Teeyana rears her head up and feigns a gasp, a hand flying to her chest. "Amara, I will always have time for you. You're my person."

"Girl, of course I'm your person, but we're both growing up, times are changing, and we need to embrace these new seasons in our lives."

"Yeah." Teeyana nods. "You make a good point." She brings her head up to look at me. "What season do you think you're in now?"

I unravel the last flat twist and turn to look at Teeyana. "Yesterday, my parents had a serious conversation with me about marriage and choosing the right person and *blah, blah, blah.*"

"Oh, really?" Teeyana's face brightens.

"Yeah. You should have heard my mom go on and on about the type of guy I should marry."

Teeyana laughs. "I'm not surprised. You're her only child and she wants the best for you."

"Of course." I smile. "But you know what this means?" I lean forward, wiggling my eyebrows.

She frowns, "What?"

I separate my curls with my fingers. "It means I need to be on the lookout for my dream man. Now that I'm venturing into the working world, I could meet him any day now, you know?"

"Yes, you could." Teeyana leans forward and rests her chin on her cupped arms. "Pray about it, trust God, and He will direct you to him at the right time."

"Yup, the right time."

Teeyana pushes herself up and yawns. "I would have liked to stay up for longer, but my body aches from checking out all the wedding venues today. I can't believe it's been three months since I got engaged and the only thing I've done is pick a venue."

"Girl, please, don't be too hard on yourself. Picking a venue is a great accomplishment and I'm proud of you."

"Aww, thank you. I wish you all the best tomorrow. You'll do great, I'm sure."

"Thanks, girl. I'll call you on my lunch break. Love you."

"Love you, too."

I end the call and pick up a black head wrap from my dressing table before using it to tie my hair up so it forms a "pineapple" shape. Then I put my satin bonnet back on and head to the bathroom.

In half an hour, I've washed my face, brushed my teeth, and now, I'm sitting up in bed with my back against the headboard and my bedside lamp on. I pick up my laptop and browse through the hospital website, clicking through all the tabs of the NICU section. My eyes land on the research page and without hesitation, I scan through the words to read more about their research program. It would be perfect for my resume and it'll give me good experience for when I want to become a NICU nurse practitioner.

But you'll never be good enough, Amara.

The dark voice returns and zaps away my excitement. For once, I want to stand up against it. I want to fight back and prove that it's wrong, but I can't do it. What if it's true? I'm sure there are many people applying for the program who have a lot of experience. I'll never be able to get in.

"There's no point." I mutter to myself and close my laptop, before looking for something else to distract me. My thoughts drift back to the conversation I had with my parents earlier today.

Be careful with these boys who will start flocking around you like pigeons.

Well, the funny thing is, I wish I was in a position where boys flocked around me—even if they were pigeons. I wish someone at least gave me some attention. It's better than having endless crushes who never reciprocate the affections. *Sigh.*

I didn't get married at an old age so my daughter too will not get married at an old age.

If I didn't know Mom well, I would have easily brushed those words off, but something tells me there was more to those words than she let on. I've watched way too many Nollywood movies to understand how girls—especially from African backgrounds—

35

get pressured to get married. I don't want to be that girl who is approaching thirty and still has no man. If that happens, Mom's critiques will be solely focused on my love life then. I just know it.

I sigh and rub my temples, trying to soothe a headache coming on. Opening the top drawer of my bedside table, I take out a packet of pain relief tablets and pop out two pills before dragging myself out of bed and walking to the kitchen.

When I get to the kitchen, I put my container of jollof rice back into the freezer and take out a glass from the cupboard. I fill the glass with water from the faucet and throw the pills in my mouth before pushing them down with the water.

An idea pops into my head as I place the glass back on the kitchen counter. I said I would be on the lookout for my dream man, which means I need to know what I'm looking for.

"You remember things better when you write them down." Teeyana once told me after giving me a lecture about forgetting things a lot. "So if I write a list of things I want in my dream man, then I'll remember them when I find him."

She has standards, and she cannot just marry any kind of person.

Mom's words echo in my mind again, and that's the one thing we agree on. "Heck yeah, I have standards." I squeal and run back to my room. Taking a random notebook out of my bag, I flip to an empty page and start writing a bold heading across the top of the page, followed by my list.

THINGS I WANT IN MY DREAM MAN.

1. *He must be tall, dark and handsome, with a beard that connects, muscles that pop out of his shirt, and a smile that melts my heart*
2. *I must be attracted to him*

3. *He must be financially upright*
4. *He must be romantic*
5. *He must know how to make me laugh*
6. *He must care about me*
7. *He must care about my family, my friends, and my culture*
8. *He must love God*

I close my eyes and let the picture of my dream man form in my mind. I can already see his face, his broad smile, his tall frame towering over me, his muscly arms wrapped around my waist, and his thick beard tickling my face when he kisses me.

I smile and turn around to lie on my back, before spreading my arms on my bed. My hand flies to my chest and I let out a long sigh as the ticktock of the clock fills my ears. When I turn my head to check the time, the shock that overwhelms me sets my heart racing.

Come on, girl. You need to be up at six a.m. I groan and close the notebook before sliding it in my bag again. I better not be late for my first day of work and I better find this dream man *real* quick.

6

RAYMOND

Every time I drive past the American flag waving in the hospital parking lot, my mind's eye imagines the Nigerian flag instead; with its green, white, green colors flying high. Then my mind always drifts off to the Nigerian anthem, reminding me about how I used to sing it every week when I was in primary school.

The teachers used to make us stand in rows and columns in front of the principal's office, hands by our sides, backs straight, and eyes focused on the Nigerian flag. Our burgundy trousers were neatly ironed, our ivory shirts were tucked in, and our big black belts kept our trousers from falling off our thin waists.

Every morning, my mother ironed out all the creases on my uniform, combed my hair, and cut my nails short, so the head teacher wouldn't send me back home for looking untidy. It's for this reason that I'll never let her see the state of my messy house; if not, she might just start pulling my ears again.

The tune of the Nigerian anthem rings in my head as I close my car door and turn around to face the hospital building. It stands tall with dark brown walls in some areas and beige in others. I place my hand over my eyes to block out the sun reflecting from the glass windows as I step on the sidewalk. On the second floor, I can make out the silhouettes of some NICU nurses with their characteristic floral scrubs.

I hum the first verse of the Nigerian anthem and round the corner toward the hospital entrance. Monday mornings at the hospital are sure to wake up any sleeping person. I've missed the banging of wheelchairs, the sirens of the ambulances, the rhythmic thumping of the helicopters flying above our heads, and the sea of colorful scrubs moving in and out of the hospital building.

Taking a week off from work was a turning point for me. It helped me focus on God and retrained my mind to know what my priorities are. I'm not the same man who was almost driven into depression because of a break-up three months ago. Kate is long gone now and just as God continues to bless me in my career, He will bless me with the right woman.

I walk past a white and blue sign which has two arrows— one pointing toward the ER, and the other toward the main hospital entrance. Whenever Joe is working, I like taking the shortcut through the ER to say hello to him before he clerks his surgical patients. But today, I'm going through the main entrance because Joe is off and I need to buy coffee.

A petite woman walks past me, wearing a hijab and a long black dress. She is holding on firmly to the arm of a boy who looks about four years old. The boy's head has a bandaid on it, and his other arm is in a sling, but he is still jumping around and singing. I love how resilient children are, how even with wounds and plasters, they can still carry on with life as if nothing has happened.

Lord, please help me be more like these children.

As I approach the hospital entrance, the automatic doors swing open and I walk past the familiar hospital logo sign which has greeted me almost every day for the past three years. If someone had told me when I left Nigeria twelve years ago that I would be working in Atlanta's biggest children's hospital, then I would have branded them the biggest liar of the century. But like the Nigerian singer Dunsin Onyekan sang, "*what God cannot do does not exist.*"

As I step into the building, the familiar atmosphere of chattering welcomes me. "Good morning." I nod and smile at a porter pushing a man in a wheelchair.

"Good morning, doctor." The porter returns my smile and walks past me.

"Good morning." A voice says from beside me, and my gaze drops to a little girl holding her father's hand.

"Oh, look who we have here." I kneel in front of her. "Where are you going today?"

She grins at me and shows me her missing front teeth. "Home." She points at the exit before looking at her father again.

"Wow. You must be so excited," I say, and she nods.

"Well, you've been a very brave girl and I'm sure your dad here will give you a special treat, right?" I stand up and smile at her father.

The man who looks about my age sends me a weak smile. Judging from the stress lines across his forehead and dark circles underneath his eyes, I know he has made some sacrifices to make sure his little girl is well.

"Everyone is so kind in this hospital," the man says. "Thank you for all your help. Now say goodbye, Tracy." He pats his daughter's head.

"Good bye, doctor." The little girl waves as her father leads her toward the exit.

I have no idea who that little girl is, but experiences like this always put things into perspective for me. Everything we do in this world matters, even if we don't always see the impact we're making.

I make my way to the coffee shop, and when I get to the front of the line, the guy behind the counter sends a knowing smile my way. He's a very hardworking seventeen-year-old boy who recently started working here. "Would you like your *usual* today, doctor?" He says before running his hand through his blonde hair.

"Yes, John, thank you." I respond before passing him the dollar bills I always carry around in my wallet. He punches in numbers into the register and then turns around to make my coffee. Five minutes later, John is back with my order.

"Thank you, John." I take my cup of black coffee with no sugar and place another ten-dollar bill in his hand.

"But you already paid for the coffee." The boy frowns.

I lower my voice and lean forward. "I know. How about you add that to your college trust fund, huh?" I sip my coffee and squeeze his shoulder before walking away.

"Thank you, Doctor Aderinto." John's voice comes from behind me.

"Have a good day, John, and God bless you." I say, but don't stick around long enough to hear his response. If I don't move quickly, I'll be late and I hate being the last one turning up to the morning meeting.

When I get to the elevator, there's a crowd of patients waiting to get in, so I turn around and head for the stairs. I open the door with my free hand and as I'm about to enter, I collide with a girl who is rushing out in the opposite direction.

My cup of coffee loosens from my grip, the hot liquid splashing on my scrubs and hers. She shrieks and steps back as the cup hits the floor, her handbag dropping too.

"Oh, no. I am so sorry. Are you okay?" I massage the spot on my chest where the hot liquid has seeped through my scrubs and touched my skin.

"Oh gosh, I'm gonna be late now." She takes out a folded piece of tissue from her bag and dabs on the coffee stain. But her efforts would have been fruitful if I had put milk in the coffee. "*Ugh!!!*" she groans at the brown patch on her floral scrubs.

"I'm so sorry..." My gaze flies to the name tag on her chest. **Amarachukwu Ikezie, RN, NICU.** *Oh, she's Nigerian.* "Amara, are you okay?" I ask, but she sends me a death glare and doesn't say a word. What did I do? Oh, no. Should I not have shortened her name? *Oh come on, Raymond, you should know better.*

I pick up the empty cup from the floor and throw it in the trash can nearby. I move closer, but the girl steps back and raises both hands up. "Please, just stay away." Her voice is snappy, and anger is burning through her big brown eyes.

"I said I'm sorry. I didn't see you coming, I promise. Are you okay? Did it burn you?"

"I'm fine." She tries to wipe the stain a few more times before kissing her teeth and picking up her bag. She fixes her big, curly puff and walks away.

"I can...I can show you where to find new scrubs."

"I said I'm fine." She says with a finality in her voice and doesn't look back.

"I'm...sorry?" I try one last time, but she doesn't respond. I watch her walk down the hallway toward the stairs leading to the NICU department.

Wow, what a way to start a new week. Letting out a heavy sigh, I drop my head and stare at the puddle of coffee on the smooth tiled floor. A million possibilities of things that could go wrong today creep into my head, but I shake them off. I head back to the cafeteria to get some paper towels and another cup of coffee. Today, I'm choosing to stay positive. Nothing will spoil my day. Absolutely nothing.

7

RAYMOND

"I heard Kate dumped him when he proposed to her three months ago." Jevon's voice is hushed, but still loud enough to make me stop in my tracks outside the pediatric cardiology staff room. I lean close to the door, which is slightly ajar, and press my ear against it.

"That girl has no shame. How could she do that to the poor doctor on his birthday? He's a nice man." Another woman, who sounds like Carla, speaks. Then Michelle shares her own thoughts, followed by Hasna and Maureen.

Are these nurses seriously having a conference about my love life?

"He has been so unlucky in love," Maureen says.

My eyebrows crease into a frown. *Excuse me? I don't believe in luck.*

"I think the problem is that he loves too hard," Michelle says.

"Or better still, he loves all the wrong girls," Hasna adds. "Everyone knew Kate was a gold-digger except him."

I have to agree with them. Kate was a big spender of my money.

"I think his problem is that he is too nice. Girls don't like nice guys. We want bad boys." Maureen says and I roll my eyes.

That makes no sense. Why would anyone want a bad boy?

The nurses talk over each other before Jevon shushes them. "Girls, instead of talking about what has already happened, we can start thinking about how we can help him."

I raise my eyebrows. *Help me? So I'm now a charity case?*

"Yes, we need to find him a nice girl," Maureen agrees.

"Too bad we're all married or in relationships. Anyone have any younger friends or sisters?" Carla asks.

"Ooh, me." Hasna speaks again. "I have a lot of cousins who are single and ready to mingle."

Alright, I've heard enough. This must stop now.

I push the door open and the nurses' heads snap in my direction, bringing an abrupt end to their conversation. "Ladies, I believe it's almost nine a.m. and we have patients waiting to be seen?"

"Yes, doctor." They reply in unison before stepping out of the room in a single file with Carla in the lead, followed by Michelle, Hasna, Maureen, and Jevon.

"Jevon." I call out and she turns around to face me. Calling older people by their first names still rubs me the wrong way. I never got away with that as a child without an elder smacking my head.

"A word, please." I bop my head toward the office.

Jevon closes the door behind her and inches closer. When she gets to me, she pushes her glasses close to her face and fixes the fringes of her new wig.

I fold my arms and look her in the eye, trying to figure out if I have the strength to be angry this morning. I promised myself and God to always choose joy, no matter what happens.

"Jevon, since when did my business become the talk of the town?" I ask, making sure to watch my tone. Jevon is the senior nurse practitioner in the pediatric cardiology department, but she's also my friend, and she has treated me like her own son since the first day I started my fellowship here.

Jevon turns her gaze to the green sofas in the office, then to the open louvers through which a fresh breeze is blowing into the room. Then she uses the pen in her hand to scratch her scalp—something I've seen my mother do many times, especially after getting new hair installed.

"I'm sorry, Raymond. I was the one who brought up the discussion with the girls. They had nothing to do with it." She straightens her back. "It won't happen again, I promise. We're just worried about you."

I close my eyes and sigh. "It's okay," I say. "How did you even find out?"

Jevon shrugs. "Well, you stopped talking about her so I suspected something was wrong and I did my research."

I blink back in surprise. "The whole hospital knows about my break-up?"

"What do you expect when the world's favorite doctor is dating a physiotherapist in the same hospital, huh? Oh, by the way, I heard Kate quit her job last week. I bet she was feeling guilty after what she did."

"Well." I shrug and lean against the desk behind me. "She's an adult and she can choose to do whatever she wants. I can only wish her well."

Jevon sighs and steps closer. "How are you feeling, though?" Worry lines crease her forehead.

"I'm okay. I just...thought she was the one I was going to marry, you know?" I turn to meet her dark gaze.

"Hon, it's her loss for rejecting you." Jevon places her arm around my shoulder. "You're an amazing man and if a woman can't see all you have to offer, then really, it's her loss."

Her words send a comforting and calming reassurance through me. "Thank you, Jevon." I squeeze her hand. "Kate is in the past now, and I've moved on. That's why I'll appreciate it if you tell the other nurses to stop talking about me and her."

"Got it." Jevon nods. "I'll do that. Just make sure you stop worrying about it because God is in control." She points upward and winks at me before heading out the door, leaving me to the sound of honking cars and screaming children coming from the parking lot outside.

Of course He is. God is always in control.

I smile and push myself from the desk, shaking away my worrying thoughts. Slipping my white coat on, I throw my stethoscope around my neck and head out of the room.

In the hallway, I walk past the playroom and sensitivity rooms for the children before stopping in front of the "Wall Of Fame." My eye catches a new addition to the photos, which is one of me listening to a baby's heart with my stethoscope. The photo was taken on the first day of my fellowship over a year ago. *Wow, how time flies.*

"Dr. Aderinto, are you ready?" Carla peeks at me from behind a computer monitor at the nurse's station.

"Yes, Carla, who's our first patient?" I turn around and approach her.

She springs to her feet and grabs a patient's file from the desk, tucking a strand of her curly black hair behind her ear as she approaches me. "We have eight-year-old David Young who is—"

"Ah yes, little Dave. I know him very well." I take the file from Carla's hands. "Please bring the monitor with you so we can check his vitals."

"Yes, doctor." Carla nods and walks off to the stack of vital sign monitors plugged into the wall. I flip through the first page of the file to remind myself of the procedure carried out on Dave before heading to his room.

I knock on the door and peek into the room which has drawings of Spiderman, Superman, and Captain America all over its blue walls. Dave, who is sitting on the edge of the bed, turns his head to look at me.

"Dr. Aderinto." Dave's face lights up and the excitement in his voice fills the room. He pushes himself up and turns to his parents, who are sitting in the chairs next to his bed. "I told you he was going to come." The boy says before running to me and wrapping his arms around my torso.

"How are you, Dave?" I squat in front of him and ruffle his silky black hair, which now falls down to his neck. "Have you been a good boy?"

He nods, and I stand again before turning to his parents. His father is wearing a leather jacket and is sitting on the edge of his seat, while his mother is wearing a sun hat and a long floral dress and is leaning back in her chair with her legs crossed.

"Hello, my name is Dr. Raymond Aderinto. I assisted Dr. Steele during Dave's last surgery. I believe we met then."

"Yes, I remember you," Mr. Young says and shakes my hand.

"He hasn't stopped talking about you since he learnt about this hospital appointment," Mrs. Young adds.

"Ah well, I thank God for using me to make an impression on him. He is a brave young man." I turn to face Dave. "You are very brave, right?"

The boy nods as I pull a chair to sit next to the family of three. "So, Dave, do you feel breathless at all?"

The boy shakes his head.

"And do you have any pain from your scar?"

Again, he shakes his head.

"Have you been able to go out and play with your friends?"

He shakes his head. "Mom and Dad don't let me go out much, but I've been playing a lot of video games with my cousins when they come over to see me."

"Ooh, interesting, and do you win?"

Dave nods. "Yes, every time."

"Now, that's my boy." I clap my hands. "Come on, *chop*

knuckle, chop knuckle." I lean forward, bringing my fist close to Dave and he pumps it with his own fist before we both lean back, making an explosion sound with our mouths. I taught him how to do that.

Carla walks into the room and checks Dave's vitals before I listen to his heart with my stethoscope and give him a chance to listen too. "You, my friend, have a cool sounding heart." I grin before straightening my back. "I'm very happy with your progress and I think you'll be running around and playing with your friends again very soon." I give him a high five before reassuring his parents.

On my way out, Dave stops me. "Dr. Aderinto, can you please show Mom and Dad your favorite dance move? You know...the one you showed me the last time?"

Ah, see me see trouble o. Does this boy want me to embarrass myself here?

I rub my neck and send Dave a sheepish smile. "I don't think your parents want to be scarred for life by watching me dance."

"Oh no, we would like to see it in person, actually. Dave has been trying to show us, but it doesn't look quite right." Mrs. Young uncrosses her legs and leans forward.

Mr. Young nods. "Yes, I think he said you called the dance move the...*Se...Seekee*?"

Ah, God, come and see o. Let me educate them.

"It's called '*Sekem*.'" I drop the file on the bed. "It's a very simple dance move, actually. Let me show you." The three of them stand in a straight line facing me.

Wow, this is a serious something.

"Okay, you need your feet apart. Then one hand on your waist, and the other hand on your chest. And then all you need to do is lean to one side and...*sekem, sekem*....like this." I move my body and dance to the side singing MC Galaxy's "*Sekem*" song in my head.

As I spend the next one minute watching the Youngs learn the dance move, Dave's determined face inspires me the most. He keeps going for longer than his parents, who give up after their first try. His child-like faith makes him believe that anything is possible and I know Dave; he won't stop until he learns the dance move. That's exactly what I need in my life—child-like faith.

Please give me grace, Lord.

~

"Guy, I now know why my last four relationships failed." I pull a chair out and place my Tupperware on the table. In the summer, Joe and I always have lunch in the hospital garden. It has tables spread out across the central open space and it is surrounded by green shrubbery and pastel-colored flowers.

Joe removes his theatre cap from his head, which has his name embroidered on it, and he places it on the table. "You do?" He occupies the chair opposite me.

"Yes *o*." I open my Tupperware and the aroma of my rice and chicken stew hits my nostrils and salivates my mouth. "I told you I was serious about seeking God's direction before taking any step." A group of doctors wearing grey scrubs stroll past us, talking and laughing.

"Mmm-hmm." Joe nods and pulls out a bottle of orange juice from his lunch box.

"Last night, I turned off my phone and took some time out to pray. While I was studying my Bible, God directed me to a sermon on TV, and guess what it was about?"

Joe leans back, a smirk crossing his face. "Why your last four relationships failed?"

I kiss my teeth and roll my eyes. "This guy, you are not a serious somebody." I say a quick prayer and start eating my food.

Joe laughs out loud, his shoulders shaking up and down to indicate how much he is enjoying this. "*Oga,* sorry *o*. Please, continue."

I place my elbows on the table and lean forward. "The sermon was about purpose, and while I've heard purpose messages a thousand times before, the preacher put a unique spin on it. He weaved in the importance of purpose when you're looking for a life partner."

"Ooh, tell me more." Joe chews on his pasta before digging his fork in for some more.

"He said it's important to find a partner whose values and purpose aligns with yours because marriage is about finding a teammate, and someone you can run the race with. Do you get?"

Joe nods. "I definitely agree. These are all things I told you before *nau,* and you didn't listen to me."

"*Ehh*, my guy, please don't blame me. Feelings are deceitful and I was blinded by pretty faces."

"Hmm, I will blame you, *o*. Look at this guy. You didn't heed to my advice before, but it's okay. That's all in the past now. I know how much you want to impact the lives of children. You could never have stayed true to that purpose if you had married those other girls."

"Exactly. Now we are speaking the same language." I put a spoon of rice into my mouth, the peppery stew making my taste buds come alive. "There are many women who love God in this country, but I need to choose one who will help me fulfill my purpose, and who will also let me help her fulfill hers." I blow out the hot steam from my mouth. "You know, after praying last night, I'm pretty sure I heard God tell me I'll be meeting my wife soon."

"*Chai,* papa G. G for general. General in America. The one and only heart doctor. You are blessed, my brother. Flesh and blood did not reveal this to you. God is involved. Shout four hallelujahs right now." Joe lifts both hands up and I shout four hallelujahs before we both burst into laughter.

I cover my mouth to stop myself from laughing too hard so rice doesn't shoot out of my nose. When I lift my head, my eyes fall on her—Amarachukwu Ikezie, the nurse I accidentally splashed coffee on this morning.

She's sitting on a wooden bench across the garden on the right-hand side, eating what looks like jollof rice and talking to someone on the phone. It looks like she found new scrubs, because the top she is wearing now has no coffee stains.

I hope she got to where she was going on time. I hope the accident didn't ruin her morning. Maybe I should apologize to her again.

"Honestly, Raymond, on a more serious note." Joe's voice brings me back to the current conversation. "I can't wait to be the best man at your wedding. It's about time I repay you the favor, *abi*?"

"Of course." I bring my attention back to my food before picking up a chicken drumstick and biting into it.

"Oh, by the way, that reminds me. Are you working the weekend in two weeks?"

I place my drumstick down and lick my fingers. "No, I don't think so. Why?"

"Ah, perfect." Joe clasps his hands together. "There's an event at my church. It's a seminar about relationships, but it's for both married couples and singles, so Josephine and I are going to it. You *have* to come with us."

I pick up a paper towel and dab the corners of my mouth, but my gaze slips to find Amara again, her African-print headband stealing my attention. "Do I have a choice in this matter?" I turn back to Joe.

"Exactly. You don't. It'll be fun, trust me. You said you want to marry before your thirtieth birthday, which is now only nine months away. You might meet someone at this event, you know?" Joe sends me a sly smile.

He's right. But I'm not going to the event just because I want to find someone. I think it'll be a good thing to experience. I'm having to unlearn everything I know about relationships and God is taking me on a wonderful journey to discover more about this beautiful thing He has created called marriage. I need to be prepared for this season. He will give me grace.

8

AMARA

"**G**irl, you won't believe I was late on my first day of work." I shake my head and lean back on the wooden bench in the hospital garden.

"What? Why?" Teeyana asks, as I press my phone against my ear. "I intentionally ended the call so you could sleep early. Explain yourself, young lady."

I pound my fist lightly against my chest and a burp escapes my lips, reminding me of the delicious jollof rice I've just consumed. *Nothing better than Mom's food to get me through today.* "I was writing a list."

I can imagine Teeyana frowning right about now. "What list?"

I place my empty Tupperware on the bench, already thinking about how I'm going to get rid of the oil stains so the container looks brand new again. "I was writing a list of what I want in my dream man. I need to be prepared when he comes, because I could meet him any day now."

Teeyana chuckles. "So you think you'll meet him soon, huh?"

I nod. "Errr...yeah, girl. In fact, if I meet him today, it'll be the perfect end to the crappy day I've had so far. After waking up late this morning, I got here with a few minutes to spare, but I bumped into this doctor who poured hot coffee on me and stained my scrubs."

"Oh, no. Did it burn you?"

"No, it didn't. Most of it went on the floor. Thank God." I sigh. "I was wearing my vest top underneath, but it left a huge stain on my scrubs. I was late for my orientation meeting but one of the NICU nurse practitioners was very nice to me. Her name is Claire, and I found out later that she's my mentor. She helped me find new scrubs." I smooth the new scrub top before adjusting the waistband of my trousers.

"Aww thank God for Claire." Teeyana sighs into the phone. "Okay, what did you write on your list?"

I knew she was going to ask. "Girl, it's my secret, but I can tell you it's a good list."

Teeyana chuckles. "Have you seen anyone yet who fits your list?"

I clear my throat and start recounting all the guys I've met today, starting with *Mr. Coffee,* who is tall, but not as muscly as I would like, and he is bald and has no beard, so that's a no-no.

Then I tell Teeyana all about the male doctors on the NICU —James, Henry, and Charlie. James is nice to look at but he's too heavy-handed with his hair styling products. I ain't gonna be fighting with him over mirror time every morning.

Henry is muscle-built and he has a nice beard but he's not very tall. If I wear heels, I'm sure I'll be taller than him. Then Charlie reminds me of the character J.D. from the TV show *"Scrubs."* He is a sight for sore eyes, but I'd prefer a melanin brother.

"Wow, you're very analytical," Teeyana says.

"Yes, of course. I have standards," I say as Mom's words flash in my memory again.

"Okay, but all the qualities you've mentioned are based on

physical looks. Are any of these guys Christian? You know we can't compromise that standard, right?" Teeyana asks.

"Girl, of course. I ain't planning on dating a non-Christian man. That's a *no-go* area. In fact, I'll have you know that being a Christian is the top thing on my list." I smile.

Or at least I think it is.

"Great." Teeyana exhales. "I'm excited that God has you in this season, but as your best friend in the whole wide world, permit me to throw in my words of caution too."

Girl, seriously? As if my parents haven't cautioned me enough.

"I know you have a list and you're trying to stick to it, but please don't be too picky. You can't cook up a perfect man and make him marry you. Ask for God's guidance because feelings are a terrible leader—I've learned that the hard way."

And who says I'm letting my feelings lead me?

I press my phone close to my ear. "Girl, I understand. But I also know God cares about my happiness and He will grant the desires of my heart, right?"

"God cares about you, Amara." Teeyana responds. "He knows who you will marry and trust me, this man might not be the perfect man you have sculpted in your list."

That's easy for you to say since you already have your perfect man.

I clear my throat and adjust in my seat. "I've heard you, girl."

"Also, you don't *have* to meet someone at the hospital. Church or church events are a good place to meet godly men. What do you think?"

"Yeah, my friend Emily from church told me about this event taking place at her friend's church two weekends from today. It's a relationship seminar for both singles and married couples."

"Sounds like it'll be fun. Are you going?"

"Heck yeah, I'm going. I wouldn't miss it for the world."

"That's great." Teeyana says. "Okay, my French lesson starts in two minutes. I need to get better at it before Jayden and I leave for Madagascar."

"Aww, enjoy your lesson. I better get back to the ward now. My lunch break ends soon."

"Alright, I'll speak to you later. Love you."

"Love you, girl." I end the call and place the phone in my bag. Sitting back on the bench, I mull over Teeyana's words. I know she means well. I know everyone means well. But this is my life, you know. "No one will choose for me." I mutter to myself as Dad's words come back to me.

An itch erupts on my scalp, and I use my fingernail to scratch that part of my head. *Frolita, you can't start itching now. I only washed you two days ago.*

Standing up, I sling my bag over my shoulder and pick up my Tupperware container when my eyes fall on *Mr. Coffee* walking toward me from across the garden.

Oh no, not again.

I quicken my steps and enter the building through the double doors, praying I'm walking fast enough so he doesn't catch up. "Amara?" His voice echoes down the hallway. I sigh and close my eyes before slowing down. I don't want to be rude and ignore him, but I also don't want to talk to him.

"Amara." He stops next to me and I turn to face him. "Sorry to bother you. I saw you eating in the garden and I thought I'd come over and apologize again." He rubs the back of his neck with one hand, the other hand carrying a plastic bag. "I still feel terrible for ruining your morning."

"I told you it was fine. I'm not mad at you." I turn to go, but he stops me again.

"Did you get new scrubs in the end?"

"Yes."

"Amara..."

"Why do you keep calling me that?" I snap. "How do you

know I don't like to be called Amarachukwu or something else?" I cross my arms and raise my eyebrows. *Nobody calls me Amarachukwu, but that's not the point.*

"I'm sorry. That's my bad. What would you like me to call you?"

I turn my head away. "Amara is just fine."

"Okay, my name is Raymond. I work in the pediatric cardiology unit upstairs." He brings his I.D. badge closer.

Dr. Raymond Aderinto. *Hmm, he's Nigerian too. That explains the accent.*

"Good to know." I continue down the hallway, and he walks beside me.

"Look, I know you say it's okay, but I'm hoping we can start again on a clean slate. Please, can I offer a peace offering and buy you lunch tomorrow?"

"I can bring my own lunch, thank you." I tighten my grip on my bag.

"Okay, can I buy you a hot drink? Maybe not coffee." He laughs sheepishly, but I remain silent. "Do you like hot chocolate?" He asks.

Yes, I love hot chocolate, but he doesn't need to know that. "I can buy my own drink, thank you." I keep my gaze fixed on the hallway in front of me, ignoring Raymond's *Hugo Boss* scent, which is caressing my nostrils.

"Okay, tell me what you want and I'll..."

"Look, Raymond." I stop and look at him, his frame towering over me, standing at least six feet. "Please, stop apologizing. I already told you it's fine. You don't have to make up for anything because I hold no grudges."

"Okay, that's good to know." His shoulders relax. "Are you having a good day so far, though?"

"Yes, but I have to return to the NICU. My babies need me." I turn around and open the door leading to the stairs.

"Okay, well...I guess I'll see you around." His voice comes through before I close the door. As much as I appreciate him apologizing and offering to make things right, I don't have time for small talk, and I don't have time for distractions or unnecessary friendships.

9

RAYMOND

"The famous author Gary Thomas said in his book *Sacred Search* that it's not about who you marry, but why." Pastor Gabriel Adekunle leans on the glass podium and speaks into the microphone. "Do you understand the significance of that statement?" He poses the rhetorical question to the crowd of a hundred people sitting across the main auditorium of Light On The Hill Community Church.

Pastor Adekunle is a speaker, a relationship coach, and the author of over a dozen books. So when Joe told me he was going to speak at this event, I knew I had to park all my reservations aside and come down here.

"Why do you want to get married?" The middle-aged man straightens his back. "There's even a famous movie called *Why Did I Get Married*? But do you think any of the reasons explored in that movie depict the real reason why we should get married?"

I cast my mind back to when I watched the movie in Nigeria. I'm pretty sure I watched it a few times, but I can't remember what it was about. I lower my head and scribble the title of the movie at the top of my notebook so I remember to watch it again later.

Pastor Adekunle adjusts the collars of his grey suit and fixes his black tie. He walks to the far left end of the stage, the click-clack of his well-polished shoes bouncing off the white walls of the auditorium. "Let me address the married couples now for a second. Would anyone like to volunteer to tell us why they got married?" The crowd is silent. A lady coughs behind me, and another man sneezes in the far right hand corner of the room, but no one says anything.

My head turns to the other half of the room, where the married couples are. Joe is sitting next to Josephine, her arm tucked nicely around his. For a moment I wonder where their daughter Chelsea is, but then I remember Joe said they were going to drop her off at his parents' house.

There are more singles than married couples in the room, so it's difficult for the couples to hide. Pastor Adekunle picks on someone like I suspected he would. "In thirty seconds, can you tell us why you got married, sir?" He points to a man wearing a brown blazer over a white shirt.

The man places his hand on his chest and asks, "Me?" Laughter erupts from the crowd.

"Yes, you, sir." Pastor Adekunle stifles a laugh. "Please tell us why you married the beautiful woman sitting by your side." He points to the woman wearing a green dress and knee-length black boots.

The man clears his throat before rising to his feet. An usher rushes to his side and holds the microphone to his mouth, but the man opts to take the microphone and hold it himself. "Sir, I married my wife because apart from her beauty and kind-hearted, she was the only one willing to support me in the work God has called me to do."

"Hmm." Pastor Adekunle smiles. "That's a very thoughtful

answer. What about you, madam?" He speaks to the couple sitting next to Joe and Josephine.

The woman who is wearing an ankara top and headgear rises to her feet and takes the microphone. "My husband and I both love God, we have the same vision and passion for the same things." She hands the mic back to the usher but then brings it back. "Oh, and we are attracted to each other. Very important." She emphasizes the word *important* and draws chuckles from the crowd.

Pastor Adekunle cocks his brows and smiles. "Very interesting." He also emphasizes the word *interesting*. "Brilliant. You all have given wonderful answers, and it looks like you have peeked at my notes for this talk." He returns to the pulpit. "I might as well sit in the crowd and let you guys teach." The crowd laughs.

"Now I'm going to combine all these answers and tell you what they are really saying. And before I do it, the one thing I want you to take away from today's talk is that marriage was God's idea and not yours." He shakes his head. "If it was your idea, then there would be no need for you to seek His direction and His guidance."

Wow, what a word.

"Let's look at it this way. Every manufacturer of a product knows exactly what you need to do to make the product work. That's why they make manuals to guide us and help us make the best out of the products. In the same way, because marriage is God's design, we have to do it the way He has purposed it." He turns to face the single section.

"If you are single, the first thing you need to know is that you were created because God has a purpose for you, and you *can* fulfill that purpose with or without a spouse." He nods.

"Your single season is not a curse—it's a beautiful gift from God, just like marriage is, so we need to learn to appreciate these gifts more. There is a time and season for everything under heaven, and God has made everything beautiful in its time. So your single season is beautiful; appreciate it, cherish it, and use it to draw closer to your Maker. If your reason for wanting to marry is to find your purpose, then you've got it all wrong. You can walk in your God-given purpose even in your single season."

That's right, sir. Preach it. The words creep to the edge of my tongue, but I bite them back.

"To answer the question, we have to ask the Maker why He created marriage in the first place, and we can't do that without looking at the Maker's manual." He opens his Bible. "Now, will you please turn with me to Genesis chapter one."

Pastor Adekunle spends twenty minutes analyzing the first marriage between Adam and Eve, emphasizing on the fact that God had already given Adam a purpose which was to tend to the garden before He brought him a help meet. "Children of God—know your purpose. If you don't know it yet, ask God to help you find it before you throw yourself into any relationship. Your purpose is not defined by your marital status. Your purpose is defined by the One who knit you in your mother's womb."

I scribble so fast in my notebook, my hand starts cramping from all the good points I'm writing down. Pastor Adekunle continues, "Singles, look for good character, vision, companionship, and the alignment of purpose above all else. Of course, never marry someone you're not attracted to, but the former things are what will make a marriage last."

Wow. Thank you Lord for this confirmation. Purpose over feelings.

At the end of the talk, there is a question-and-answer session followed by a ten-minute break. Contemporary worship music fills the air as I meander through the crowd to meet Joe. "*Ayy,* papa G." Joe says before shaking hands with me. "How are you finding the event so far?"

"Honestly, guy, *e be like say Pastor Adekunle know my story o.* The guy was preaching to me directly."

"Ah, you see. What did I tell you? The Spirit is one."

"Yes *o*. Madam, *how body nau*?" I ask Josephine, and she smiles at me.

"I'm fine, thank you Raymond and you?"

"I'm doing well. You're looking very *correct* tonight. This my brother is treating you right *o. See as you don baff up.*" I place both hands on my hips.

"*Eh, eh. E don do,* my brother." Joe places his hands on my shoulders and pushes me away. "You didn't come to this event to hit on my wife. *Oya,* go and find a single woman. Go, go, go."

Joe spins me around toward the single men and women chatting in small groups while sipping on their drinks. One guy dressed in a white shirt and black bow tie is talking to a lady wearing a red dress. The lady is twirling her wineglass in her hand and laughing at whatever the guy is saying. Another guy wearing a grey suit keeps dabbing on his forehead with a white handkerchief as the lady in front of him talks and every time he leans closer, the lady takes a step back.

This is going to be a long night. I shift my gaze to the left and it lands on...her. I shake my head and wipe my eyes to make sure I'm not hallucinating, but my eyes aren't deceiving me. It's Amara...I mean Amarachukwu. Oh, wait, no, she said it was okay for me to call her Amara.

She's wearing a floral skirt and a black long-sleeved top. Her black heels make her look much taller than I remember but she's still looking up at the man she's talking to. Her make-up is simple, yet sophisticated and elegant. She is wearing her hair down, and her thick curly strands are grazing her shoulder. Her afro makes her stand out unapologetically from the crowd, and I can do nothing but stare with my mouth open.

"*Ahem.*" Joe clears his throat and brings me back to earth. "Have you found someone already?"

"Guy, you see that girl over there in the floral skirt?" I try to be subtle by pointing with my bottom lip. "She's a NICU nurse at the hospital. I mistakenly spilled coffee on her a few weeks ago and I don't think she likes me very much."

"Oohh, look at how God works. *Oya,* go and talk to her." Joe tries to push me, but I stiffen.

"Guy, are you even listening to me? I said the girl doesn't like me."

"*Abeg,* leave that thing, *jor.* You know working at the hospital is stressful and that can make some people seem a little hostile."

Okay, he has a point there.

"She looks like she's in a good mood from the way she's flashing all thirty-two of her teeth. Go and speak to her *o.* You have nothing to lose. *Oya,* go."

When I look back in Amara's direction, she has finished her conversation and is now heading toward the snacks table.

Okay, this is my chance. Remember, it's purpose over feelings. I have to look past her beautiful exterior. Purpose over feelings, Raymond. Come on.

"Hello." I cut in front of Amara and she stops in her tracks. "Good to see you again." I grin, excited about the possibility of us making a fresh start, but she doesn't reciprocate my enthusiasm.

Amara rolls her eyes and places one hand on her hip. "It's you again." The irritation in her voice wipes away the smile on my face.

"Yes, it's me indeed. Small world, isn't it?" I force another smile.

She shakes her head. "Why do you always catch me at a bad time?"

"Oh, sorry. I didn't...I didn't think you were busy—"

"I was heading to the bathroom and you just...blocked my way." She crosses her arms.

"Okay...I'm sorry. I guess I'll..." Before I can finish my sentence, she walks away without another word.

Hmm, na wah o. Is she still mad about the coffee, or am I missing something?

I clench my jaw and turn around to head back to my friends when the sound of clinking glass stops me. We all turn our attention to the event coordinator—Mrs. Willoughby, a short, round woman with curly brown hair. "Attention, everyone." She speaks into a microphone. "We're moving on to a very exciting part of the evening where we can make new friends.

"As promised, we're going to be having a speed-dating session for the singles, and also a fun games session for the married couples. Since there's a lot of us, we can't all be in the same room. Please, look at the card on your seat to find out which room you'll be going to. Thank you."

I turn around and wave at Joe and Josephine as they leave the room. Looking at my card inside my notebook, I realize I don't have to move rooms. I walk over to the table and pull out a chair before settling into it like the other guys. The seats are barricaded with wooden dividers, so we can't see who is sitting in the chairs next to us.

"Attention everyone," Mrs. Willoughby speaks again. "Just to go over the rules for this session; you have ten minutes with each lady. You can either answer the question on the cards or start up a whole new conversation of your own. Just speak as the Holy Spirit leads. I don't know about you, but I'm excited to see the connections God makes today. Oh, don't forget to exchange phone numbers." She gives a broad smile before walking away.

I close my eyes and say a quick prayer to calm myself before the bell goes and more contemporary worship music starts playing again from the overhead speakers. The women flood into the room in groups, bringing with them a row of chatter and laughter. The first girl who sits across from me has the name "**Kate**" written on her name tag and my chest tightens. "Hello, my name is Raymond. Nice to meet you." I force a smile.

"Oooh, Raymond. That's a nice name." She leans forward and flips her loose curls, exposing her big hoop earrings and her long slender neck.

Ah ah, weti dey do this one?

"What do you do for a living, Raymond?" She says my name as if it is the brand name for the medication that will cure all her problems.

"I'm a doctor." I say. "A pediatric cardiologist to be precise."

She gasps. "Really? Like a doctor, doctor? Wow, you must be rich."

I clear my throat. "What about you, Kate? What do you do?" I try not to vomit while saying the name out loud again.

"I'm a massage therapist, and let me tell you, these hands can work some real magic...doctor." She flashes me a weird smile again before leaning further forward so the neckline of her top drops to show more skin.

Hia, I thought they said this was a Christian event.

I lean back and avert my gaze, occasionally glancing at the clock as Kate goes on and on about all the people she has worked her magic on. When the bell goes, Kate writes her number on a card and slides it under my notebook before winking at me and walking over to the next table. I use the notebook to push the card away, as if it is cursed.

God forbid I get myself entangled in this.

The next lady is called Debbie, and she's an investment banker. She has locs, wears glasses, and has kind eyes and a funny personality. Our conversation flows smoothly and by the end of the ten minutes, I find myself wanting to know more about her.

"Debbie, I hope you don't mind me asking, but can I have your number?"

She smiles and bites her pink bottom lip. "Of course. Here you go." She scribbles on my notebook while I write my number on a card and hand it to her.

"I'll call you." I say when she stands up to leave and I hold her gaze until she sits at the next table, failing to notice the new girl sitting in front of me.

Sharon is the next girl—a lawyer, followed by Lola—an event planner. Then there's Ynas, Charlotte, Peace, Kelly, and Sarah. To be honest, I can't say very much about the latter girls because I keep thinking about Debbie's charming laugh and cute smile.

I grab a bottle of water and sip on it before Mrs. Willoughby comes to the microphone again. "We're down to the very last date guys, so use your time wisely." Again, she shrieks and then runs off to the corner before the bell goes. *Wow, who would have thought this thing could be so exhausting?*

To my greatest surprise, Amara rocks up in front of me and freezes for a second when she sees me. The way she clenches her fists and presses her lips together makes me stifle a laugh. "Well, look who we have here." I grin and lean back in my chair.

She rolls her eyes and reluctantly takes a seat. "What's so funny?" She asks as she places her small clutch purse on the table.

I shrug. "The fact that God has a wonderful sense of humor."

She frowns. "What's that supposed to mean?"

I clear my throat before leaning forward. "That you can run, Amara, but you can't hide."

She raises her eyebrows. "Why would you think I'm running?" She focuses her big brown eyes on me, and for the first time, I can stare into them without her looking away.

I shrug. "It's obvious from your actions you don't like me." I reply and she snorts.

"I never said that. That was your own assumption."

"Oh, really?" I place my elbows on the table, taking in her scent of roses. "Then prove it."

Her eyes widen. "What? How?"

My fingers intertwine on the table. "They say actions speak louder than words, so if you like me like you claim, you'll let me buy you hot chocolate. I know it's your favorite hot drink."

Actually, I don't know, but she seems like a hot chocolate kinda girl.

"How did you...it's...it's..." She fumbles.

"So I'll take your inability to respond to mean I'm right. Hot chocolate it is." I lean back again, feeling really pleased with myself.

Amara clears her throat and picks up a card from the stack in front of us as I hold down my urge to laugh. "I believe we have a question to answer." She says, and I keep my eyes on her as she reads. "Who's your favorite person in the world and why?"

Her gaze slides up to meet mine. "You go first."

I shake my head and smile. "Nah, ladies first."

She sends me a glare and then clears her throat. "My best friend. Her name is Teeyana. She's like a sister to me. We've been friends since high school and even though we're many miles apart, our friendship is still going strong."

So she knows how to make and keep friends. That's great.

"Your turn." She says, tucking a strand of her curly hair behind her ear. "Who's your favorite person?"

"My dearest mother." I say, with no hesitation. "She has sacrificed so much for me. She's an amazing woman and I love her *very* much."

"I see." Amara drops her gaze to the card in her hand. "That must be nice." She says and then turns her head sideways, allowing me to have a better look at her hair.

"Your hair...it's very beautiful." I blurt out, and she turns to look at me again, her lips stretching into a small smile.

"Thank you." She says. "Sometimes, *Frolita* cooperates with me."

I smile. "You named your hair *Frolita*?"

She shifts in her seat. "Erm...well, no, it's just—"

"I think it's a lovely name." I say, and her shoulders relax. "If I ever grow out my hair again, I would definitely give it a name. Maybe you can help me pick one."

Amara smiles, and then the bell goes. She stands and picks up her clutch purse from the table.

"Amara, please wait." She pauses and looks at me. "Can I have your number? If I'm going to buy you hot chocolate, I need to know where you are." I smirk.

"In your wildest dreams, Dr. Aderinto," she says, and the sweetness of my name in her mouth gives me chills. "If you *really* want to buy me hot chocolate, you're gonna have to find me."

Hia, see me this girl o. Na me she dey do shakara for?

"You have a good night." She says and then walks away.

"Have a good night, Miss Ikezie. I'm looking forward to our date." I laugh when she turns around and rolls her eyes at me, but this time, another smile breaks on the corner of her lips. It was a small smile and easy to miss, but I saw it, and that's enough for me to hold on to the hope of some kind of friendship.

10

AMARA

I'm looking forward to our date. *Ugh*, who does he think he is? That boy has got some nerve. How could he laugh at my demise and make a joke out of it? I felt like throwing my clutch purse at him before walking out of that room, but of course I didn't do that because the other guys were watching.

Speaking of other guys, there were some *real* cute guys out there tonight. Too bad the ones I was interested in didn't ask for my number while the ones who annoyed me—aka *Mr. Coffee*— or Raymond, or whatever he said his name is, asked for my number. He's *so* annoying, *ugh*.

I take off one of my black stilettos and hop on my shoeless foot to my bed as I take off the other. After plopping down on my mattress, I lean forward and massage my temples to soothe the headache threatening to come on.

Letting out another groan, I throw myself backward on my bed and land close to my Bible. The impact with which I hit the bed acts as a reset button in my brain because images of all the kind things Raymond has done to me flashes in my memory.

I thought it was cute that he guessed my favorite hot drink, offered to buy me lunch, and even asked for my number. He gave me the most attention tonight, and he was nice about it.

Seriously, why don't I like him? Okay, so he spilled coffee on me and ruined my scrubs on one of the most stressful days of my life. But he has apologized a thousand times, so what is my problem? In this world full of many not-so-nice people, how many times will someone wrong me and go the extra mile to make things right like he has done?

First of all, holding a grudge is not a very Christian-like thing to do and second of all, if the tables were turned and he gave me the same attitude I've been giving him, I wouldn't have apologized to him. Why do I keep giving him such a hard time?

Come on, girl, give him a break.

I push myself up and place my Bible on my lap as a nudge of guilt pinches through my chest. I take my phone out of my clutch purse and Google a Bible passage which talks about forgiveness. The first link opens to the book of Romans, chapter twelve, and verses seventeen to eighteen. I flip to the same passage in my New Living Translation Bible, reading the words out loud to myself. "'Never pay back evil with more evil. Do things in such a way that everyone can see you are honorable. Do all that you can to live in peace with everyone.'"

I sigh and lift my head, my gaze meeting my reflection in my dressing-table mirror. My shoulders slump and I sigh. "In my case, I have paid back good with evil." I place my Bible on my bed and clasp my hands in front of me. Closing my eyes, I let the words out as they come to me.

"Lord Jesus, I haven't been the best at showing love to others the last few days—especially to Raymond. Please forgive me, and give me an opportunity to at least apologize to him. Thank you Lord, in Jesus' name."

Before the word "amen" comes out of my mouth, a vivid scene of a girl pops into my head. It's a teenage girl, with beautiful long braided hair, sobbing in front of me. I can only see the back of her head, but I'm holding her shoulder and praying for her as she sobs. I don't know who she is, or why she's crying, but her emotions surge through me with a force I can't explain, so I pull her in for a hug and then, my eyes flutter open to meet the familiarity of my room again.

"What...what just happened?" I turn my head slowly and let my gaze linger over the room. It darts from my dressing table to my bedside lamp, and then to the Scripture art prints on my wall. "What was the meaning of that?" I ask again, as if I can provide the answers I know I don't have. "Man, I didn't know fatigue could cause hallucinations. I need to sleep."

I yawn and shake my head when my gaze drops to my Bible again. Images from my speed date with Raymond flash in my mind and a sigh escapes my lips. I close my Bible and place it on top of my bedside table before heading to the bathroom. I'm going to apologize to him tomorrow. I hope he'll be more forgiving and pay back evil with good.

I suppress a burp as I chew on the last of Mom's signature spicy jollof rice. That was good while it lasted. Now I have to go back to cooking my own boring food. I shake my head and place the empty Tupperware on the bench. Picking up my water bottle, I bring it up to my lips and tilt my head back until the cool water runs down my tongue and into my throat.

"Hey." A familiar voice startles me and the water diverts into my windpipe, sending me into a coughing fit. I place the bottle down and lean forward, pounding my fist lightly against my chest to clear my lungs.

"Oh, no. I'm so sorry." Raymond towers over me in his dark

blue scrubs. He places two cups on the bench and kneels beside me. "Are you okay?"

I stop coughing and lift my head to meet his soft gaze, his face only a few inches away from mine. "Yeah…" I clear my throat. "Yeah, I'm fine."

Unable to control myself, I burst out laughing, confusing the poor boy. Raymond tries to stifle a laugh, but the look of concern on his face can't be missed. "Amara, are you sure you're okay?"

I nod and try to find my words in between giggles. "Don't you think it's time we meet under normal circumstances when you're not spilling coffee on me, stopping me from going to the bathroom, or trying to choke me?"

Raymond sends me a sheepish smile. "Yeah, I think that'll be great." He scratches his head.

"I forgive you, by the way." I say and slide along the bench to make room for him.

"Really?" He picks up the two cups and occupies the space next to me. "Wow, wonders indeed shall never end." He stresses his Nigerian accent.

I chuckle. "My mom always says that."

"Well, your mom is the real MVP." He smiles and for the first time I notice how bright his teeth are. *Makes me not want to show my own teeth now.*

"Hot chocolate?" He hands one cup over to me. "I guessed you would like creamer and sugar."

I blink back. "Wow, are you always this good or am I just very predictable?"

He shrugs and smiles. "It's the Holy Spirit, my dear."

I cringe at his use of "my dear"—reminding me of something my dad would say. Sipping my drink, I let the warm liquid caress my tongue, the sweetness making me feel more awake. "Hmm, this is good."

"Yeah, my friend, John, who works at the coffee shop, knows

how to work his magic." He takes a sip of his coffee before leaning forward. "Okay, I have a very serious question to ask."

"Erm...okay?"

"What happened between Saturday night and today? I'm pretty sure you hated me then, but now you're gracing me with your beautiful smile?"

Again, I chuckle and look away, trying to hide the smile on my face. *Girl, why are you smiling, though?* "I thought about it, prayed about it, and God showed me the error of my ways. I'm sorry about my attitude before. I was rude to you and that wasn't okay."

His eyes widen. "I'm even getting an apology? *Wawu.* This is a serious something."

I chuckle again. I love how he just switches to a Nigerian accent at will. It's actually kinda cute.

"Honestly, I was bracing myself for how I would convince you to accept this peace offering." Raymond says. "This is some Damascus experience I'm witnessing with my own *coro-coro* eyes."

I laugh. "You exaggerate too much, Ray."

"Hmm, Ray." He repeats the nickname I just called him. "I like the sound of that."

I cover my mouth to stop myself from smiling some more, but my effort is useless. *Girl, what is wrong with you? He's not even your type.*

"So how long have you been working as a nurse?" He asks, pressing into my thoughts.

"Hmm, let's see." I tilt my head and swirl the hot chocolate in my cup. "One month, to be precise."

"Wait," Raymond squints. "You're a new grad nurse?"

"Yup."

"I knew I hadn't seen you around the hospital before. Do you like working here?"

I adjust in my seat before answering. "Yeah, I do like it here. Everyone is nice and supportive."

"That's good to know."

"So, have you always wanted to be a pediatric cardiologist?" I ask, glancing at his name badge again to make sure I'm right.

"Hmm, I won't say *always*. I love children, so I'm not surprised I'm doing this job. But regarding pediatric cardiology specifically, God was the one who directed me here."

Okay, so he's not just a Christian by label but a Christian who talks about God. I guess that's a good thing, but it doesn't always mean he's living a Christian life. For starters, he's a Nigerian who grew up in Nigeria. How do I know he's not going to turn into some domineering husband who would stop his wife from working and turn her into a baby making machine?

"What about you?" Raymond's voice snaps me out of my thoughts.

"Huh?"

"Why did you decide to become a NICU nurse?" He asks, his warm smile making me feel more comfortable.

"I was a premature baby and my mom always talks about how amazing the NICU nurses were to me back in Nigeria. When I decided to do nursing, it felt right to go back to the NICU. Children are the future, so it's a privilege to serve the leaders of tomorrow. Who knows, I might look after the future president of America, or a future New York Times best-selling author. It's amazing to be a part of that."

"Wow, that's a wonderful way to look at the job we do." Ray smiles at me and excitement flutters around in my chest, encouraging me to open up even more.

Before I can stop myself, the words spill out of me. "Someday, I'd like to be involved in research. I'd love to be part of improving the care we provide to these children."

"Someday?" Raymond tilts his head. "Why someday? Why

not now? You know the NICU department runs a research associates program, right?"

"Yeah...I know, but..." I avert my gaze, trying to find an excuse to explain why I've chosen to believe the dark voice hovering in my thoughts. "I mean, I probably won't get in, anyway. I'm only a new grad nurse with no experience." Saying the words out loud to someone else makes me sound like a pathetic, sore, loser.

That's because you are. The dark voice speaks and I force myself to look at Raymond in a bid to silence it.

"It doesn't matter if you have no experience." Raymond turns to look at me, the genuine kindness in his eyes pushing away the dark voice in my head. "My best friend, Joe, is a surgeon and he joined the program for a short time last year. I can assure you that there are opportunities for all levels of experience. It'll boost your resume and if you ever want to become a NICU nurse practitioner, it'll work in your favor."

"Yeah, I want to be a NICU nurse practitioner someday." I smile at the fact that he may have just read my mind.

"And that's *exactly* why you shouldn't let this opportunity pass you by," He says. "It's always good to start early. You have nothing to lose."

I sigh. "Okay, but...did your friend, Joe, say the recruitment process was intense?"

Ray shakes his head. "Not at all. I've met the leader of the program—Dr. Miller. I was recently elected as the lead for diversity and equity, so I've met Dr. Miller a few times at our quarterly meetings. He seems alright."

I sigh. "Okay."

"So...you promise you'll apply?"

"I promise," I say quickly before the dark voice can talk me out of it.

"Good." Ray smiles and we both lean against the bench and sip our drinks in sync. The silence that passes between us is both calming and reassuring. He seems like a nice guy. I'm glad I apologized.

"Amara, can I ask you something?" Ray breaks the silence.

"Yeah, sure."

"I'm organizing this event at my church for the teenagers. Last year it started as a way to raise health awareness, but over time, God led me in a different direction. I'm hoping not only to mentor and coach them, but also to help them attain spiritual prosperity and to teach them basic life skills. So next Saturday, I'll be teaching the boys how to cook jollof rice."

My eyebrows shoot up and my jaw drops. "You...you cook? Really?"

"Yes *o*. Baby girl, if you want jollof rice, fried rice, okra soup, *eba*, chicken stew, or pounded yam, then I'm your guy."

I cover my mouth as chuckles escape my lips. *Baby girl? Pfft, boy, don't get ahead of yourself.*

"I saw you eating jollof rice the other day." He says, his gaze sliding to my empty, oil-stained Tupperware on the bench. "And today from the looks of it." He grins. "I know you love it, so if you're free that day, I'd like you to join us."

Okay, let's take a moment to think about this. Not only is this guy a Christian, but he's nice, funny, and loves children too? *Too bad I'm not attracted to him.*

"I think I'm free that weekend, so I'll make sure I come so I can watch you teach your boys how to cook jollof rice. I pray it's good because my taste buds are very critical." I nod with a sly smile.

He shrugs. "Please, my food is going to scatter your taste buds *gbas gbos*." He makes cutting motions with his hands.

Laughter erupts from my core, and I open my mouth to ask him what the last thing he said meant when a piercing scream flies across the garden. We both snap our heads in the direction of the sound.

"Somebody help me!!! Help me, please. My child...my child is dying!!!" A woman's shaky voice follows short screams and we both spring to our feet.

Oh, no. An emergency? What...what do we do?

"Amara, come with me." Ray says before running toward the distressed woman. It wasn't a question or a plea. It was an instruction.

"Yes, doctor." I reply and fast-walk behind Ray, struggling to keep up with his long strides. A weakening sensation creeps up my legs and knees as the hairs on my arm and nape of my neck stand on edge.

At the scene, a woman who looks like she's in her thirties is hunching over a young boy lying on the sidewalk, who looks to be about ten years old. The boy's legs and arms are stiff, his eyes are rolled back, and his whole body is jerking as the woman cries.

"Please help me, doctor." The woman extends a shaky arm to Ray, the other arm tucked behind her son's head.

Ray immediately takes charge and turns to me. "Amara, please start the timer on your phone, and get some head support for the boy." Then he turns around and points to another nurse who is approaching the scene with the words "**ER**" embroidered on her burgundy scrubs. "Nurse, can you please get a crash cart ready?"

The nurse nods before running toward the ER as the crowd of onlookers grows, everyone talking in hushed tones. I start the timer on my phone before approaching a nurse wearing dark blue scrubs, who is holding out her hoodie to me. "Thank you." I take the hoodie from her and return to the scene before placing the folded hoodie under the seizing boy's head.

"Madam, please breathe." Ray swaps places with the woman as she settles at the boy's feet. His voice is calm, yet in control, and it puts me at ease. "Is this your son?" He asks the woman, and she nods as tears stream down her face. "Did he hit his head when he fell?"

The woman shakes her head.

"Please, tell me what happened." Ray pushes away a small stone in the boy's path and gently unbuttons the boy's shirt.

The woman takes a deep breath and exhales. "He hasn't...he hasn't been feeling well for the past three days. He had a high fever this morning, and we were on our way to the ER when he collapsed."

"Has this ever happened before?"

The woman shakes her head. "Please, he is my only child, don't let anything happen to him." The woman grasps Ray's hands.

"Madam, we will try our best to take care of him." Ray squeezes her shoulder before turning to me. "How long?"

I look at my phone. "Three minutes and twenty-three seconds."

Lord, please let him stop seizing.

Ray turns to the woman again and asks whether the boy has any medical history or if there are any medications he's taking. The woman sobs and shakes her head to both questions as the ER nurse returns with the crash cart, along with a porter and a wheelchair.

They park well away from the scene. "How's he doing, doctor?" The ER nurse asks Ray. He turns to the boy and brushes his curly black hair away from his face.

The boy's shaking slows to a stop, and then he starts crying and groaning. "He's coming around." Ray says, and a sigh of relief escapes my lips.

Thank You, Lord.

"Amara, let's get him into the recovery position."

I lean across and place one hand on the boy's shoulder and the other on his knee. Ray does the same on the same side, his large hands brushing against mine. His hands are warm, and for a brief second, I wonder what it would feel like if he touched my arm...or my face.

Focus, girl. Come on.

"Ready...on three." Ray instructs. "One, two, three..."

We turn the boy slowly on his side and then Ray gestures for his mom to come and soothe him as his cries increase. The woman rushes to his head and kneels beside him, planting kisses on his forehead. "I'm here, baby. I'm never leaving you."

Ray stands up and mutters to himself. "Thank you, Jesus." He pinches the bridge of his nose and turns to look at me. "Thank you, Amara." He gives my arm a gentle squeeze and my cheeks warm up.

As the crowd slowly disperses, Ray walks over to the ER nurse standing behind me. "He's stable now, but I think he needs to be seen immediately to check for infection and hypo-glycemia..."

Their conversations fade in the background, drowned out by the loud thoughts in my head. Ray is so calm, so gentle, and he involves God in everything he does. How can one guy have so many good qualities? *Again, too bad I'm not attracted to him.*

11

RAYMOND

Last night, as I was sitting on my bed and reading my Bible, a prayer of thanksgiving came to me. It was a strange prayer, but now I understand what it meant. Four months ago, I was getting ready to propose to a woman who wasn't right for me.

God removed me from a situation which could have caused me a lifetime of unfulfillment and even though it crushed my heart, that pain was necessary for me to get to where I am today. So last night, I was thanking God for letting Kate dump me.

I never thought I'd ever pray that kind of prayer, but it's true. Everything has changed since I started being intentional about seeking God. I could have easily slipped into bitterness or wallowed in anger toward Kate. I could have gone stagnant and let the devil use Kate's rejection to wreak havoc in my life, but I'm now realizing that God has been removing stumbling blocks from my path. Every day, I'm more reassured that everything will fall into place.

I've been thinking about Amara a lot. In fact, soon after my prayer last night, before I fell sleep, I thought about the way her lovely curls frame her face, and the way she always laughs at my jokes and covers her mouth so I won't hear her snorting.

I haven't seen her since we helped the little boy and his mother two weeks ago. I've mostly been on night shifts and I still don't have her number. My youth event is in three days and I need to give Amara the venue address, which is why I'm carrying myself down to the NICU to see her.

O boi, this is too soon o. Abeg, cool down. Joe's voice rings in my head. That's how he'll caution me if I mention this to him, but I shake my head as I walk past the commotion of nurses, porters, and patients in the hallway.

Tapping my ID badge on the intercom, I open one side of the double doors and walk in. I've always loved the calm NICU atmosphere, the beautiful white walls, the spacious hallway, and the many rooms which have at least a dozen incubators.

When I walk by one of the double-glazed windows, a sight draws me to a halt. My eyes find her—the one girl I've been wanting to see again for the last two weeks. Amara is standing beside an incubator with one arm inside, and she's saying something to the sleeping baby.

She has tucked her hair underneath big cornrows, the tips of the extensions kept together in a low bun. She checks the stickers attached to the baby's chest before gently adjusting the baby's position to lie on their side. She leans over and rubs the baby's head softly, before wrapping the baby in a cozy-looking white blanket.

Her lips move again, although this time, I think she's singing. I want to enter the room and draw closer so I can hear her singing, but unless I want her to call me a creep, I better not try that.

I can only imagine what her voice sounds like—it must be a sweet melody to the ears, a sweet, sweet melody, I'm sure. But wait. Everything is happening the same way it did the last four times; I meet a girl who says she's a Christian, her beauty draws me in, I fall in love, but then she dumps me. I don't want that to happen again. Not this time. Never again.

Lord, I know you said I'll meet my wife soon, but is this her?

Even if it's her, how do I know for sure?

Purpose over feelings. The words ring in my head again, putting some rationality back into my thoughts. Okay, it's a well-known fact that Amara is a beautiful woman, but so were the other girls. The only thing I know about Amara is that she loves children, too, but I need to explore her world and find out whether our purposes align.

Lord, please help me.

"Raymond?" A familiar voice jerks me out of my thoughts. A tall, blonde, middle-aged woman approaches me.

"Hey Claire." I push myself away from the glass window, wondering if she had seen me staring at Amara. "Long time no see." Claire is a NICU nurse practitioner, and two years ago, I assisted during a heart surgery on her son, Jamie.

"That's true." She throws her arms around me and squeezes tight. "How are you?" She breaks the hug and lowers her voice. "I heard about what happened between you and Kate. I'm so sorry."

Wow, Jevon was right. News really spreads around this hospital like a wildfire.

"It's okay. It's all in the past and I'm doing great now by God's grace. What about you?"

She sighs before blowing a breath, moving her fringe upwards. "I see you're still going on about this God of yours."

"Of course. He wants to be your God too." I lean in, reminding her of all our conversations before about God, Jesus, and the Bible. Claire has made it clear she's atheist and I see nothing has changed...yet; because *what God cannot do does not exist.*

Claire shakes her head. "Nah, I'm good. With work being busy and me going back home every day to my troublesome teenager, I think I already have enough to worry about."

"Ah, I was just about to ask, actually. How's the big man doing? Does he still remind you every day that he's no longer a boy?"

Claire laughs. "Every single day. Soon, he'll be going off to college and I'll be moping around the house wondering what to do with myself."

I tilt my head. "Oh, please, you can always come to my house, so you can finally taste all the Nigerian food I've been telling you about." We both laugh.

"What are you doing here, by the way?" Claire asks.

"Oh right, erm..." I clear my throat, throwing another glance at Amara on the other side of the glass window. "I came to see my friend." I smile at Claire. Even though I *am* telling the truth, I still feel the same way I did whenever my mother caught me stealing meat from her pot when I was younger.

"*Oooh*, a friend, huh?" Claire's gaze shifts to Amara and then back to me. "I see." A smirk creeps up her lips. "So you've met my mentee?"

I raise my eyebrows. "Amara is your mentee? That's amazing."

Look at God. The opportunity to find out more about Amara has finally presented itself. Boaz inquired about Ruth from the harvesters in the Bible. So here's my turn.

"So Claire." I rub my palms together and smile at her. "What do you think of Amara?" I nod toward the glass window.

Claire squints and steps back. "You mean as a mentee or a potential girlfriend?"

I roll my eyes. *Why are women like this? Somebody will ask a question and you're asking me another question.*

"I mean as a person, you know, her attitude, professionalism, *everything.*"

"Hmm." Claire shifts her weight onto her right leg before tucking her hands into the pockets of her scrubs. "That's a smart move." She smirks. "Well, if you must know, *Mr. Detective,*" Claire teases. "Amara is amazing, kind, tender-hearted, and you can see, she loves the babies she looks after." Claire turns to look at Amara again, and I follow her gaze without hesitation.

Of course she does. God lives in her and He's the one empowering her to love those babies the way she does.

I smile, and before I can open my mouth to say anything else, Claire speaks again. "She has been doing so well on the unit. We love having her here. We're waiting for Dr. Miller's response regarding her application into the research program, but I know she'll get in with no problems." She turns to me, but my gaze stays fixed on Amara. "She's doing great, Raymond."

Chai, look at the favor of God at work.

"Okay, so now that I've given you the information you asked for, will you tell me why you're here?" Claire asks, and I give her a sheepish smile.

"Erm..." When I glance at Amara again, I lock eyes with her and my heart drops a little. I smile and wave at her, but she only gives me a blank stare.

Oh, no. I hope she doesn't think I'm a creep.

I turn to face Claire again. "Well, I...uh... I already said I came here to see my friend."

"Mmm-hmm." Claire crosses her arms and shakes her head as Amara walks toward us. "I know the real reason you're here."

"And what's that?" I swallow as my tongue sticks to the roof of my dry mouth.

A sly smile creeps across Claire's face. "I think the heart doctor has got *goo-goo* eyes for the new nurse."

Hia. Which one is goo-goo eyes again? Sounds like juju o. I no dey there.

"Claire, I...hey, Amara." I straighten my back when Amara opens the door and steps out of the room.

"Hey," she says before looking at Claire. "You guys know each other?"

"Yeah, Raymond and I go way back." Claire nods at me. "He's such a brilliant doctor."

"I mean, I try my best." I interject, but Claire wouldn't let me finish.

"Oh please, you do so much more than someone who tries, Raymond. Let the lady here know how wonderful you are." She squeezes my shoulder and then turns to Amara. "I'll see you at that meeting at two, right?"

"Yeah, I'm right behind you." Amara nods and then steps close enough for her rose perfume to tease my nostrils. "Ray, I'm busy right now. Is everything alright?"

"Yeah, everything is fine. I'm so sorry for showing up unannounced like this." I clasp my hands and search for the right words. "I...um...I realized I invited you to the youth event but never gave you the address."

Amara raises her eyebrows in that cute little way she does, which makes me think she doesn't believe me.

"I wasn't sure if you were working today and I didn't know if I would see you again before Saturday," I add.

"Okay?" she says. It's not irritation in her big brown eyes, but a slight indifference. "Do you have the address written down or something?" She extends her hand.

"Oh, well, since you're busy, I have a better idea. Can I get your number instead?" I smile and when she doesn't respond, I explain further. "So I can text you the address?"

She sends me a blank stare.

"If I write it on a piece of paper, you might lose it. Plus, what if you get lost? I'd love to find you." I flash her another nervous smile, my heart suddenly picking up pace.

She stares and crosses her arms against her chest. Then finally, after what feels like forever, Amara cracks a smile and shakes her head. "You never give up, do you?"

Wow, look at those beautiful teeth. Fine girl. Omoge.

I scratch my head. "Are my efforts going to be in vain?"

She kisses her teeth and extends her hand again. "Where's your phone?"

12

RAYMOND

"*Chai,* so this is how my brother has landed a woman just like that." Joe teases as I press my phone against my ear to hear him better above the music. "Guy, please, where were you hiding these skills all this time?" He asks.

"What are you talking about? Is this why I called you? See this guy *o.*" I kiss my teeth and turn around to face the group of teens who are arranging furniture in the church event room.

"*Ahn, ahn.* Bros, cool temper, *nau.* We're not fighting." Joe's laugh comes through the phone and soon I'm laughing, too. Although I sometimes wish my best friend would learn when to be serious, his ability to make everything light-hearted helps me think less about the negatives.

"Uncle Raymond, where should I put this?" Matthew, a sixteen-year-old boy with glasses, walks up to me holding up a chair.

"Bro, one second, please." I take the phone away from my ear and glance around the room. The teens have arranged twelve chairs in a semi-circle and the central table at the front has all the notecards and stationery I'll use for the interactive exercises. "Over there, big man." I point toward the stack of chairs against the wall at the back. "Please, pile up all the extra chairs there because we might need them if more people come, okay?"

"Yes, Uncle." The boy nods before walking away.

I turn to the boy arranging the notecards and pens on the table. "Hey Brian, could you please turn down the volume of the music?"

"Yes, Uncle." The boy places the notecards on the table and heads over to the laptop playing Mary Mary's "*Shackles.*"

I bring the phone up to my ear again. "Hello?"

"*Yes, Uncle.*" Joe snickers and I roll my eyes.

"Okay, I think it's time for you to go."

"No, no, please wait. When is *madam* coming?" Joe asks, and a tight pressure settles in my chest.

"I texted her the address and the time, so she should be here soon." I swallow to wet my dry mouth.

"Okay, so how are you feeling about all this?"

I frown. "About what exactly?"

"*Ah, ah.* Your first date since Kate, *nau.*" Joe's questions rattle memories in my brain. I remember the countless times I invited Kate to come to one of my youth events, but she always declined. If it wasn't an eyebrow appointment, it was a spa day with her friends, or a shopping trip to change her wardrobe. And guess who paid for all those adventures? Yours truly.

I have no problem with a woman wanting to treat herself. Amara seems to be quite the fashionista herself and I love it— but life goes much deeper than that and Amara is the first girl who has shown interest in what God has called me to do.

"Guy, when I think about all the expensive places I took Kate to, this barely strikes me as a date," I respond.

"Oh, but it is. You two are getting to know each other, so it's a date. Please, let me go and enjoy my wife's company, but I'll be praying for you. I wish you all the best in your endeavor to *woo* Amara."

I laugh. "*Woo?* Does anyone use that word anymore? Please be going, *abeg*. You're a village man."

After ending the call, I join the teenagers to finish preparing the room. In less than ten minutes, the room is ready, and then I ask Brian to take the bag of groceries to the kitchen. He takes the plastic bag from me and disappears round the back.

I look like I'm busy, but God knows the only thing I'm thinking about is whether Amara will show up. It's four o'clock, and she's not here. I glance at the door, just in case she slipped in while I wasn't looking, but she's nowhere to be found.

Maybe she's running late? I take my phone out of my pocket and press on the home button, but no messages from her. *I guess she would have texted if she was running late?* I put the phone back in my pocket. "Guys, well done for all your hard work," I say to the teens. "Let's spend the next five minutes gathering all the mess we've made and then we can start."

The boys and girls nod and walk around, gathering scraps and bits of paper, before putting it in the trash can.

Okay, surely Amara will be here before we start. But five minutes pass, then ten minutes and then fifteen minutes, and still, Amara is not here.

"Uncle Raymond, it's fifteen minutes past four." Tessa points to the clock on the wall and I drop my shoulders before smiling at her.

"Thank you, Tessa." I turn to the rest of the group. "Alright everyone, find a seat so we can say an opening prayer."

One by one, the boys and girls, dressed in their t-shirts, jeans, and sneakers, all settle in a chair. First, there's sixteen-year-old Tessa who is outspoken and into makeup and fashion. I can already see her clicking with Amara because they have similar interests. Then there's Breonna—Tessa's shy best friend, who sometimes struggles to speak up for herself, and who lets Tessa do all the talking for her.

Matthew always gets the girls' attention—especially Tessa's. He obviously loves the attention and can sometimes come across as arrogant, but he is a nice kid. Fifteen-year-old Brian is quiet, humble, and very hardworking. He was the first one to arrive today and has done most of the work.

Fourteen-year-old Taiwo recently joined the group with his twin sister Kehinde. Taiwo is very protective of his sister, but she loves her independence, so sometimes they clash. Kojo is the bubbly sixteen-year-old boy who loves making jokes out of everything, and sometimes struggles to know when to be serious. Sometimes he reminds me of Joe.

Finally, there's fifteen-year-old Ekene who has a beautiful voice and who is always singing with his childhood best friend Nicole. So altogether, there are four girls and five boys and hopefully, when more parents see what God is doing here, they'll let their teens join the group too.

"Uncle Raymond, are you expecting someone?" Tessa asks, pointing to the door behind me.

I whip my head around and, of course, Amara is standing there in all her beauty. *Yes!!! Thank You, Jesus.* "Amara."

She sends me a small wave as she approaches me and I have to stop myself from running to her. She is wearing a blue jumper over black jeans, with a matching blue headband, hoop earrings, and flat shoes. I have to clear my throat to bring myself back to earth, so I don't look like a fool staring at her.

"You made it. I thought you got lost."

"Sorry, Ray." She tilts her head and presses her lips together in a cute way which tugs at my heart. "African timing, I guess?"

Can you imagine this girl?

I laugh and shake my head. "That's okay." I smile before bending over to give her a side hug. The scent of her rose perfume fills my nostrils, followed by the scent of coconut and lavender radiating from her hair, which is still tucked away in big, neat cornrows.

Chai, this girl go make me catch cold o.

"*Ahem!!!*" Kojo clears his throat, reminding me of our audience.

"Oh, hey, everyone." I turn around to face the room of teens with a smile on my face. "Please allow me to introduce you to a friend of mine—Amara."

"Hello, Aunty Amara." They all greet her in unison.

"Hello, everyone. Nice to meet you all." She sends them a smile big enough to capture anyone's heart.

"Amara will join us today, so please be nice to her." I gestured for her to take the empty seat next to Tessa. Amara walks over and places her very tiny bag on the carpeted floor before sitting down. *I wonder whether she can even fit her fist in that bag.*

Closing my eyes, I finally say the opening prayer and after everyone echoes an "amen," I pick up my Bible and give a short talk about seeking God's face through His Word.

As I teach from the book of Proverbs, I can't help but steal glances at Amara, and every time I do, I find her big brown eyes focused on me—always concentrating and always paying attention. When I give out the first activity, I break up the group into pairs, but since Tessa is the last one, I pair her with Amara.

I hand out pens, sheets of paper, and note cards which have different Bible passages written on them. "It's very important that we learn how to approach God's Word with an open mind, so we don't misinterpret it. I want you to discuss these passages on your notecards with your partner and one person from each pair will tell us what they have learnt at the end of the exercise. Got it?"

"Yes, Uncle." They all reply.

"Okay, your time starts now."

Everyone gets to work and I turn up my Afrobeat gospel playlist on Spotify. My gaze sweeps across the different groups, but it lingers more on Amara and Tessa. I watch how Amara interacts with Tessa, the way she is gentle with her, asking her questions, flipping through the Bible pages, and helping her find passages to help with the exercise.

Amara is such a natural with children, but judging only from how hesitant she was to apply for the research associates program, I can tell there's something holding her back. I'm hoping to find out what that is as I get to know her.

After fifteen minutes, I wrap up the exercise and a representative from each group shares what they've learnt. Kojo is the last one to speak and after a round of his jokes, and making everyone laugh, he finally goes back to his seat.

"Okay, who's ready for the fun part?"

"Is it time for food?" Kojo asks. "My stomach is playing drums right now."

"Yes, Kojo. You guys know we always buy food, but there's a twist today. There's no food."

Displeased groans pass around the groups, and I spot Amara's chuckle before she sends me a knowing glance. "There's no food because the boys are going to be cooking for us." I stifle a laugh when I see the shock on the boys' faces.

"What?" Matthew exclaims, his jaw dropping.

"Yes, that's right. Last time the girls cooked, so today, it's your turn. If you boys want us to eat on time, you better get over here and I'll show you how to do it."

"Are you being serious?" Taiwo asks as he walks over to me. "Why do *we* have to do it?"

"Because cooking, my friend, is an important life skill *everyone* needs to learn irrespective of gender." I hand out aprons to Brian and Kojo. "Come on, Ekene, the food won't cook itself. Maybe you can sing to us, so we don't get bored."

The boys drag their feet toward the kitchen, and I can feel Amara's eyes watching me. To be honest, I'm not bothered. It doesn't get any more real than this and if I must *"woo"* her, then she needs to see the real me.

In the kitchen, I show the boys how to cut the vegetables, and they take out the onions, tomatoes, and bell peppers from the bags. Soon, all the vegetables are chopped and ready to go. As the boys work, I walk back to the main room to meet Amara, who is now talking with all four girls. "Hey, are you alright?"

They all turn to face me, and Amara smiles. "Yeah, these lovely girls are keeping me company." She squeezes Kehinde and Tessa's hands.

"Are you sure they're treating you well? You can always tell me if Tessa is giving you trouble."

Tessa feigns a gasp. "Uncle Raymond, I'm behaving, I promise."

"Alright, I'm watching you." I squint at her.

"Make sure you give the boys a hard time—especially Matthew." Tessa smirks.

"Well, I hope if he says that about you next time, you won't be offended." I smile and head back to the kitchen. Over the next hour, the boys and I blend the vegetables before frying and adding the rice. Half an hour later, the jollof rice is done, and ready to be sampled.

"Who wants to be the first to taste?" The boys and I approach the ladies with a bowl of rice in my hands.

"I think Aunty Amara should go first." Tessa says before her gaze finds Matthew as usual.

"That's a brilliant idea." I stretch the bowl of rice toward Amara. "The people have spoken."

"You sure?" Amara asks, looking at the boys.

"Aunty Amara, if it tastes bad, please blame Uncle Raymond." Kojo says and everyone laughs.

"Hey, cut it out. The food will taste delicious. Boys, trust your hard work." I say, before turning to Amara again.

She takes the bowl from my hands before leaning forward and taking a whiff of the aroma. "Hmm, this smells delicious."

"Careful, it's hot." My heart races as we all watch her. *Wait, did we even add the Maggi seasoning?*

I hold my breath as Amara puts a forkful of rice in her mouth and I watch her face as she chews.

"Hmm." She moans before taking another forkful and another, and another. "Ray, this is...this is delicious."

"Yes!!!" The boys clap.

"I bet it tastes better than the girls' food," Matthew adds.

"No, it does not." Tessa responds and then Matthew and Tessa start bickering in the background, but all I'm thinking about is the fact that Amara loves my food.

"We should do a cookout in the future," Nicole suggests. "It's the only way we can know for sure who is the better cook."

"Yeah, it's on," Kojo says.

"Alright, alright, let's all relax." I say. "We can decide on a cookout later but for now, can we eat please?"

Everyone stands up and heads to the kitchen, leaving Amara and I behind. "Thank you for helping me today."

She holds my arm and squeezes. "No, thank you for all you do, Ray. This is amazing. Well done."

Amara smiles and walks in front of me, leaving me to fight the urge to break into a *zanku* dance step. *Thank You, Lord, for softening her heart toward me.*

13

AMARA

"So how is it over there in Madagascar? Have you seen a lion yet?" I snort when Teeyana rolls her eyes on my phone screen. "You know I'm only kidding, girl." I shake my head as I lay the edges of my hair using a toothbrush and some hair gel. I don't have time to wash my hair yet, so these feed in cornrows are gonna have to hang on for another week.

"Life over here is very interesting," Teeyana says. "It's so hot and I've been sweating in places I didn't even know I could sweat. I also have mosquito bite marks all over my legs and I've been drinking so much water because my mouth is always dry after speaking to so many people every day." Teeyana says, before turning her phone camera to show me the long line of men, women, and children sitting in the shade outside the Good News Hospital in Mandritsara.

I spot Jayden at the back, speaking to a woman cradling a baby in her lap, and behind him is a grey brick building. The sandy earth is reflecting the sun's rays, and patches of sunlight are scattered across the grey cemented floors of the building. The imagery transports me back to the one time I visited Nigeria when I was fifteen years old. *Man, it's been so long.*

"Wow, that's a lot of people." I place the toothbrush down and bring my phone close to my face. "It looks like you guys are doing great work, though."

"Only by God's grace." Teeyana nods. "I've met men and women in the last few days who have experienced so much grief, so it's a blessing to help them in their journey of healing."

"Hey, Amara." Jayden squeezes his head into the frame, a grin plastered on his face.

"Hey, lover boy." I wave at Jayden briefly before frowning at him. "I hope you're taking care of my BFF. If not, I'll be whooping your butt with my slipper." I use my stern *"Nigerian mom"* voice but we all end up laughing instead.

"You know she's in good hands." Jayden plants a kiss on Teeyana's cheek before leaving us again.

Throughout the four years Teeyana and Jayden have been dating, I've never, and I mean *never,* felt a hint of jealousy until today—until now. Is it wrong that I want the conversation to be about me for once? Is it wrong that I want to talk about a guy who is giving me attention too?

"I went out with Raymond." I blurt out before my brain registers what I've said.

Teeyana frowns. "Raymond? Who's Raymond?"

Amara, what are you doing? You know he's just a friend. "Erm, the guy who spilled coffee on me, remember?"

Teeyana's eyes widen. "Wait, what? You went on a date with him and you didn't tell me?" Her eyes almost pop out of her head. "Amara, you better start spilling."

A grin spreads across my face, signifying the satisfaction in my heart. *I'm loving this attention already.* "He invited me to a youth event he organized at his church and he taught the boys how to cook jollof rice for me and the girls. It was so cute."

"Wait a minute. He cooks? Jollof rice?" Teeyana's voice rises with every question. "Dude, where did you find this guy?"

I laugh and glance at my reflection in my dressing table mirror. Satisfied with how my edges looks, I stand up and pick up my work bag. "Girl, my night shift starts in an hour. I have to leave now." Well, technically I don't have to leave now, but Teeyana's gotta work to get the information out of me.

"No, wait. You can't spring this on me and then up and leave. Give me details, please."

Another smile of contentment creeps up my lips as I sigh and sit on the bed again. I tell Teeyana about how Ray and I met again at the relationships seminar, how he offered to buy me hot chocolate, how he came to the NICU to get my number and how he literally treated me like a queen at his youth event. I might not be attracted to him, but it feels good to have a guy show me attention.

"Wow." Teeyana brings her hands up to her mouth. "You never told me you were speaking to him this whole time."

"Girl, there's nothing to tell. I don't think it'll lead to anything."

"But...but it sounds like he wants to be more than your friend." Teeyana leans in. "Listen, you have to give me updates every single day. I don't want to wake up tomorrow morning and find out you're married."

I tip my head back and laugh. "And yet, you call me a drama queen." I stand up again and sling my backpack over my shoulder. "He's a really nice guy, but I can't see myself being with him. He's not my type." *Although, his bald haircut doesn't look too bad up close. He has a nice head shape for it and it suits him.*

Teeyana's brows knit together. "Hmm, let me guess, he doesn't tick the boxes on your list?"

"Nope." I shake my head.

"Okay, but have you told him you're not interested? You know, so he doesn't keep his hopes up?"

I shrug. "Nah. I just want to have fun with the process, you know?"

Teeyana wipes away a bead of sweat on her forehead and steps into the shade. "Amara, don't you think it'll be best to tell him sooner rather than later?"

What, and then lose all the attention I've been getting? Heck, no.

I resist the urge to roll my eyes because I know she's right. I'll still do it my way though, because it's my life. "Of course," I respond. "I want to know him a bit more. Something might change. You never know with these things."

Teeyana nods. "That's true, but you'll pray about it, right?"

"Of course," I say, even though I don't see the point. I'll go ahead with my current plan for now and see how that turns out. "Thanks, girl." I pick up my house keys from the bed. "I'll keep you updated."

"You better. I want to sing *Amara and Raymond sitting on a tree. K-I-S-S-I-N-G.*"

"*Ugh*, go away." We both laugh as I end the call and stand up.

Half-way across the room, my gaze falls on my laptop on my bed and I stop in my tracks. Ray's words come flashing back to me, *"So promise me you'll apply?"* and before I know it, I'm retracing my steps back to my bed again.

Opening my laptop, I scroll through the hospital website and pull out the application form for the NICU research associates program. Two days ago, I attended a brief lunchtime talk led by Dr. Miller and I was able to ask him a few questions. Ray was right. Dr. Miller seemed nice, so when I got back home, I filled out the application form and saved it.

I can't shake off how much Ray believes in me even though he barely knows me. I've heard those same words from my mom, my dad, and Teeyana. But hearing Ray say it made me realize that I have to try. No matter how scary it is, I have to at least try, so I won't spend the rest of my life proving to the dark voice that its opinion about me is right.

Reading through my saved answers one last time, I hit send before closing my laptop. I exhale slowly and smile. "See, it wasn't too bad, was it?" I stand up and head out the door. "Just take it one step at a time, girl. One step at a time."

The view in the hospital garden at night is a sight worth beholding. Lights line the sidewalk on each side and ignite the path, the benches, and the garden. It's past one a.m. now and I'm on my first break for the night. The smell of the shed autumn leaves on the grass awakens my senses as the coffee cup warms my fingers.

I don't like coffee, but boy, I don't think I'll survive this night shift without it. The breeze presses against my skin as I walk down the sidewalk to my favorite spot. A man and woman dressed in burgundy scrubs cross the garden in the opposite direction going toward the ER. An ambulance is leaving the premises and turning into the main road, while the automatic doors at the main entrance open and close as people walk in and out of the hospital.

The weird thing about this night shift is that I've been thinking about Ray more often than I would like. I think it's because of the conversation I had with Teeyana before work, but to be honest, I'm not sure. *I need to do something about this Ray situation.*

"You did really well with the girls, you know?" Ray told me after his youth group session two weeks ago. *"The girls love you."*

I shrugged, finding it hard to take the compliment. *"Yeah, well. I didn't do anything."*

"Are you serious? You were great. I've never seen Tessa pay this

much attention during a session since I met her. She always finds a way to talk about Matthew. You know how to relate with them and it's so inspiring to watch."

A smile tugs at my lips and the butterfly feeling I felt that day comes flooding back as I remember how Ray showered me with praises. If I didn't know myself, then maybe I'd believe him easily. But unfortunately, I know myself too well to believe that I can add value to someone else's life when I'm still struggling through mine. Look at how long it took me to send a stupid application form for the research associates program. If little things like that scare me, how can I inspire and encourage others?

I sit down on the bench and place my cup on its cold, hard surface. The truth is, I enjoy Ray's company and I want to know more about him. But I also don't want to narrow down my options too soon. He's the first guy who has ever shown interest in me, so I think this is making me too excited.

Don't let anyone pressure you, Adamma. Dad's words cling to my thoughts. I stare across at the pond not too far away and after sipping on my drink again, my phone vibrates in my pocket. When I take it out, my heart skips a beat when Ray's name appears on my screen.

Raymond: Hey, sorry I forgot to message you earlier. I was still recovering from my night shift.

Me: Hey, it's okay. You needed to rest, so I don't blame you.

Raymond: I remember you said you had your first night shift tonight?

Me: Yeah, I'm on my break now

Raymond: Oh, great. How is it going?

Me: It's going well, but I just want to know why you're still awake at this time

Raymond: I'm awake because I'm thinking about you

My heart somersaults in my chest, and I bite my lip to stop myself from squealing. "Oh, he didn't just say that." I put my phone back in my pocket and shake my head. "Snap out of it, girl. Snap out of it."

My phone starts vibrating continuously and when I take it out, Ray's name flashes on my screen again. *Why is he calling me?* My thumb hovers over the end button. "This boy is tryna get me in trouble." I mutter before swiping green and pressing the phone against my ear. "Aren't you supposed to be sleeping?" An involuntary smile forms on my lips as I ask the question.

He laughs for a few seconds, and the richness of his voice stirs up happiness in my heart. "I've spent the whole day sleeping, my thumbs are too tired to type, and I wanted to hear your voice."

Aww, why is he so sweet? He is not making this easy for me.

"How are you?" Ray asks and I pause. So many people ask me that question all the time, but there's something about the weight on Ray's voice, the intonation, and the emotion it carries, that makes me believe that he truly cares.

"I feel tired because I'm sitting down now, but when I get back on my feet, I'm sure I'll be fine." I sip on my coffee.

"Yeah, first night shifts are hard, but trust me, your body will get used to it. The hours will pass and morning will be here in the blink of an eye."

I sigh. "I really hope so."

"So, do you have any plans for the morning?" He asks.

I raise my eyebrows and laugh. "Errm....sleep all day? You don't want me running a marathon after my night shift, do you?"

Ray chuckles. "No, I'd like to buy you breakfast. You finish at 7:30, right?"

Aww. "Yeah, I do." My mind races as I try to imagine what he's planning.

"Okay, in the morning I'll be at your favorite spot in the garden. There's a good breakfast place not too far from the hospital."

I press my lips together to stop myself from squealing into my phone. "Okay," I say after forcing a calm composure.

"Well, I won't take much of your time. Please, make sure you stay hydrated because I don't want you getting headaches."

His tone is warm, yet very serious, which gives me no other option but to reply with, "Yes, doctor."

As I end the call, I lean back on the bench and finally let out the squeal I've been holding in. *Why do I feel this way?* I thought I knew what I wanted, but now I'm not too sure. The more I talk to Ray, the more I want to talk to him.

I stand up and toss my empty coffee cup into the nearby trash can before walking back to the main entrance. I should pray about this like Teeyana said. I thought Ray was only going to be my friend so why am I getting butterflies, squealing, and smiling like a fool every time I hear his voice? *Lord, please help me.*

14

AMARA

I drag my aching feet toward the double doors of the NICU, my eyes begging for sleep, and my stomach growling at me. My hand flies to my abdomen and I kiss my teeth. I knew drinking coffee on an empty stomach would do me no good.

I wish these NICU incubators were much bigger, because the Lord knows I would rather crawl into one of them and sleep. But it's okay. Six more hours and I'll be back in my bed. *Come on, girl, you can do this.*

As I tap my ID badge on the intercom and open the door, my gaze falls on a doctor walking away from the nurse's station and down the hallway toward me. Over the last few months, I've worked with a lot of doctors here at the NICU, but not *this* doctor.

He has a serious expression on his face, his big strides are purposeful, and when he rolls up the sleeves of his white coat, I take a peek at his veiny, muscular forearms.

When he is close enough, I catch a glimpse of his full, pink lips, and his neatly trimmed beard which connects. His facial expression softens as he walks past me. "Hey," he says and flashes his bright white teeth before continuing his walk.

My stomach flips inside of me, sleep clears from my eyes, and I almost trip on my shoelaces. *Oh, my gosh. He just spoke to me.*

"Hey." I wave and freeze on my spot as I watch him walk out the door, his strong back muscles almost bursting out of his white coat.

I stand there for a few seconds before a gust of draught coming in through the open window slaps me back to my senses and forces me to move my legs.

When I finally get back to the nurse's station, I find Claire, Imani, and Aaliyah sitting down and talking. I place my elbows on the desk and support my tired head with one hand. "Girls, who was that?" I say, before glancing at the door one more time.

Imani leans forward and follows my gaze before using her rubber bands to tighten her space buns. "Who? The doctor who just left?"

"Yeah, who is he? I've never seen him before."

Claire stands up. "That's Jamar. He's one of the locum PICU doctors. He comes over to the NICU sometimes to borrow our equipment."

"I see." My gaze travels to the door again, hoping that the handsome doctor would walk back in.

Aaliyah adjusts her green hoodie over her scrubs. "Why you asking, though? You think he's hot, don't you?" A smirk crosses her lips and my cheeks warm up.

"No...I was just asking." I swallow and push myself away from the desk.

"It's okay, Amara. You can admit it," Imani says. "We all think he's very attractive. I mean, it's not every day you meet a tall, dark, and handsome man with charming blue eyes. Do you know how long we've been trying to get him to notice us? You can join the queue, sister."

"Well, even if Amara thinks Jamar is handsome, I'm sure she's not interested because another *special* doctor has his eyes on her." Claire winks at me and my heart drops to the floor.

Really Claire? You choose to bring up Ray now?

"*Oooh.*" Imani and Aaliyah both sing-song.

"Come on, Amara. Tell us all about it," Aaliyah says.

"Yeah, who is this mystery doctor?" Imani asks.

I flash them a nervous smile, and my hand flies to the back of my head as I scratch my scalp. "I..uh..I think my break is over now. Aaliyah, you're next." I turn around and check the monitor on the wall, focusing on the heart tracing for the babies I'm looking after before walking away.

There's nothing wrong with admiring someone else. I mean, it's not like Ray has asked me to be his girlfriend or anything. I'm still single and ready to mingle.

I go about the rest of my night shift, trying not to think about Ray or about the handsome new doctor who I'm sure I will never see again. Unfortunately, I fail at doing both and soon, my thoughts are occupied with both Ray and Jamar. What if I see Jamar again? What if he is a Christian and he asks me out on a date? What will I do then?

The hours pass just like Ray said they would, and now my first night shift is over in the blink of an eye. "You did great." Claire hugs me before I pick up my bag to leave. "Now, go get some rest, okay?" She sends me a warm smile, even though her own fatigue is obvious from the wrinkles on her forehead and the dark circles under her eyes.

"Thanks, Claire." I return a small smile with all the strength I have left in me. As I walk out of the hospital, the sun's morning rays warm my face, and even though I tried not to think about Ray all night, I'm excited to see him this morning.

If my feet weren't aching so much, I would be skipping down the sidewalk leading to the garden, but I'm choosing to keep my composure today.

My heart rate quickens, and I let out short breaths as I round the corner with a big grin on my face, expecting to see Ray's tall frame, waiting and smiling back at me, but my grin disappears when Ray is not there.

I stop in my tracks and something shifts in my chest. My gaze sweeps through the whole area as an ambulance parks in front of the ER and cars drive in and out of the parking lot. Different doctors and nurses walk into the hospital to start their morning shift, but not Ray. I can't find him anywhere. *I don't understand. He said he'd be here.*

I search for my phone which is buried underneath all the crap I carry around in my bag. When I turn it on, there are three missed calls from Ray, a voicemail, and a text message.

I'm about to open the text message when a call comes in from Ray. "Hello?"

"Hey. Good morning. Are you okay?" He asks and his caring voice soothes some of the disappointment in my heart.

"Yeah, I am. Sorry I missed your calls. Are you still coming?"

He lets out a deep sigh. "Please don't hate me for this. I'm so sorry, but I can't come for our breakfast date this morning. I was about to leave when my pastor called. I was supposed to have a meeting with him this afternoon but he moved it up because he's going to be busy for the rest of the day. If I had come to the hospital first, I would have been late for the meeting. I'm really sorry. Please forgive me?"

"It's okay. You don't have to apologize." I say, trying to hide my disappointment.

"Thank you. I'll make it up to you. I *promise,*"

"Okay," I respond. "Well, hope you have a nice day."

When I get off the phone with Ray, my growling stomach

forces me to find the breakfast place he talked about. After a five minute walk, I'm sitting at a table and flipping through the menu, the pictures of pancakes, sweet cream butter, and syrup making my stomach growl even more.

"Is this seat taken?" A voice says from above and I snap my head up. My gaze meets the same charming blue eyes, pink lips, and bright smile I saw a few hours ago. The night shift was hard on me, but at least now I know I wasn't hallucinating.

"Eerrm...no, it's not." I say, pulling my bag from the table and placing it on the floor next to me.

"Sorry, I was about to order some breakfast when I saw you sitting here by yourself. You were the one I saw last night at the NICU, right?"

Aww, he remembers me. How cute is that?

"I thought I'd come over here and introduce myself." He smiles and extends his hand to me. "My name is Jamar, and I locum on the PICU sometimes. What's your name?"

Oh, my gosh. He wants to know me? Okay, girl, calm down and tell him your name.

"Amara..." I force the word out of me as if it's foreign. "You already know where I work I'm sure." I reach for his hand and he covers it with his, the softness of his palms sending a warm sensation up my spine.

He laughs and licks his lips—his full, pink lips—the same kinda lips that can make a girl forget her name. *I'm surprised I didn't forget mine.*

"Yeah, I figured that's where you work," he says. "Can I buy you something?"

"Oh, no, you don't have to. I can—"

"Please, I insist." When his blue gaze meets mine, my breath catches in my throat and I can no longer refuse.

"Okay." That's all I say before going back to watching him as he studies the menu.

Is God trying to tell me something? This man looks like He took him straight out of my list. Did He prevent Ray from coming this morning so I could meet Jamar again?

Oh, hold up. Is this guy even a Christian?

I clear my throat. "Erm...sorry to interrupt, Jamar, but I'll need to leave in about an hour because I have a church meeting to attend after my nap." I lie. I have to do it because I need to see his reaction when I mention church. The Lord knows if he tells me he's anything other than a Christian, then I'll be fleeing away from this temptation.

"That's okay. We won't be long. I go to church too, so I know you need all the energy you can get." He smiles before closing his menu and giving me his undivided attention.

Okay, that's it. That seals the deal. Teeyana didn't think God could bring me a man who ticks all my boxes? Well, God proved her wrong. This is a sign for me to explore my options. I'm not committed to anyone. I never made a promise to Ray, so I don't have to put all my eggs in one basket. *Yaas, Jesus.*

15

RAYMOND

Sigh. I really wanted to take her out that day. I had a whole plan and I was looking forward to spending more time with her. But as I was about to leave the house, Pastor Ben called me.

It's not that I forgot about the meeting. We planned for it to be at two p.m. In fact, the plan was to spend some time with Amara, take her home, and then go to church. But obviously, it didn't work out that way.

I hope she doesn't feel like I ditched her or that I'm someone who goes back on my word. I'm not like that at all. I need to make it up to her somehow.

"Mr. Lover." Joe's voice makes me jump slightly in my seat. "Are you even listening to me?"

I stare blankly at Joe, who is furrowing his eyebrows at me. After my initial meeting with Pastor Ben, he loved my idea of doing more activities with the youth. He asked me to come up with more activities for the whole year and bring it to him at our next meeting so we can talk about funding. Joe has kindly come over to help me brainstorm.

I kiss my teeth. "I'm listening, *nau.*"

Joe side-eyes me. "*Ehe-heh?* So what was the last thing I said?"

I sigh and drop the stack of papers I'm holding on the round table separating the two of us. "I need a coffee break." I push my chair back and the resulting sound vibrates the fruit bowl at the table's center. "Do you want one?" I ask, but I don't wait for Joe's reply as I walk over to the cupboard and take out two mugs. When I look back at Joe, he is staring at me. "What?"

"Trouble in paradise?" Joe leans back, crossing his legs on top of the chair I just vacated and I resist the urge to roll my eyes at him.

"Not really." I respond, pouring coffee into both mugs before placing the coffee maker back in its usual position. "I want to tell Amara about my intentions." I walk over to the fridge and take out a bottle of creamer. "It's not too soon, is it?"

Joe straightens his back, and his mouth stretches into a grin. "Wow, you want to make things official? This is a serious something."

I pour the creamer into Joe's cup and stir it before approaching the table again. "You...don't think I'll scare her away? We've known each other now for almost two months, so...it's a good time to let her know how I feel, right?" I place both mugs on the table.

"Yes." Joe nods. "I think you should tell her you like her, so you don't end up in the friend-zone."

"Exactly." I place the cups of coffee on the table before making my way across the kitchen and standing next to the window.

"Bro, you've never had a problem telling girls how you feel. Why are you hesitant about this one?" Joe asks.

I sigh and focus on the cars passing on the street, and the skyline of the buildings. "Because I've been praying about this for the past two months and I think Amara could be the one."

"And that scares you because?"

I turn around to face Joe. "I don't want to do anything that would ruin my chances or make her leave like the other girls did."

"Mmm hmm." Joes shakes his head and leans forward. "I'm not worried about you *doing* anything. Bro, if you continue relying on God, Amara will see for herself how amazing you are. Plus, if she's the one, then you don't have to worry about her leaving because she won't."

Joe's right. How could I ever think for one second that I have control over this? God has been orchestrating my journey from the beginning and He's still in control. "Thanks, man. I really needed that reminder."

"Anything for you, Mr. Lover." Joe smirks and sips on his coffee.

I kiss my teeth. "See your head. *Oya,* remove your legs from my chair, *jor.*" I walk back to the table and push his feet off before occupying my seat again.

"So as I was saying before your mind vacated the premises and started thinking about your woman." Joe grins and I send him a glare. "I was suggesting a retreat for the teens. You could take them to a place they've never been to before—someplace nice."

I click my fingers. "Yes. That's a brilliant idea. It'll help them build friendships."

"Exactly." Joe says. "You can have different workshops about Bible study, prayer, and even mental health."

Joy bubbles in my chest as the picture of the retreat forms in my mind. "Yes, they're not too young to learn about the Biblical view of sex and marriage. I think some of them really need it." I say as Tessa comes to mind. "And you know what?" I grin. "Amara could come with us too. I think the girls would really love that."

"Exactly." Joe leans back and crosses his legs over the empty chair next to us. "Don't forget you'll need parents' consent for this, so give plenty of time when you pick a date."

I pick up a pen from the table and scribble some words on the paper in front of me. My hand writes fast, as if the ideas would fly away if I write any slower.

Just then, my phone vibrates, and a text message pops up on the screen from Amara. I drop my pen and pick up the phone, tapping on her message and scanning through it.

Amara: Hey. Sorry for the late reply. I fell asleep as soon as I got back.

Ray: That's okay. No need to apologize. Did you rest well?

Amara: Yeah, I did. These night shifts are honestly a killer. I don't like them at all.

Ray: But you still survived three nights in a row, so well done. God will continue to strengthen you.

Amara: Amen. Thanks, Ray.

"Uncle Raymond? Is Aunty Amara going to join us again soon?" Tessa asks at the end of our Hallelujah Fellowship which we had instead of Halloween. If I didn't know the girl any better, I would have brushed off her question as innocent. But one thing I've learnt from working with these teens is that they know way more than I think they do.

I stack the chair I'm holding on top of another before turning to her. "I don't know. Would you like her to come back?" I smile.

"Yeah." She leans against my stack of chairs, one finger making invisible circles on her phone screen. "She's nice, intelligent, and very beautiful."

I laugh. "You're right about that. She is *very* beautiful."

Tessa squeals. "I knew it. I knew you liked her."

"*Shhhh*. Can you please keep your voice down?" A finger flies to my lips and I glance around to find that all the teens have left the room, leaving only Tessa and Breonna behind.

I arch an eyebrow and lean back, looking down at Tessa. "And what makes you think I like her?" *This should be interesting.*

"Well, *duh*, I saw the way you kept looking at her when she came here. The way you kept smiling at her every time your eyes met. I even saw the way you keep smiling at your phone now. She calls you Ray and nobody calls you Ray." The teen nods and crosses her arms, mischief written in her eyes. "So...are you still going to deny it?"

I scoff. "Tessa, nobody is denying anything. I just—"

"*Aha*, so you like her." She grins and turns to Breonna, who is sitting in one of the lower stacked chair towers. "Bree, he likes her. I told you."

Breonna looks up from her phone and pushes herself up. "Really?" She approaches us with a grin which matches Tessa's. "You should ask her to be your girlfriend, Uncle. I'm sure she'll say yes."

Wow, I've been with these children for almost a year, but I'm always shocked by how direct they are.

"Yes, you should." Tessa echoes. "I'm sure she'll say yes."

I never had these discussions with my elders while I was growing up. My mother always said that anything to do with sex and relationships was a taboo. I wish they had taught us about these subjects in church instead of us learning about them the hard way.

"Uncle Raymond?" Breonna's voice shakes me out of my thoughts. "Will you ask her then?" The girl's eyes widen behind her glasses.

I sigh. "Breonna, when you grow up, you'll realize that life is not as simple as you think."

Tessa frowns. "Yeah it is. I don't understand why grown-ups like to make it complicated."

I raise my eyebrows at her wise words. "Oh, really?"

"Yeah." She nods. "It's like me and Matthew, for example. Crushing on someone without telling them is stupid and a waste of time, so I told him I like him and guess what? He likes me too."

I frown. "Well, Tessa, I don't want to burst your bubble, but you and I know your mom doesn't want you dating yet."

"But why, Uncle Raymond?" She whines. "It's no big deal. Everyone's doing it. Why do African parents have to be such killjoys?"

I throw my head back and laugh before taking a seat on the carpeted floor. Tapping the space across from me, I invite Tessa and Breonna to sit too. "Listen, girls. I know how frustrating it can be when we're told what to do. I know it's annoying when parents impose rules on us when we don't understand. I know because I was once a teenager and my strict Nigerian mother never let me out of the house."

"Wow, that sounds awful." Tessa says and Breonna giggles.

"My point is, we always see rules as restrictions, but have you ever thought about seeing them like a barrier to protect you?"

"Hmm, let me think about it." Tessa taps a finger on her chin. "Nah, I still see only restrictions."

I roll my eyes and move closer. "You'll soon realize that not everything is good for you, Tessa. It is important to obey your parents. They love you and want the best for you." I turn to look at Breonna. "Jesus wants you to obey your parents, right, Breonna?"

The shy girl nods and pushes her glasses close to her face.

Tessa drops her shoulders with a heavy sigh. "Well, that's

disappointing. I was hoping you'd bully my mom into letting me date Matthew."

I snort. "*Abeg.* I don't want trouble." The girls giggle as I stand up. "Come on, it's time to go."

"But Uncle Raymond, I—"

"Tessa? I'm sure your mom is waiting for you. We will discuss this again another time."

"Bye, Uncle Raymond." They turn around and head for the door.

"Oh, Tessa? One minute please." I call out and Breonna hugs Tessa before walking out the door, and leaving her friend behind.

"Yes, Uncle?" Tessa approaches me again.

I sigh and look at her. *Lord, please give me wisdom.* "Tessa, what's really going on between you and Matthew?" I start, and the teen averts her gaze, choosing to look at the walls instead of me.

"Erm...nothing. We like each other, that's all." She fiddles with her fingers.

I shift my weight to my right leg and tuck my hands in my pockets. "I saw both of you in one of the meeting rooms during the church service on Sunday. I already spoke to Matthew earlier today, so you don't have to lie to me."

"It was only a kiss." The teen blurts out as she shakes her head. "I promise we didn't do anything else."

I raise an eyebrow. "Are you sure?"

She nods vigorously. "Yes, I'm sure. Please don't tell my mom. She'll kill me if she finds out."

I open my mouth to speak but the words evade me when I catch a glimpse of the tears moistening her eyes. Sighing heavily, I shake my head and take my hands out of my pockets. *Lord, please help me.* "Okay, fine. I won't tell your mom. But you *have* to promise, the same way Matthew promised, that this won't happen again. The fact that you two were hiding only proves that you know what you're doing is wrong."

"I'm sorry, Uncle Raymond." Tessa lowers her head. "It won't happen again."

"It's okay. You're a good kid, Tessa. Matthew is too. Please don't let the devil lure you into doing something you'll regret later." And I hope I don't regret my decision later.

16

RAYMOND

I pace the length of my balcony with my phone in hand before pausing and leaning against the metal barrier. Inhaling the chilly November air, I watch the cars pass down below and exhale deeply. Every day, for the last week, I've come out here and dialed Amara's number; but every day, I've talked myself out of it.

You should ask her to be your girlfriend. Tessa's words echo in my mind again. Even though the girl has a lot to learn, I have to agree with her. I can sometimes make things too complicated for myself. "Give me faith, Lord." I whisper. "Please give me faith to trust that you have this under control. I have kept you at the center of this whole process since I met Amara. Please help me with this one. If this is your will, then please go ahead of me and favor me. But if this is not your will, then Lord, I don't want it."

I take a seat in the only chair on my balcony and rest my arms on the table. Dialling her number, I bring the phone up to my ear and wait for her to pick up.

"Hello?" Amara's soft voice comes through the phone.

I clear my throat. "Hey. I hope this isn't a bad time."

"No, it's not. You okay?"

"Yeah...erm." I shut my eyes and let out a heavy sigh. "Are you free on Saturday?"

"Hmm, let me check my calendar." There's a pause on her end followed by a shuffling noise in the background before she speaks again. "Aww no, unfortunately I'll be working on all my weekends for the rest of the month."

"Oh, I see." My heart sinks and I ransack my brain to find an alternative.

"But I'm free on the first Saturday in December," she says.

"That would be perfect," I reply, relief surging through my heart.

"Perfect for what, exactly? Do you have another youth event coming up?"

It dawns on me that I haven't told her why I'm asking about her availability. "Oh no, no. Erm...I'd like to take you out to dinner." I bite my bottom lip.

There's silence on her end for a few moments. Then she finally speaks. "You mean, like a date?"

I gulp. "Yes, exactly. I'd like to take you out on a date."

"Erm..." There's another pause. "Yeah, I suppose I could. That would be fun." Her voice perks up.

Thank You Jesus.

After ending the call with Amara, I slip underneath my covers at ten p.m., so I can wake up early for my shift tomorrow. When I close my eyes and start drifting off, my phone vibrates on my bedside table.

Ugh, I thought I turned this thing off. I groan and move my pillow away from my head before grabbing my phone. I swipe up to turn on the night time mode setting, but the message on my screen makes me pause.

"Debbie?" I rub my eyes before turning my bedside lamp on. "Oh no." My hand flies up to my forehead as memories from our speed-dating session flash in my mind. I promised I would text her when I got back home that night after the seminar, but the thoughts of Amara stole my attention and I forgot. I open her text message.

Debbie: Hey, long time no speak. Just checking you're still alive

Reading her words festers a tightness in my chest. I hunch over to start typing, but pause, my thumbs hovering over my keypad. There's no way I'll be able to explain myself over a text message. I dial her number instead and bring the phone up to my ear. It only rings once before she picks up. "Hey, Debbie."

"Hey, Raymond. I hope my text didn't wake you up." Her voice brings back memories of that night, those wonderful, joyful ten minutes we shared.

"No, it didn't at all. I'm so sorry I didn't call you. The last few weeks have been crazy."

Debbie chuckles and I imagine her beautiful smile. "It's okay. I understand. That's why I'm calling."

"How have you been?"

"Well, to be honest, I've been looking forward to speaking to you again. I thought you had forgotten about me and I almost talked myself out of texting you tonight. But I'm glad I did."

I lean forward and pinch the bridge of my nose. I can't do this to her. It's not fair. I don't want to ruin the foundation I've built with Amara. *Lord, please help me.*

"Raymond, are you still there?" Debbie nudges me out of my thoughts.

"Yeah...yeah, sorry, I'm still here." I let out a heavy sigh and rub the back of my neck. "Listen, Debbie. I really appreciate you checking up on me. But...I don't want to lead you on. I'm really sorry...there's someone else in my life and...I don't think it's fair to drag you two along. I'm sorry."

Debbie sighs. "That's okay. I had a feeling that was the case. But at least now I know. Thanks for being honest with me. Whoever she is, she's very blessed to have you. I hope she knows that."

My heart swells at her kind words. "I appreciate you, Debbie. Thank you so much for understanding. I know God will direct you to that godly man who will love you right."

"Amen *o.*" Debbie responds. "Thank you so much."

We bid ourselves good night, and I turn my phone to night mode. When my head hits the pillow again, my eyes remain open, staring at the small beam of light filtering through my curtains into my dark room. *Lord, please, I hope I just did the right thing.*

I jolt out of sleep in the middle of the night when my phone vibrates again. In confusion, I turn around to see the device flashing on my bedside table. *Oooohhh, who is it again?*

My eyes drift to my clock, which reads two a.m. I frown and reach for the phone, holding back the urge to fling it across the room. But when my gaze lands on the caller ID, I stop myself.

I sit up and bring the phone to my ear. "Hello, Mommy?"

"*Oko mi? Eyaa,* my son. My only son. You have finally picked up my call today. *Jesu ese oh.*"

"Mommy, is everything okay? Are you okay?" A million and one possibilities run through my brain about why she's calling me at this time. Maybe she still hasn't understood that I live in a different time zone and that her seven a.m. is my two a.m., or maybe something bad has happened, and I always dread the latter.

"I am fine *o*. Everyone is fine. I woke up for my morning prayers and thought of you, so I said let me call since you have refused to call me for the past one week."

I let out a sigh of relief before laying on my back. "Mommy, *e ma binu*. Please, don't be angry. Things have been so busy at the hospital, that's why I've been making sure to message you every day. I read your prayers every morning and I always respond to them."

"*Eeeh,* but *Oko mi*, you know I don't like these text messages you keep sending, *eh?* I want to either hear your voice or see your face. Is that too much to ask, my son?"

I use my free hand to massage my temple. "Mommy, I'm sorry. I'll try my best to call you when I get back from work this evening. You have to stop calling me at this time because it's two a.m. for me now."

"Oh, oh, oh. I'm sorry, my son. This thing you call time zone or *kini kan*, keeps shifting from one place to another, *eh?* Can it just not stay in one place for once?"

"No, Mommy, this is America. Things change all the time." I chuckle before rolling on my side to admire her new display photo of her wearing an African print dress with a matching head wrap. "I love your new profile picture. Mommy, you're looking very beautiful."

"Eh, thank you very much, my son. But I will like you to have a woman in your life who you will be telling all these sweet words to. You can't tell me for the rest of your life."

Oh no, not again. "Mommy, please, it's two a.m. I need to be up in four hours. Can we please talk about this when I call you later?"

"Okay, *o*. That would be good because then I can tell you about the nice girl I found for you to marry."

My eyebrows shoot up and sleep disappears from my eyes. "Mommy? Which girl again?"

"Do you remember Feyi? You people used to go to Sunday school together. She is Mama Adetunde's daughter, *nau.*"

Of course I remember Feyi. I used to have a crush on her. She was the most beautiful girl in Sunday school—I think. I was so convinced I was going to marry her when we grew up. I even dreamt of saving up for her bride price when I finished university. But the day Mama Adetunde came to our house to announce that she and Feyi were moving to Kaduna, it was as if my heart was wrenched out of my chest. That's in the past now and none of it matters.

"Yes, Mommy. What about her?"

"*Ehhee, oko mi,* so you haven't heard? This is why we need to speak often so I can update you on what's going on down here. Feyi is back from Kaduna and she is now a banker. A very big banker *o.* I even saw her in church on Sunday, and she told me she has come to stay in Abuja for good. I told her I was going to inform you she was back."

I frown. "Mommy, I hope you didn't tell her anything about my previous relationships."

"*Ah,* no. I didn't. I just told her that you are very single and I will call you and give you her number."

I shake my head when Amara comes to mind. "Mommy, I might be single now, but God willing, I won't be for too long."

"Eh? *Oko mi,* what are you saying? Have you found a wife? Raymond, don't tell me you went and got married without telling me, your mother? Aahhh, Raymond, they had to cut me open to take you out of my body *o.* Why would you ever do such a thing to me?"

"Ah, Mommy, please calm down. I never said I got married."

"Then what are you saying? Do you want Feyi's number or not?"

"No, I don't." I press my lips together, trying to figure out the right words. "I...I met someone. She's very special to me and I don't want to ruin it by speaking to someone else."

"You met someone? Heeyy, *Oluwa ese o.* I've always known my enemies will never prevail. They have tried to destroy your life four good times with these girls you have been meeting, but they will not succeed. My God will prevail. *Oluwa* is involved."

"Amen." I yawn and turn to lie on my side. "Please, can I sleep now?"

"*Ah, ah* but *oko mi,* you can't just give me good news like this and not give me the details? Who is she? Where is she from? Is she a Christian? Does she love God?"

"Mommy, yes, she is a Christian, and yes, she loves God. I will tell you more about her later." I pull my duvet cover over my shoulders.

"Okay, but when will I be able to meet her?"

"Mommy dearest, you will meet her when the time is right. Please don't worry your sweet head. I will call you when I get back from work tonight."

Finally getting my mom off the phone, I place it on the nightstand again before covering my head with my pillow. A smile breaks on my lips when I think about how happy my mom was to hear about the possibility of me finding love again. *Lord, please help me to always put a smile on her face.*

17

AMARA

I love the attention Ray is giving me, but he's not my type, and I've been honest with myself about this from the beginning. Jamar is handsome and I'm attracted to him. Again, I've been honest with myself about this from the beginning. I don't know Jamar as much as I know Ray. That's why I agreed to go on a date with Jamar next Friday—so I can know him better.

When Ray asked me out on a date, I wanted to say no, but it's not like he asked me to be his girlfriend. It's *just* a date. Ray is gentle and sweet, but that's not enough for me. I don't want to settle for less when I know my heart wants more. Maybe I'll find that *"more"* with Jamar. I won't know if I don't explore my options. But I also need to be sure things will work out with Jamar before saying no to Ray.

"Amara, are you okay?" Ray's deep voice breaches into my thoughts and my grip tightens around his arm as we walk down the street. When I turn to look at him, his soft gaze is on me. He has been talking to me for the past five minutes, but I have no idea what he has been saying.

"Hmm?" I tilt my head, and press my lips together.

"Is everything okay?" He halts and places his hand over my arm.

"Yeah, I'm okay." I place my free hand on top of his, giving it a gentle squeeze before smiling at him. "It's just that...this is my first proper date with anyone, so I'm a bit nervous." My gaze drops to my black heeled boots.

Ray turns to face me squarely and gently tips my chin up so I can meet his gaze. "It's just me...Raymond...not the queen of England." He laughs and draws a giggle from my lips too. "You're going to be fine, okay?"

I nod and we turn around, our arms linking again as we continue our walk. The beautiful Atlanta skyline comes to view, but it's the colored lights hanging from the Christmas trees and tinsels wrapped around the street pillars that steal my attention.

I can't remember the last time I went out for an evening walk like this. Since I moved to Atlanta for nursing school four years ago, I've never taken the time to explore the city or visit the beautiful buildings I walk past on my way to work.

I've never even tasted the delicious food in the hundreds of restaurants I've heard about. I thought I would get more time as a new grad nurse, but boy, I lied to myself. *Adulting is a scam.*

"We're almost there." Ray says as we turn round another corner. "That's our destination." He points at the sign of the restaurant shining a few miles away. I tighten my coat's belt around my waist and the cold air hits my face. My heels click-clack against the sidewalk as we approach a man dressed in a red Santa suit ringing a bell.

Ray stops in front of him and pulls out some dollar bills from his wallet before dropping it in the red bucket. To this, the man rings the bell even louder and shouts. "*Ho, ho, ho.* Merry Christmas!!!"

A Caucasian man dressed in a white shirt and black bow tie ushers us into the restaurant and shows us to our table. "I'll be right back to take your orders." He smiles at us before walking away.

Inside the restaurant, a warm breeze glides across my skin as we walk further into the spacious room with tables and sofas arranged in neat rows and columns. Well-dressed men, women, and children are chatting over their food, and soft music is radiating from the speakers above our heads.

A blend of spices and flavors hits my nostrils and my mouth waters as we approach the table closest to the glass window. I hope the food tastes as good as it smells. *Ain't nobody got time for bland food.*

Ray helps me take off my coat, revealing my red ruffle midi dress. I spent half an hour on FaceTime with Teeyana trying to pick an outfit, and we both concluded that the red dress was a good fit for the occasion. It matches my red lipstick, while my black shoes match my black clutch purse. *Frolita* cooperated with me today and my twist-out didn't turn out badly at all.

"Wow," Ray says, his gaze sweeping over me from head to toe with a twinkle in his eyes. "You look very beautiful."

Aww, boy, stapp it! Heat rises to my cheeks and I turn my face away to hide my smile, even though I know he has already seen it. "Thanks, Ray."

He rushes to my side and pulls my chair out, allowing me to slide underneath the table before pushing the chair in again.

As he returns to his seat to settle in his own chair, I study him, fishing for a compliment to return. He looks good in his blue shirt. I love the way it makes his dark eyes pop and how it brings out the white of his teeth. I can't believe I'm saying this, but Ray is actually...not as bad looking as I once thought.

"You look good in blue," I finally say as I grab a menu from the table, and his mouth curves into a broad smile.

"Really?" He smoothes the top of his shirt. "It's my favorite color."

I nod. "I can see why."

Outside the glass window is the most breathtaking view I've ever seen. I place my elbows on the table and rest my chin in my cupped hand as I stare at the view from hundreds of feet above the ground.

Two skyscrapers stand tall, only a few miles apart, one shaped like the tip of a pencil and the other like a rectangle. The traffic is moving at a steady pace on the swervy road below, and bright lights are flashing from the cars. "It's beautiful," I say absentmindedly.

"Still not as beautiful as you." Ray responds and I turn to face him, his own head resting in his hand, but his gaze fixed on me.

I pull out the menu and study it, and my eyes widen when I see the prices of the food. *Wow, that's expensive.* I glance up at Ray as he concentrates on his menu.

The Lord knows I would've been in total disarray right now and shifting in my seat if Ray hadn't made it clear beforehand that he was going to pay for everything tonight. If Dad was here, he would have shaken his head and walked out, refusing to pay so much for such little portions.

The waiter returns to our table like he promised. He greets us again with a warm smile and asks what we would like. After giving our orders, he takes the menus from us and leaves.

"So, tell me more about you." Ray rubs his palms and I chuckle, his question reminding me of my interview for the NICU job.

"What would you like to know, Dr. Aderinto?" I smirk, trying to practice my *"Nigerian accent."*

"Ahh, I love the way your accent changes every time you pronounce my name. You should try pronouncing my *full* name."

Being up for a challenge, I straighten my back and keep my chin up. "Bring it on."

Ray takes out his phone from his pocket and types something on it before handing it over to me. My eyebrows furrow in concentration and I practice it a few times in my head before speaking out loud. "Raymond Oluwagbemiga Aderinto?"

"Nice try. You have to hit the *gbe* correctly though," he says. "It's pronounced Oluwa*gb*emiga." He accentuates.

"Oluwa*gb*emiga?" I try again, cringing at my horrible pronunciation.

"Well done," Ray says, clapping softly. "You finally got it."

"Really?" I ask, surprised. "My Nigerian accent is not the best."

"Baby girl, you need to give yourself some credit."

Baby girl. It's the second time he has called me that. The first time he did, it annoyed me because it sounded patronizing. But this time, it sends a tingling sensation down my spine. There's nothing wrong with wanting to be someone's baby girl, is there?

"Okay, it's my turn now," Ray says, forcing me out of my thoughts. "I have to try pronouncing your name."

"*Pfft.* You and I know that's not fair. Of course you're going to know how to pronounce it." I whine as I type out my full name below his.

He feigns a gasp. "You can't be sure of that. I might surprise you."

He takes the phone from me and after looking at it for only a few seconds, he looks up at me again. "Amarachukwu Ifeoma Ikezie."

The smoothness of his tongue and perfection of the accent makes my heart flutter. "See, I told you. You pronounce my own name better than I do." We both laugh. "It's not fair. Please don't ask about my Igbo." I shake my head and Ray raises his brows.

"You can't speak Igbo?"

Hearing the surprise in his voice, I close my eyes briefly and press my lips together, before searching for an explanation. "Not fluently. Blame my parents." I lift my hands up in surrender as I anticipate Ray's look of disapproval, but it doesn't come.

"We moved to the US when I was five years old," I continue my explanation. "Even though my parents speak to me in Igbo all the time, I always reply in English. I guess I could try speaking it if I put in the effort." I reach for the glass in front of me and take a sip, the cold water refreshing my dry throat. "I'm sure I don't need to ask if you know how to speak Yoruba."

A bright grin crosses Ray's face as he picks up his own glass. "Of course, *nau. Nne,* I can speak it very well." His forced accent makes me chuckle. "And don't worry about not knowing how to speak Igbo. I will gladly teach you Yoruba. I'm sure your parents won't mind."

We both laugh and he looks at me as if there's something on his mind—something he wants to tell me. "What?" I ask.

He stares for a few seconds, but then shakes his head and smiles. "Nothing."

I open my mouth to press him further, but the waiter returns, carrying a large tray of food. In very smooth movements, he places our starters in front of us—my jumbo lump crab cake, and Ray's smoked pork ribs with BBQ sauce.

"How did you and Claire become so close, anyway?" I ask as we dig into our food.

Swallowing his pork ribs, Ray uses the serviette to wipe the corners of his mouth. "My residency years stretched and challenged my faith in many ways, so when I started my fellowship eighteen months ago, I prayed that God would help me have a better experience at this hospital." He clears his throat before continuing.

"One day, my supervisor, Dr. Steele, asked me to assist him with some surgeries and I was shocked because I had only worked there a month." He rubs his chin and places his arm across the table.

"I wanted to tell him I wasn't ready, but I knew if I wanted to grow into a better doctor, I had to challenge myself, you know?" He stares at me, his dark brown eyes searching mine. I nod and lean in, totally being able to relate with him, especially since starting this NICU job.

"Dr. Steele briefed me on the first procedure; it was a twelve-year-old boy with dilated cardiomyopathy. He collapsed while playing football and his mother—who turned out to be Claire, was very anxious about the situation." He sips on his water.

"After many grueling hours of surgery, Dr. Steele asked me to speak to Claire and tell her the surgery was successful. I still remember the look in her eyes when I broke the news to her, how she wept for joy and thanked me for saving her son's life since she didn't want to lose him the same way she lost her husband."

"Oh yeah." I say, as realization dawns on me. "She always talks about how her husband captured her heart the first day she laid eyes on him when she was on holiday in Jamaica."

Ray nods. "Yeah, sadly, he died of heart failure after doing a marathon for charity. It wasn't long after that when Jamie, her son, collapsed at school."

"Wow. The woman has been through a lot. Yet, she is such a joy to be around. I'm so blessed to have her as my mentor."

Ray nods, his gaze still fixed on me. "Claire and Jevon—one of the nurse practitioners in my department, make the ache of missing my mother less. Unfortunately, I've been trying to invite Claire to church, but she doesn't want to hear any of it. I pray that one day, God will heal her heart and save her soul."

"Amen," I say, and without thinking about it, I cover Ray's hand with mine, giving it a gentle squeeze. I'm not sure what this action suggests, but a tugging on my heart forces me to speak up. "You're an amazing person, Ray. I haven't known you for long, but the way you care for your patients is very inspiring." I smile and his face brightens.

"Thank you so much." He places his free hand on top of mine, the warmth of his touch sending a tingling sensation up my back. "You have no idea what your words mean to me."

At that moment, the waiter returns, forcing us to break our contact. He smiles at us and takes away our empty plates, before returning with our main courses of a grilled Colorado rack of lamb for me and a Springer mountain half chicken for Ray.

"Oh, by the way, have you received a reply from Dr. Miller regarding your application?" Ray's eyebrows furrow.

I shake my head and chew on some lamb, hoping my face doesn't show the disappointment twisting my insides. "I don't know why it's taking so long." I shrug. "It's okay, though. Maybe it's not meant to be after all."

Ray places the rib he is holding back on his plate and looks at me. "Amara, can I ask you a question?"

I adjust in my seat, taking note of the seriousness in his voice. "Erm...sure."

"Please, don't take this the wrong way, but...I've noticed that you seem to always settle for the negative. Can I ask why?"

After a long pause, I swallow the chewed bits of lamb in my mouth and sip on some water. "Well, I think it's easier that way. I don't like putting my hopes up and then getting hurt or disappointed." I shrug, trying to convince Ray that that is all there is to it. But I can tell from the way he's still looking at me, that he's not buying it.

Ray sighs and leans forward. "But why? Why do you think it's easier?"

I drop my gaze to the half-eaten food on my plate. Oh, this boy is treading on dangerous grounds. I don't want to open this can of worms. I don't trust myself to keep my emotions together.

I also don't trust that Ray won't judge me and call me a pathetic, sore loser like the dark voice in my head.

"Hey." The warmth from Ray's hand envelopes mine and brings me out of my thoughts. When I lift my head, I meet Ray's soft gaze which sends my doubts flying away. "Please, trust me."

That's how I spend the next fifteen minutes telling Ray about Olivia Hastings—my high school bully. When my parents and I moved from Brooklyn to Boston, I attended Coverton High, where Olivia and her friends used to tease, mock, and throw out racial slurs at me every day. For many months, I believed I was only a piece of trash that could amount to nothing, and Teeyana was the one who finally reported the bullies to the principal because I was too scared to defend myself.

Now many years later, the impact of those hateful words are still etched in my memory. Teeyana has moved on and is doing well, but here I am, still fighting a stupid voice in my head. "Olivia made me believe lies, so I find it easier to stand back and do nothing than to fight, you know?"

Ray says nothing, but instead he maintains a thoughtful look on his face as he keeps his eyes on me.

"Yeah, I know you probably think it's all stupid and I should just get over it, but..."

"Oh, I'm thinking about a lot of things right now, but 'stupid' is definitely not one of them." Ray squeezes my hand gently. "Amara, you are a beautiful and talented woman. God has equipped you with the passion and drive to change the lives of children and He is working in and through you. You're not doing this on your own. If there's ever a day you struggle to believe that, text me or call me, and I'll be there to remind you about how blessed you are. Okay?"

Tears threaten to fall out of my eyes as Ray's words temporarily lift a weight from my shoulders. "Wow. That's...that's the nicest thing anyone has ever said to me." I smile. "Thank you, Ray."

"You're welcome." He returns my smile before picking up his pork rib. "Regarding Dr. Miller, you could pass by his office sometime. Maybe the application is sitting in his junk mail?"

"Oh, yeah." I tilt my head. "I never thought about that. I'll do that when I get the chance. Thanks, Ray."

For the rest of the evening, we talk about different things, which gives me the opportunity to know more about Ray. He tells me more about his childhood, his mom who lives in Nigeria, the passing of his father from a heart attack, and his Uncle Seun who took him in when he moved to the US.

While having dessert, Ray tells me all about his past relationships and what the girls did to him. It would be interesting to hear the girls' perspectives, though. I can imagine how painful a heartbreak is, but to get dumped four times? Boy, I would die from pain and sorrow if that ever happened to me.

The more I get to know this guy, the more I admire his tenacity. For someone who has been through so much, he is always positive and friendly toward others. A little smile crosses my lips when I think about how Ray said God has a sense of humor. If I wasn't running late that day and if Ray hadn't spilled coffee on me, we wouldn't be here right now.

"So do you have a favorite baby yet?" Ray says as he helps me put my coat on. I narrow my eyes at him and he tilts his head back and laughs. "I mean at the NICU."

"Oh, right." I chuckle as well. "Do you remember the baby I was with the first time you came to see me?"

"Yeah, I remember." Ray says as he opens the door and waits for me to step out in front of him.

"Her name is Emily. She was with us over a month ago, then she got better, but then she came back with another infection last week. The poor girl has been fighting her respiratory distress since she came in."

"Aww, that's sad. Babies are good fighters, though. They can be unpredictable sometimes. I pray God grants her a quick recovery in Jesus' name."

"Amen." I respond. "Thank you, Ray."

He smiles at me before sticking out his bent arm. I link my arm with his, and we walk back down the street to his car.

It's ten p.m. when Ray parks in the street across from my studio apartment. We drove for over half an hour in his very cozy car. The perfect lighting, perfect temperature, and perfect music set the right atmosphere for me to doze off.

Ray played a lot of Nigerian worship songs from his Spotify playlist. I recognized some of them from either my parents or church, but most of them were new to me. I've always wanted to add more Nigerian songs to my playlist, so here's my chance.

"We're here." Ray's voice wakes me up from my slumber. "Sorry, it was a long drive. I tried to get you home as quickly as I could, but the traffic was an enemy of progress."

I chuckle, recognizing the use of the term "enemy of progress" from all the Nollywood movies I've watched with my parents. "It's okay, Ray. Thank you so much." I sit up and stretch before yawning.

Ray steps out of the car and walks around to my side. He opens the door and I unbuckle my seatbelt. I take his hand and he helps me step out. My heeled feet find the slippery ground and I falter in my steps, almost slipping, but Ray holds me with a firm grip around my waist.

My heart rate picks up the pace when my face ends up only inches away from Ray's chin. He looks down at me and smiles. "Are you okay?"

I swallow, realizing how close we are, and how good his cologne smells. "Yeah, I'm fine." I push against his chest as I try to stand on my own. Ray's grip on me loosens, but he holds my hand until I'm safe on my feet again. *Ugh, girl, you should have brought flats. What were you thinking?*

Ray walks with me across the road until we're at my door. We climb up the stairs and I take out my keys from my bag before turning to him. "I had a lot of fun tonight. Thank you for everything." I insert the key and twist to open. Maybe if I leave his presence, my heart rate will return to normal.

"Please, wait." Ray says and I pause mid-step. "There's something I need to tell you."

My heart sinks at his words. I know what he wants to say. I've seen the way he looks at me, the way he studies me, and everything he does for me. I know why he is doing these things and I appreciate them, but I'm not ready to give him an answer yet.

Ray takes my free hand and brings it up to his lips, before planting a soft kiss on it. He locks eyes with me again, and the softness of his gaze sends warm sensations up my spine. "I'm not here to play games with you. I've been hurt so many times and I've learnt to appreciate a special woman when I meet one."

Oh, no. He's not making this easy for me.

"I have no doubt that we share something special and I'm certain God's hand is in this." He nods. "I like you very much and if you let me, I'd like to share your world with you, meet your parents, and Teeyana." He smiles.

Aww, he remembers Teeyana's name.

"I want to pursue a relationship with you that will hopefully lead to marriage someday." He rubs the back of my hand with his thumb. "I don't know if this is too soon for you, but I couldn't hide my feelings any longer. I just wanted you to know that. What do you say?"

His eyes search mine as I try to press down on the guilt rising in my chest. Of course I like him too. But I can't tell him that. If Ray had told me this before I met Jamar, then I may have given it a shot. But now, I need to know what Jamar has to offer. I don't want to hurt Ray, so I won't say yes yet. "Thanks for telling me. I appreciate your honesty."

He doesn't say anything, but his eyes keep searching mine. "I...I have to pray about it first." I drop my gaze to the floor, my heart tearing a little. "I'm afraid I'm not as sure as you. I need more time."

His shoulders drop slightly as he gives me a weak nod, but his bright smile returns only seconds later. "Of course," he says. "Take as much time as you need. I'll be here."

18

RAYMOND

"**G**uy, it couldn't have gone any better. Thank you so much for recommending that restaurant. It was beautiful, but it was nothing compared to the beautiful girl I spent the evening with." I smile as I place my phone on the kitchen counter.

"*Eisshh,* come and see *Mr. Lover.* You have seen your wife, *abi*?" Joe says, referencing the lyrics of an afrobeat song.

"*Ah, ah before nko*? I have seen her *o.* One plus one is one indeed." We both laugh as I dish out rice from the rice cooker to my plate.

"So, does this mean you guys are now official? As in, officially official?" Joe asks, and my shoulders drop as I remember Amara's words to me last night. I was hoping she would say yes. I hoped I'd be able to tell the whole world she's my girlfriend, but as much as I'd like to be a married man by my thirtieth birthday, I don't want to pressure her. If she needs time, I'll give her time so God can confirm it to her.

"No, she only said she'll pray about it. She asked me to give her time."

"Okay, no *wahala*. At least she didn't say no, so that's good news."

I nod. "Yes *o*, my brother."

"God is not a God of confusion. This thing He has revealed to you, He will reveal to her too."

"Amen *o*."

"Even if it takes twenty years, *we die here o*."

My smile fades. "*Ah*, guy, please, which one is twenty years again? It's because you have a wife and a child, that's why you are letting this rubbish come out of your mouth, *abi*?"

Joe bursts into laughter. "Bro, if God decides to reveal it tomorrow, who am I to stand in His way?"

"Thank God you are not God." I spread spicy beef sauce over my rice and put the plate in the microwave.

"Oh, that reminds me. How far with the youth project? Have you presented it to Pastor Ben yet?"

"Not yet." I turn the microwave on and walk over to my dining table. "I had a brief meeting with him a few days ago and I gave him a summary. He seemed to like the idea, but I'll meet with him again early January to discuss the details and finances."

"*Ah*, okay, no problem. I'm sure God will favor you. Who would have thought that this youth ministry you had been praying about for the past two years would finally kick off this year?"

"I know, right. God works in mysterious ways." My microwave dings and I push myself up from my chair, walking over to it. "And who would have thought that I would find a wife this year?"

"*Abi o.* But, bro, please. Since Amara has said you should give her time, make sure you do that. Your thirtieth birthday is now five months away, and while I believe there is nothing impossible with God, the last thing you want to do is make her feel like you're forcing her to be with you."

I shake my head as I take my hot plate out of the microwave. "I've heard you. I'm just learning to take this slow, and to trust God's timing. All I can do is to keep showing her how much I care about her."

"Exactly. In fact, you should bring her around our house sometime. Josephine and I would really love to meet this girl *wey don make you kolo.*"

I laugh. "I'm sure she would love to meet you guys."

After work on Saturday night, I take off my white coat and toss it into one of the laundry bags on my way to the dressing room. I'm always excited to leave work on time, but I have a date with Amara tonight, which adds even more to my excitement.

I whistle a popular Nigerian praise song called "*every thing na double double*" as I walk down the corridor, meandering past patients, relatives, and staff. "Hey man, how you doing?" I wave to my porter friend whose name I keep forgetting.

He nods and smiles at me. "Have a good evening, doctor." The older man grins as he pushes a wheelchair past me.

"You too, my friend." I push open the door into the dressing room and with no hesitation, I open my locker and grab my backpack before changing out of my scrubs and into my jeans and t-shirt.

I'll be picking Amara up from her house so we can drive down to Joe's place. This is a big step for me because Joe is my best friend and I've always trusted his good judgment of character. I want someone else to see the same thing I see in Amara.

I grab my coat from the hanger and swing my backpack over my shoulders before making my way out of the dressing room.

As I'm about to get out of the hallway and down the flight of stairs, someone shouts my name from behind, and I turn around.

Jevon is fast-walking toward me in her blue scrubs and crocs. "Please wait a minute, hon."

"Hey, Jevon. Are you okay?" I hug her when she gets to me.

"Yeah, sorry, Raymond. I've been so busy today, but I wanted to speak to you about something important."

I frown. "Is...everything okay?" I hold her hand as we step aside so we're standing close to the wall and away from the passing crowd.

"Yeah." She squeezes my hand. "I just wanted to check up on you."

Ah, just Jevon being her usual self and worrying about me. "I'm fine, Jevon." I flash her a grin. "In fact, I have a date this evening."

She steps back and cocks her eyebrows. "Oh, really?"

"Yeah."

"With who?" She asks with a high-pitched voice, and I laugh.

"With Amara, of course. I told you I'm interested in her. I really like her."

"Ray, are you sure? Do you trust her?" Jevon uses a tone she's used on me before. It's either because she's worried about me, or she knows something I don't.

I sigh and lean against the wall. "What's wrong? What's on your mind?"

"Ray, I just worry about you. You trust people too easily and I'm worried you're rushing into this."

I straighten and place my hands on her shoulders, squeezing gently. "Jevon, I'll be fine. God is in this one, trust me." I hold her gaze.

She tilts her head and opens her mouth to say something, but closes it again.

I frown. "Jevon? Is there something you want to tell me?" I slide my jacket sleeve up my arm to check the time on my watch. "If I don't leave in the next five minutes, I'll be late."

"Okay, okay. It's just that I saw Amara talking to some other doctor. I think his name is Jamar and I hear they've been spending a lot of time together and he—"

"Please stop." I step away from her.

"Ray—"

"Stop it." I raise my voice and she flinches. "I know you care about me, and I appreciate that. But I'm a grown man. I can choose who I want to be with without you meddling."

The look in Jevon's eyes tells me my words have hurt her, but there's no way I'll stand here and let her coerce me into having doubts about Amara. Amara told me she's still praying and asking God for direction, but if there's someone else involved, I'm sure she'll tell me.

"Look, Jevon." My voice softens and I inch closer, taking her hand in mine. "I appreciate your concern for me, but like I said, I know this time will be different. Amara is not like the other girls. You'll see." I wink at her—a gesture we often do to each other. But instead of returning the wink like she always does, Jevon sighs and puts her free hand on top of mine.

"If you say so, hon. I'll be praying for you. I *really* hope this works out for you."

I bend over and give her a long hug. "It'll work out. You told me to trust God, and that's exactly what I'm doing."

I break the hug and open the door. "Now, you be good and I'll see you tomorrow." My last words to Jevon leave my lips in a rush as I shut the door behind me and rush down the stairs.

Joe ushers Amara and I into his dining room, which has food spread out across the dining table. At the center of the table, there are two silver trays made up of grilled fish and ringed bell peppers decorating the perimeter of the trays.

To the left of the fish trays is a serving pot with jollof rice and another filled with *puff-puff*—the delicious-looking dough balls making my mouth water.

"*Chai*, my brother. This aroma attacking my nostrils is so strong, it can carry somebody's child back to Abuja."

Josephine smiles at the compliment as she emerges from the kitchen, wiping her hands with a kitchen towel and untying the apron around her waist. "Raymond." She says and approaches me for a hug. Releasing her hold, she turns to Amara and smiles. "You're Amara, right?"

"Yeah." Amara steps forward. "Josephine?"

"Yes, that's right. It's so good to finally meet you." Josephine reaches over and hugs Amara too. "You're welcome to our home." She holds Amara at arm's length. "You're so beautiful. I love your head wrap."

I grin when Amara's face lights up. She smiles in the same shy, cute way she does whenever I compliment her. "Thank you." Amara says and touches the head wrap. "My mom takes regular trips to Nigeria, so she brings back a lot of them."

"Wow, you need to tell your mom to hook me up, then. I've been—"

"Uncle Ray-Ray!!!" Chelsea runs out of the living room while waving her doll and we all turn to her.

"*Ayyy*, look at my big girl." I bend down and pick her up in my arms, carrying her around while making fake airplane sounds with my mouth.

The child giggles and screams as I alternate between throwing her in the air and flying her around. After ten minutes of our airplane game, I stop to catch my breath and carry

Chelsea in my arms. "Have you been a good girl?" I ask, and the child nods. "And have you been looking after mommy and daddy like I told you to?"

"Yeah." She responds and pats her doll's afro hair.

"Okay, Chelsea, I would like you to meet my special friend." I turn to face Amara, who is already smiling at the child.

"Hello." Amara says and when she reaches over to carry the child, Chelsea stretches her arms out willingly. "You are so adorable." Amara balances Chelsea on her hips.

"Wow, she has never let a stranger carry her like this before. This is amazing." Josephine says.

"I know right. The first time I carried her as a baby, she wanted to scream my head off." We all laugh as I cast my memory back to the day when I saw the joy in Joe's face as he handed me his baby. I know I'll experience that joy someday with the woman standing next to me right now.

"Is this your friend?" Amara points to the doll and Chelsea nods. "What's her name?"

"Chelsea," the child responds with a big smile. "Because she looks like me." She brings the doll close to her face so we can all see how their chestnut brown skin tones match and how they both have kinky curly hair.

"Awww," we reply in unison.

"You are raising a beautiful queen right here," Amara says to Joe and Josephine.

"Indeed, she has brought nothing but joy since she came into our world," Josephine says and places her hand on Amara's shoulder.

Amara's gaze drops to the apron in Josephine's hand. "Oh, do you need help in the kitchen?"

"If you don't mind, that would be great."

"Of course. Come on, Chelsea, let's go help mom in the

kitchen," Amara says to the girl before the ladies walk to the kitchen.

"Papa G." Joe turns to me. "G for General. General in Atlanta. The one and only heart doctor. My brother, I hail you *o*." Joe runs on the spot while waving both arms above his head.

"This man, you are a joker." I laugh and shake his hands before giving him a brief hug. "So, what do you think of her?" I lower my voice and look over my shoulder before settling on one of the sofas in the living room.

Joe walks over to the dining table and grabs two bottles of Supermalt. "Guy, *this your babe na fire o.*" He says before opening the drinks and walking back to meet me. After handing me a bottle, he sits on the sofa across from me and leans back. "Seems like Josephine and Chelsea love her, so do I even have a choice?"

"Honestly, you have no idea how relieved I am." I relax in my seat as I imagine us receiving this same warm response when Amara and I eventually visit my family in Nigeria. I can only imagine my mother's reaction, how my uncles, aunts, and all our neighbors will rush out of their houses, eager to see the *Americanah* I've brought back home as my wife.

Everyone will see how beautiful, intelligent, and hard-working Amara is. She will be my pride and joy. I would have to hold her close to my side the same way market women hold their purses close to them. If not, someone might steal her away from me on those busy streets of Abuja. God knows I can't wait to make her mine.

"Okay, food is ready," Josephine announces as the three ladies emerge from the kitchen carrying plates and silverware. Joe and I stand up and walk over to the dining table. We settle in the chairs with Amara sitting next to me, Joe and Josephine sitting across from us, and little Chelsea in a high chair next to Josephine.

One reason I love visiting Joe and his family is not only the fact that Josephine is a good cook but also the fact that she cooks Cameroonian meals, which I'm not used to.

The last time I was here, Josephine made what she called *poulet DJ,* which is French for chicken DJ. It is a delicacy made up of fried plantains and chicken mixed together in a wonderful blend of spices. Today, I can't wait to try this *puff-puff,* seasoned grilled fish and pepper sauce.

"Amara, are you okay with spicy food?" Josephine asks, raising her brows as she picks up a serving spoon.

Amara laughs. "Trust me, growing up with Nigerian parents means you have to be more than okay with spice. I'm good, girl."

"That's great." Josephine bends over to serve Amara's food. "There's a place in Cameroon called Limbe beach and they sell grilled fish on the roadside, so visitors can eat while they enjoy the beach view. If you want to enjoy this food to the fullest, you have to use your hands. It doesn't taste the same with a knife and fork."

"Bring it on, girl. I'm ready." Amara rubs her palms together.

When the food is placed in front of us, we wash our hands and dig in. Chelsea is the only one using a spoon as her mom helps her eat her mashed fish and puff-puff.

"So tell us, Amara." I say, shifting my gaze to the beautiful queen sitting beside me. "Now that you've tasted Cameroonian, Ghanaian, and Nigerian jollof rice, which one would you say is better?"

"Nuh-uh. Ray, we're not going to start that jollof war here." Amara shakes her head and we all laugh.

After dinner, we settle on the sofas in front of the TV as Joe picks a Nollywood movie on Netflix. Chelsea settles in Amara's lap and as she cradles the child, my mind can't help but wander off to when she will cradle our own child in her lap. We start talking and soon, our conversations take up our time and the movie fades to background noise.

"So...Josephine and Joseph, huh?" Amara says to my friends. "How did that even happen?"

Joe shrugs, and Josephine smiles at him. "Honestly, God has a wonderful way of working things out. If someone had told me I would meet a Cameroonian girl in this country who is literally the female version of me, I wouldn't have believed it."

"Yeah, God writes the best love stories and till this day I can't believe I found a man like him." Josephine looks at her husband and the grins on their faces brings them closer until they finally kiss.

"Our eyes are bleeding o. *Abeg*, get a room." I say, and we laugh. We spend the evening talking about different topics—our jobs, the church, ministry, and of course, Africa, and soon we start talking about afrobeat songs and dance moves.

"Did Raymond tell you he is a good dancer?" Joe blurts out, and I almost choke on my saliva.

Amara turns to look at me with wide eyes. "Really?"

"Yeah, this guy can dance for Africa." Joe adds.

I shake my head. "Actually, I can't—"

"He even dances for his patients," Joe jumps in again.

"Really?" Amara gasps. "You dance for the children? How did I not know about this?"

I sigh and lean forward, sending Joe a death glare. "I've only danced for one patient and the only reason I did it was because he was feeling low about being stuck in hospital and not being able to see his friends at school. Since then, the boy has been asking me to teach him the dance steps every time he sees me."

"Wow, no wonder everyone loves you. The measure in which you go above and beyond for your patients is incredible, Ray." Amara says, resting her hand only a few inches away from mine. It takes a lot of self-control in me not to hold it.

"Thank you." I shrug. "It's nothing, really."

At first I was thinking of a way to fight Joe later for running his mouth, but seeing the admiration in Amara's eyes now makes me believe that this new revelation has scored me more points.

"Okay, I believe it's time for the heart doctor to teach us those same dance moves."

I whip my head around to face Joe, who now has a smirk on his face. "Guy, are you okay?"

"Yes o. Please, we are all here to learn from the master." Joe and Josephine leap to their feet, followed by Amara, and soon everyone is chanting, "dance, dance, dance."

"Dance, Uncle Ray-Ray!!!" Chelsea screams, and now I know I'm trapped.

"Alright, this one is only for you." I say to Chelsea before pushing myself up. Joe takes out his phone and plays the song "Sekem" on Spotify.

In less than a minute, we're all dancing, including little Chelsea prancing around the living room with her doll. For someone who says she doesn't dance much, Amara is picking up the dance moves really well. There's no stiff bone in her, and it's impressive how her body flows with the music so effortlessly. With a little more practice, she'll be the "Sekem" queen dancing by my side. I'm impressed. *Very* impressed.

As bouts of laughter and singing fill the room, my heart swells at how comfortable Amara is around my friends. This is what I prayed for. She may not have given me an answer yet, but I know it'll be positive.

Thank You Jesus.

19

AMARA

If today was a dream, then I would never want anyone to pinch me out of it. I can't believe that four months ago, my dream man was only a list on paper, and today, I'm going on a date with someone who ticks all my boxes. Who says God doesn't answer prayers? Who says God doesn't care about what I want? I prayed, I handed it all to Him, and He delivered. *Yaas, Jesus.*

Last night, I stayed up until two a.m. researching mistakes I should avoid on a first date. Then my anxious brain woke me up at six a.m. this morning to find the perfect outfit as I was too tired to choose one last night.

"This would be perfect." I smooth my hands down my black top with polka dot mesh sleeves. I've tucked the top into my blue skinny jeans and I'm going to match it with my black thigh-high boots to complete the look.

My phone buzzes and sends me fast-walking across the room to my bed. A text notification from Jamar pops up on my screen, announcing that he's waiting in his car outside my apartment.

"Oh no. He's here? How can he be here? I'm not ready." I run back to my full-length mirror to check my afro puff before grabbing my boots from the shoe stand. After wrestling with the boots and forcing my feet and lower legs into them, I straighten my back and sit on my bed, waiting for my heart rate to calm down.

How come I never felt this nervous when I had my first date with Ray? Maybe it's because this date means a lot to me. It's with my dream man, so I think I'm allowed to be nervous. My phone buzzes again and another text notification pops up.

Jamar: You ready?

Me: Yes, I'll be out in a minute.

As if my heels have been struck by the speed of lightening, I grab my cross body bag and my jacket and dash out of my apartment. Across the street, Jamar is leaning against his car with a wide grin on his face and his gaze roams over me from head to toe as I walk down the stairs to meet him.

When I'm standing a few steps away from him, he makes a whistle sound with his mouth and pushes himself to stand up. "Mamacita, you look good."

My eyes widen at his comment, but I just stand there, smiling like a fool, and not knowing how to respond. Okay, so he's a little expressive with the way he appreciates his woman, but I'll take that over someone who says nothing. "Erm...thank you." I flash him a sheepish smile in return, before silently praying he doesn't notice my shaking hands.

As if sensing my nerves, Jamar inches forward and takes my hand. He pulls me in for a hug, and the strong scent of his perfume—*Dior,* or maybe *Tom Ford,* fills up my nostrils. But I ain't gonna lie. It still doesn't smell as good as Ray's *Hugo Boss* fragrance.

"Should we go?" He jerks his head toward the car when we break the hug.

"Okay." I nod and he opens the passenger door for me, allowing me to step in. After shutting the door, he walks around and jumps in. In less than a minute, the car engine revs and he drives off.

I keep my eyes on the road, focusing on the cars outside, but not failing to notice Jamar's quick glances from time to time. I bite my bottom lip to suppress my smile, but I'm too nervous to turn around and look at him or start up a conversation.

"You're really nervous, aren't you?" Jamar asks and I turn to meet his blue eyes staring at me.

I clear my throat before responding. "Yeah, I'm sorry. I'm new to this dating thing."

He laughs. "I can tell. But don't worry, you're in good hands. I don't blame you for feeling nervous. Apparently I have that effect on a lot of women." He winks at me before facing the road again.

Hmm. He has that effect on a lot of women? I don't know if I feel comforted or worried about that statement. A part of me feels like I should ask what he means by that, but another part of me doesn't want to know. Surely he won't be seeing other women while seeing me, right? Oh, who am I to talk? I'm seeing both him and Ray.

After another five-minute drive, Jamar pulls into a space at the parking lot outside the movie theater. He opens the door for me and I step out into the cold, the bright-colored building coming into my view. Jamar leads the way as we walk past clusters of people chattering and laughing inside the building. The sweet-smell of popcorn hits my nostrils and my stomach rumbles. *I knew I should have eaten before leaving.*

"Wait a minute." Jamar stops in his tracks and turns to look at me. "I just realized we haven't decided on a movie."

"Oh, yeah...." I had no time to think about that since I've been too busy being nervous. "Should we look at the list and decide?" What I really want to do is make sure I find a good romcom with a good love story.

"Yeah, we'll just pick anything that is action-packed." He says. "You don't mind action, do you?"

Well, now I don't. "Of...course I don't mind. I love action." I force a smile to hide my disappointment.

"Okay, that's great because I once dated this girl who refused to watch anything but romantic comedies. *Ugh.* Don't you girls ever get tired of those?"

Well, no sir, I can never get tired of romantic comedies. I bite down the words and force another laugh. "I know right. We need to realize there are other genres besides romantic comedy."

"Exactly." Jamar responds and we start walking again. "That's what I tried to tell her, but she had none of it. I'm so glad you're more open-minded."

"Yay me!" My voice comes out more high-pitched than I would like. If this boy wasn't so fine, I would have smacked him unconscious with my bag right now. But what good would that do? It's only a movie. Only a few hours. So what if we don't appreciate the same movie genres? I can sit through a few hours of blasts, explosions, and gunshots. It's no big deal.

"Come on. Let's go." Jamar extends his hand to me and I slip mine into it without hesitation. The warmth of his fingers around my hand melts away all the building frustration I had a few seconds ago. Who cares about rom-coms? My dream guy is holding my hand, so nothing else matters.

Jamar leads the way and he pays for our tickets, food, and drinks. As we walk to the theater, Jamar talks about his favorite action movies, and how he always wanted to be an actor when he was growing up before he realized he couldn't act to save his life.

"There's a fair share of action in Nollywood dramas." I sneak in some information to advocate for my country.

Jamar scrunches his brows. "Nollywood?"

"Yeah, the Nigerian movie industry. My parents love watching their movies and there are a lot of them on Netflix."

"Oh really, I've never seen any of them, but I would love to watch them with you."

My heart skips a beat when he smiles down at me. "That would be great." Hmm, so he's interested in my culture. *Check.*

I get more comfortable the longer Jamar holds my hand and before I know it, I'm leaning my head on his shoulder as we watch the movie. Two hours pass by really quickly and I try my best to savor the moment without focusing too much on the loud sounds, but unfortunately as time passes, a pounding headache threatens to ruin my evening.

"That was a good one." Jamar says as we walk out of the movie theater. "I really hope they make a sequel."

"Yeah, it was epic indeed." I massage my temples as I walk closely behind him. My pounding headache drowns out Jamar's chatter and when we get back to the car, I realize I haven't been listening to anything he's been saying.

"Amara, are you okay?" He says, drawing my attention to him.

"Yeah, sorry. I just have a horrible headache."

"I'm sorry about that. Should we skip dinner, so I can take you home?"

My first instinct is to scream "no." I want to spend more time with him and I want us to talk a bit more about other things besides movies, but if I don't lie down soon, I'll be battling this headache at work tomorrow. I hate working with a headache, so I'll count my losses for today.

In less than ten minutes, we're back in front of my house and Jamar walks me to my door. He holds my hand again and squeezes it gently. "I'm sorry you don't feel well. Maybe next time, we'll choose a movie that's not too loud." He chuckles, accentuating his beautiful blue eyes, his straight teeth, and his perfect, neatly-shaped beard.

Next time? Aww, he wants to go out with me again.

"Yeah, that would be great." I smile in return and turn around to open my door.

"You owe me dinner." He says as he retreats to his car.

"Of course." I wave at him before entering the house and closing the door behind me. For a few minutes, I lean against the door and bite back a squeal so Jamar doesn't hear me all the way from his car.

When I change out of my clothes, I take a quick shower and heat up some rice and stewed chicken in the microwave. The spicy food is probably not good for my headache, but it's what my taste buds need after eating so many sweet things tonight.

With my plate of food in one hand, and a bottle of Supermalt in the other, I sit at the dining table and take my list out of my bag. "Jamar ticks almost all the boxes." I say to myself as I go through it and place little ticks next to each criterion.

Jamar is tall, dark, and handsome with a beard that connects and muscles that pop out of his shirt. His smile literally melts my heart, I'm attracted to him and he has a stable job. He is romantic, he is funny, and he cares about me enough to recognize when I need rest.

He is also interested in knowing more about my culture, which is a good thing, and he...well I think he loves God. We didn't get the chance to talk about God today, but I'll blame this stupid headache for cutting our date short. The good thing is, he wants to see me again, so I have more time to learn more about him.

Jamar and Ray are so different, but I have to admit that there was something missing from this date and I can't figure it out. All I know is that Ray would have never had any problems

watching a rom-com with me and I would have never ended up
with this stupid headache.

20

AMARA

Raymond: *I told you they would like you. If anyone meets you and doesn't like you, then their head is not correct* 😂

I chuckle when Ray's text message pings into my phone. Rolling over on my bed, I prop myself up to lie on my belly. The news presenter on the TV is chatting away in the background, but I pay no attention to him; my eyes are glued to my phone. My fingers linger over my keypad as I bite my lip, staring at the words and feeling playful. Without thinking about it, I start typing.

Me: Haha so...does that mean you like me too?

As soon as I hit the "send" button, Ray starts typing. My heart thuds against my rib cage and I bite my nails as I watch the three dots floating at the bottom of the screen. One minute passes, and Ray is still typing. *Oh no, why did I ask him that? What if he thinks I'm desperate? What if he—*

Raymond: *You know I like you, Amara. I like you a lot and I hope my actions have proven that. I told you I'm not here to play games. You're the girl I want to be with and that's the honest truth.*

My fingers freeze around my phone, and I'm unable to move my thumb. Of course he likes me. What was I expecting him to say? I already knew the answer but I asked him anyway. What is wrong with me?

Raymond: *Do you like me too?* • •

Oh, no. What have I done? A pang of guilt rises in my chest and I turn around to lie on my back. The last few days have been torture for me. Since the day Ray took me to see his friends, I haven't been able to get him out of my head. *How did I get here?*

I barely liked Ray when we first met. I couldn't stand the sight of him. I was annoyed about how nice he was, how he wouldn't stop apologizing, and how he kept bumping into me. But now he has found a home in my thoughts.

The most surprising thing is that I find myself not even bothering about his looks anymore. I steal glances at him when we are together, hoping to take a peek of his charming smile, his soft gaze, and just to bask in the kind and patient demeanor he radiates. *How did I get here?*

Ray may not look like my dream man, but he sure knows how to make me feel like a queen—like a prized jewel. He makes me feel like I'm the only girl in the world, and I haven't even said yes to him yet. The truth is, I want to say yes, but at the same time, I don't.

Raymond: *Actually, you don't have to answer that. Please forget I asked.*

A wave of relief washes over my heart, followed swiftly by another wave of guilt. I feel I haven't given Jamar a fair chance to show himself. I'll go on a few more dates with Jamar and then I'll decide. If only God could take Ray's personality, and visions, and put them into Jamar's attractive body, then I would have my perfect man. If only.

Me: I should go now, Ray. I have to work in the morning.
Raymond: Yes, of course. Goodnight, Beautiful 🩶
Me: Goodnight, Ray.

"Eeeek!!! Girl, I'm so excited for you. You're gonna be looking real good in your dress." Teeyana and I squeal and link our arms as we walk down the street to Kleinfeld Bridal store. Behind us are Teeyana's mom, her dad, her brother Danny, her Aunt Bella, and also her grandpa.

"Amara, I'm so nervous. What if I don't find the dress here? We'll have to start all over again." Worry lines crease up her forehead.

I ain't gonna lie, I've thought about that too, but now is not the time to let my worries reflect on Teeyana. I need to keep making her believe everything is possible.

"Nuh-uh." I hold her at arm's length as we pause in the middle of the sidewalk. "Repeat after me, 'I am going to find my dress today.'" I stare at her dark brown eyes.

Teeyana sighs and pulls down her winter hat. "I...I will find—"

"Nuh-uh, that ain't loud enough, girl. You better say it with your chest now."

Teeyana chuckles, and the worry disappears from her eyes. "I will find my dress today." She lifts her chin and nods as she says it louder.

"There you go. That's my girl. Now, let's go find that dress." We link our arms again when our crowd meets us. Grandpa Thompson is walking hand-in-hand with Aunt Bella, balancing on his walking stick.

Mr. and Mrs. Sparks are holding Danny's hands and walking beside him. It's a week before Christmas and the streets of Atlanta are buzzing as always with Christmas music, excited children, and stressed adults running around trying to make the money to get them through the holiday season.

We drove down here from Grandpa Thompson's house in

two cars, which are now parked five minutes away from the bridal shop. We're all dressed in our thick coats, winter hats, and snow-friendly boots. It snowed the night before, but since the sun is back up this morning, there are only sparse heaps of snow scattered along our path.

Walking past several restaurants, a library, and two coffee shops, we finally reach the bridal shop. Outside, a glass window looms over us, and behind it are two mannequins with the most beautiful and classy wedding dresses on them. One of them is an A-line dress with a halter-neckline while the other is a ball-gown with an off-shoulder neckline, lots of bling, and lots of lace.

Teeyana and I stop in front of the dresses, staring at them as if we've just seen a UFO drop from the sky. Without saying a word to each other, we turn around and squeal together. Teeyana has to try on the ball gown.

Mr. Sparks pushes the front door open and walks with us to the reception area where we check in. Then, in a single file, we head to the waiting area and make ourselves comfortable on the white sofas.

Behind the sofas is a long line of white and ivory sample wedding dresses on hangers stretching farther than my eyes can see. There are different styles of lace, chiffon, taffeta, and satin. Across the hall on the other side are pink and purple dresses.

"Wow, this is so beautiful." Teeyana comments as we take in the view.

"Hello, everyone." A woman who looks to be in her late twenties walks up to us with a warm smile. She's wearing a black dress, black stilettos, a black satin scarf tied around her neck, and red lipstick. "Welcome to Kleinfeld Bridal. My name is Lorita, and I'll be your bridal consultant for today. Who is my bride?"

"That's me." Teeyana lets out a little squeal before shuffling forward, bringing me with her. "My name is Teeyana."

"Welcome, Teeyana. Who have you brought with you today?" Lorita asks and Teeyana goes around introducing us. "Hello, everyone. It's lovely to meet you all." Lorita waves at us before turning to Teeyana again. "So, do you know what kind of dress you're looking for?"

Teeyana nods. "Yeah, my wedding is next December because I've always wanted to be a winter bride. I think a ball-gown will be perfect and I'd *really* like to try the one on display on the mannequin." Teeyana points to the store window.

"Of course. I'll make sure we get you to try that one on." Lorita says. "So what's your budget?"

Everyone turns to look at Teeyana's dad, who smiles at Lorita. "If my baby girl loves it, I'm going to get it for her."

"That's what we like to hear." Lorita says and we all laugh.

"Aww, thanks, Dad." Teeyana reaches over and hugs Mr. Sparks.

"Alright, let's go find your dress, Teeyana." Lorita says, and we all spring to our feet.

We walk down the hall, past other brides who are trying on dresses with their friends and family watching them. Then we enter another room at the back with a lot more dresses than the one outside. Even though it's not my wedding, it feels like I'm shopping for myself. I feel like a kid who has been let into a candy store.

We work together to pick out different dresses from the hangers, so Teeyana can try them on, and, of course, the ball gown from the mannequin. When we're done, we head back to the waiting area while Teeyana follows Lorita into one of the dressing rooms.

As we wait for Teeyana to come out with the first dress, my

phone vibrates in my pocket and when I take it out, it's Ray. Of course it's Ray.

Raymond: *Good morning, Beautiful. I'm not sure if you've left to go bridal shopping already, but I hope you have a lot of fun :)*

I haven't spoken to him much since he asked if I liked him. I told him I was going wedding dress shopping with Teeyana today, but nothing more. On one hand, I feel terrible for letting things get this far. But on the other hand, I just want to grab Ray by the shoulders and shake some sense into him.

How can he like me this much already? We've only known each other for four months. What if he doesn't know what he's talking about? He has four failed relationships under his belt, so why is he certain that things will work out between us?

Sometimes, I'm scared about how confident he is, but he knows what he wants and his actions have always been consistent with his words from day one. Maybe I'm the one who needs to be shaken in the shoulders so I can believe him. This is so hard. *How did I get here, Lord?*

"Here's dress number one, everyone." Lorita walks into the waiting area and ushers Teeyana in. We all gasp as she walks out in a white mermaid sleeveless dress, with a bling sash and a ruched bottom. When she steps on the pedestal, the smile on her face and the way she turns and admires herself in the mirror from all angles warms my heart.

"Girl, you are gorgeous." I say, speaking for everyone else in the room. "This one does a lot for your figure."

"Oh, my baby." Mrs. Sparks stands up and walks over to Teeyana with tears in her eyes. She wraps her arms around her daughter and they share a hug for a few minutes before she returns to her seat.

"Wow, everyone seems to love this dress, but it's only the first one. Do you want us to stop here or do you want to try on a few more?" Lorita asks Teeyana.

Teeyana turns around to look at us. "Yeah, I'd like to try on two more. The one with the sleeves, and then the ball gown."

"Okay, let's go."

Teeyana and Lorita go back inside and five minutes later, Teeyana reappears wearing an A-line lace dress with an off-shoulder neckline. "I like this one, but not as much as the first one." Teeyana says.

"Yeah, I can see it in your face." Lorita says. "Let's try on the last one, then."

"Eeeek!!! I'm excited." I say, moving to the edge of my seat. Teeyana squeezes my hands before walking away. My phone buzzes again and when I check, it's another text message, but this time, it's from Jamar.

Jamar: Hey, I had a lot of fun last week and I wonder if you want to hang out again. Are you free on Christmas Eve? I'd like to take you to dinner.

Yes. The word almost leaps out of my mouth, but I compose myself when I remember I'm not alone. I've been praying for another date with Jamar and God has answered me as an early Christmas present.

Me: Hey :) I had fun too. I'd love to, but I'm going back to Boston today to spend Christmas with my parents.

Jamar: Okay, that's fine. I'll take you somewhere nice when you get back.

Me: Okay, that sounds good. Where will we go?

Jamar: It's a surprise. Just make sure you wear something real nice.

I frown. What does he mean? Haven't I always worn something nice? Or is he going to take me to some fancy restaurant like Ray did? Oh, what am I going to wear? Maybe Teeyana will help me pick an outfit. *Oh, shoot.* She doesn't know about Jamar, so she can't help me.

Ugh. How did I get myself into this mess? *Come on, girl. What are you doing?* I put my phone away before leaning forward and taking a deep breath.

"Here we go. Our star dress for today." Lorita walks in one more time and when Teeyana steps out in her dress, I gasp again, holding my breath as I take in the scene. She is wearing the ball-gown from the display mannequin. It has a sweetheart-neckline with capped sleeves, and the bottom is blingy and puffy. It hugs her waist well and the tiara and veil on her head makes her look nothing short of a queen.

"Girl, you are...so beautiful." My voice breaks, and I swipe tears away from my eyes. "Come on, why am I crying?" I stand up and walk up to her, and we share our own hug. It lasts a few minutes with us taking turns to sniff. Only God knows how much we've endured together since high school. I can't believe we made it through college and our bond is still as strong as ever. My sister is really going to be a wife soon.

Everyone stands up and joins us for a group hug, with Danny being squished in the middle. Mrs. Sparks is sniffing, and even Grandpa Thompson's eyes are glistening. I knew Mr. Sparks wouldn't cry. "Girl, Jayden has no idea what is waiting for him. If he doesn't shed a tear when you walk down that aisle, then you better turn around and start again coz the boy's vision would need to be clearer."

"Hallelujah." Bella says and we all laugh.

"So, is this your dress, Teeyana?" Lorita asks, but before Teeyana opens her mouth to answer, Danny cuts her off.

"Yes!!! This is the dress!!!" The boy screams at the top of his voice and we all burst out laughing.

21

RAYMOND

Amara might have said she doesn't like me, but that's okay. Wait, no. She didn't say she doesn't like me. I didn't give her a chance to answer because I didn't want her to think I was pressuring her. I won't let that discourage me, though. She needs time and I'll wait. But should I have waited before asking if she likes me back? She asked me the question, and I had to know what she was thinking.

Oh no. Is that why she hasn't responded to my text messages these past few days? It's the first week of the new year and I haven't seen Amara since she went to spend Christmas with her parents in Boston. I did mostly night shifts over the Christmas holidays, so I didn't speak to her much. She told me she would be starting work today, so maybe she's busy? Or maybe not? *Oh, what have I done?*

Do you really trust her? Doubts pierce into my thoughts.

Are you sure she hasn't found someone better than you?

Are you sure she won't leave you like the other girls did?

"Dr. Aderinto?"

I flinch and lift my head, locking eyes with Carla, who is staring at me.

"Are you okay?" She asks, a concerned look on her face. "I've been trying to get your attention for the last minute."

I clear my throat and push myself away from the desk I've been leaning on. "Sorry, Carla." I sigh. "What were you saying?"

"The last patient is ready for you." She tucks a strand of her curly dark hair behind her ear before handing me the clipboard.

"Thanks, Carla." I take the clipboard from her and walk down the hallway to room ten. I stop in front of the room for a brief second, letting out a sharp breath before entering.

"Hello, Happy New Year." I smile and close the door behind me. The parents of baby Ayobola Makinde are both sitting on the bed and playing with him.

"Hello, doctor. Happy New Year to you." Mr. Makinde, a man with glasses, stands up to greet me. He's a little taller than me with a similar skin tone, but he has a head full of hair. He extends his hand and gives me a firm handshake.

"My name is Dr. Raymond Aderinto and I'll be assessing Ayo today." I say, before turning to his wife and shaking her hand too.

"Ah, look at my fellow Yoruba brother." Mr. Makinde's demeanor immediately relaxes as he shakes my hand again. "I knew there was something different about you as soon as you stepped into this room."

"Wow, thank God." I drop the clipboard on the table before grabbing a mini train from the toy box in the corner of the room. I stoop next to the bed where nine-month-old baby Ayo is bouncing and babbling. "How is Ayo doing today?" I ask Mrs. Makinde, a petite woman with short curly hair, wearing blue jeans and a striped shirt.

"He has been very active today, which is the first time since the surgery." She rubs Ayo's head softly. "He has been eating a lot too. He even tried pounded yam for the first time yesterday."

"Ah, that's good. You're doing well, big boy, aren't you?" I reach over and tickle Ayo's tummy when his mother pulls down his overalls to expose his chest. Ayo leans forward and grabs his feet, giggling and spitting on me as I hand the mini train over to him.

I take my stethoscope from around my neck when the train catches his attention. "Oh, look...what is this? Where is your heart? Right here? Shall we listen to it?" I place the stethoscope on my chest and then on his chest, going back and forth a few times. When he starts laughing, and warming up to the strange instrument in front of him, I use that opportunity to listen to his heart and examine the scar on his chest, looking for any signs of infection.

Ayo wraps both his hands around my finger, flinching at the feel of the metal against his bare chest. "Your heart sounds really good." I say to him before pressing the stethoscope on his back. "And your lungs sound perfect too." I stand up and step back to speak to his parents.

"His heart tracing and scans have all come back normal. His scar is healing well and I'm happy with his progress. We will see him again in three months." I place the stethoscope around my neck again.

"Thank you so much, my brother. God will bless you. You have no idea how relieved we are." Mr. Makinde says.

"Yes, thank you, doctor." Mrs. Makinde stands up and balances Ayo on her hip. "We spent almost all our savings on Ayo's surgery. We're so happy he's well now, thanks to you."

"Mmm-mmm." I shake my head. "I had nothing to do with it. God takes all the glory. The amazing team who was involved in Ayo's surgery deserves some accolades too."

"I'm so glad to see my brother in an influential healthcare position like this," Mr. Makinde adds. "May God bless you and may your life continue to shine to impact these children."

"Amen and Amen. Thank you so much, my brother." My

heart warms at their encouraging words as I leave the room. It's always refreshing to meet kind people and I would love to have a family like that where we stick by each other through thick and thin.

After a few minutes of musing, my thoughts switch again to Amara. I need to speak to her. I approach the nurse's desk and hand the clipboard back to Carla. "Here you go. I'm going to step out for a minute to get coffee and also to see a friend. Page me if you need anything urgent." I roll up the sleeves of my white coat and turn toward the door.

"Is this person you are going to see called Amara by any chance?" Jevon's voice comes from behind me.

I turn around and give her a quick nod with a smile on my face. "Yes, Jevon."

"That's what I thought." She lowers her glasses and shakes her head, a smirk forming on her lips. Maureen and Carla giggle as I turn around again.

On my way to the NICU, I check my phone again to see if Amara has responded to my text messages, but still, there's no reply. *Lord, please, if I offended her, give me the chance to make it right.*

"I don't want to blow this again, Lord, please," I mutter as I enter the NICU department. Quickening my steps, I walk past the room with the glass windows I saw her in last time, but she's not there.

Further down the hallway, I spot a group of nurses in front of the nurse's station, chatting in hushed tones. At the center of the huddle is Amara, dabbing at the corner of her eyes with tissue as Claire squeezes her shoulder.

My heart sinks at the sight. A million and one possibilities run through my mind. What has happened? What is going on? "Amara?" The group of nurses turn to face me, sullen looks on their faces.

The crowd disperses slowly until it's just Claire and Amara left. "You can take a break now, dear. Take as much time as you need." Claire says to Amara before turning to me. "Hey, Raymond." She sends me a small smile and then walks away.

Amara dabs her eyes once more before crumpling the tissue and tucking them in her pocket. She sniffs and lifts her head to look at me, her eyes puffy and red.

"Hey." A small smile forms on her lips. "Sorry, I didn't reply to your messages earlier. Today has been horrible and—" Her voice breaks and tears stream down her face.

"Please, don't apologize." I inch closer, taking her hand into mine. "Come on. Let's take a quick break, so you can have some fresh air." I nod toward the door. "I promise, I won't take you away for too long." When Amara looks over her shoulder at Claire, the older woman gives us two thumbs up and we walk out of the NICU holding hands.

My mind is so clouded by what the problem might be that I can't even internally rejoice about the fact that Amara is letting me hold her hand while we walk. I don't know what she's about to tell me, but whatever it is, I'm ready to be there for her and comfort her, no matter what it takes.

We grab our jackets and walk out of the hospital, down the sidewalk, and into the garden until we get to our favorite spot. When Amara settles down on the bench, I plop down next to her, placing both my palms on the bench.

"Are you okay?" I ask after a few minutes pass, and she leans forward, the view of an ambulance driving into the ER entrance catching her attention.

She shakes her head and the tears return. "Emily died this morning."

My heart drops, trying to search my brain for a time when she mentioned the name before. "Emily?" I ask, the tone of my voice making it clear I have no idea who she's talking about.

"You remember my favorite baby on the ward? The one I was looking after the first time you came to see me at the NICU?"

The images from that day quickly flash back into my memory. "Oh yes, yes. The one who had respiratory distress because of her viral infection?"

Amara nods. "She desaturated overnight and had to be intubated. Despite all our efforts, she kept deteriorating, and they finally pulled the plug on her this morning." Amara's bottom lip quivers. "I feel so sorry for her parents—especially her mom. They had so much hope that Emily would get better." Amara buries her face in her hands and sobs.

My hands fidget by my side, itching to reach out and hold her, to hug her and cradle her. I want to tell her everything will be okay, but I don't know what to say or how to say it. Finally, I give in to the itch and place my arm around her shoulder, pulling her gently toward me. "That's a horrible thing to go through." With those words, Amara turns to me and buries her face in my shoulder, her tears soaking my scrubs and her breath warm against my neck.

She's wearing her hair up today, a puff at the back and curly bangs at the front. It's the first time I've seen her wear this hairstyle, but she looks beautiful as always. I rest my chin on her head and the coconut oil scent from her hair wafts into my nostrils. If I could, I would stay like this forever, protecting her, and providing the comfort she needs.

It's always a shock when we experience our first death as healthcare professionals—especially if the patient was someone we were fond of. I still remember the first death I witnessed to this day. It was my first year of residency and during a night shift; I saw a young girl who had come into the ER with breathing difficulties.

We suspected she had a blood clot in her lungs and she was receiving treatment for it. But one moment, I was chatting with her, and she was smiling at me, and the next moment, as I turned to get her the cup of coffee she asked for, she lost consciousness and her heart stopped. In the end, after forty minutes of CPR, we had to pull the plug.

One thing I know about comforting someone is to give them time to air out their frustrations. Of course I want to tell Amara that God is still in control and that He will work everything out the way He has planned it from the beginning. But now is not the time. I know God will eventually lead Amara to that realization. But for now, all she needs is a friend, not someone to preach to her.

A few more minutes pass and her sobs quiet down, then she sits up and looks at me. "Sorry you had to see me like this." She sniffles, and her beautiful smile returns.

I shake my head. "There's nothing to be sorry about. You're human and you're allowed to cry. It shows you have a big heart and you care about the babies you look after. It's beautiful." I thumb the tear sliding down her cheek. "You're beautiful." The words leave my mouth so freely now. I was hesitant about telling her before because I didn't know if it would make her feel uncomfortable. But now that she knows how I feel about her, there's nothing left to hide.

"Thank you, Ray. Thanks for staying with me and making sure I'm okay."

"I'm here for you anytime." I say before leaning forward. "And I think I know *exactly* what will make you feel better."

Amara leans back, a knowing smile appearing on her face. "Hot chocolate?"

"*Eisshh*, baby girl, you're in the spirit today." I spring to my feet and extend my hand to her again, so she slips her hand in mine and we walk back to the hospital.

~

"Thank you so much for agreeing to meet with me, Pastor Ben." I shake the middle-aged man's hand before he ushers me to sit in the chair across his desk.

"No, I should thank you for being so patient with me." He settles in his own chair before arranging the stack of documents on his desk. "It has been a very busy month for the church."

I smile and clasp my hands in front of me. "I understand that, sir." Every time I come into this office, it reminds me about how haphazard my life was during my med school days. I used to lock myself up in my room for three days without seeing daylight. It was just me, my books, food, water, and the four walls of my room.

"So, tell me more about this vision of yours." Pastor Ben's deep voice forces me out of my thoughts. He leans forward and rubs his greying beard and moustache before adjusting his glasses.

I clear my throat, thinking about the best way to start. I practiced my pitch with Joe, Amara, and to myself several times in front of the mirror. It sounded great then, but now that I'm in front of the man, waves of doubt are surging through my brain and turning it upside down.

What if this is not a good idea after all? Is it even worth a try? What if he just dismisses me? I would have spent the last few months preparing for nothing.

"Raymond?"

I jolt out of my daydream to meet Pastor Ben's raised eyebrows, and when I open my mouth to say all the words I practiced before, it hits me that I don't have to do that. I just need to relay the vision to Pastor Ben the way God laid it on my heart. *Lord, please help me.*

"There are over fifty young people in this church who are within the ages of fourteen and eighteen years old." I start, letting the words flow out without putting pressure on myself to get them right. "I believe this age group is very critical because this is when they learn to adjust to the pressures and challenges from the world. Since children are the future, I believe we need to guide them, mentor them, and teach them the ways of Christ. Doing this will encourage them to stay in the ways of the Lord and they'll realize that the world has nothing to offer them."

"Hmm." Pastor Ben picks up a blank sheet of paper from the stack next to him. He takes the pen from behind his ear and starts scribbling on the paper. "Continue."

I adjust in my seat and keep talking. I tell him about my plans for the bi-monthly youth services where I would organize interactive sessions to teach the teens about topics relevant to them. I tell him about the retreat, how I plan to make it a yearly thing, and how I want to choose a different location each time, so the teens would look forward to it.

"In a nutshell, I want it to be a space where these teens can grow together. When they get to eighteen, a lot of them will go off to college and we won't see them very often after that. A fellowship like this will ground them and prepare them for what the world is going to throw at them. It will show them that they need to rely on God, whether their parents are watching or not."

Pastor Ben keeps scribbling as I talk and by the time I finish with my last sentence, he has filled the A4 sized sheet of paper with words I can't make out. He drops his pen dramatically on the table and looks up at me, a smile appearing on his face. Then he nods and leans back in his chair. "I am very impressed, Raymond. You have a great passion for this."

I return his smile. "God gave me this vision, sir. I'm simply obeying Him."

"And I'm sure our good Lord is very pleased with you for doing that." The older man picks up the piece of paper and hands it to me. On the paper are figures and potential expenses for the next year. At the bottom is a total budget and a tick next to it. "After you told me about the idea last month, I discussed it with the other church leaders and we are all on board. I believe God can use this project to do wonderful things in the lives of our young people, and I think you're the best person to handle it."

"Really?" My heart swells with joy and I exhale sharply. "Thank you so much, Pastor Ben." I stand up and shake his hand. I can't wait to see Amara's face when I tell her.

Speaking of Amara, I think it's time to tell Pastor Ben about her. "Erm...Pastor Ben, before I go, I just wanted to say I met someone. Her name is Amara and I would like you to meet her sometime in the future."

Pastor Ben's face brightens up. "Wow, really? This is great news. Out of all your relationships, this is the first woman you have wanted me to meet."

Something tugs at my chest as my mind flashes back to how miserable I was in those relationships—how those girls constantly made me doubt my abilities, my vision, and my faith in God. That was then. This is now. I know better.

"What has changed this time?" Pastor Ben asks.

"God is in this one." I respond. "I got confirmation and I'm sure she's going to be my wife."

"In that case, please bring Amara over whenever she's ready. It would be my pleasure to meet her."

22

AMARA

When Jamar cancelled our date on the first Saturday of the year, I was a little worried. He was so nice when he sent the text message and told me he was going to be staying late at work, so rather than disappointing me at the last minute, he cancelled the dinner and rescheduled.

I thought that was very sweet of him, but one part of me kept wondering if he cancelled because he was no longer interested in me. Even though he texted me ten minutes ago to say he is on his way to pick me up, I'm still expecting him to call and say he has changed his mind.

I scoff and shake my head as I fluff my curly puff with my wide-tooth comb. "If he's not interested, then why does he keep coming back?" I talk back to the dark voice without giving it a chance to speak to me first.

After admiring my make-up in the mirror, I place the comb down and my mind flashes back to what Ray told me on our first date. *Amara, you are a beautiful and talented woman. God has equipped you with the passion and drive to change the lives of children, and He is working in and through you.*

The softness of Ray's voice in my head brings back the peace

I felt when I heard those words come out of his mouth. That's what I should do. I should speak these words of affirmation to myself. It's one step toward defeating the dark voice.

Clearing my throat, I straighten my back and point at my reflection in the mirror. "Amara, you are a beautiful and talented woman. You can do this." I repeat the words two more times, and before I know it, I'm feeling a little better.

But I'll be honest and say the words sounded more believable coming out of Ray's mouth. I wonder what they'll sound like coming out of Jamar's mouth. *Oh shoot.* Jamar would be here any minute and I need to finish getting ready.

Half an hour later, Jamar and I walk into the bowling alley filled with excited shrieks and squeals from the people playing games. My eyes adjust to the dark blue lighting as we approach the far left-hand side where the bowling lanes are. Soft RnB music is playing from the speakers above us, giving the place a relaxing atmosphere and I'm so happy the music isn't loud. At least I know I won't be leaving with a headache today.

We were only supposed to have dinner tonight, but Jamar told me his friends are in town today, so we're going to meet them first. Jamar waves at a group of people who are changing into bowling shoes and they turn their heads to us. "Hey, look who it is." A tall, bearded man with a similar build to Jamar shouts out. He greets Jamar with a brief hug and a clap on his back, before turning to me. "Who's this pretty lady you've brought with you?"

Jamar laughs and pulls me close to him. "Hey, you back off now, young man, this one is mine."

The other man steps back and lifts both hands up in mock surrender. "Yes, boss. You always get the good ones. Who am I to compete with you?" They both laugh and I force a smile, ignoring the fact that I now feel like a piece of meat they're going to have for dinner.

"Oh, I'm so sorry about my manners." Jamar holds my hand. "Amara, this is Jason, my best friend. Jason, this is Amara."

"It's a pleasure to meet you, Amara. Such a nice name." He extends his hand and I reluctantly put mine in his.

"Thank you and it's nice to meet you too, Jason." I say, before removing my hand from his grip. Something about the way he looks at me is uncomfortably familiar—it's the same way Jamar looks at me.

"This is André and his fiancée—Jayla." Jamar walks over to the couple sitting on the bench next to the bowling lane.

André is shorter than the other two guys and has an afro. He also doesn't have a neatly-shaped beard like the other two, but his jawline is framed with stubble. "Nice to meet you." I shake André's hand before turning to Jayla. She's also a few inches taller than André and wearing a bone-straight waist-length wig. Her smile is warm, but her artificial nails are so long, I wouldn't want them coming anywhere close to my eyes.

I'll be surprised if she doesn't break a nail before we leave today. "It's nice to meet you, Jayla."

"And you too, girl. Jamar has told us a lot about you."

Good things, I hope. The words roll to the edge of my tongue, but I swallow them back in.

"So, are you ready to beat these boys at bowling?" Jayla asks.

"Yeah, sure." I follow the rest of them and change out of my own trainers into the bowling shoes before we move to the bowling alley. Our first game starts and even though there's an uneven split, Jayla and I stick together as a team versus the boys.

Jayla is the first one to go and like a skilled bowler, she throws the ball and smashes down all the pins without breaking a sweat. "You take that, boys." She turns around and sticks her tongue out at our opponents.

"Not bad, not bad." Jamar says as he picks up a ball. "But don't gloat just yet because soon, we'll find out if that was a skilled shot or a fluke." He winks at Jayla before walking to the lane to throw his ball. His shot misses one pin, and this sends Jayla into a hyper mood as she jumps up and down while pumping her fists in the air.

"Sorry, I get really competitive sometimes," she says after calming down.

I can see that. "That's okay." I smile and pick up my own ball. Walking up to the lane, I throw the ball without putting much thought into it and it knocks down half the pins.

"Ah, that's okay, girl. We'll still beat them." Jayla says as André inspects the different balls.

"So, how did you and Jamar meet?" Jayla asks.

"We work together." I respond. "I'm a NICU nurse and Jamar does locum shifts at the PICU sometimes."

"I see." Jayla folds her arms as we both watch André throw the ball. "Jamar has always struggled to make up his mind about what he wants. That's why he does locum tenens shifts instead of settling on a speciality." She turns to me. "He used to be like that with girls when we were in med school. He ended up stringing a few of them along because he couldn't decide who he wanted to be with." She chuckles and shakes her head. "But I'm glad he has found something special in you. Welcome to our tribe, Amara." She squeezes my shoulder and picks up another ball. "Now get out of the way, loser," she yells at André who only knocked down two pins.

Wow, this girl really doesn't know how to paint her friend's good side, does she? I was right about my suspicion. Jamar is a lady's man. I'm doing the same thing with him and Ray, but it feels different being on this side of the equation. If Jamar is speaking to other girls, then there's no guarantee he'll choose me in the end.

He definitely won't choose you.

"Hey." Jamar's warm touch jolts me out of my head. "It's your turn."

I lift my head to find Jayla and the others staring at me. "Oh, right. Sorry."

"Are you okay?" Jamar holds my hand. "You don't have a headache again, do you?"

"No, I'm fine." I smile at him. "Thank you." I proceed to throw the ball, knocking down all the pins this time and I pump my fists in the air before giving Jayla a high five.

Even if I was brave enough to ask Jamar about what Jayla said, this is not the right time. I'll get to know more about him when we have some time alone.

The rest of the evening flies by and we share lots of giggles and playful arguments, but every time I look at Jamar, more doubts sink their teeth into my skin and I start asking myself what I'm doing and why I'm interested in him.

So many thoughts run through my mind as I sip on a cup of coffee during my lunch break. I wrap my jacket around me and lean forward, staring at the ground as Jayla's words flash in my memory again.

The bowling date with Jamar was two weeks ago and since then, I've stayed up late at night many times thinking about what Jayla said. What if Jamar is still the same person he was when he was in med school? That would mean I'm totally wasting my time.

There's a famous African proverb that says *no matter how hard the rain falls, it can never wash away a leopard's spots.* But if Jamar is a true Christian and his heart has been changed, then I have nothing to worry about. The problem is, I know nothing about where Jamar stands with his faith. Every time I try to talk about God or church, he brushes off the subject, so I'm not sure what to think.

A hand squeezes my shoulder, shaking me out of my thoughts. I lift my head to meet Ray's soft gaze. "Hey, are you okay?" He stoops next to me as I lean back.

"Oh, hey. How long have you been standing there?"

"Not long." He stands up and sits next to me. "Are you okay?" He asks again.

I nod. "Yeah, I am. I just had a rough night, that's all."

He drops his gaze to the cup of coffee in my hand. "Wow, it must have been really rough for you to drink coffee." He laughs and I can't help but join him too.

"You know what they say. Desperate times call for desperate measures."

"Is there anything I can do to help?"

There he goes again, always knowing the right thing to say. I know he'll do anything within his power to make me feel better, but me being tired and restless is entirely my fault. I smile and shake my head. "No, I'm okay for now. But thank you so much."

"The teens have been asking about you," Ray says, and I frown.

"Really? Me?"

"Yeah. I told you they loved having you around the last time —especially Tessa. She won't let me drink water and she keeps asking when next you'll be around."

I chuckle. "Aww, we had a great time."

"So you should come again." Ray turns his whole body to face me. "Okay, I have a proposition. The youth retreat is coming in May and I plan to cover a lot of topics with them. I was thinking maybe you could...lead one session at the retreat?"

My heart drops and I shake my head. "Oh no, no. Ray, I'm not a leader. I can't lead anything. I'm happy to just help out in the background."

Ray sighs and holds my hand. "Amara, remember what I told you a few weeks ago? I believe God has equipped you, but you need to stop quitting before you even start."

"Ray, you don't understand." I exhale sharply. "I've never done this kind of thing before. I don't know where to start."

"I'll do it with you." Ray places his palm on my cheek. "Okay, what do you think about starting with something casual like a question and answer session, and then when you're ready, you can lead a session?"

"Ray, I don't know…"

"I'll help you." He squeezes both my hands. "Please, trust me."

I sigh and turn my head to the double doors of the ER when my gaze lands on a familiar face walking toward the parking lot. *Oh, no. It's Jamar. I forgot he was working at the PICU today.*

I remove my hands from Ray's grip and stand up. "Erm…sorry Ray, I have to go now. I have a meeting."

"Amara…"

Without waiting for him to respond, I fast-walk into the building using a different door, so Jamar doesn't see me.

Ray doesn't give up and he follows closely behind me. "Amara, please wait." He catches up to me and walks by my side. "Okay, I'm sorry I asked. I don't want you to feel pressured into doing anything. If you're not ready, then that's okay." Ray steps in front of me, forcing me to stop walking.

When I glance outside the window, I catch a glimpse of Jamar's car driving out of the parking lot and I let out an internal sigh of relief.

"Amara?" Ray follows my gaze to the parking lot.

"I'll do it." I respond to divert Ray's attention back to me.

"Really?" He smiles. "That's great. Thank you so much."

"That's okay, Ray. As long as you help me like you promised."

"Of course, I've got you. You've just made my day. I'll pick you up after work and we can discuss the details and paperwork, okay?"

I nod. "Sure, that sounds good."

"Okay, I'll see you later." He squeezes my arm before walking in the opposite direction back to his department. I rub my forehead and start walking back to the NICU.

Phew. That was close. When I agreed to date both Ray and Jamar, I never considered the possibility of them meeting. If that ever happens, it'll be a disaster. They'll find out I've been lying to them and they'll hate me forever. *Oh, no. What have I gotten myself into?*

23

AMARA

I've spent the last few days pacing, biting my nails, and pulling at *Frolita* while trying to choose an outfit for my date with Jamar. I prayed for this day, so I don't understand why hesitation is seeping through me. I thought my heart would be dancing with joy, but this whole ordeal feels wrong.

I started feeling like this after Ray hugged me at the hospital. The Lord knows I was emotionally, physically, and spiritually drained that day. I needed comfort and someone to listen to me. The nurses were brilliant and helped me through that tough time.

But when Ray showed up, he knew exactly where to take me, when to hug me, when to say something, and when to be quiet. When he hugged me, I wanted to stay in that position for a lot longer. The warmth of his embrace was so reassuring. It spoke a thousand words—words I could understand.

Since that day, I've thought about hugging him again. I've replayed the hug over and over in my head—the same way I replay cute scenes when I watch romantic comedies; like when the guy pulls the girl in for a hug and they end up kissing. Or when the girl slips and he catches her and then they stare in each other's eyes. Or when they're trying to reach for the same object and their hands touch.

It feels like I'm living in my own romantic comedy. I want to feel the tingling sensation I had when Ray held my hand that day. I want my stomach to flip on the inside and the warmth of his hands to send my heart racing again, like a wild horse that can't be tamed. I want all of that again, and that's why I'm wondering why I'm still going on this date.

It's been weeks since Jamar and Ray narrowly missed each other at the hospital, but I've been feeling nervous every time Jamar has a shift at the PICU. I had to stop Ray from coming to the NICU today to reduce the chances of them meeting.

It's Valentine's Day tomorrow and I already agreed to spend the evening with Ray, so I convinced Jamar to have dinner with me tonight instead. I also lied to Ray when he asked me what I'm doing tonight. I don't like doing this, but I don't have a choice. I just need to keep them away from each other for a little longer until I make up my mind.

Beep. A car horn from outside my studio apartment shakes me out of my thoughts. I push myself from my couch, balancing on my wedged heels, which add an inch to my height. I pull down my black fitted puff organza sleeve dress before rushing to my window. The car horn beeps again and Jamar winds his window down before nodding at me to come outside.

"Why won't he come to the door like Ray does?" I mutter to myself. "It's not like he's a cab driver picking up a passenger." I take out my red lipstick from my clutch purse and smother a little bit more on my lips before fluffing out *Frolita*'s curls and leaving the apartment.

The cold air wraps around my legs as I walk down to Jamar's car, which still has the engine running. When I'm a few yards away, he steps out and walks up to me, taking me by my hand.

Finally, he decides to step out.

"You look beautiful." He smirks and his gaze slides from the top of my head to my feet before settling on my chest.

"Thank you." I respond and pull my jacket forward to cover my chest. Removing my hand from his, I get in the car and we drive off.

A few minutes into our journey, I turn to look at him, his eyes focused on the road and his beard framing his jawline perfectly. He looks really handsome in his white shirt and blue blazer, but his silver necklace is the icing on the cake.

Come on, girl, stop staring. I clear my throat and adjust in my seat as he turns the radio up to some station playing a hip hop song I don't recognize. "So...where are we going?" I ask, trying to fill in the awkward silence.

He turns to look at me with a smirk. "You'll see." He uses his tongue to wet his lips before facing the road again. The colored lights from the cars on the street shine in front, behind, and beside us.

Street lamps line the streets, illuminating the sidewalks and highlighting the pedestrians walking on them—some in groups and others in couples. The full moon is already shining in the distance, immersed in a sea of stars spread out across the dark sky. One moment, I'm admiring how beautiful the view is and the next, my mind is drifting back to Ray and wondering what he's doing right now.

"So do you like working at the NICU?" Jamar's voice impedes on my thoughts and I turn to face him again.

"Well, yeah...some days are better than others, but overall, I love working there." I say as Emily's innocent face comes to mind. "I watched my favourite baby die a few weeks ago and it wasn't the best experience."

"Oh, that's okay. I'm sure you'll get over it." He says in a dismissive tone as he steers the car into a parking lot.

I'm taken aback by his response. *That's okay? How is that*

okay? Is he even listening to me? You know, for a pediatrician, he doesn't seem to have much empathy.

"We're here." The car pulls to a stop and Jamar opens the door and walks round to my side. He extends his arm to me, and I wrap my arm around his as we walk to the restaurant.

"Here we are, m'lady." He opens the door to the restaurant and ushers me in. The sound of jazz music envelopes me as the waiter greets us at the door and shows us to our seats. We order our food and when the waiter goes away, the chatter of customers around us replaces the awkward silence.

Jamar stares at me and smiles, but something about the way he does it makes me feel uncomfortable. It doesn't send the warm sensations down my spine the way Ray's looks do. I might find Jamar more physically attractive, but he doesn't make me feel the way Ray does.

So girl, what are you still doing here?

When I lift my head, Jamar is staring at me again, so to stop his gaze from wandering to my chest, I ask a question. "How was your week at the hospital?"

He leans back in his seat and adjusts his blazer. "Oh, just the same old. Nothing new."

Really? Is that it?

I force a smile and sip on my glass of water before lifting my gaze to admire the chandeliers hanging from the ceiling. Okay, here's my chance to know more about Jamar. That's why I agreed to come on this date, not to sit here in silence and watch him stare at me like a hungry dog.

"Jayla told me about your previous relationships in med school." I say, watching his facial expressions,

Jamar clears his throat. "She did?"

"Yeah. She said you used to have trouble deciding who you wanted to be with and..."

"That was years ago." Jamar cuts me off. "I was naive and

stupid back then. I think I know better now." He picks up his glass. "And Jayla had no right to run her mouth about my personal life."

Yeah, she had no right. But I'm glad she told me, because at least now I know Jamar has changed. "So." I speak again as Jamar sips on his drink. "What would you say your purpose or calling is?" I cringe as the words leave my mouth, but I have to change the subject and I have to know where Jamar stands spiritually.

He shrugs and leans forward. "It's simple. To help people."

Ooh, good answer. "What motivates you to help people and how does God fit into it?"

He stares at me with a blank expression on his face. "God helps me and then I help people. It's that simple." He shrugs again, a sheepish smile forming on his mouth. "I'm not sure what you want me to say."

Okay. That didn't go as planned, but I need to have my answers today. "Jamar, how would you describe the relationship we have?" I say, gesturing my finger between the two of us.

He averts his gaze and clears his throat again. If I didn't sense that this is an uncomfortable conversation for him, I would've genuinely thought there's something stuck in his throat.

"Jamar?"

"Honey, listen." He finally looks at me and reaches for my hand. "I don't like being pressured into defining relationships. We're getting to know each other and we're having fun while we do it. Please, let's just enjoy each other's company and see where it goes. Okay?"

Pressured? He now sees me like someone who is pressuring him?

"Okay." I respond and sink back in my seat. "What church do you go to again?"

"What?" He asks, staring at me as if I'm a ghost.

"Your church." I frown. "You said you go to church too."

"Right, oh yes...church." He clicks his fingers. "I go to...to..." his voice trails off as the waiter returns with our food. When the waiter leaves, Jamar quickly changes the subject and we spend the rest of the evening talking about our families, college and hobbies. He tells me he loves playing golf and that he comes from a family of five with two younger sisters.

I always see a different side of Jamar when we're talking about him, his family, or his interests. But whenever I ask a question to aid my understanding of his goals and his views on life and faith, he literally blanks on me and forgets how to form sentences. So I'll stop asking, so he doesn't think that I'm putting pressure on him.

I miss the deep conversations with Ray; conversations which make me think about the meaning of life, why I'm here and how I can commit to making every day meaningful. Those are the conversations I want to have. Not this shallow chatter.

When Jamar pulls up on my street after our date, I'm wide awake. I didn't fall asleep this time like I did with Ray. Throughout the journey, I was thinking about a hundred and one things, and Ray was eighty percent of those things.

"So, what do you say we go inside, get a drink, and watch one of those Nollywood movies you talked about?" Jamar places his arm over my shoulders and leans in. The smell of his cologne gets stronger and it churns the food in my stomach. *Ugh, what is he doing? Does he want to kiss me?*

A few months ago, this situation would've been a dream come true and an answered prayer, so why are there alarm bells ringing in my head and asking me to get out? My heart rate quickens, saliva dries from my mouth and I press myself against the window as Jamar closes the gap between us. Something about this doesn't feel right.

Jamar's gaze drops to my mouth, and he licks his lips again. His hand slides behind my neck and he pulls me closer, but I turn my face away just in time and his lips press against my cheek instead.

"I think I need to go now." I unbuckle my seatbelt and Jamar lets out a heavy sigh before pulling away. "I'm sorry." I push the door open and step out into the cold air.

"That's okay. I'll call you." Jamar says as I shut the car door and power walk to my front steps without looking back. His tires screech against the road as he reverses his car and speeds off.

When I'm inside my apartment, I close the door and lean against it while tilting my head back. *Boy, that was close.* After taking deep breaths to calm my heart rate, I drag myself to my room and take out the list from my bag. I run my hands down the eight things I thought I wanted in a guy and Jamar ticks most of the boxes. He is handsome, I'm attracted to him, he is financially upright, he is romantic, and he is a Christian—well, he says he is.

But if this is what I want, why am I running away? Why does Ray keep popping into my head every second? Why do I crave Ray's presence, his smile, his touch, and his words?

I drop to my knees in front of my bed and look at my list again, but all I can think about is Ray, and then, realization dawns on me. *How did I get here, Lord?*

Scrunching the list into a ball, I toss it in the trash can and sink to the floor before bringing my knees up to my chest. "Lord, I'm sorry it's taken me so long to bring this to you. I don't know what's going on with me, but...I think I like Ray." I sigh before continuing. "Do my feelings even matter? I'm sure I'm not the right woman for him, anyway. Lord, please show me what to do. I'm so confused."

As I continue praying, the vivid scene from before pops into my head again. It's the same scene of a teenage girl, with beautiful long braided hair, sobbing in front of me. I can still only see the back of her head, but she's sitting closer to me now and I'm holding her shoulder and praying for her as she sobs. I still don't know who she is or why she's crying, but like the last time, I pull her in for a hug and then open my eyes.

"Lord, I don't understand." I whisper to myself as a cold shiver travels down my spine. "Who is this girl and why do you keep showing her to me?" Shuddered breaths escape my lips as I catch a glimpse of my Bible.

An unexplainable urge to read it forces me to push myself up and grab the book before opening it on my lap. It's been a while since I did my personal Bible study. I know the Bible has all the answers, so I need to find the ones I need. "Please, help me understand, Lord."

I flip open to Genesis and start reading from the first page, word after word, and sentence after sentence, until time is no longer my concern.

24

AMARA

I don't have time to buy the special Valentine's Day hot chocolate this morning because I'm late for work. I didn't fall asleep until three a.m, but at least this time, I wasn't writing some *stupid* list. After that weird dream or trance, or whatever that was, I spent a few hours studying my Bible. I might feel like a zombie right now, but I don't regret it.

Teeyana and Jayden have been bugging me for months to join them in studying the whole Bible in one year, but I prefer taking my time to savor every word, and reading them over again until they sink in.

Last night, I studied the story of Isaac and Rebecca and it's now one of my favorites. Rebecca went out of her way to help Abraham's servant, but I realized that this servant was looking for more than just a woman who could give him water and feed his camels.

Rebecca's actions showed the servant that she was extraordinarily kind, and that she could show compassion and care. Rebecca was a woman of character, a helpmeet, and the comfort Isaac needed to fulfill his purpose. Coming to that realization last night made me excited, but it also made me feel a little deflated.

Now that I know I have feelings for Ray, I can't tell him yet because I still don't know if I'm the Rebecca to his Isaac. I don't know if I have the good character and qualities he's looking for. I know he thinks I'm the woman for him, but what if he's wrong? What if he finds out I have nothing to offer? He'll probably dump me and then I'd die of a heartbreak.

I push open the door leading up to the stairwell and sling my bag over my shoulder. With my new afrobeat gospel playlist blasting through my headphones, I run up the stairs and resist the urge to skip some steps as I know my short legs would betray me and land me face down on the floor. My chest constricts and my legs turn to jelly when I make it to the top. I press one hand against the wall and bend over to catch my breath. *Darn it, girl, you're so unfit.*

My phone vibrates and when I take it out of my pocket, it's a text from Jamar asking if we could meet for lunch. I roll my eyes and delete the notification. "Not today, satan."

As I'm about to turn into the corridor leading to the NICU, a strong arm wraps around my waist and turns me around to meet the loving gaze and bright smile I've been thinking about.

His chest is only an inch away from my face and his familiar cologne wafts into my nostrils, slowing my heart rate down. *Eeeek.* I bite my bottom lip to stop myself from squealing with the excitement of seeing him—even though I only just saw him yesterday.

"I've been calling your name." Ray says before taking a step back and placing a hand on his hip. A white t-shirt is peeking out of the V-neckline of his scrubs and something about the teal color makes him look especially handsome today. *Stahhpp it, girl. Focus.*

"Sorry." I smile sheepishly and take off my headphones. "I was listening to the new playlist you shared with me."

"Ah, I'm glad you're enjoying it. Are you running late?"

"Yeah, I got carried away reading about Isaac and Rebecca last night so I slept late and missed my alarm."

"Oooh, come and see a true woman of God." He hails me and heat rises to my cheeks. This is why I love talking to him. He makes me want to tell him even the smallest details of my life—the same way I've learnt to communicate with God.

"Ray, I need to go. I'm already late." I turn around, but he stops me with a gentle pull of my hand and goosebumps travel up my arm.

"Wait, you're forgetting something." He hands me a cup of hot chocolate, which I didn't notice before. "For you."

My hands fly to my chest. "Aww, you got me the Valentine's Day special? That's so sweet." My voice comes out sounding squeakier than I would like, but I ignore it and take the hot chocolate from him, admiring the red heart stamped on the front of the cup.

"I just had a feeling you'll need one this morning. Happy Valentine's Day." Ray smiles and my heart dances around in my chest.

Okay, somebody call the fire department because my chest is about to blow up.

"I won't hold you up any longer." He places his hands on my shoulders and before I can recover from his touch, he pulls me closer and plants a soft kiss on my forehead.

His warm lips linger for not one, or two, but three seconds—long enough to rile up all sorts of emotions inside of me. When he lets go, he brushes my chin with his thumb and saunters down the hallway, leaving me to fight the strong urge to cartwheel all the way to my destination. *What just happened? Did he...did he just...did he just kiss me?*

During our ten-minute coffee break, we rush into the staff room as the sweet smell of Claire's homemade brownies envelopes us. I grab a heart-shaped brownie and sink into the couch in between Aaliyah and Imani before biting into the chewy, chocolatey goodness.

As the girls talk about the upcoming Valentine's Day special episode of *Grey's Anatomy,* I take out my phone to read Ray's message. His text buzzed in half an hour ago, but I didn't want to read it in between changing diapers and preparing milk bottles for my babies.

Ray: Hey, I hope you weren't offended by the kiss. I didn't realize how excited I was to see you this morning 😳

Boy, don't be sorry. I would do anything to feel the softness of his lips against my forehead again. Everything about that moment felt right, and I'm so glad I didn't let Jamar kiss me last night.

Me: I didn't mind the kiss at all. It was nice.

My heart flutters as I imagine what it would feel like kissing Ray's lips. I smile to myself before exhaling deeply when Imani elbows my side and forces me to lift my head.

Everyone's curious eyes are on me and I didn't even realize they had stopped talking about *Grey's Anatomy.* "What?" I ask, heat rising to my cheeks as I try to take an oblivious stance.

Imani leans over to look at my phone, but I guard it close to my chest as if it's some pot of gold. "Who are you texting?" She asks, and I swipe my screen shut, embarrassed to let them see the reason I'm smiling like a fool.

"Yeah, does Dr. Aderinto know he's distracting you from talking about the greatest show ever made? Hmm?" Aaliyah wiggles her eyebrows.

"Errm…" I clear my throat. "We're just…just…"

"Oh, come on, ladies. Leave the poor girl alone." Claire comes to my rescue. "Let the young ones fall in love. It's a beautiful thing." She stares at me with a pleasant smile.

My gaze moves from Claire to Imani and then to Aaliyah, but before I can say anything more, Claire adds, "I've known Raymond for many years and I'm glad he has finally found someone who makes him happier than he already is. You should have seen him when I bumped into him this morning. He looked like he was about to do a cartwheel."

A warm sensation travels up my chest. *This morning? That must have been after he kissed me.* Despite Ray's apology, I won't be surprised if he kissed me on purpose.

"I see you guys sitting in the garden all the time." Imani chimes in.

"Yeah, you both look so cute together." Aaliyah adds as she picks up another brownie from the tray.

A wave of guilt overwhelms me and turns the warm sensation I felt earlier into nausea. How can I sit here and take all these compliments when I went on a date with someone else last night? I'm a fraud. I'm lying to everyone—including Ray.

"Actually." I clear my throat, determined to make some rectifications. Maybe that will take away the guilt raiding my chest right now. "Ray and I are not official yet." I lower my head to hide my shame.

"You don't have to be shy about it, honey." Claire stands up and makes her way to the door. "We all know there's something special going on between you two." She winks at me before turning to the others. "Alright, ladies, break ends in five minutes." Claire adds, before walking out of the room and shutting the door behind her.

As soon as Claire is out of sight, Imani and Aaliyah shuffle close and start firing questions at me. "Okay, Claire is gone, so you can tell us. What's the deal between you two?" Imani asks, and my heart picks up the pace, pounding loud against my rib cage.

You're a fraud, Amara. You don't deserve to be with Ray. The dark voice swirls around in my mind and I drop my gaze to my finger nails. Maybe if I focus on how long it has been since I put nail varnish on them, I will fight this voice.

"Yeah, has he asked you out yet?" Aaliyah slips in.

He's way too good for you. He deserves someone better.

"Come on, Aaliyah, I'm sure he already has." Imani says. "The real question is, have you guys kissed yet?" Imani makes smooching sounds with her lips and goosebumps creep up my arms. Words catch in my throat, the walls start closing in on me, and the questions flying out of the girls' mouths make it difficult for me to think straight.

"Yeah, how was it, was it gentle and filled with passion?"

"What are you both doing for Valentine's Day tonight?"

You have nothing to offer him. You never will. You're a fraud.

I push myself up from the couch and the girls lean back. "I'm sorry, but I have to go now." I skitter out of the room, ignoring the confusion and disappointment on the girls' faces.

Outside the office, I step back into the familiar chaos of the NICU as I try to find a hiding spot, but after a quick scan, I give up and head for the bathroom.

As I make a u-turn and turn into the narrow corridor, I bump into a man heading in the opposite direction. "I'm so sorry—" I pause when I recognize his face. "Dr. Miller?"

I swallow my anxiety and smile at the brown-haired Caucasian man, whose features are clearly expressing how unimpressed he is. "Sorry if this isn't a good time, but I spoke to you months ago at the research associates introductory meeting. You encouraged me to apply for the program."

He frowns at me before shaking his head. "It doesn't ring a bell." He lifts his chin and pushes his glasses close to his face.

Now it's my turn to frown. "But...Dr. Miller, the deadline to get a reply was a month ago and everyone else has received an email except me. I just wanted to make sure—"

"Listen, young lady." He takes a step back, his frown now creasing up his already wrinkled forehead. "I have an important meeting starting in two minutes. Could you please step out of my way?"

The shock I'm experiencing at this moment is nothing compared to the anger boiling up in my chest. *Why is he being so rude?* I take a deep breath in through my nose and out through my mouth as I try to calm my nerves. "I apologize for inconveniencing you, Dr. Miller. It's just that I've been to your office four times now since the meeting and I haven't been able to—"

"There's no space left on the program," he cuts me short. "You're wasting my time, so I'd appreciate it if you step out of my way."

A lump builds in my throat as I'm transported back to high school when Olivia Hastings and her friends bullied Teeyana and I. All those emotions of not fitting in and not being wanted or appreciated come rushing back in one solid wave.

Coupled with my previous state of anxiety and guilt, my eyes start watering and my legs suddenly become too heavy to move. But Dr. Miller steps aside and continues down the hallway without any care in the world.

What were you thinking, Amara? The dark voice returns like it never left.

"What a jerk." Claire says behind me.

Did you really think you could get into that program?

"I know right." Someone else says, whose voice I don't recognize.

"Is he allowed to do that?" Another voice asks.

You're not good enough and you'll never be.

As I lean against the wall, the palpitations return and tears blur my vision. Soon, my once heavy legs resume their original journey toward the bathroom, my feet hitting the ground faster than they ever have.

Don't cry, Amara. You can't cry in front of these people. My pep talk only helps me until the end of the hallway because as soon as I open the bathroom door and enter an empty stall, the tears flood out of my eyes without any mercy.

25

RAYMOND

I whistle to myself as I make my way to the NICU to pick Amara up for lunch. I had to ditch Joe today, but he definitely understands. With the way I'm feeling right now, only my lack of talent is stopping me from doing the moon-walk down this hallway.

I don't even care if anyone thinks I'm crazy because they don't know I kissed Amara. Seriously, I don't know what came over me. The girl was looking too *fine* and I couldn't help myself. Today is going to be a wonderful day; it might even be the day Amara says yes to me.

When I get to the double doors, I pause and turn to face my reflection in the glass window. I fix the neckline of my scrubs to lie flat, and if I had a beard, now would be a good time to check it's in shape, but thank God I don't have to worry about that. I reach into my pocket and take out a small tube of vaseline—the one I always carry around to prevent me from getting chapped lips in Atlanta's harsh weather.

Satisfied with my now moisturized lips, I shrug my shoulders playfully and scrunch my eyebrows before bursting into laughter. *"O boi, weti dey worry you?"* Joe would ask if he was standing next to me right now. *"Please, be going, jor."*

I open the door and walk straight to the nurse's desk, spotting Claire's blonde hair behind it. "Hey, Claire. Have you seen —" My smile disappears when Claire lifts her head.

"Oh, Raymond. I'm glad you're here." She drops the file she's holding and walks around the desk to meet me.

My smile disappears and a twinge of worry settles in my chest. "What's wrong?"

"It's that horrible man." She lowers her voice as she approaches me. "Come on." She pulls me by the arm toward the staff office.

"What horrible man?" I ask when she shuts the door behind her.

The older woman shakes her head and lets out an exaggerated sigh. "You know Dr. Miller—the research associate lead?"

"Yes?" I step back, trying to figure out what business Claire has with the man.

"You remember Amara has been wanting to get into the research program?" Claire asks, and my eyes widen.

Oh, no. "What did he do to Amara? Is she okay? Where is she?" I start walking toward the door, but Claire stops me.

"She's fine." Claire says, and the muscles in my shoulders relax. "But she wasn't fine earlier. She has gone out for a short break."

"What did Dr. Miller do to her?" I ask again, my patience weaning as anger bubbles in my chest at the thought of anyone making Amara uncomfortable.

"He embarrassed her in front of everyone and refused to give her a spot on the program."

"What? Why would he do that? She meets all the criteria."

"Exactly." Claire places one hand on her hip. "And the worst thing about it is the way he talked down at her and treated her like a piece of trash. In front of the whole NICU."

"Oh, God, no." I run my palm down my face. Amara already struggles with insecurities. She doesn't need anyone making her believe them. This is not good. "Claire, where did she go? I need to speak to her."

"Ray, please wait." Claire holds my arm. "I think she needs some space. It took her about ten minutes to get out of the bathroom earlier. I've never seen her so upset about anything for the last six months I've been working with her. I think Dr. Miller pushed some sensitive buttons, so I'd say wait until she tells you about it herself."

My shoulders slump as I let out a frustrated groan. "But...what do I do now?"

Claire shrugs. "Help her. You're the lead for diversity and equity at this hospital. Your voice matters, especially in situations like this. You have to say something."

Claire is right. Now's the time to prove how much I care about Amara. I straighten my back and nod. "Thanks, Claire."

The staff room door squeaks open as Claire and I step out into the ward again. "Please tell Amara I stopped by to see her." I scratch my bald head, the stubble reminding me I'm due another trip to the barber's.

Claire nods and I make my way back toward the exit when a familiar face emerges from the other end of the NICU. Dr. Miller strolls past the nurses scrunching up his nose as if the air smells of feces—well, at least that's the way my mother would describe it.

I grit my teeth and ball my hands into tight fists as I redirect my steps toward him. I'm a lover and not a fighter, but one thing I know is that no one will mess with the woman I love and go free.

This place is too public to have this kind of discussion, but he didn't think about that when he embarrassed my girl in front of everyone. "Dr. Miller?" I block his path and force him to slow down.

"Ah, Dr. *Adireentu.*" He smirks. The butchering of my name makes my skin crawl and I grit my teeth even more.

"It's *Aderinto*" I force a smile. "But you can just call me Raymond." I say, trying to curb the rising urge to give him a Yoruba pronunciation lesson.

"Pardon my ignorance," he says in the most insincere tone of voice ever. "Can I help you?" His greying eyebrows furrow.

Lord, please give me the right words. "Yes, I have a quick inquiry, actually." I lift my chin before crossing my arms against my chest. "It's about your research program."

Dr. Miller shifts his weight to his right leg before crossing his own arms. "What about it?"

I clear my throat, trying to remember how confrontations happen in the Hollywood movies I've been watching. Maybe I should try the Nollywood style?... Nah, Hollywood it is. Nigerians can be overly dramatic sometimes. "It has come to my knowledge that your recent behavior toward a colleague of ours suggests you are breaching the guidelines of inclusivity that this hospital has been advocating for many years. To be more specific, I've been informed that you have publicly denied one applicant an opportunity to take part in your program without a justifiable reason."

The older man snorts. "And where would you get such unreliable information from?"

I frown at him. He is trying to divert, but I won't let him. "May I remind you, Dr. Miller, that the board takes allegations like this seriously, especially since our new plan for this year is in action. May I also remind you in case you have forgotten that as the lead for diversity and equity in this hospital, it is my duty to flag up cases like this, and I can assure you that we act on these cases immediately."

He steps forward and stares at me intently, but I don't flinch. "Are you threatening me, Dr. *Adireentu?*"

I now have my confirmation that he is butchering my name on purpose, so I laugh it off. "I don't do threats, Dr. Miller. I only stand for what is right. You can't go about disrespecting colleagues for your unjustifiable reasons."

"And who says my reasons are unjustifiable?" He raises his eyebrows.

Ah, see me this guy o. Is he being serious right now? "By all means, state your claim, Dr. Miller. Tell me why you won't give Miss Ikezie a place on your research program even though you and I know she is overqualified."

"I owe you no explanation." He shakes his head. "You have no proof. It's going to be my word against yours."

"Oh, really? I guess you didn't think about that when you embarrassed her in public, did you?" I use my hand to make a sweeping gesture over the NICU, bringing his attention to all the nurses and doctors watching us. "I have more than enough proof."

The muscles in Dr. Miller's jaw twitch and that's definitely a sign that he's cracking. He opens his mouth to say something, but closes it again before walking past me, his exaggerated strides reminding me of a child throwing a tantrum because his parents have refused to buy him a toy. *And I thought only Nigerians were dramatic.*

"It's the end of the road, Dr. Miller. If you don't give her a fair chance like everyone else, I *will* bring this up at the next board meeting. You know what that would mean for your reputation?" My voice rises as he continues walking down the hallway. His strides get even longer and after brushing past a nurse, he rushes out of the NICU and shuts the door behind him.

I sigh and drop my gaze to the floor. *Lord, please take control.* A hand touches my shoulder gently and I turn around, hoping to meet Amara's soft gaze, but that's not the case.

"That was beautiful, Raymond." Claire squeezes my shoulder. "You really care about her, don't you?"

I nod. "There's no doubt about that. But this isn't just about Amara. It's about doing the right thing. Dr. Miller has been pulling on a long string all these years. He has finally come to the end."

After our twelve hour Valentine's Day shift, I stand outside the hospital at our favorite spot, waiting for Amara to walk through the double doors. I sent her a text message five minutes ago asking her to meet me here.

It's cold, but the two hot drinks in my hands are providing some warmth for my fingers. My jacket, scarf, and winter hat are not enough to protect me from this forty-degree Fahrenheit weather. Can you imagine that after living in this country for over a decade, I'm still shaking like a leaf whenever the winter hits? I guess it's true what they say; *you can take a man out of Africa, but you can't take Africa out of a man.*

I smile when I spot *Frolita* among the sea of people walking out. I still remember how mesmerized I was when Amara first told me she named her afro. I thought it was funny at first, but now *Frolita* matters to me too.

"Hey." She gives me a small smile, but it's not bright enough to disguise her puffy eyelids, or the fact that she looks tired and drained.

"Hot chocolate?" I offer her one cup, and she takes it without hesitating. *Thank God this hot chocolate trick still works. If it ever stops working, then God, I'll need divine intervention.*

"How was your day?" I ask, hoping she'll tell me about Dr Miller. Before leaving the NICU, I told Claire and the other nurses and doctors not to tell Amara about my conversation with Dr. Miller. I worry that if Dr. Miller gives her a spot on the program and she finds out I confronted him, she might take it the wrong way and think she didn't deserve the spot. I now regret speaking to Dr. Miller in public. I should have done it privately, but what is done is done.

"Nothing much." Amara shrugs. "Just the usual work stress." She lowers her gaze, but I use my finger to prop her chin up, so she can look at me.

"Come on, I can tell you've been crying. It's written all over your face. Do you want to talk about it?"

She looks at me for a few seconds, then she slowly shakes her head. I'm not surprised. She didn't mention Dr. Miller when she replied to my text messages after lunch, so I know she's not ready to talk about it yet.

"Okay, but you know I'll always be here if you need to share, right?" I say and she nods. "If you ever need a shoulder to cry on, mine are here, *kampe*—no shaking." I tap my shoulder so hard I almost pop it out of its socket.

Amara chuckles and the sound brings joy to my heart. "Thank you, Ray."

I open my arms wide and give her a hug, inhaling her rose scent. The warmth of her embrace is so satisfying I wish we could stay like this forever. When I finally let go of her, she looks up at me, her gaze moving from my eyes to my lips, which I'm sure are now chapped because of this cold weather. God knows I want to kiss her lips so badly, but I refuse to take advantage of her vulnerable state. One day that kiss will happen and it'll be perfect, but that day is not today.

This isn't how I thought Valentine's Day would go. My plan was to take her to dinner, and then a long walk where we can chat; but I know the kind of day she's had. The best gift I can offer her is time alone to rest. I plant another kiss on her forehead, this time not thinking twice about it. "Come on. I'll take you home."

26

AMARA

I walk out of the dressing room wearing a teal floor-length dress with a halter-neck. As I hover in front of the full-length mirror in the hallway, I pull the dress over my wide hips so it doesn't crease, while simultaneously keeping the hem off the floor so I don't trip.

My phone pings as a text notification comes in. It's Jamar asking if we can hang out after work next week. I shake my head and delete the notification. One of these days, I'll get the courage to tell him I don't want this anymore. That day is not today.

"That dress looks really good on you," a voice says from behind me, making me jump slightly. I turn around and lock eyes with Heather—Teeyana's ex-college roommate.

"Thank you." I say. "Yours looks good too." I gesture toward her purple tea-length dress. "I love the bling sash and it goes really well with your hair color."

I smile and step aside as Heather settles in front of the mirror. "Thank you," she says and fluffs her shoulder-length auburn hair.

"So, what have you been up to? I haven't seen you since Teeyana's engagement party."

"Yeah, things have been a little crazy in my life." Heather sighs softly as we both walk to the waiting area.

"Oh? What happened?"

"Well, I moved into my new studio apartment in Brooklyn and I've officially launched my social media marketing business."

"Girl, that's amazing. Congratulations." I pull her in for a hug. "You know my parents and I used to live in Brooklyn before we moved to Boston, right? I really miss that place so I'll find any excuse to go back. Let me know if you need any help moving in, okay?"

"Thanks, Amara. I appreciate that." She smiles at me as we enter the room where Teeyana is waiting for us.

We both walk up to the pedestal and strike a pose as Maggie, the middle-aged consultant with platinum blonde hair, describes the dresses we are wearing. Teeyana is sitting on the sofa across from us, her dark brown gaze darting from my dress to Heather's. "Hmm, Amara, please turn around." Teeyana says, and I give her a little twirl before returning to my pose.

Teeyana squints and tilts her head when she looks at my dress. "Amara, I really like the neckline and fit of your dress." She says and then looks at Heather's dress once more. "But I prefer the color of Heather's dress."

Of course she'll prefer it. Purple is Teeyana's favorite color.

"Do we have Amara's dress in purple?" Teeyana asks Maggie, and the older woman nods.

"Yes, we do. I will show you our catalog, so you can pick the color you want." Maggie smiles at Teeeyana.

"Great." Teeyana stands up. "So this is the dress." She walks up to the pedestal and hugs both me and Heather.

"Congratulations, girl." I say when we break from the hug. Maggie and Heather head back to the dressing room, but I stop Teeyana and hold her at arm's length. "Girl, it's officially ten months until your wedding. You still holding up good?"

Teeyana nods. "Yes, I am. Some days are great, but some days, I want to pull my hair out."

I feign a gasp, my hands flying to my chest. "Nuh-uh. Girl, not the hair. You cannot, and you will not. Do you know how many years it took you to grow this out? Teeyana Joy Sparks, you are not gonna give me a heart attack, do you hear me?" I try to imitate my mom's scolding voice, but it just sends Teeyana and I into a fit of giggles.

"But seriously though," I continue, "God's got your back, and I'm sure Jayden has been supportive."

A warm smile spreads across Teeyana's face as I mention Jayden's name—the same smile that has always been there since they met in college. I wonder how they've stayed attached to each other for so many years.

"Jayden has been amazing." Teeyana says. "Last night, when he came to see me at Grandpa's house, the caterers called to cancel because they did a double-booking. Poor Jayden had to listen to me rant for half an hour. Then when I was done, he drew me into his arms, kissed my forehead, and simply said, 'I understand you're upset, babe. But tomorrow, we'll call more caterers and I'm sure God will help us find another.'"

"Aww. That is *so* cute." I say as I remember the day Ray comforted me when Emily died.

"Yeah, sometimes you need someone who will remind you of the truth. Someone who will help you to be more rational. It's a blessing."

"Exactly. You are blessed and you have nothing to worry about." I add as an email notification chimes into my phone.

"Huh?" I frown before bringing the phone close to my face.

"What's up?" Teeyana asks and helps me get off the pedestal.

I narrow my eyes at the email and scroll through it. "It's from Dr. Miller."

Teeyana's eyebrows shoot up. "The same Dr. Miller who embarrassed you two weeks ago?"

I nod.

"What does he want now?"

"He said I've been accepted into the research program and he's inviting me to their first official meeting tomorrow with the rest of the group."

"Really? That's great." Teeyana hugs me briefly. "Congratulations. It's what you wanted, right?"

I stare at my phone again. "Yeah, but...don't you think it's strange he changed his mind?"

"Well, maybe God changed his mind and worked it out in your favor. That's great news, so we need to celebrate. Go, change out of this dress so we can go get something to eat." Teeyana pushes me toward the dressing room.

Everything else she says after that is drowned out by my loud thoughts about the oddness and strangeness of this situation. Something is not right.

Later that evening, I lay on my bed, staring at Dr. Miller's email on my phone as my thumbs hover over the keypad. What game is he playing? Is he just trying to cover his back? There must be a catch because he can't just change his mind like that, can he?

My phone's vibrations jerk me out of my thoughts and when I look at it, a photo of Ray's smiling face is staring back at me and my heart flutters. "Calm down, girl." I exhale slowly before bringing the phone up to my ear. "Hey, Ray." I keep my voice calm, a contrast to the parade of emotions dancing in my chest.

"*Nwanyi oma*." He responds, and I chuckle.

"Really? Who is giving you Igbo lessons on how to make a girl catch feelings?" I push myself up as my heart pounds faster —as if it has never heard someone call me a beautiful woman before.

"It's *Mr. Google* o. He's a wonderful teacher," Ray laughs. "How are you?"

My smile fades and I sigh. "I'm good, but I've been pondering over this weird email I received from Dr. Miller."

"Dr. Miller?" A shuffling sound comes from Ray's end of the line before he speaks again. "What did he say to you?" His tone is firm now.

"That he has accepted me into the program and he wants me to attend the introductory meeting tomorrow." At first, I refused to tell Ray about what Dr. Miller did and said to me, but in the end, I couldn't keep it away from him because I trust him. I didn't tell him about my breakdown and crying in the bathroom though.

"Wow, that's...that's wonderful news...right?"

I frown. "Really? You don't see anything weird about it? Ray, this man made me feel worthless in front of my colleagues and now he expects me to forget about what he did without an apology?"

"Maybe he wants to apologize in person. Have you thought about that?" Ray asks, and my shoulders slump.

"No, but he should have hinted that in his email and—"

"Amara, God knows how to work miracles and change people's hearts." Ray's gentle voice takes over. "Dr. Miller wronged you and you deserve an apology from him, but if he has realized the error of his ways and wants to make things right, won't you let him?"

Ray makes a good point. God is working for me and fighting my battles. Dr Miller's behaviour was an obstacle, but God came through for me. "Yeah, you're right. I'll go to the meeting and see what he says."

"That sounds like a good plan. If Dr. Miller does or says anything mean to you, please tell me first, okay?"

"Okay." I smile. "Will you fight him for me if he does?"

Ray's laughter bubbles from my phone, pulling a chuckle from me as well. "Ah, no. Fight *ke*? Baby girl, I'm a lover, not a fighter. But I have my ways."

The butterfly feeling in my belly returns. "Thank you so much, Ray."

"No problem, *arewa mi*. I'm here for you anytime."

I frown. "Erm, hello? You forget I don't speak Yoruba."

"I know you don't, but like I said, *Mr. Google* is a wonderful teacher." Ray snickers and I roll my eyes.

"*Ugh*, you're so annoying." I chuckle as I remember what Teeyana said earlier about having someone who reminds you of the truth. Ray is that person for me. He has been a blessing since he came into my life. Now I know why I've developed feelings for him. He is good to me; but can I really be his Rebecca?

I've been praying about this more, but I haven't told anyone yet about my feelings for Ray—not even Teeyana. I think it's time to seek older and wiser counsel—something I should have done earlier.

When I was in nursing school, I had a spiritual mentor at my college church. She helped me through a lot of issues I was dealing with then, and she encouraged me to deepen my relationship with God. We were close during my freshman and sophomore years, but when all the stresses of final year hit, I started withdrawing so I could focus on passing finals and my N-CLEX exam.

She still checks on me from time to time, but I'm sure she

has a lot to deal with now. She won't have time for my troubles. That leaves me with no choice but to go to my parents. If I could, I would only tell Dad, but I know the fuss Mom would make if she finds out later that I didn't involve her from the beginning. *Lord, I know Mom has beef with Yoruba men, but please, let Ray's case be different.*

27

AMARA

"Chai, *Adamma*, my beautiful child. The way you are shining today, *eh*? *Omalicha m.*" Mom leans closer to the screen to look at me. Heat rises to my cheeks, and I cover my face with both hands. "*Ah, ah.* Look at this child *o.* Why are you shy? Is this how you will be covering your face when the boys start approaching you?"

"Mom. Please, stop." I whine.

"*Obi m*, leave her alone, *nau.*" Dad comes to my rescue.

Mom turns to Dad. "But *obi m,* I am giving her tips on how to be correct." Mom squares her shoulders. Today she managed to get the camera in the perfect position so both she and Dad can fit in the frame. *Finally.*

"*Ehe*, she will learn with time. Leave her for today." Dad squeezes Mom's hands and then turns to face me. "*Adamma,* don't mind your mother. How are you doing, my dearest daughter?"

I smile at him, pulling the sleeves of my sweater forward to cover my cold hands. "I'm fine, Dad. I haven't had a weekend off in a long time, so I'm glad to be relaxing at home today."

"God will strengthen you, my daughter." Dad prays. "All this hard work you are doing will not be in vain. God will continue to bless and keep you in Jesus' name."

"Amen." Mom and I respond. "Thank you so much, Dad. Mom, how is the business going?"

Mom adjusts her wrapper around her chest. "Business has been very good. We have been catering for one event after the other; birthday parties, naming ceremonies, and, of course, weddings. You know, they cannot resist your mother's sweet food."

"And she has been dragging me to all these events." Dad adds. "Now I have to be the one resolving the conflicts when people fight over the leftover food. Can you imagine?" Dad says, and we all laugh. When I was in high school, I was the one Mom dragged to all these events. Now poor Dad has to take my place.

"It's okay, Dad, you will survive. I hope you are saving some jollof rice and chicken for me, though."

"We don't need to." Mom cuts in. "I'm sure that soon, we will eat jollof rice and chicken at your own wedding."

Here we go again. Mom has a special skill of turning every conversation into one about marriage. "So, how is it going?" She leans forward, giving me a mischievous smile. "Has anyone approached you yet? Because if no one has, I can introduce you to the very handsome and rich sons of my friends at the Boston Igbo women society."

"*Ah, ah*, this woman, leave this child alone, *nau.*" Dad tries to save me again. "If she has someone she will tell us."

"Yes, but sometimes she might be too shy. That's why I want to give her a little push."

As my parents go back and forth, bickering at each other, my idea of telling them about Ray becomes more appealing. My heart thuds and I place my fidgeting hands under my thigh. Exhaling, I clear my throat before opening my mouth to speak.

Lord, please, if Ray is the one for me, let Mom approve of him.

"Erm...Mom? Dad?" My parents stop bickering and turn their heads toward me. "There's actually someone I want to tell you about."

"Eh?" Mom and Dad say in unison.

"Really? Heeeey, *Chineke dalu o, dalu.*" Mom breaks into an Igbo song and starts shaking her waist in front of Dad, who tries to push her to the side.

When Mom finishes dancing, she lowers herself on her sofa again. "*Obi m*, did I not tell you?" She turns to Dad. "My enemies have failed."

"*Ehe*, now that you have finished dancing, can we hear more?" Dad says, their eyes fixed on me. "My dear, well done. Please, tell us. What is his name and what does he do?"

I bite my lip to hide the smile on my face. "His name is Raymond..." Ray's surname creeps to the edge of my tongue, but I stop myself. I should make them love him first before mentioning he is Yoruba. "He is a doctor at the hospital I work in."

"Chai!!! *Omo*, doctor." Mom hails. "Wow. This is a serious something. Is he Nigerian?"

"Yes, Mom."

"Oh, that is very good. Now which part of Nigeria is he from?" Mom asks, and my heart sinks to my stomach.

Darn it. She just had to ask, didn't she?

"He used to live in Abuja before he moved to the U.S."

"Okay, but I mean what tribe is he from?"

"Ermm...he is Yoruba." I put on a confident smile as I straighten my back to meet Mom's gaze, only to find the smile on her face disappearing as quickly as it appeared.

She presses her lips into a thin line, her jaws tense, and her forehead creases. Her silence is loud enough to deflate the hope rising in my chest like a popped balloon.

"Oh, that's good." Dad shuffles forward, oblivious to Mom's silent reaction. "How long have you two known each other and has he made his intentions known?"

"Intentions, *ke?*" Mom shouts and I jump in my seat. "Nnamdi, which intentions?"

"*Ah, ah.* Intentions to marry her, *nau.*" Dad says. "Or don't you want her to marry again?"

"Hmm, hmm." Mom closes her eyes and shakes her head. "My daughter cannot marry a Yoruba man."

My throat closes up as I open my mouth to protest, but no words come out.

"And why is that?" Dad asks as he takes off his glasses. "Does he have two heads?"

"No, but he is Yoruba and I will never accept a Yoruba man as my son-in-law." Mom stands up. "If that ever happens, it will be over my dead body." She hits her chest with both hands and then shoots me a glare before walking away.

"Njideka? Njideka, come back here. Come back here and explain yourself right now." Dad stands up, but then sits down again and looks at me. "*Adamma*, please don't worry. Don't mind anything she is saying. I will speak to her." He follows Mom out of the room, leaving me with the view of their black leather sofa.

A heavy feeling travels through my chest and my back. Each breath I take becomes labored, and the hot tears blurring my vision fall down my cheeks. *Lord, why is this happening?*

I've heard a lot of horror stories about people who have struggled against their parents' tribalistic actions. I've also heard that this can cause psychological and emotional instability and sometimes even violence. I have listened to these stories from afar, but I never thought it would happen to me.

My mind flashes back to all the times Mom expressed her hatred for the Yoruba tribe, and how I turned a deaf ear to it. I never thought it'd matter, never thought it'd come back to bite me like this. *Lord, is this it? Is this the answer to my prayer?*

I close my laptop and reach for the throw pillow in front of me, before bringing it up to my chest. Then I take a deep breath and bury my face in the pillow as I let the tears flow out as freely as they come.

28

AMARA

"What? Amara, you're kidding, right?" Teeyana props herself up on the chair across from me and I shake my head, wondering if I made a mistake by telling her what Mom said. Teeyana is staying over at my place this weekend. Last night, she helped me wash *Frolita*, and I helped her wash her own hair. It was just like old times in Boston, except both of us now have natural hair, which makes our wash days even more fun. After not seeing each other for months, we're treasuring this time we have before she returns to Boston tomorrow.

"No, she actually said those words." I adjust the satin bonnet on my head and drop my gaze to the bowl of cereal in front of me.

"And what did you tell her?"

I lift my head again to meet Teeyana's raised eyebrows, her dark brown eyes focused on my every move. *My daughter will never marry a Yoruba man.* Mom's words cleave to my heart and snatch away the words from my mouth.

I slurp the soggy cereal and milk from my spoon, my appetite vanishing like my breath on a cold winter night. "Nothing." I shrug, trying to act unbothered, even though the guilt continues to tear at my chest.

"Nothing?" Teeyana raises her voice, making me flinch. "Amara, you know what she said is wrong, right?" She pauses, waiting for me to respond, and when I don't give her an answer, she leans forward and tries to meet my gaze, which has now returned to the soggy bits of cereal floating around in my bowl of milk. "Right?"

I will never allow it. If that ever happens, it will be over my dead body.

I drop my spoon in the bowl and look at her. "Girl, what was I supposed to do?"

Teeyana frowns. "What do you mean? You have to speak up about it."

"Do you think it's that easy?" I push the bowl of cereal away, my voice rising. "I've spent the last few months trying to choose between Ray and Jamar. Sometimes I stay up all night worrying about making the wrong choice that will ruin my life forever. Do you think I love being in this situation?" I blurt out without taking time to consider my words.

"Wait, what?" Teeyana shakes her head, a frown settling on her face. "Who's Jamar?"

Oh darn it, girl. Darn it. I look away as my best friend keeps staring at me, waiting for me to spill. I know she won't like this and that's why I never told her in the first place. But maybe if I had said something, she would have talked me out of it and I wouldn't have found myself in this mess. "He's another doctor who does locum shifts at the PICU sometimes."

"Okay?"

"He asked me out on a date a few months ago and we've been on a few more dates since then." I pause to think about my words. "Ray has a good character, but Jamar has all the physical qualities of my dream man. I've been trying to choose between them and I don't know what to do."

Teeyana sighs and rubs her forehead with her palm. "I feel like I already know the answer but...does Ray know about Jamar?"

I gulp as the guilt creeps back in, flipping the cereal in my stomach and sending a burning pain up my chest. "No." I shake my head and swallow the metallic taste at the back of my mouth.

"You know that's kinda cheating, right?"

I snap my head up to look at her, her words feeling like a heap of salt in my already stabbing wound. "No, it's not. Ray and I haven't made things official."

"If it's not, then why didn't you tell him about Jamar?"

I open my mouth to protest, but when no words come to defend myself, I close it again.

"You know Ray wants a relationship with you," Teeyana continues. "You've told him you're praying about it, which I'm sure you are, but have you ever thought about how he would feel if he finds out you've been seeing another guy behind his back? When you say you won't say anything to your mom, is that because you can't do it, or because you don't want to?"

"Girl, it's not as straightforward as you make it sound." I rest my arms on the table. "It's easy for you to sit there and judge me because you're not the one who was born into Nigerian culture where everyone treats singleness like a disease. You were fortunate enough to snag Jayden in college and you don't have to deal with dating in the working world. You also don't have to deal with the guilt of letting your parents down, while also feeling like you're being forced to make a choice you're not sure about. You're not in my shoes, so you'll never understand." My voice breaks and I push myself up from my seat.

I walk over to the grey couch in my living room and sit on it, my shoulders shaking as I sob into my palms. Only a few seconds pass before Teeyana sinks into the couch next to me. "I'm sorry. I didn't know you felt this way." She wraps her arms around me and leans her head on my shoulder. "I want to support you, I want to be here for you, and most importantly, I want to understand."

Her words are accompanied by a reassuring squeeze, and for the first time in forever, I feel I can speak about this without being judged. "I have feelings for Ray. I wasn't attracted to him initially, but now I am. It's not just his looks I'm attracted to; it's his vision, his values, and what he stands for. Hanging out with him is a breath of fresh air, and he makes me love God and myself more every day."

"But?" Teeyana asks as she rests her chin on my shoulder.

"But he's very popular at the hospital and I feel everyone is expecting me to choose him. He has had four failed relationships in the past and now everyone expects me to be the right one. I don't know if I'm the kind of woman Ray needs. He is so driven by purpose and knows exactly what he wants out of life, but I feel I'm not at that level yet. I don't know what I want or what God wants me to do with my life. I just feel like...like he's too good for me."

Saying the words out loud and not just letting them mope around in my head forces more tears out of my eyes. "Before I told my parents about Ray, I prayed that if he is the one for me, then God should make my mom approve of him. Maybe this is God's way of saying I should let Ray go."

Teeyana sits up and holds my hands. "Or maybe you've accepted the situation because you're scared to confront your mom?"

I shake my head. "I'm not scared of her. I just don't want her *wahala*, that's all. I don't want to be the source of strife in my family. If God wanted it, then he would have made it easy."

"Or maybe God wants you to fight." Teeyana objects. "Maybe

he wants you to stand up against your mom so she can see the error of her ways. Come on, Amara, don't let fear make you throw away a man who is perfect for you. I don't believe this is the end, so we have to keep praying about this. You've only told me positive things about Ray, and it seems he really cares about you. Your mom doesn't know him, and she hasn't given him a chance yet. It's unfair for her to write him off without even meeting him. If you feel the whole situation is putting you under pressure, then speak to Ray about it, so you both can slow things down."

Teeyana lifts my chin, so I can look at her. "I don't know Jamar and I can't vouch for him, so please be careful. You need to rely on God to help you make the right choice. Okay?"

I let out a heavy sigh because I know Teeyana is right. I have to sort this out once and for all. "Thanks, girl." I pull her in for a hug.

We spend some time praying about it and to cheer me up, Teeyana finally watches *Grey's Anatomy* with me after many years of begging her. I help her do mini twists on her hair and she helps me do my favorite flat twist updo.

Soon, our conversation slips back into wedding planning as we brainstorm wedding favor ideas for the guests. Teeyana mentions she has finally started her freelance Graphic Design business and has gotten her first few clients.

"Yaas, girl. You are slaying it." I click my fingers at her.

"Thank you." Teeyana smiles. "I have to start saving up for the future because adulthood is a scam."

"Girl, I'm with you on that one." We both laugh and continue watching the medical drama.

When Jayden shows up the next day to take Teeyana back to Boston, Teeyana and I hug for a long time, and my heart goes heavy when I realize I don't know the next time I'll see her. "Let me know when you're off work and I'll come visit you again," Teeyana says as they drive off and I nod.

Back in my apartment, I carry myself to my bed, and take out my Bible. "Lord, please help me. I don't know what to do. I don't want to make the wrong choice."

I wait in silence for a still voice, another vision...something, and once again, I'm back to the scene with the crying teenage girl. This time, the sensory details are clearer. The cool breeze brushes against my skin, the girl's lavender perfume fills my nostrils, her tears wet my neck, and I can feel the rough texture of her braided extensions against my fingers.

In the midst of all that, a still voice speaks for the first time— a voice I've never heard before. It's so gentle, yet it echoes into my soul.

My beloved Amara. I love you.
Follow Me with all your heart.
I will never lead you wrong.

The hair at the back of my neck stands on edge as a cold shiver travels down my spine. I open my mouth to say something, but no words come out. Then the girl lifts her head, but before I can look at her face, everything fades away and I'm back in my room again.

I stand up and pace the length of my room, my gaze once again darting around, as if the answers I seek are hiding in the corners of the ceiling. I still don't know what this vision means or why I only get it when I pray about Ray. "Lord, please make me understand." I lift both hands to my head and let out a heavy sigh when the words "Follow Me" echo strongly in my heart.

"Follow me." I repeat, before rushing to my bed and picking up my Bible study notebook. "God wants me to follow Him." I say to myself as my gaze sweeps through the lined pages, which are covered in black and blue-inked words. When I get to the page I'm looking for, I run my fingers across as I read the highlighted Bible verses to myself. It's a personal study I did months ago about what it means to follow Jesus.

As Jesus was walking beside the Sea of Galilee, He saw two brothers, Simon called Peter and his brother Andrew. They were casting a net into the lake, for they were fishermen. "Come, follow me," Jesus said, "and I will send you out to fish for people."
-Matthew 4:18-19

Following Jesus requires a lot of faith and trust in His character. When the first disciples accepted the call, they abandoned their lives as fishermen and followed the Giver of life. They had no idea what the road was like in front of them, but they knew they had found treasure in Jesus, and that was something that was more precious than anything the world could offer them.

I flip over to the next page and read the next Bible verse I've written down.

"Lord, if it's You," Peter replied, "tell me to come to You on the water."
"Come," He said.
Then Peter got down out of the boat, walked on the water and came toward Jesus.
-Matthew 14:28-29

When Peter stepped out of the lake, he had no certainty that he was actually going to walk on water, but he trusted in Jesus' good character to keep him standing. So he abandoned the safety of his boat, and stepped out into the raging storm, knowing that the Master of the waves was watching over him, and that if Jesus could walk on water, then He could empower him to do the same. Following Jesus may require you to step out of your comfort zone, to face your fears, and to do the impossible. Following Jesus will mean standing for the Truth, and accepting instructions you may not understand. Following Jesus means denying yourself and losing your life. It's not an easy journey, but it's worth it because it brings ultimate life and joy which is found in Jesus alone.

Tears fall out of my eyes as a calming presence washes over me. I swipe my hand under my eyes to catch a tear. "Lord, I'm so scared, but I will follow You. Show me what to do. I will follow You." A satisfying feeling engulfs my heart, giving me the assurance that God is with me. I'll keep praying. I'll keep trusting. God will shine His light in my darkness. He will give me clarity.

29

RAYMOND

"**M**ommy, I've told you to leave it, *nau*. You'll meet her when she's ready." I prop my iPad against my microwave, so my mother can have a better view of me cooking. My *egusi* soup is simmering on the stove and the aroma in my kitchen is strong enough to make me salivate for a whole year.

"But, *oko mi*," Mom protests, "that is what you said in November. It's now the end of March. Is she still not ready to let me speak to her or can you not even show me her picture?" She leans toward the camera.

I grab the last bunch of *ugwu* leaves from the plastic bag on the kitchen counter and slice them on the chopping board. "Mommy, there's no rush. When the time is right, I will tell you all about her."

"Hmm, okay *o*." She folds her arms and turns her head away, but knowing my mother, she won't be giving up anytime soon. "I don't understand how you people do things in this generation." She says, as if talking to herself, but clearly she's talking to me. "You tell a woman you are interested in marrying her and instead of introducing her to your family, you are hiding her. What is there to hide?"

I sigh. "Mommy dearest, there's nothing to hide." It's not that I don't want to tell her about Amara, it's that I won't tell her until Amara has officially given me her answer.

I add the chopped *ugwu* leaves in the pot and stir them into the egusi soup before tapping the end of my wooden spoon on my palm and tasting the soup. "Hmm, Mommy, this thing is sweet *o. Chai*, a lot of pepper. Aren't you proud of me?" I smirk when she tries to suppress a smile.

"Of course I'm proud of you, my son," she responds. "But if you had your wife here, she would help you cook. See how you've come back from work and you won't even rest properly."

"Mmm-mmm." I shake my head. "Mommy, even if I had my wife here, I will still cook this *egusi* soup because I don't think she will cook it better than me."

Frustrated by my refusal to give her answers, she starts firing questions at me again. "Okay, but please, can you tell me her name? Is she *oyinbo*? Tell me *o*, so I can start preparing myself to eat salad and orange juice when I come to see my grandchildren."

I drop the wooden spoon and burst into laughter. "Mommy, you are so funny, honestly." I cover my pot and lower the intensity of the flame before turning to face her squarely. "First of all, some *oyinbos* can cook and not all Nigerians know how to cook. Second of all, her name is Amara. Amarachukwu Ifeoma Ikezie." I lean back on the counter, recalling the day I read her full name from my phone.

Mom's face lights up. "Wow, such a beautiful name. *Ah*, she's even Nigerian. That is *very* good."

"Yes, she's a nurse at my hospital, but not my department. She works in intensive care with the newborn babies."

"*Eya*," Mom tilts her head. "So she must be a very caring person."

"She's amazing. You will love her."

"Erm, but, *oko mi,* does she love Jesus?"

I smile because I know she won't let me get away without answering this question. "Yes, Mommy, Amara loves Jesus."

"*Ah*, praise the Lord. *Oluwa e se o.*" She rubs her palms. "So why have you not proposed to her yet?"

"*Ah, ah.* Propose *ke*? I will propose eventually, but not now. Everything takes time." I can just imagine proposing to Amara now when she hasn't even said yes to me officially. She'll definitely run away.

"Yes, but you are not getting any younger, *oko mi.* In two months' time, you will be turning thirty, so it's time you settle down."

Ah egba mi o. She's talking as if I don't want to settle down. Although I wanted everything to happen in my own timeline, I prefer how things have taken time to build the bond between myself and Amara.

"In my own time, your father proposed and gave me a ring before I ever introduced him to my parents. We did everything *quick-fast* and our marriage still worked out well until my good Lord called him home." Her voice breaks.

"Aww, Mommy it's okay, *nau.*" My heart breaks for her whenever she talks about my father. I know she misses him. I miss him too and it hurts to know that she has to wake up each day and fight the pain and grief on her own.

A tear streams down her cheek and she uses the corner of her wrapper to wipe it. "Sorry if it feels like I'm pressuring you, *oko mi.* You are my only pride and joy, and I just want the best for you. Your father was a good man, and he treated me well. Every day, I pray that you also find a woman who you can build a life with and serve God with. I want you to have that before my Father calls me home too."

"Ah, Mommy, God is in control. I can't force His hand on this matter." I pick up my iPad and bring it close to my face after wiping the lone tear threatening to escape my eye. "I love you and I believe that very soon, God will answer all your prayers."

"*Loruko Jesu. Amin o.* Thank you, my son." Her smile returns and the wrinkles on her forehead deepen as the grey hairs peek out of her head wrap.

"I can't wait to see you in December," I say. The last time I was in Nigeria was two years ago, but I need to go back for the fifteen year anniversary of my father's passing to glory.

Mom cracks a smile before her playful side returns. "*Ehe,* and maybe you can even bring Amara with you." We both burst into laughter.

"Yes, Mommy. By God's grace."

When I end the call with her, I turn off the hob and make some pounded yam with the new yam flour I bought. I have a personal mission to try different brands of yam flour until I find the one which tastes closest to the pounded yam my mother makes.

When I finish, I stand back and wipe my forehead as I admire my perfect rolls of pounded yam on the plate. Then I take off my apron and head out of the kitchen.

As I walk across the living room, I pick my bag off the floor and my jacket, which is lying at the other end of the room. *Honestly, I ask myself why I have clothes hooks in this house when I don't even use them.*

Taking one last look at my living room and satisfied by how organized it is, I head to the bathroom to take a shower. Half an hour later, I return to the kitchen and eat my own portion of the hearty meal before scrolling through the unread messages on my phone.

I asked Amara if she was up for dinner this evening, but she said she wasn't feeling well, so she decided to stay home. I'm sure she'll feel much better if she tries some of this *egusi* soup. They say chocolates and roses can warm a girl's heart, but I say delicious *egusi* soup does a much better job. *Who roses epp, sef?*

Without thinking twice, I place my dirty dishes in the dishwasher before ransacking my drawers for a Tupperware container. I always bring back a lot of food containers from Nigerian parties, but I can never find one when I need it.

When I finally find two containers, I dish out some egusi soup in one of them and two rolls of pounded yam in the other. After wrapping both containers in cling film, I place them in a plastic bag and grab my car keys. Then I slip my jacket on and head out the door. *I hope Amara loves this surprise.*

30

AMARA

Today I'm going to tell Ray how I feel about him. But first, I need to end whatever is going on between myself and Jamar. I'm done with this game. I know who I want to be with now. I'm ready to take a chance with Ray. It won't be easy standing up to Mom, but having Dad on my side is a plus. I have to at least try to fight. If I don't, I'll regret it for the rest of my life.

Jamar will be here any moment now. I invited him over, even though it's not for casual talk. Well, at least I don't think my text sounded like that.

Me: Hey, are you free this evening? We need to talk.

I read the text over and over again in my head. Yes, I'm sure he knows this is about something serious. Everyone knows that if someone says 'we need to talk' then a breakup is coming—although we're not official, so this is technically not even a breakup.

Jamar: Hey pumpkin, is everything okay? • •

I cringe as I read out the word "pumpkin." *Boy, what am I, a five-year-old?* I told Jamar to drive by my house on his way home from work. I don't have the heart to do this over the phone or via text message and I don't want to wait until the next time I see him at work, so we're gonna get it done today.

I won't let Jamar into my apartment. This conversation will be short and sweet. Hopefully, he'll understand and just walk away and that'll be the end. Yes, that's the plan. Short and sweet.

The doorbell dings, alerting my attention. I drop my hands from my face as a wave of nausea rises to my throat. Exhaling, I swallow and rise slowly as I walk to the door. I'm wearing a thick jumper, a pair of jeans, and UGG boots. Hopefully that'll be okay to give me warmth until I can tell Jamar everything I need to tell him.

I open the door to Jamar wearing only a thin shirt. "Hey, sugar." He shivers and his breath fogs up as it rises in front of him.

Oh no. The words creep to the edge of my tongue, but I swallow my shock horror and straighten. "Jamar." I force a smile. "Where's your jacket?"

"Oh, sorry, I left it in the car." He nods toward his car parked on the other side of the street.

You don't say. I resist the urge to groan. I mean, I could still leave him out in the cold, but even Jesus wouldn't want me to do that. "Okay, come in."

I step out of the way so Jamar can get in before giving myself a face palm. *Lord, please give me strength.*

"You have a nice place here." Jamar says as he looks around. "It's warm too."

Boy, no one asked you not to wear your jacket. I shut the door behind me and resist the urge to roll my eyes. "Thank you. God helped me find it when I needed a place of my own."

"Right." He makes a sweeping motion toward the sofa. "Can I?"

"Yeah, sure. Please, forgive my manners." I take a few steps toward him as he lowers himself on my sofa. "Would you like me to get you anything?" I ask, hoping he'd say no.

"Erm, do you have wine?" He smirks and licks his red lips. *Okay, I don't know how I ever found that cute because it's just annoying. Boy, keep your tongue in your mouth.*

"Sorry, I don't drink alcohol." I tuck my hands in my hoodie pockets.

"Oh." His smirk disappears and his shoulders slump. "Okay, in that case, I'll be fine."

Thank God. I walk up to the sofa and occupy the one across from him.

"Why are you sitting all the way over there, *sugar*?" He taps the space next to him. "Come sit next to me."

Okay, clearly he got the wrong message from that text. "Listen, Jamar." I ignore his invitation. "I asked you to come because I want to tell you something very important."

He leans back and places his arms on the armrest. "Sure, hit me up."

I take a deep breath and exhale. "I can't do this anymore. I don't know what's going on between us, but I would like to end it, please."

Jamar frowns and leans forward. "Really? Why? Did I do something wrong?"

"No, you didn't. It's just me. I made a mistake and I shouldn't have led you on."

"So, you're saying you weren't interested in me this whole time?"

"No, I'm saying that..." I raise my voice before realizing myself and pausing. *Lord, please give me strength.* "I was interested at the beginning and that's why I agreed to go on the dates with you. But as time passed, I realized we don't...really have much in common in terms of life goals, purpose, and vision.

"You're a nice guy and I'm sure you'll find a girl who appreciates you for who you are. That girl is not me." The words come out freely from my mouth and the more I speak, the more I'm convinced I'm doing the right thing.

Jamar clears his throat. "Are you sure about this, Amara?"

Finally, he can use my real name. I thought he'd forgotten.

"Are you sure this isn't some sort of phase?" He gestures toward me, and I frown.

"No, this isn't a phase. You and I don't value the same things. I want to grow in my relationship with God but I don't think I can do that with you."

"Ouch." Jamar's hands fly up to his chest. "That's a pretty harsh assumption, don't you think?"

"Oh really? Okay, when was the last time you went to church?" I raise a brow and watch him mumble.

"Well, Easter Sunday? No, Christmas. Or was it Halloween? Do churches do anything for Halloween these days?"

Wow, I can't believe I got myself here.

"Listen, sugar, does any of this God-stuff even matter?"

"Yes, it matters to me."

"But what about all the fun we've had? Come on, you can't tell me none of that matters."

"No, you're not listening to me. Please, don't make this harder than it already is. I can't do this anymore." My tone is now desperate.

Jamar taps his foot on the carpet and rubs his palms, the lines on his jaw tightening.

Lord, please help me.

"Okay, fine." Jamar finally says and stands up. I breathe a sigh of relief and stand up with him as he walks to the door. He opens it and steps out into the cold again, but half way down the stairs, he turns around. "I really like you, Amara."

Guilt tugs at my heart and I lower my head, refusing to let his intense gaze trick me into going back on my decision. "I'm sorry, Jamar..." I start saying something else, but before I finish my sentence, Jamar is in front of me again. He wraps one arm around my waist and the other around my neck, before pulling me close and descending on my lips.

I mumble under the harshness of his mouth and push against his chest, but his strong arms pin me close to his body until he releases his hold on me. "How dare you?" My palm collides with his cheek, forcing his head sideways. "What part of '*I'm not interested*' don't you understand?"

Instead of remorse or getting an apology, Jamar shrugs as he rubs the back of his neck. "I'm sorry. My kisses have always worked their magic in the past. It was the last trick up my sleeve."

"Jamar, please leave." Tears pool in my eyes as I wipe my lips. This isn't how I imagined my first kiss and certainly not with Jamar.

"Amara, I'm sorry—"

"Go away." I sniffle as the tears fall. I wait until Jamar enters his car and drives off before wiping my eyes again. A smacking sound forces me to lift my head and right there across the street is the last person I thought I'd see today. In one second, the world around me comes crashing down.

31

RAYMOND

Is that Amara? I stop on the sidewalk and squint in the darkness, my vision trying to make out the face of the girl kissing a guy in front of Amara's doorstep. *Is that really her?* I ask myself again, the plastic bag of pounded yam and *egusi* soup in my hand suddenly feeling like a ton of bricks.

No, it can't be her. I shake my head as a million thoughts fly through my mind. She must have a friend who came to visit her, or a sister, or better still, a twin I didn't know about.

"It can't be her." I repeat to myself, hoping that by saying it out loud, I'll convince myself that I'm not looking at *Frolita*, I'm not looking at one of Amara's favorite Ankara headbands, and of course, I must be at the wrong house.

The girl pushes the guy away and slaps him across his face. I quicken my steps and run toward the house, but when the guy turns around, I halt, my feet refusing to move any further. "Jamar?" I whisper.

I saw Amara talking to another doctor. I think his name is Jamar. Jevon's words ring in my head as Jamar walks down the steps, gets into his car, and drives off. The sight I'm left with sends a tearing pain through my chest.

"She's been seeing someone else?" The plastic bag slips from my hand, and the flat base of the tupperware lands on the sidewalk, sending a smacking sound across the street.

Amara lifts her head and locks eyes with me. For a few seconds, she doesn't move, then she calls out. "Ray?" She hurries down the stairs and power walks for most of the way before stopping a few meters away from me. "Ray,...what are you doing here?" She looks at me and then glances down the street where Jamar's car is no longer in sight.

"It's not what you think. I promise I can explain," she says, the glint of the street light reflecting from the tears lining her eyes.

This is the last thing I want to hear her say. It sounds like a line from a movie where someone gets caught in the act.

"Ray, he kissed me," she continues, her voice breaking now. "I didn't kiss him back."

Yeah, because that's supposed to explain everything?

"Ray, please say something." Her voice forces me out of my thoughts and I turn away from her, using both hands to massage my temples.

"Ray." She walks toward me. "Please, you have to believe me."

I turn to look at her now, tears leaking from her eyes as she blinks.

"So...so you're not ill?" I ask, and her bottom lip quivers as more tears stream down her face.

I sigh and shake my head. "Okay, please answer this *one* question." I point a finger down the road. "Are you seeing Jamar?"

"No." Amara takes a step closer and then stops. "I mean, yes. I was, but not anymore."

"Wow." I shake my head. Jevon was right this whole time. I

should have known. I should have seen the signs. I can't believe this is happening again.

"Ray, I was confused." Amara sniffs. "When Jamar first approached me, he was everything I wanted in a guy. He ticked all the boxes on my list and I didn't want to miss out on that."

"Your list?" I scoff. "So I'm now a product you sample to see if I have all the ingredients you need and then you toss me to the side like trash when you find me wanting?"

"No." Amara shakes her head. "Ray, I've always valued you and you know that."

"So why have you been lying to me for seven months?"

Amara closes the gap between us and reaches for my arm, but I turn away. "I'm sorry. We weren't official and—"

"Can you please stop?" I raise my voice and she steps back. Heat rises in my chest as I pace the width of the sidewalk. "I've been honest with you from the beginning about my feelings. If you weren't interested in me and you thought Jamar ticked all your boxes, then why didn't you just tell me?"

"I didn't know what I wanted, okay?" She cuts in. "I just ended things with Jamar tonight, and do you know why? It's because I've been praying about this for months and God has led me back to you."

She steps closer, but I back away again. I want to believe her. I really want to, but the image of Jamar kissing her is now permanently etched in my mind. *Lord, why did You let this happen again?*

"Ray, I'm sorry."

I finally turn to look at her. "I'm sorry too." I pause. "I thought you were different from the other girls and—"

"The other girls? Are you kidding me?" Amara's jaw tightens. The remorse in her eyes disappears and in its place, there's a hard, cold stare. "I know I'm not perfect and you can call me out on my mistakes, but I won't let you stand there and compare me to your ex-girlfriends. If you think I'm anything like them, then maybe you don't know me after all." She turns around and walks away.

"Well, maybe I don't," I say, trailing behind her. "How am I supposed to believe anything you say now?"

"If you don't believe me then go away." She turns to face me as she sobs. "I never said yes to you because I didn't want to hurt you and become like the other girls."

"Well, you hurt me anyway, so you accomplished nothing by lying."

The expression that washes across Amara's face tugs at my heart. She lowers her head and wipes her eyes again. I want to reach out to her, pull her into my arms, but I'm so confused. I don't know what to believe anymore.

"If you can't trust me now," she sniffles, "then maybe we shouldn't be in a relationship."

The searing pain in my heart intensifies with her words. I want to fight. I want to hold her and tell her everything will be okay. But I don't have the strength to do it. "Maybe...maybe we shouldn't." My gaze drops to the plastic bag next to my feet as silence crosses between us. "Enjoy the pounded yam and *egusi* soup." Exhaling, I turn around and drag my heavy legs back to my car without once looking at her again.

32

AMARA

"I didn't mean to do it. Please, girl, you have to believe me." I press my phone against my ear and wipe away a tear sliding down my cheek.

My confrontation with Ray half an hour ago has turned my chest into a giant dump hole of emotions. My brain is swelling up as I fight the waves of hurt, anger and disappointment trying to pull me away. I need to explain to someone who understands the turmoil I've been through for the last few months. Maybe that'll take away some of the guilt suffocating me right now.

"Aww, girl, I believe you, okay? Now, please take a deep breath, and tell me what happened." Teeyana's voice is soft, and she pauses, giving time for my brain to communicate with my mouth, so they can form coherent words.

Leaning forward on my sofa, I rest my elbows on my thighs before dropping my head in my hands. "I prayed about what you told me last time and I felt God leading me to fight for my relationship with Ray." I pause before continuing. "So I decided it would be the right time to end things with Jamar."

"Okay?" Teeyana responds.

"I didn't want to wait any longer, so I asked Jamar to come over to my place to talk."

"Oh...." Teeyana's voice trails off.

"Nuh, uh, girl, I wasn't planning to let him in. I wanted to tell him while we were standing outside, but the boy wasn't wearing a jacket when he came to the door and he left me with no choice but to let him in."

"I see." Teeyana's voice softens again.

"I went straight to the point and I told him I didn't want to see him anymore. I thought he understood, but when we got outside, he forced himself on me and kissed me." My voice cracks and I wipe my eyes as the memory comes to my mind again. "I pushed him away and slapped him."

"Yes and he'll be getting another slap from me if I ever see him. I'm glad he didn't hurt you." Teeyana says.

I nod, and more tears flow out of my eyes. "I was so scared of what he would do to me after I slapped him, but thank God he just got into his car and drove off. But I didn't realize Ray was standing on the sidewalk across the street."

"Oh, no."

"Yeah exactly. You can imagine how shocked I was to see him."

"Wait, but why did Ray come to your house in the first place?"

I wipe my eyes and sit up. "He texted me earlier today to ask if he could take me out to dinner and because I had already told Jamar to come to my house after work, I didn't want to complicate things for myself, so I told Ray I wasn't feeling well and would stay home for the rest of the night. I didn't think Ray would surprise me with pounded yam and *egusi* soup."

"Awww, he cooked for you?" Teeyana's high-pitched pierces into my ear. "That's so adorable."

241

"I know." My voice breaks again. "Ray has always gone out of his way to make me happy, but all I cared about was my stupid list. I'm a fool. I can't believe I let this happen."

"Okay, listen to me." Teeyana protests. "You're not a fool. Everybody makes mistakes."

"Yeah, but this is different. You warned me about this, but I refused to listen. I got myself into this mess and I blew my chance with Ray." The lump in my throat turns into an explosive sob and I run to the bathroom to grab some tissue.

Teeyana waits for me to blow my nose before she speaks again. "Amara, you made a mistake, but it's all in the past now. We need to think about how to fix the situation."

"Girl, there's no fix for this. Ray thinks I'm a liar, and he even compared me to his exes." I lean back on my sofa and put one arm over my head. "I ruined everything. It's all over."

Teeyana blows out a breath before speaking again. "You can't be sure about that. Ray should have given you a chance to explain. Maybe it'll help if someone else talks to him—someone like me."

"You?" I frown and shake my head. "Nah, girl, please, you don't have to do this. I don't want the situation getting any worse."

"Oh, so you think I'll say something that'll make things worse?"

"Not really, but I don't know what Ray is thinking and I don't want him to interpret it differently."

"Okay, fine," Teeyana says. "It's a good thing you've realized your mistake, but please don't give up. Let's keep praying and asking God for direction, okay?"

"Okay." I respond, even though my heart has already accepted that Ray would want nothing to do with me even if I apologized for a thousand years. I always knew I wasn't right for him. This incident has only proven I was right. He deserves someone better—someone who has the qualities that will suit his vision. My gut instincts were right after all. I'm not his Rebecca.

33

RAYMOND

I slam the door shut and take off my jacket as I walk toward my living room. After dropping my jacket on the floor, I take off my shoes and plop down on the sofa.

I can't sit still; one second I'm leaning forward, and the next second I'm tapping my foot on the carpet and wiggling on the sofa.

How could she do this to me? Images of Jamar kissing Amara torture me as Amara's words swirl around in my thoughts again and again.

Ray, he kissed me. I didn't kiss him back.

I want to believe her, but why did Jamar think it was okay to kiss her? She even said it herself that she was seeing him. I trusted her and she lied to me. *I'm such a fool.*

I spring to my feet and walk to my window before taking a deep breath in and exhaling. But even the view of the skyscrapers and cars passing on the freeway is not enough to distract me from thinking about Amara's words. *Jamar ticked all the boxes on my list.*

I shake my head. "So this whole time I was her second best. She kept me on the sidelines in case things didn't work out with her perfect man." The words come out in a whisper. I lift my head to look at the black, starry sky. "How did I get back here, Lord? I thought this was your will for me. Why am I here?"

My phone vibrates in the pocket of my jeans, and I ignore it. Honestly, if it's Amara, I don't want to speak to her.

When the vibration stops, I push myself away from the window before taking the gadget out of my pocket to see who called. "Oh." I frown when Pastor Ben's name pops up on my screen instead of Amara. Before I'm able to call him back, my phone starts vibrating again. "Hello, Pastor Ben?" I press the phone against my ear.

When he responds to my greeting, the tone of his voice is low, and he doesn't sound as upbeat as he usually does. I'm not surprised though—it's late in the evening. "Sorry to call you so late, but there's an important development regarding some members of your youth group and it requires your immediate attention."

My thoughts spin wild as I try to decipher what he's trying to say. "Important development? What happened, sir?"

"I don't think this is something I can discuss over the phone. I was calling to ask if you are free to come in to see me tomorrow morning. If not, we can reschedule to when you are free and…"

"No, tomorrow is fine with me, sir," I cut in. "I have a night shift tomorrow, so the morning works well for me."

"Alright then, I'll see you tomorrow at ten a.m. Good night and God bless you." With that, pastor Ben ends the call, leaving me to ponder on his words all night. *This doesn't sound good.*

"Good morning, brother James." I shake hands with Pastor Ben's secretary in the hallway. "Pastor Ben?" I point a finger toward the pastor's door.

James nods and smiles. "Yeah, he's expecting you." He says before fixing the collar of his long-sleeved shirt.

"Thanks, bro. Hope you have a wonderful day." I walk further down the narrow hallway as James continues in the opposite direction.

Finally, I get to Pastor Ben's office and when I check the time on my watch, it's *9:50 a.m.* "Lord, please, let this not be bad news." I whisper to myself before knocking.

Pastor Ben's voice is clear from the other side as he ushers me in. When I open the door, he is sitting in his usual spot behind his desk. Nothing has changed since the last time I was here. There are still stacks of papers piled in front of him, but today, there's also a coffee-stained mug on the table.

"Morning, Raymond. Please take a seat." He gestures to the chair across his desk and I sit down. I open my mouth to ask a question, but Pastor Ben speaks first. "You're early, so we'll have to wait for the others to join us," he says, and then returns to scribbling on the paper in front of him.

Others? What others?

"Yes, sir." I nod and rub my palms on my knees, suddenly feeling the urge to take off my jacket as a rush of heat creeps up my spine. It's only at this moment, I notice the other two chairs next to me. "Erm, Pastor Ben? Can I ask who is joining us?"

"You be patient, Raymond. They'll soon be here." He says without looking at me and soon, the only sounds in the room are the scratching of his pen against the papers, and the rustling sounds made when he transfers the signed copies to a different pile. The next ten minutes are painfully slow, but at last, a knock on the door expels the silence.

"Come in." Pastor Ben lifts his head.

When I turn around, Tessa's mother—Mrs. Adebayo, and Matthew's father—Mr. Etomi walk into the room.

Oh, no. I push myself up and bow my head respectfully. "Good morning, Sir. Good morning, Ma."

Mrs. Adebayo's gaze slides from the top of my head to my feet. She kisses her teeth and then greets Pastor Ben before occupying the seat next to me.

Hia, wahala dey oh.

"Good morning, brother Raymond." Mr. Etomi sits in the other chair and takes off the black face cap he is wearing.

Oh, no. What did Tessa and Matthew do?

"Good morning everyone." Pastor Ben places his pen on the table and clasps his hands over the stack of papers, which have now significantly reduced. "Now that we're all here, I think it's important that we discuss the issue at hand."

Pastor Ben meets my gaze for the first time since I entered the room. "Raymond, you know I've always supported your goals and visions..." he starts and I shift in my seat.

"You know I want to see you reach your full potential and achieve everything God has set in your heart. I was excited about the idea of you starting a youth ministry here at Grace Baptist church, and over the past few months, I've gotten good reports from parents." He glances at the older man and woman before turning to me again. "But yesterday evening I received some disturbing news and that's why we're here."

I swallow the lump in my throat and all the saliva disappears from my mouth. "Please, what happened, sir? Did any of my teens do something wrong?"

"Hmm," Mrs. Adebayo shrugs her shoulders and looks away.

Pastor Ben sighs and leans back. "As a matter of fact, yes. Yesterday, Tessa and Matthew were caught in Matthew's bedroom, all alone, performing...sexual acts."

"Oh, no." I drop my head in my hands.

"Point of correction, Pastor Ben," Mrs. Adebayo jumps in. "My daughter is a good girl and she would never do such a thing." She turns to face Mr. Etomi squarely. "You should ask Mr. Etomi here what his son has been teaching my daughter." Then she turns to me. "And then you should ask this man here, whatever his name is, whether he has been doing his job to teach the teenagers—especially the boys, about purity."

"Excuse me?" I frown at the woman, heat rising in my chest.

"Hmm." Pastor Ben leans forward. "Sister Joy, I beg you to please calm down. That's the reason why we're here; to get to the bottom of this."

Mrs. Adebayo leans back in her seat and doesn't say another word. She wraps her arms around herself before closing her eyes and tapping one foot.

Pastor Ben turns to Mr. Etomi. "Brother Ayoola, can you please confirm that the children did this?"

"Yes, Pastor." Mr. Etomi speaks for the first time. "I caught them myself. I spoke to both of them and they admitted it. Then I told sister Joy here about it and she suggested we bring the matter to you."

My chest tightens, and I take a deep breath before speaking. "Did they...did they sleep with each other?"

"No." Mr. Etomi responds. "I questioned them thoroughly and they assured me they've never gone that far."

Oh, thank God.

"But if I hadn't caught them," Mr. Etomi continues, "who knows what would have happened?"

Mrs. Adebayo stomps both feet and leans forward, placing one hand on her hip. "Pastor Ben, I know what my daughter can and cannot do. She is a good girl and she was doing well until she joined this youth group. These teenagers are spending *way* too much time together and it is serving as a breeding ground for these kinds of things."

I straighten my back. "Ma, please, with all due respect, I believe God put me in these children's lives to mentor them and that is *exactly* what I've been doing. I have planned to address relationships at the retreat and to teach them about the Biblical view of sex and marriage. These are teenagers and you can't always keep tabs on *every* single thing they do. I don't think it's fair that you blame Tessa and Matthew's actions on the youth group. You are Tessa's mother and you also have a duty to train your child in the right way." As soon as the last few words leave my mouth, regret engulfs my whole being.

"Ahhh!!!" Mrs. Adebayo explodes into sobs as both hands fly up to her head. "Ahhh!!! Pastor Ben, are you hearing this? This boy is now calling me a bad mother. Me? Joy Oluwafunmilayo Adebayo? A bad mother? Ahhh!!!"

Slowly shaking my head, I raise both hands. "I'm sorry, Ma. I didn't mean to..."

"Sorry for yourself." She stands up and Mr. Etomi stands with her, holding her arm, and stopping her from getting close to me. "Were you there when I was toiling and working to provide food and money to take care of her? Do you know about all the sacrifices I've made to give her a good life?" Her voice breaks. "How dare you sit there and call me a bad mother?"

Frustration builds in my chest as I try to get words out in between her sobs. "I'm sorry, Ma. This wasn't what I planned. I never wanted this to happen." *Lord, please help me.*

Pastor Ben stands and stretches both arms across his desk. "Sister Joy, please sit down."

"I'm sorry, pastor. I'm just wounded in my spirit." She pulls her hand away from Mr. Etomi's grip and sits down.

Pastor Ben lets out a deep sigh and turns to me. "Raymond...please, I have one question." He places both hands on his desk and locks his fingers. "Did you know anything about Tessa and Matthew's relationship?"

Oh no. I feared this. I had a feeling this would come back to bite me. *Oh God, please help me.* My gaze drops to the table in front of me. "Erm...yes, I did. I saw them kissing months ago after the church service."

"Eh?" Mrs. Adebayo leans forward again. "You knew about it and you didn't tell us?"

Pastor Ben raises a hand to silence Mrs. Adebayo before turning to me again. "Please, Raymond. If you knew about this, why didn't you tell their parents?"

"I talked to both of them. I cautioned them and I made them promise they wouldn't do anything they weren't supposed to do. I agree that I should have done more and I'm sorry. But I never thought things would get this far."

Mrs. Adebayo stands up. "Pastor Ben, I can't sit here and listen to any more of this. Please, I want you and the church leaders to re-evaluate the essence of the youth group and whether it is really helping our children." With those last words, she storms out of the room and shuts the door behind her.

Mr. Etomi sighs and inches toward me. "Brother Raymond, I appreciate everything you have done for my son and the other children. No matter what happens, please forgive them. They are truly sorry for what they did."

"I hold no grudge against them, sir. Thank you for your kind words."

Mr. Etomi picks up his hat and leaves the room as well.

Pastor Ben sighs and lowers himself on his chair again. "Raymond, I'm sorry to do this, but the church has decided to cancel the youth group meetings temporarily, including your upcoming retreat until further notice."

"What?" I shuffle to the edge of my seat. "Pastor Ben, these teens need this group. They need to learn how to relate with each other. Why would you let everyone else suffer for the mistakes of two people? You were here when I moved to Atlanta four years ago. You have mentored me and watched me grow into the man I am today. You know I love these teens and I want nothing but the best for them."

"I know that, Raymond, and I know how passionate you are about this." Pastor Ben wipes his face with his handkerchief. "But the church leaders just need some time to talk about what has happened so far. This is only a temporary suspension and I'll let you know what we decide about the future of the youth group."

A sigh of defeat escapes my lips and my shoulders slump. I want to protest more, but I can only bring myself to say two words. "Yes, sir."

~

"So they suspended everything? Why?" Joe places his elbows on the table, almost knocking over his cup of tea. It's another busy Sunday afternoon at the *Holy Granules* coffee shop.

I stir my cup of coffee as an ambulance rushes past us. "The church leaders have to discuss whether they want to keep the youth group or not." I drop my head and shrug. "If they decide not to reinstate it, then that's the end."

"Listen, bro. You have nothing to worry about. God has your back, so please, chill."

I glance down the street as the swooshing sounds of the passing cars fill my ears, but they're not loud enough to drown out my thoughts. Sighing, I stare into the coffee in my cup, as if the black liquid has the answers to the questions in my head. "Joe?" I lift my head to look at my best friend, who is finishing the last sip of his tea.

"Yes, my brother," he says and places his cup down.

"Do you...do you think Mrs. Adebayo is right?"

Joe frowns. "Right about what, exactly?"

"About the fact that..." I pause and exhale. "Maybe I'm not

cut out for this youth ministry. I knew about Tessa's unhealthy crush on Matthew, but I did nothing about it. I should have known better and acted fast, but I was so distracted by Amara. It's all my fault."

"Mmm-hmm." Joe shakes his head. "Raymond, stop this. What are you saying?" He leans forward again. "This is the calling God has given you, and no one else will do it, but you. Do you think the devil is happy you're obeying God? Do you think he'll sit back and celebrate without fighting back?"

Joe shakes his head before continuing. "Of course not. The devil is not happy, that's why he's fighting you. Don't let this discourage you. The devil won't succeed. God is fighting on your side. He is the one who called you, so He will vindicate you. Okay?"

I nod because Joe is right. When God gave me this vision two years ago, I knew I would face challenges along the way. I just didn't expect the challenges to come so soon.

My phone rings in my pocket and I take it out, hoping it's Pastor Ben calling with good news. But no. It's not Pastor Ben. It's Amara. I sigh and place the phone on the table as it continues ringing.

"*Ah, ah*. Bro, pick up the phone and hear her out, *nau*. It's been two weeks. Why are you doing this?"

I shake my head and wait for the vibration to stop before speaking. "Guy, I'm tired of this whole relationship thing. She has already explained herself and there's nothing to talk about. I don't like when people lie to me, you know that."

"Yes, I know." Joe pulls his chair forward as a couple strolls past us, laughing and holding hands. "But, bro, she has apologized many times. Surely you guys can talk about it and try to work things out?"

I rub my temples and ponder on Joe's words. But every time I want to think about Amara and me, my mind drifts to Tessa and

Matthew and my current ministry dilemma. The truth is, I'm tired of it all.

I just need to forget about how much I've embarrassed myself and learn how to move on with my life. I'm so tired of girls in this country and now I'm seriously considering this Feyi girl my mother has been suggesting for me back in Nigeria.

"I just...I just need some time away from this place," I respond. "I've booked my flight at the end of this month to go see my Uncle Seun and his wife in Phoenix."

Joe nods and puts on his sunglasses. "Okay, bro. Do whatever you think will help. You know I'll always be here to support you."

34

AMARA

I drag my suitcase toward the red front door of my parent's house, wondering how Teeyana convinced me this was a good idea. I mean, it sounded like a good idea to get out of Atlanta for a few days after spending the last four weeks wallowing in self-pity. I agreed to this because I thought it'll help me get my mind off Ray—but deep inside, I know I'm wrong.

Spending the weekend with my parents won't help me forget about Ray, but taking a break from Atlanta is a good start. Given that Mom and I are still not talking to each other, I'm happy knowing I'll be getting comfort only from Dad.

This weekend was supposed to be the youth retreat and Ray's thirtieth birthday is on Monday. The teens and I were planning to do an early birthday celebration for him, but none of that matters now. Maybe I'll think about this someday and not have tears running down my face. I can't believe I sabotaged my first relationship before it ever started.

I carry my suitcase up the stairs before turning around to stare at the road again. Further down, the road divides into two; one road leading to Teeyana's parents' house, and the other leading to Coverton High—my old high school.

It's crazy to think that only a few years ago, Teeyana and I were running on these streets and thinking we were invincible. Even though we had our own challenges in high school, we didn't have as many responsibilities. All we had to do was homework, family time, church, movies, and then talk about all the boys we had crushes on. I mean, what more could a girl want, right?

I throw my jacket over my shoulder and turn around again. As I drag my suitcase to the door, the rumbling of its wheels against the wood drowns out the growling of my stomach. The last good meal I had was Ray's *egusi* soup a month ago and trust me, I'd do anything to have that again.

It's not that I don't know how to cook *egusi* soup or any other African delicacies. Mom made sure I learnt all her recipes when I was thirteen. But Ray's food tastes different. I wish I could explain, but I can't. The sad thing is, I'm never tasting his food again.

The doorbell only rings once before Dad opens it, wearing a big smile on his face. "*Adamma,* welcome back, my darling daughter." I step inside and hug him, the warmth of his embrace already making me feel better. Dad is wearing a grey t-shirt and joggers—the first time I've seen him in proper lounge wear.

"I've missed you, Daddy." I say, my head buried in his neck as I inhale his Nivea scent. "Hmm, *nna m,* what happened to your white vest top and wrapper? You're not wearing them today?" I fix the neckline of his t-shirt.

He laughs as we break the hug. "Your mother bought these for me, so I said let me make sure I wear it once a week to make her happy." He leans close and lowers his voice. "You know how she gets when we don't wear her gifts, *abi?*"

I chuckle and nod. "Yes, she doesn't let us drink water."

"Exactly." Dad reaches for my suitcase behind me and I help

him bring it into the house. "So how was your trip?" He asks as we walk down the dimly lit corridor.

I shrug. "It was good, but I'm so tired now. You know how much I hate long journeys." I yawn and lean against the wall at the base of the stairs.

"Yes, but we thank God you are here safely." He hands the suitcase over to me. "*Oya*, your room is ready for you. Go and shower, and then come down and eat your food."

My mood immediately perks up at the mention of food. "What did Mom cook?" I say as I take the suitcase from him.

Dad frowns. "You mean what did *I* cook?" He nods toward the kitchen. "Your mother doesn't know you are here. She went to visit Nkechi, who delivered a bouncing baby boy last night."

"Aww, congrats to her. I'll call her before I head back to Atlanta." Nkechi is the daughter of my mom's childhood friend who lives in Nigeria. Mom mentioned a few months ago that Nkechi was pregnant but I didn't know she was almost due. I'm just relieved that I don't have to face Mom—at least not for a few hours.

"Mama Nkechi was supposed to come from Nigeria for *ommugwo* this week, but she fell sick," Dad continues.

"Aww no, that's sad." Every Nigerian woman looks forward to having her Mom there with her during the first few weeks postpartum. I can only imagine how devastated Nkechi would be.

"Yeah, so your mother has gone to help Nkechi with the baby. She won't be back until Sunday. You didn't tell her you were coming and I know that was intentional, *abi*?" He looks me straight in my eyes, the same way he always looks at me when he knows I'm up to something.

"Yes, Daddy. It was." I send him a sly smile. I love that he can still see through me. That's why I'm more open with him than I am with Mom.

"Anyway, no *wahala*. I took out *oha* soup from the freezer. By the time you come down I would have made pounded yam for you, or is it *eba* you want?" His turns his palms up to face the ceiling.

My jaw drops open at his last sentence. "You?" I point at him. "Make *eba* for me?" I point at myself. "Dad, is everything alright?" I stifle a laugh.

He frowns. "*Ah ah,* what is that supposed to mean?" He shifts his weight to his left leg. "You think I cannot cook?" He cocks his eyebrows, which now look greyer than the last time I saw them.

I shrug. "It's just that I've never seen you do it."

"*It's just that...it's just that.*" Dad juts out his bottom lip, using a mocking voice to imitate me. "So, how do you think I survived all my bachelor years at the university of Nsukka? I used to cook for myself, *nau*. It's just that having a very skilled wife and daughter all these years has made me lazy, but I can cook very well." He gives me two thumbs up and I cover my mouth to stop myself from laughing.

"Okay, I believe you. I can't wait to taste it." I carry my suitcase upstairs as Dad retreats to the kitchen. At the top of the stairs, I walk past the first door on my right, which is my parents' room, the second, which is the bathroom, and then finally push open the third in front of me.

The warm atmosphere envelopes me as I step in. Even though I was only here a few months ago, the room still feels strange every time I walk into it. My posters from high school are still up on the wall. They all have my favorite Bible verses on them, but I bought new posters for my apartment in Atlanta, so I left these here.

I made up my double bed with white sheets and a floral duvet cover. My desk is stationed not too far away from my bed and next to the window. That's where I spent the most of my time in high school studying for exams.

I walk up to the window and slide the curtains apart to check out the street view. The sun is fully up now, alerting us it's midday. My breath fogs up the glass and absent-mindedly, I draw out a heart shape with my finger.

After realizing what I've done, I wipe it and laugh at myself. "Wow, girl, you need help." I push myself away from the window and walk back to my bed before plopping down on the soft mattress.

I've spent the last month thinking about Ray and I never thought I could miss someone this much. I've missed his smile, his comforting hugs, his words of encouragement, and how he constantly pushed me to embrace my identity in God.

Tears run down my cheeks and threaten to ruin my makeup, but I let them. Maybe someday it won't hurt as much as it does now and I'll be able to move on from it. But for now, I'll just let the tears run until I can heal.

Hours later, after showering and changing into more comfortable clothes, Dad and I finish our delicious meal of *eba* and *oha* soup. "Honestly, Dad, that was really good." I say, licking off the remnant of the soup from my fingers. "What's the secret?"

"You mix the yam flour with the garri. It makes the taste different, but still good." He says, before his gaze drifts back to the Nollywood drama on the TV.

"Wow, I have to try that." I wash my hands and then bring a bowl of fresh water for him to wash his hands. When he's done, I clear the table and take the dishes to the kitchen.

"*Oya, Adamma,* come and sit down." Dad says when I return to the living room. "Please pass me the TV remote." He says after I've sat down and I shake my head. *Some things never change around here.*

After giving him the remote, he lowers the volume and then turns to face me. "When you called me and told me you were coming, I knew something was wrong. You might want to hide it from me, but what an old man sees sitting down, a child cannot see even if they climb the tallest tree." He points to the ceiling. "So, tell me. What is bothering you, my child?"

I sigh. "It's a long story, Daddy."

He sips on his glass of water and leans back on the sofa. "I have time. Please talk to me. Is it because of what your mother said about Raymond? I have told you that—"

"It's not about that. Even if it was, it doesn't matter now because Ray will never speak to me again."

Dad reaches out and touches my hand. "What happened?"

I explain the whole situation to him from the beginning. When I get to the end of my story, regret settles in my chest and tears run out of my eyes like there's no tomorrow.

"It's okay, my dear." Dad pats my back the same way he used to do when I was a child; when I used to run to him after falling down and scraping my knees, or when the other church kids would be mean to me.

"No, it's not okay." I wipe my eyes. "Ray won't pick up my calls and I went to his hospital department to speak to him but he told me he was busy and couldn't talk."

Dad sighs. "Okay, let's look on the bright side of this. What have you learnt from this situation about marriage and relationships?"

I shift in my seat before looking at him. "That honesty is key and communication is very important."

"Exactly." Dad nods. "But I'll also try to teach you something from a different angle. I'm sorry, this is something your mother and I should have talked to you about before." He reaches over and holds my hands.

"*Adamma*, marriage is about commitment," he says. "When Jesus, who is the Bridegroom, accepted to come down to earth to die for us—His bride, He made a commitment to complete this purpose no matter the difficulties He faced. They spat on Him, abused Him, and even whipped Him, but He didn't back down. He was committed to His purpose, which was to save us.

"Marriage goes far beyond feelings and physical looks. Once you make that vow under God, you choose to stay committed to that person till the day you die. You choose to be patient when he annoys you, to show mercy and to forgive him when he hurts you, and to show kindness and compassion when he feels down. Choosing to love someone is not just about your feelings toward that person; it means you are choosing to stay committed to their purpose and to put them before yourself, no matter what happens."

Wow, no one has ever put it to me like this before. That's the one mistake I've made with Ray. Teeyana warned me about it. She said I can't eat my cake and have it, but I ignored her. I was too afraid to make the commitment to Ray because I felt he might be the wrong choice for me.

Dad rests his hand on my shoulder. "I want you to know that I don't support how your mother handled this issue. She thinks she is protecting you, but she doesn't understand that fear is the major driving factor for her actions. *Biko*, don't hate her."

"I don't hate her, Daddy. I can't hate my own mother, no matter how hard I try." I shake my head. "But what do I do now? How can I fix this situation?"

"Before you think about how to handle your mother, you need to be sure about your commitment." He raises his brows. "From what you've told me, it seems this young man—Raymond Aderinto, had made the commitment to love you. But what about you, *Adamma?* Do you love him?"

Dad's question mulls over in my mind. The day I broke up with Jamar, I was so convinced I wanted to be with Ray. But why? Apart from the fact that I now find him attractive, what makes me so drawn to him? Do I truly love him? Do I see myself marrying him, fulfilling purpose with him, serving Christ and doing life with him?

As the memories of the past eight months float around in my head, my only answer to myself is yes. Yes, I want all those things with Ray and so much more. I want to be a part of his world, to help him and not hurt him. I want to stay by his side and encourage him so he succeeds in whatever God has called him to do. I have no doubt that Ray will be right there to support me as I embrace my purpose too.

I gasp and my hand covers my mouth. "I love him." Tears blur my vision as I turn to Dad. "I can't imagine myself being with anyone else."

Dad's greying moustache spreads out across his face, almost touching his ears as he grins. "I knew it, and I'm glad you have realized that for yourself."

I wipe my eyes and exhale. "Okay, but what do you suggest I do now?"

"To be honest, if the young man doesn't want to talk to you, then there's nothing else we can do. We can't change his mind about you now, but God can. I suggest we keep praying that if this relationship is God's will, He should come to our aid and show us what to do. But if it is not His will, He should help us accept it. Okay?"

The thought of accepting that Ray is not God's will for me aches my being. But yes, if that is the case, then I have to accept it. "Yes, Daddy."

"Remember that I will be right here by your side and together, we will stand up to your mother. If it is God's will to join the two of you together, then no man or woman has the power to put asunder—not even Njideka Ikezie."

I throw myself on my bed and pull the covers up when my head hits the pillow. My room is dark, but because of the many years I've slept in this bed, my eyes can still trace the edges of the dangling chandelier above my head.

My conversation with Dad could not have gone any better. We spent some time praying together and my heart doesn't feel as heavy anymore. Now I know for sure I love Ray, but what can I do to rebuild the trust he once had for me?

"Oh, Lord, please help me." I whisper. "Show me what to do. Please, Lord."

My phone vibrates on my nightstand and I push myself up to look at the caller ID. "Hey, Claire." I press the phone against my ear.

"Hey. Sorry I'm reaching out to you so late. How are you?"

"I'm good, thank you. How are you? I hope Jamie isn't giving you trouble."

Claire laughs. "Well, boys will be boys. I'm doing my best to make sure he understands I'm still the boss in this house."

I laugh. "You go, girl."

"So, how are you holding up? Has Raymond called you yet?"

I sigh. "No. Not yet." I told Claire about what happened between Ray and me because she kept prodding until I cracked.

"Aww, he'll come around, I know it. I know he needs time to think about things, but he will soon realize he loves you too much to let you go." She adds. "Seriously, the day he stood up to Dr. Miller on your behalf, I knew Ray really cared about...." Her voice trails off. "Oops, forget I said that."

"Wait, hold up." My eyes widen. "Ray did what?"

"Huh? What?"

I reach for the switch on my bed-side lamp and turn on the light, as if the darkness is stopping me from hearing properly. "Claire, what did you just say about Ray standing up to Dr. Miller?"

"Errm...Raymond made me promise not to say anything to you, but...the day Dr. Miller embarrassed you in front of everyone, Raymond confronted him after you stepped out for a walk."

"He did?"

"Yes, and he threatened to report Dr. Miller to the board if he didn't give you a fair chance like everyone else."

"Aww, he said all that?"

"Yes, and that's why Dr. Miller gave you a space on the program. Of course he did. Dr. Miller is not stupid, and he knows what a bad report like that would do to his reputation."

"I can't believe Ray did all that and didn't tell me." *He loves me. I know he does.*

"I guess he didn't want you to feel like he was trying to buy your love?" Claire says. "I spoke to him last night, and he has traveled to see his uncle in Arizona. Unfortunately his retreat and youth fellowship were suspended, so..."

"Whoa, whoa, slow down. Suspended?" I raise my voice. "Why? Is Ray okay?"

"Yes, he is." Claire replies. "He said some teens were caught performing...sexual acts, whatever that means..." My mind trails off as Claire starts ranting about why she doesn't trust religion and its rules.

Oh, no. Could it be Tessa and Matthew? Ray mentioned Tessa's crush on Matthew a few times and how he wanted to teach them about purity and relationships. But why would they cancel the youth group and the retreat? Ray cares about these teens and he would never encourage them to engage in things like that.

"...I mean these are modern times and these teens need to be left alone to explore their sexuality, in my opinion." Claire rounds off her rant, and my attention returns to her again.

"Thanks for checking up on me, Claire. You have no idea

how this conversation has helped me. Have a good night and I'll speak to you soon."

"Wait, Amara, please don't tell Raymond I told you any of these things."

"Okay, I promise." I end the call before Claire can put in another word. I search for Ray's number and bring the phone up to my ear. It rings twice but as usual, he doesn't pick up. I sigh and let my head fall in my hands. "Lord, what do I do? Please, Lord. How can I help him?"

I pick up my phone again and dial Teeyana's number and she picks up after one ring. After telling her about everything Ray did to Dr. Miller and what has happened to his youth fellowship, Teeyana and I talk about how we can help him. Then, after a few minutes of silence between us, Teeyana finally speaks. "Okay, I think I have an idea."

35

RAYMOND

"You were right all along, Jevon. She was seeing Jamar." I rub my forehead.

"Oh, Raymond. I'm so sorry this happened again." Jevon says from the other end of the telephone line.

I lean back on the sofa in Uncle Seun's living room. "It's not your fault. I didn't listen to you after you warned me. You can now gloat and tell me you told me so."

"Why would I do that?" she asks. "Do you think that's all I care about? Being right? I was hoping I was wrong. I want you to find a girl who will love you back. Please don't give up, honey. Don't blame yourself, either. We are all adults and we should take responsibility for our actions and the choices we make."

I sigh. "Thanks, Jevon. I really appreciate all you do for me."

"Raymond, you're like the son I never had. Too bad both my daughters are married, I would have wanted you to officially be part of my family." We both laugh before she speaks again. "So when will you be coming back to work?"

"Monday."

"Your birthday, right?"

"Yeah." I sigh. Almost a year ago, Kate broke up with me on my birthday, and this year I'm experiencing yet another heartbreak. *What a life.*

"Well, the girls and I are going to make sure you have a wonderful birthday. Enjoy your weekend and say hello to your aunt and uncle for me."

"Thanks, Jevon. I will. See you on Monday." I end the call, put my phone on silent, and slide it into my pocket. As I run my hands on the sofa, memories from my pre-med days flood into my brain. This is the same sofa I used to have power naps on during my study breaks.

The clanging of pots travels across the room, followed by Aunty Lara and Uncle Seun's voices and then laughter. I tried to convince Aunty Lara to let me help her in the kitchen, but she refused. When I was studying for my medical college admissions test, Aunty Lara only let me cook or clean the house during the weekends so I would get time to study during the week. They practically spoiled me when I was living here.

Uncle Seun opens the kitchen door and the smell of Aunty Lara's *efo riro* soup wafts into my nostrils. He walks toward me carrying two glasses and a bottle of non-alcoholic wine.

"*Ah,* no, Uncle, you don't have to do this." I say, rising to my feet as I take the bottle of wine from his hand. "This house is my house, *nau*. Why are you treating me like a visitor?"

"Ah, Raymond, you are my August visitor *o*. I must serve you well, my son." Uncle Seun places the glasses on the table and adjusts his kaftan before lowering himself on the sofa across from me. "I haven't seen you since last year and you've been very busy with work."

"Yes, I know, Uncle, and I'm sorry." I lean forward and place the bottle on the glass table in front of us. "I'm sorry I only thought about coming to see you when I got myself into trouble."

Uncle Seun shakes his head and leans forward too. "Raymond, the reason for your visit doesn't matter. I'm just glad God has given me another opportunity to see you again and for that, I must thank God." He takes the bottle from the table and lifts it up before saying a prayer in Yoruba.

"*Oluwa e se o.* Lord, I thank you for bringing Raymond here to see us. Thank you, that we can commune together again. May this meeting bring you glory. In Jesus' name we have prayed."

"Amen."

Uncle Seun places the bottle on the table and I pop open the bottle of wine before pouring some into his glass first, and then mine. We clink our glasses and take a sip before Uncle Seun speaks.

"So," he starts. "What is this trouble you have gotten yourself into?" He focuses his brown eyes on me the same way my mother would after asking a question.

I swallow the sweet liquid in my mouth and place my glass on the table. "Uncle, I don't know what I'm doing wrong. I need your help."

Uncle Seun adjusts in his seat and clasps his hands. "Son, what do you need help with? Is it a woman?"

Uncle Seun knows about my previous relationships. I told him everything after Kate dumped me last year. He gave me a lot of support and guidance, so I don't know why I never told him about Amara.

"Yes, Uncle." I nod. "Her name is Amara and we met seven months ago. She's a nurse and we work in the same hospital. She's also a Christian and we have so much in common. I love spending time with her because she has a good character and she inspires me to be a better man every day." My gaze drops to my toes, which are peeking out of the slippers Aunty Lara gave me to wear around the house.

"But?" Uncle Seun says, his eyebrows rising.

"But I found out a month ago that she has been lying to me and seeing someone else too." I shake my head to erase the memory of Amara kissing Jamar.

"Hmm." Uncle Seun rubs his moustache. "Please tell me you got the chance to talk to her about it?"

"Yes, I did."

"Okay, good. What did she say?"

I shrug. "She apologized and said she has ended things with the other guy. She said she was initially confused about who to choose, but after praying about it, God led her to choose me."

"Okay," Uncle Seun says. "Do you believe her?"

I pause. To be honest, I hate the fact that I have let my opinion of Amara drop so low because of this incident, but I can't help myself. How can I trust again after everything I've been through with my past relationships? "I don't know." I finally respond.

"You want to believe her, don't you?" Uncle Seun asks, and I nod. "But you're not going to because of what those other girls did to you, *abi*?"

I lift my head to look at him, my eyes begging for him to put some sense into my brain. "It's hard. Am I being unreasonable?"

"Not entirely." Uncle Seun shakes his head and leans back in his seat. "You're responding in the way anyone would if they've been burned before."

I nod again, more to comfort myself than anything else.

"But son, I have to be honest with you." He looks me straight in the eye "Just because you've been burnt many times before, doesn't mean you have to respond by burning others too."

I frown, trying to decipher what he's saying. "But Uncle, she—"

"Yes, I know she wronged you, and I'm not justifying what she did. But everybody makes mistakes, and do you know what?" He leans forward again. "Whoever you marry will make mistakes too. The question is, will you be willing to forgive?"

I lower my head, fiddling with my fingers and trying to decide whether I agree or disagree with him.

"Pride, my son." Uncle Seun continues, forcing me to bring my head up again. "Pride causes so many people to live in misery in their marriages." He picks up his glass and swirls the wine in it slowly. "Marriage is not perfect and your relationship won't be perfect either. It seems like you are putting some unrealistic expectations on this relationship before it even begins."

I open my mouth to protest, but instead pause to think about his words. *Is he right?*

"Be careful, my son. Marriage is not a bed of roses. You need to expect challenges and expect your partner to make mistakes. But this is it. This is why God created marriage."

I frown and tilt my head. "For us to make mistakes and hurt each other?"

Uncle Seun laughs at my ignorance, and I rub the back of my neck. "No, to make us more like Him and to teach us about forgiveness." He sips his wine, making a loud slurping sound before continuing. "When Jesus died on the cross for us, the people who nailed him to the cross were the same people He loved so much—you and I. We crucified Him, yet He still died for us and forgave us. Marriage is like that. If you're going to live with this person for the rest of your life, then you have to learn to forgive way more than 77 times 7 times. That count doesn't start when you get married though; it starts now.

"I won't tell you what to do, but if God has confirmed to you, like you said, that Amara is your wife, then please, temper justice with mercy and forgive her because it seems she has truly repented. But if you have prayed, and God has shown you otherwise, then please, let her go and ask God for help to move on. No matter what you decide to do, never let pride take precedence, because that will be dangerous for any relationship you ever go into. Do you hear me?"

I nod, taking his words in slowly. "Yes, Uncle."

Aunty Lara walks into the room with her long, flowy dress. She is carrying serviettes and plates and is heading toward the dining table. "Boys, food is ready. We need to set the table."

Uncle Seun and I push ourselves up and when we're facing each other, he places one hand on my shoulder and looks me in the eye. "Choosing the right person to marry is a big risk, my son. Even when we get our confirmation from God, we still can't say what will happen tomorrow, so it requires a lot of faith." He leans closer and drops his voice to a whisper. "Child-like faith." He nods again before turning around and walking to the dining table.

Child-like faith.

The words race through my mind a million times as I pace the length of my old room. Some of my pre-med textbooks are still stacked on the table, and my posters of the bones and muscles of the human body are still on the walls. *So many memories.*

The *efo riro* soup and pounded yam Aunty Lara cooked was delicious, but throughout dinner, I couldn't stop thinking about what Uncle Seun said.

When I take my phone out of my pocket, I find three missed calls from Amara. She must have called right after I got off the phone with Jevon. I stare at my phone for a few minutes as my mind fights a battle with my heart.

The events of that night play out again in my head, me standing there, watching Amara's lips pressed against Jamar's. But this time, something doesn't feel right. I sit on my bed and rest my elbows on my thighs, trying to form the memory of what exactly I remember.

Jamar was leaving when I saw them and stopped across the street. But instead of continuing on to his car, he turned around, wrapped his arms around her waist and neck and pulled her close to him. Everything happened so quickly and before I knew it he was kissing her. She whimpered and struggled under his grip before finally pushing him away and slapping him.

Amara looked visibly shaken after he left and she even had tears in her eyes when she came running down the street to meet me. She tried to tell me Jamar harassed her and all I did was shut her out and blame her for everything. Jamar could have hurt her and done worse, yet I stood by and did nothing to help her.

"Oh Lord, what have I done?" My head collapses in my hands. "I love this woman, Lord, you know I love her."

Child-like faith.

My mind races back to the little girl at the hospital entrance who trusted the doctors' decision to let her go home. Also, little Dave who trusted me to teach him how to dance, even though he knew he had no rhythm. And even Chelsea— Joe's daughter, who fell in love with Amara at first sight, trusting her to be a good friend, even though they had never met before.

Child-like faith.

As the events of the last few months come rushing back in my memory, the anger in my chest slowly turns to guilt. "Amara loves me." I whisper. "I didn't hear her say it, but I know she does."

I swipe up on my phone screen and stare at the last message Amara sent me two weeks ago, where she apologized again and begged me to answer her calls. My thumb hovers over my keypad until I finally give in.

It's midnight and she might be sleeping, but I'll take my chance. The phone rings only twice and she picks up.

"Ray?" The warmth of her voice feels like medicine to my soul, a soothing balm for all the hurt I've inflicted on myself for the past four weeks. My words elude me and I wait for her to speak again.

"Ray? Are you there?" Her voice brings me out of my head.

"Hey. Yes, yes, I'm here." I lower my voice. "Sorry, I wasn't sure if it was okay to call now. Are you working tomorrow?"

A long sigh comes from her end. "No, I'm at my parents' house for the weekend."

"Oh, I see. Sorry I missed your calls earlier. I'm visiting my Uncle Seun and his wife in Phoenix and we had a lot to catch up on."

"It's okay." She cuts in. "You don't have to explain. I guess...I deserve a cold shoulder after all."

"No, you don't." I pinch the bridge of my nose and close my eyes. "Amara, I'm sorry for ignoring your calls. I'm sorry for not listening to you and I'm sorry for shutting you out."

"It's fine, Ray." She sniffles.

"No, it's *not* fine." Another pang of guilt sears through my chest, announcing the fact that my actions have contributed to the tears she's shedding now. I need to fix this. "Amara, I miss you." I blurt out without thinking. I'm finding it difficult to pick a sentence from the jumbled words in my brain right now.

"I miss you too."

"We need to talk. Please, can I see you?" I pause, waiting for her response.

"I'd really like that."

Oh, thank God. "I don't mean on FaceTime. I mean in person."

"Sure." She giggles.

How I've missed her laugh. Lord, please, don't let me mess this up again.

"I'll see you on Monday, then?" she says.

"Monday." I repeat.

"At the usual place?"

A smile tugs at my lips. "Of course. No other place will do. Goodnight, Amara."

"Goodnight, Ray."

36

AMARA

Mom came back earlier than we expected. Before leaving, she told Dad she would be back tomorrow, so I was surprised when she stormed into my room last night and started firing a million questions at me.

"*Adamma, so you have been back in Boston for a whole day and you didn't even bother to tell your own mother?*" Mom woke me up from a dream where Ray was about to kiss me. *Come on.*

"*Mom?*" I said, rubbing my eyelids and squinting in the darkness. Her silhouette standing in front of my bedroom door didn't help my disorientation.

"*Yes?*" She flipped the light switch on and I shielded my eyes with my hands. Still dressed in her dashiki dress and leggings, she walked into my room and continued asking her questions. "*So it's true, Adamma? You really came back without telling me?*"

I groaned when my senses cleared and I realized what she was talking about. "*Mom, it was a last-minute decision, and I didn't know you were traveling.*" I leaned back and covered my face with my pillow, trying to drift back into the sweet dream I was having. Mom went on a rant about how we needed to talk, but all I could think about was Ray.

"Amarachukwu, are you listening to me?" She tapped my leg and woke me up from my slumber again. Kissing my teeth, I pulled my blanket away from her and groaned. *"Mom, please, I'm trying to sleep. Can we talk about this in the morning?"* I said from underneath my pillow. I don't remember if she said anything else, but the next thing I heard were retreating footsteps and the door slamming shut.

Today, Mom seems calmer—well, I hope she is, because the last thing I want is to argue with her before going back to Atlanta. Since there's a chance of Ray and I getting back together, I need to understand Mom's point of view.

"Lord, please help me." I whisper to myself when Mom struts into the living room, Dad following closely behind her. She pushes my suitcase out of the way before occupying a space on the sofa.

Dad walks past me and gives me a reassuring nod before settling in the seat next to Mom.

Leaning forward, Mom clears her throat and starts talking. "Amarachukwu, I have to say that I am very disappointed." She shakes her head. "Have things become so bad that you have started avoiding me—your own mother?"

Mom only ever uses my full first name when she's angry and this case is not different. A swallow to wet my dry mouth and my heart rate quickens.

"How could my own child," Mom points at her chest, "who I carried in my womb for nine months," then she points at her belly, "find my presence so irritating that she has to sneak in and out of the house?"

I sigh, trying to find the right words. Mom can be so dramatic sometimes, but that's how she's always been. She knows what the problem is; yet, she chooses to act oblivious, as if she didn't hurt my feelings by blatantly refusing to tell me why she won't approve of the man I love. *Oh my goodness. I still can't believe I love him.*

"Amarachukwu, I'm talking to you." Mom's words make me flinch.

"It's not like that, Mom." I try to reason with her.

"Not like what? That you will come back to see only your father and not even bother to—"

"Mom, please drop it." I raise my voice, the height of my frustration reaching its peak. I meet Dad's gaze and he tries to calm me with his facial expression, but I ignore him and carry on, taking on a confidence I've never possessed before. "You're beating around the bush. Why don't you go straight to the point and address the elephant in the room."

Mom's mouth hangs open for a few seconds before she speaks. "*Bia*, come *o*, Amarachukwu, is it me you are talking to like this?" She pushes herself up and Dad stands up with her. "So it is because of that *Yoruba demon* that you have developed a sharp mouth *eh*?"

"Mom, please stop this nonsense." I stand up as well. "Do you think I'm still a five-year-old girl you can control?" My voice cracks as I fight the lump building in my throat. "You know nothing about Ray. You have no idea how much he has helped me over the last eight months, you don't know about his goals, his dreams, and his aspirations and yet, the first thing that comes out of your mouth is a disdainful presumption."

"*Hia*, Amarachukwu, *moi*?" Mom turns to Dad who has one of his arms around Mom's shoulder. "Nnamdi, can you hear what your daughter is saying?"

"*Obi m,* calm down and hear the girl out, *nau.*" Dad steps in. "You're taking this thing too far."

"Taking *what* too far?" She talks over Dad's protest. "Is this how I brought her up? To disrespect her elders? Leave me alone, *jor.*" Mom jerks her shoulder away from Dad's hold.

I keep my head down and tap my foot, waiting for when to step in and what to say. *Lord, please help me.*

"I am not discussing this matter again." Mom finally turns to me. "You cannot bring a Yoruba boy into this house. Period."

Something snaps inside of me and all the emotions I've been suppressing for so long rush up at once. "You have no power to put a period on my life." I say, as the little patience I had at the beginning of this conversation dissipates from me. "You are not God and you will *never* be." With determined steps, and not caring about the consequences, I turn around, grab my suitcase, and head for the door.

"*Adamma*, please." Dad steps in front of Mom and holds my suitcase.

"Where are you going?" Mom asks, but I ignore her.

"Dad, please let go." Then I turn to Mom, tears already leaking out of my eyes. "I'm going back to Atlanta since you don't want me here."

"Amarachukwu, if you step out of that door without us resolving this issue, then Heaven and earth will not contain both of us."

In exasperation, I drop the suitcase and groan. "Mom, for the love of God, what do you want from me? All you've done this past year is talk about me getting married early and choosing a good man. Now someone is interested in me and you keep acting as if he's an alien.

"You claim you're rooting for my happiness yet you're the same person trying to crush it with your bare hands. Have you even asked me how I feel? You're very selfish, Mom. You never listen to me and you're always so quick to criticize me. That's *exactly* why I'm not sorry about always running to Dad first." I turn my head away, but not before noticing the hurt in Mom's glistening eyes.

"*Adamma*, please, let us settle this matter before you go." Dad says, but I shake my head.

"*Nna m.* I've tried my best. I can't do this anymore. I'm sorry." I hug him. "You can keep your wife. Whenever she's ready to have a proper conversation, she can call me." I drag my suitcase and step into the hallway.

"*Adamma*, please wait," Mom says and I stop in my tracks, not because she spoke, but because of the emotion in her voice. When I turn around, tears are streaming down her face.

"Please let me explain everything to you." She takes a few steps toward me.

I hesitate, but finally let go of my suitcase and walk over to the sofa I just vacated.

Mom sits and Dad again lowers himself beside her. "*Adamma*, you are young and you don't understand—"

"Then make me understand," I say, without letting her finish. "You can't keep imposing rules on me without a rational explanation. I'm not a child, Mom. You need to explain."

"Okay, I will explain." She lowers her head before continuing. "You know my sister, your Aunty Chinonye was once married to a Yoruba man, right?"

I frown, casting my mind back to the many conversations Mom has had with Aunty Chinonye about her ex-husband. I know he was a Yoruba man and I know they were having issues which led to their divorce, but Mom never gave me specifics. Even when I speak to Aunty Chinonye over the phone, she never mentions him and I wouldn't expect her to since she's now happily married to Uncle Chibuzor with two children.

"Of course I know that. But why is that important?" My gaze alternates between Mom and Dad.

Mom dabs her cheeks with the hem of her dress. "Chinonye was so in love with Dayo; he was all she could talk about, and she didn't listen to anything anyone told her. That's how she entered into a marriage she was not ready for."

I frown, still not following her explanation. "What exactly was she not ready for?"

"Everything." Mom shrugs. "She was marrying into another tribe and she didn't know much about their traditions and customs." Once again, Mom uses the corner of her dress to wipe her tears.

"Two years into their marriage, after Chinonye had many miscarriages, Dayo's family started putting pressure on him to get another wife. At first, Dayo supported Chinonye and reassured her she had no reason to worry. But as the pressure grew, especially from his mother and sisters, Dayo's attitude started changing."

Dad reaches for Mom's hand as she continues. "Dayo turned on her, refused to eat her food, started keeping late nights, and some days he didn't even come home at all. One day Chinonye came back home from work and found Dayo in bed with his secretary, and when she confronted him about it, he beat her up and called her a witch who was eating up all her children." Mom pauses and closes her eyes. "He almost disfigured my sister's face. She ended up in the hospital with so many injuries. If that other woman was not present in that house, Dayo would have killed my sister."

Oh wow. I remember in senior year of high school, when Mom woke up one morning crying and packing her bags, saying she was going back to Nigeria because Aunty Chinonye was in the hospital. Now that I think about it, it was after that trip that she started making all her side comments about Yoruba men being *demons. Why didn't she tell me about this before?*

Mom blows her nose into a piece of tissue, the sound pulling me out of my thoughts. "Before Chinonye married Dayo, she thought he was the perfect Christian man. No one would have been able to convince her that he would do that to her. Neither of us ever thought he could change like that." Mom lifts her head and looks at me, her eyes red and her eyelids swollen.

"*Adamma*, my good God knows I love you with everything I have. I'm sorry if I've been too hard on you, but I don't want your story to end up like my sister's. I will never forgive myself if—"

"God forbid, Mom, that will never be my story." I walk across the room and kneel next to her, using my thumb to wipe the tears on her face. "What Uncle Dayo and his family did to Aunty Chinonye is despicable and I understand your fears. But Mom, Uncle Dayo didn't do all those things because he had a tribe problem. He did all those things because he had a heart problem." I glance at Dad, who nods in agreement.

"It's so easy to attribute people's actions and behaviors to their tribe, but we forget that things are much deeper than that. I know you're afraid of other cultures and you want to stick to what you know, but there are so many Igbo men who cheat on their wives too. You know that, right?"

Mom nods reluctantly. "Yes, that's true. Mama Nkechi has been dealing with this for many years. Her husband keeps running after all the small girls in Lagos."

"*Ehe*, I'm glad you acknowledge that too. So Igbo men can also beat and mistreat their wives. It doesn't matter whether the man is Igbo, Yoruba, Hausa, or even from another country altogether. What matters is the state of his heart."

Mom's moisture-covered shaking hands cover mine. "I don't want you to make a mistake, *Adamma*. You're the only child we have."

"I don't want to make a mistake either. That's why I came to you and Dad for accountability. Of course I want your blessing, but you can't help me if your vision is already blurred by your self-imposed biases." I cover her hand with mine. "I'm not saying Ray is perfect, but he is a wonderful man. He loves God, he loves me, and...I love him."

Mom sighs and wipes her eyes. "Are you sure?"

I nod. "Yes, Mom. I would love for you to meet him. But you have to promise me you'll have an open mind, please?"

"Please, *obi m*." Dad chimes in, squeezing Mom's shoulder and then he leans close and whispers in her ear. "We can interrogate the young man together."

We all burst out laughing and Mom's face lights up again, her cheeks marred with dried tears. "Okay, fine," she says. "I would love to meet this suitor of yours whenever he is ready."

"Thank you, Mom. I love you." I wrap my arms around her and plant a kiss on her cheek.

My knuckles collide with the wooden door three times before I drop my arm by my side. I wait and shake my hands when a voice responds from inside. "Come in."

I wrap my knuckles around the doorknob and twist, saying a quick prayer before pushing the door open and walking into the office. "Good morning, sir." I say to the middle-aged man sitting beside the desk.

When Teeyana talked to me about this idea, I initially refused to do it because I didn't think I could pull it off. But one thing Ray has taught me is not to shy away from things God has placed on your heart. If you do, then that would be disobedience and then you would miss out on a chance for God to use you. Besides, this is for Ray, so I have to do it.

"Good morning." The man lifts his head and locks eyes with me. He takes off his glasses and places them on the table next to the stack of papers in front of him. "Please, take a seat, young lady." He points to the chair across his desk. "I don't believe we've met before. Are you a new member of Grace Baptist Church?"

I shake my head before sitting down. "No, Pastor Ben, but I'm here on behalf of someone who attends your church."

"I see." He says. "What's your name?" He picks up his pencil and places it behind his ear.

"Amara." I respond and his facial expression loosens, as if he has just had a lightbulb moment.

"Amara?" He asks and I nod. "Hmm. Who have you come on behalf of?"

"His name is Raymond Aderinto. He's the youth leader at your church, sir."

"Ohh, of course. You're Amara." A wide smile spreads across his face.

I frown. "Have you heard about me before, sir?"

"Yes, I have. Raymond is my spiritual mentee and he has mentioned you before. He spoke very highly of you, so it's an honor to have you here. How can I help?"

My cheeks warm at the revelation and I adjust in my seat, praying for the right words to come. "Sir, I know there's a possibility that you might not like what I say, but please, all I'm asking for is that you consider it."

"You have my word." He nods.

"I came to beg you to please reinstate the youth fellowship you suspended." I watch the lines on his forehead reappear. "Before you ask, no, Ray didn't send me to you. He never told me about the suspension and he doesn't even know I'm here, but I attended one of Ray's youth programs and I helped him plan the retreat.

"He has nothing but good intentions toward these teens and he goes above and beyond for them. Ray is not after a title and he doesn't have an ulterior motive or a selfish ambition. He just wants to see these teens attain spiritual prosperity. He is one-of-a-kind and even though people have taken him for granted in the past—including me—he continues to pursue the purpose God has called him to do."

I sigh, fighting back a tear. "I never had this opportunity when I was growing up. If I had more conversations about friendships, prayer, Bible study, and relationships, then I would have avoided so many mistakes. Please, sir, God has been using Ray to work in the lives of these teens.

"If we don't train them now, then the world will try to turn their hearts away from God. So before you think about cancelling the youth fellowship permanently, all I ask is that you think about everything these teens will be missing out on. I care a lot about this vision because Ray does, and whatever matters to Ray matters to me. "

"Hmm." Pastor Ben leans into his hands and rubs his beard. "Amara, I have to say that this meeting today is an answered prayer."

My heart leaps in my chest. "Really?"

He nods. "Yes, my dear. Since we suspended the youth fellowship, I've been very weary in my spirit, and for the past week, I've been asking God to help me make the right decision. Last night, I had assurance that God would give me an answer, but I never expected you to walk through this door and give me confirmation."

M bottom lip quivers as tears slide down my cheeks. *Lord, thank You. Thank You for doing this for Ray.*

37

RAYMOND

"Happy Birthday, Raymond!!!" Cheers and whistles erupt when I walk into the staff room. I smile and step back to take in the scene. A blue birthday banner is hanging on the wall, and the cake on the table is shaped like a white coat with a stethoscope and a number thirty candle on it.

"Aww, thanks everyone. This is so beautiful." I place my backpack on the sofa as Carla fixes a blue party hat on my head. Then I walk around the room greeting everyone from the department who has come to celebrate with me. I blow the candles on the cake and cut out my first piece before Carla shares out the rest of the slices.

"Happy birthday, sweetheart," Jevon says as she hands me a cup of fruit punch.

"Thanks, Jevon. You shouldn't have." I take the cup from her.

She places both hands on her hips and shakes her head. "Nuh-uh. Honey, we would do so much more for you. We love you, Raymond," she says, her kind words warming my heart.

Carla and Maureen join us and after a group hug, we spend an extra ten minutes talking about birthday milestones before the crowd disperses and everyone returns to their duties. As I walk in and out of the rooms seeing patients, I glance at the clock every two minutes, counting down the hours, the minutes, and the seconds until I can speak to Amara.

I stayed up until one a.m. last night trying to structure out my apology, and how to convince her to take me back after pushing her away. But then I remembered what Joe told me months ago—that the best thing I can ever do is be myself.

Finally, at one p.m., I hand over the last patient's file to Jevon. "It's time. If you need me, page me." I turn toward the exit, my strides quickening with each step.

"Raymond?" Jevon says and I turn around to meet her gaze. She places both her elbows on the nurse's desk and lowers her voice. "All will be well." A broad smile appears on her face.

"Thanks, Jevon."

"Anything for you, boy." She winks at me.

I wink back at her and head out the door, the saliva drying from my mouth as I push open the doors leading down the stairs. I drag my heavy legs across the corridor, my breathing, oh God, my breathing is quickening too.

All will be well. Jevon's words echo in my thoughts as I continue down the stairs. I told Jevon about everything I learnt during my weekend in Arizona. I had to admit the truth. Amara is not the only one who made a mistake. I did too, and I'm tired of playing the blame game.

My phone vibrates in my pocket and I pause in the hallway, the crowd of people meandering around me to get to their destinations. My heart sinks at the sight of the caller ID and I bring the phone up to my ear.

"Hello, Pastor Ben?"

"Good afternoon, Raymond. How are you?" His cheery voice takes me by surprise. He has been checking up on me every week since our meeting with Mr. Etomi and Mrs. Adebayo. He told me he would let me know when the church leaders have made a decision.

"I'm fine, sir. Is everything okay?" I ask before heading toward the cafeteria. I need to get a hot chocolate for Amara. It's the only peace offering that has worked so far.

"Yeah, everything is fine. Sorry to call you while you're at work."

"No, it's okay. I'm actually on my lunch break now." I approach the counter and mouth to my friend John, "*the usual*" and then signal a "*number 2*" with my fingers. John nods and turns to the machine behind him.

"Oh, that's good. So I guess this is the best time to tell you the good news."

I freeze. "What good news?" I ask, trying not to get my hopes up.

"The church leaders have decided to reinstate your youth fellowship program."

My mouth drops open. "Really? Are you serious?"

"Yes, Raymond. This past week, I have seen God work mightily in your favor." He pauses. "I have no doubt that this is truly what He wants you to do, and I refuse to stand in the way of His plans. I haven't been at peace since we suspended the program. The investigations only went on to prove that you are a man of integrity. These teens need you and just like a wise young lady told me, God has sent you to help them attain spiritual prosperity and I can't wait to experience that at Grace Baptist Church and beyond."

"Wow, thank you so much, Pastor Ben." I smile as joy envelopes my heart. "This is wonderful news." I pause, considering his words some more. "Wait, what young lady?"

Pastor Ben laughs. "Well I believe you know her very well. No wonder you were so eager for me to meet her. I have to agree with you; she is a special one."

"Wait, Pastor Ben—"

"We'll talk some more on Sunday. Have a nice day and God bless you."

Before I can get in another word, he ends the call as John balances two cups on a holder in front of me. My gaze drops to the cups, one with my name, and the other with Amara's name. Then it hits me.

Amara.

"That'll be six dollars, Dr. Aderinto." John's voice drags me out of my thoughts. I tap my phone on the card reader and slip John another five-dollar bill from my wallet before picking up the cup holder. "Thank you, my good man." I smile at him before turning toward the exit.

As I rush out the double doors, the sun's rays warm my skin, and when I turn round the corner toward the garden, I spot an old friend, *Frolita*. Her kinky coily strands are standing high up in a puff and the African queen who wears her proudly is sitting on the bench, waiting.

Amara locks eyes with me and my heart swells with so much joy, I have to stop myself from running to her. I keep my head high and take reasonably paced strides until I'm standing in front of her.

"Hey." She stands up and pushes her curly bangs away from her eyes.

"Hey." My gaze meets her big brown eyes, the same ones I've missed looking into. *She's so beautiful.* "Thanks for speaking to Pastor Ben on my behalf."

She smiles and lowers her head. "I only returned a favor."

I frown, but before I can speak again, she adds, "Yes, I know what you did, Ray. Claire told me everything. I can't believe you confronted Dr. Miller."

I shrug. "I had to. No one messes with the woman I love." Her cute giggle returns and soon, she's biting her bottom lip and turning her face away like she always does. I'm so glad I still have that effect on her. "Please, forgive my manners. This one's for you." I hand her the hot chocolate as we both sit on the bench.

"Aww, it has my name on it." She brings the cup close to her face.

"Yeah, to make sure you don't get black coffee with no sugar instead."

"Oh, gosh, that would be poison to my sweet tooth."

"I know." We both laugh and then a moment of silence passes between us before she looks at me.

"Ray, I'm sorry for lying to you. I didn't mean to hurt you." She exhales. "You have a beautiful support system and everyone is rooting for you. I didn't want to choose you because everyone expected me to. Love is a choice and I've chosen to love you. I know I'm still trying to figure things out, but I'm willing to learn with you. Please, forgive me and give me a second chance."

I take her hands in mine and press my lips against her fingers. "Amara, I'm so sorry for pushing you away when you needed me the most. I condemned you instead of extending grace to you—the same grace God has shown me so many times after I ignored His directions and chased after girls I should've had no business chasing. I'm sorry I ever compared you to my exes. I was a fool for letting those words come out of my mouth. You're nothing like them. I love you, Amara. You're good for me and I don't want to be with anyone else but you."

I lean forward and plant a kiss on her forehead, my lips lingering for longer than they did the last time. Then breaking the kiss, my gaze slides down to her lips. "Amara, I don't have it figured out either. I'm only following God's lead and learning to take a leap of faith." Her rose scent wraps around me as I slowly give in to the overwhelming urge to kiss her. "Amarachukwu Ifeoma Ikezie, will you please be my girlfriend?"

"Yes, Dr. Raymond Oluwagbemiga Aderinto, I would *love* to be your girlfriend. I love you." Taking me by surprise, she leans in and closes the gap between us, allowing our lips to touch for the first time.

I wrap my arms around her waist and bring her close until our bodies touch. She presses into me and brings her arms up to my shoulders, her soft lips parting and giving way to mine. I kiss her slowly, softly, and tenderly, but when my lips and body beg for more, the Holy Spirit whispers words of caution in my ears and I pull away gently.

She leans in and pecks my lips again. "That kiss was as sweet as the *egusi* soup you cooked for me."

"Oh, no." I shake my head and cover my eyes with my palm. I never want to remember what happened that night. *Lord, please, if I ever walk away from her again, slap me back to my right senses.* "I'm so sorry I did that to you. I can't believe you ate the food."

She frowns and pulls my arms down. "Of course I ate it. I knew you put a lot of love into it, so I couldn't let it go to waste."

I smirk. "That's true. Can't you see my biceps bulking up? It's from all the pounded yam I've been stirring."

"Ooh yes, I'm *very* impressed." Amara laughs and wraps her arm around mine, her closeness forcing me to realize she's really my girlfriend now. "Happy Birthday, Ray."

I gasped and lean back. "You remembered?"

She raises her brows. "What kind of girlfriend would I be if I didn't? I got something *real* nice for you, but shipping was delayed so it's still on its way."

"Please, don't be sorry." I take her hands and kiss them softly. "You are the best birthday present God has ever given me."

"Aww, Ray."

I lean forward and claim her lips again when my phone starts vibrating. *Oh, who is this person trying to ruin my moment?*

When I take out my phone, my mother's photo is staring at

me. "Do you mind?" I ask Amara. "She still doesn't understand this time zone thing. She just calls whenever and hopes for the best."

Amara lets go of my arm, but doesn't respond.

"Hey, are you okay?" I ask her.

"Yeah, I'm fine, but you said your mom is the most important person to you so...what if she doesn't approve of our relationship because I'm Igbo? What will happen then?"

I turn to face Amara squarely. "Baby girl, today, I give you my word. As long as God is in this, I'm ready to fight anyone who tries to come between us."

"Even your mom?"

"Of course. Even my mother." I say. "But you don't have to worry about that because she loves you."

Amara frowns. "And how do you know that?"

I straighten my back and plant a soft kiss on her lips "Because she already knows who you are, where you're from, and what you look like."

Amara's face brightens. "Really?"

"Yeah, she has been waiting to meet you since November." My phone vibrates again—a video call this time. "Do you want to see for yourself?"

Amara fluffs her hair and pulls up her scrubs top. "Wait, how do I look?"

"Like the beautiful queen you are." I kiss her forehead and then answer the call. "Mommy, *e kaaro o*. You won't believe who I have here with me today." I wrap my arm around Amara and draw her close to me so my mom can see her face. "This is Amara, my sweetheart."

Mom's eyes almost pop out of her head. "Ahhh. Amara-chukwu? Is this really you? Oh God, thank you. Ohhh, you're so beautiful, my darling."

Amara smiles and tucks loose strands of hair away from her face, "Thank you."

"Ah, *Arewa*. Wonderful. *Oko mi* you need to teach her Yoruba *o*."

I smirk. "Don't worry, Mommy. I've got her covered."

Not long into the call, Mom starts talking about getting engaged and going to Nigeria to meet the whole family. Amara relaxes more into my hold and engages in the conversation throughout. But soon, my senses tell me to wrap up the call before Mom's questions start making Amara uncomfortable.

When we get off the phone, we kiss again, and then cheers erupt from the second floor of the building behind us. When Amara and I turn our heads, Jevon, Maureen, Carla, and Claire are waving at us from the window.

Amara and I wave back before facing each other again.

"You know they'll be watching our every move from now on, right?" I say.

"Mmm-hmm." She nods and leans in to kiss me again, but I move my head back.

"You're okay with that?"

"Of course." She smiles. "I have nothing to hide. Do you?"

I shrug. "*Mba o*, *Nne*, my hands are clean." I pretend to wash my hands, the same way I've seen some mothers do in Nollywood movies.

"You're such a drama king." Amara chuckles and leans closer, allowing me to claim her lips once more.

38

AMARA

I can't stop myself from smiling as I sit at the back of the room and listen to Ray teach the teens. I should be paying attention to his talk about being pure in heart, but I can't stop thanking God for how good He has been to me.

Ray and I have been officially dating for a month now, and after the church reinstated the youth fellowship, we both dived straight into planning the logistics for the retreat. Joe and Josephine volunteered their time and helped us find a retreat venue.

We hired a cabin in the woods for the weekend, and all the teens agreed to come—including Matthew and Tessa. I'm surprised Tessa's mom agreed to it after everything that happened, but I'm glad she did. Pastor Ben helped us hire the church bus, and the journey took us approximately two hours before we arrived at our destination.

The wooden cabin house is in an open space surrounded by tall trees. It has a balcony with stairs leading up to the front door. Behind the house is a slope leading deeper into the forest, with paths going in different directions, and five toilet stalls stationed at the edge of the open space.

I made sure Ray picked a cabin house with enough toilet stalls, as I wasn't ready to fight with these teens for toilet time. Inside the cabin, there's a kitchenette, two upstairs bedrooms, and a living room space with a TV and a sofa. It's not too spacious, but it's not crowded either. There's just enough space for everyone.

When we arrived on Friday night, Ray and I made quick pasta bolognese as the teens claimed to be too tired to move a bone. I introduced them to the game of charades and Bible trivia, just like we used to play at my home church back in Boston. After watching a movie, Ekene and Nicole led us in worship and prayer before everyone went to bed.

Yesterday, after breakfast, we kicked off the morning with another session of worship and prayer and Ray talked about the importance of spending time in God's Word. At the end, Ray shared his personal Bible study routine and then he asked me to share mine. I told them about my chronological Bible study routine and how I learned so much about the story of Isaac and Rebekah. From there, more relationship questions started flooding in.

"*Aunty Amara, do you and Uncle Raymond study the Bible together?*" Breonna asked as she wrapped her arm around Tessa, who had been quiet during the whole retreat.

"*We make sure we have our own individual Bible study time, but we always share with each other what we've learnt every week.*" I responded.

"*We've also started reading a book together.*" Ray chimed in. "*It's so fun when you have a buddy to discuss books with.*" He turned to me and winked, sending my heart into an erratic dance.

After the study, we went out for a hike in the woods. Kojo loved it and he convinced Matthew, Taiwo, Ekene, and even Bryan to climb up the slopes with him. Everyone loved watching the waterfall, and we sat and talked on the river bank for a while before heading back to the cabin. On our way back, the girls stuck with me and asked more questions about my relationship with Ray.

Tessa seemed withdrawn the whole time and chose to lag behind. For the first time, Breonna was talking a lot more and finding the confidence to express herself. I wrapped my arm around Tessa and pulled her close to the group, asking her questions until she joined in the conversation.

Today, we're rounding up the retreat with talks about relationships. We intentionally left it till the end because we want it to mull in their brains as they leave. Ray has been looking forward to this one. I love hearing him teach. He has an extraordinary gift for breaking things down into simple terms. It's so clear from his hand movements, the rise and fall of his voice, his broad smile, and the way he gets so excited about the Bible, that he truly loves God. I'm so blessed to call this man of God *mine*.

After the talk, Ray takes the boys to the kitchen to work on their famous fried rice for lunch while the girls and I stay back in the living room to paint each other's nails. Last night, the girls made rice and stew, so it's our turn to chill.

Breonna still has her arm wrapped around Tessa, but as usual, Tessa isn't talking. I've had a tugging in my heart to speak to Tessa all weekend, but I've been too afraid to poke my nose into something that doesn't concern me. I couldn't sleep last night, and the thought of leaving this retreat without doing what God wants me to do keeps haunting me.

"Tessa, can I speak to you for a minute?" I touch her arm gently and she looks up at me. After saying something to Breonna, she leaves the group and follows me to the stairs outside.

Tessa takes up the space next to me and for a minute, we take in the view and listen to the birds chirping in the distance.

The wind blows through the trees and they dance around under the influence of it. A whooshing sound follows, and we both exhale at the same time.

When we turn to look at each other, we both break into a giggle and I playfully nudge her shoulder. "I've missed your beautiful smile." I flip a few strands of her platinum waist-length braids to the side so I can see her face clearly. When I tip her chin, she finally meets my gaze. "You're a wonderful girl, you know that, right?"

Tessa shakes her head. "My mom doesn't think so and I'm sure the other girls are talking about me behind my back. My mom keeps reminding me every day about what I did and how much I've wronged God. Nothing I do will ever be good enough for her now and I know God feels the same way." She wipes a tear running down her cheek.

I open my mouth to interject, but close it again. Tessa is very fragile and I need to tread on this ice carefully. "Tessa, look at me..." I wait until she has finished wiping her eyes. "First of all, none of the other teens know about what happened between you and Matthew. Secondly, everyone makes mistakes. I have made many mistakes in my life, your Uncle Raymond has, and I'm very sure that even your mom has."

Tessa sniffles. "What mistake have you made?"

When I lift my head, I lock eyes with Ray, who is standing on the other side of the glass window in the kitchen. He has an apron tied around his waist and a wooden spoon in one hand. He mouths, "Are you okay?" and I nod and smile at him. Then I send him an air kiss and he gladly receives it before heading back to the boys.

"You really love him, don't you?" Tessa's voice brings me down from cloud nine.

I nod, my cheeks warming up. "But it wasn't always like this. I actually didn't like him in the beginning."

"No way." Tessa's eyebrows shoot up. "How is that even possible? Everyone loves uncle Raymond."

I explain to her how we met, about Jamar, and how all of that blew up in my face. "If I could go back in time, I would have never gone on any dates with Jamar."

Tessa nods. "Yeah, I agree. Maybe that would have saved you all the tears."

"True." I chime in. "But God has a wonderful way of using our mistakes to teach us lessons and draw us closer to Him. It's not the mistake that matters, Tessa. It's God's grace and forgiveness through it and what that tells us about His love for us."

Tessa sighs. "I agree with you, but it's hard when my mom keeps rubbing my mistakes in my face. Will it ever get easier?" Her dark gaze pleads for some words of hope and I cast my mind back to my relationship with Mom. I'm hoping that we'll learn to understand each other more from now on, but dealing with her endless criticisms while growing up wasn't easy.

As much as mentoring the teens, we need to be intentional about educating the parents about how to best relate with their children. Ray and I have talked about this and we know so much work needs to be done.

"I think we should be hopeful, but I can't promise things will get easier." I shake my head "Our parents are human beings too and they make mistakes. Have you asked God to forgive you?"

Tessa nods. "Yes, I have and I don't want to do it again."

"That's great. Are you willing to live your life fully as a Jesus girl?"

Tessa nods again. "Yes, I am."

"Then that's all that matters because God now sees you as flawless."

"He does?" She asks as tears pool in her eyes.

"He sure does, girl. So even if your mom reminds you of it,

remind yourself that Jesus has forgiven you and that's all that matters, okay?"

"Yes, aunty. Thank you," she says before hugging me.

The cool breeze brushes against my skin, and Tessa's lavender perfume fills my nostrils. Her tears wet my neck, and I can feel the rough texture of her braided extensions against my fingers. When I close my eyes, realization hits me. This is my vision—the same one I've been having repeatedly for the last ten months every time I pray for Ray. It's no longer just a vision. It's now my reality. I close my eyes and say a prayer. *Lord, is this what you've been trying to tell me?*

My beloved Amara. I love you.
Follow Me with all your heart.
I will use you for My glory.
But Lord, how can You use me? I'm not good enough.
I know you're not. But I am more than enough.
I live inside you, so depend on Me.
Depend on Me, my beloved.

Tears leak out of my eyes when I open them. This moment right here is an answered prayer. All this time I was praying for God to show me how He wanted me to serve Him. I didn't know the answer was right in front of me.

"Aunty Amara?" Tessa's voice pulls me out of my thoughts, her head still on my shoulder. "Please, will you be my mentor?"

A lump nudges in my throat as tears blur my vision. All this time God was leading me to this moment and many more to come. The teenage girl in my vision wasn't just Tessa, but also Breonna, Kehinde, Nicole, and every other teenage girl he will send my way.

The One who loves me has done this. He has opened my eyes to see that this was never about me. God's love has fought for me and stood by me even in my stubbornness and disobedience. His love broke through my insecurities and brought me out of my comfort zone. It lifted me up and showed me the light.

I tried to follow my own way, but God knew this was the best path for me, so He kept me. He had mercy on me and brought me back here. He favored me with someone as wonderful as Ray, who I can share this vision and purpose with. All this time, I was focusing on my inadequacies instead of looking at the power of God. Of course I'll never be good enough, but God is enough for me. I refuse to go back to the bondage of believing the lies in my head. This is my purpose and I will serve God with all my heart.

"Of course, I'll be your mentor." I respond as I let the tears fall. I want to say more, but I'm too overwhelmed. The only words that graze my mind are *Thank You, Jesus.*

39

AMARA

One thing Mom and Ray have in common is their love for food, so I think they're already one step ahead in their bonding process. When Ray and I had a video call with my parents last week, we arranged to meet today, and I've been praying a lot about this meeting.

I ain't gonna lie though, last night I had a nightmare that Mom poured a bucket of water on Ray and chased him out of the house with a cutlass. I blame it on all these Nollywood movies Ray has been making me watch.

"*Ehe*, did I not tell you that her sister will steal her husband?" Dad's voice sweeps in from the living room as the dramatic music of the Nollywood movie they're watching plays in the background.

"Yes *o*. But Daddy, she will soon come back from work and catch them red-handed." Ray responds, clearly also invested in the movie.

I chuckle and shake my head as I hold out the last serving bowl for Mom to dish out the jollof rice. She tries to send me a glare, but it fails when a small smile tugs at the corners of her lips. We both burst into laughter.

"Those two might as well get their own house and watch Nollywood all day," Mom says.

"I know right. It's so good to see them bonding." I look at Mom, hoping she'll tell me what she thinks of Ray, but she avoids my gaze.

After dishing out the last bit of rice, Mom places the pot in the sink and turns on the faucet.

"Don't worry about that, Mom. I'll wash it later."

"Okay." Mom picks up a napkin and wipes her hands, but when she turns to carry the bowl of rice, I stop her. "Mom, come on. You're not gonna tell me what you think of him? You're killing me here."

Mom shrugs and clicks her fingers over her head. "God forbid. I'll never kill my own daughter."

I roll my eyes, and Mom laughs at my frustration. I pout and cross my arms against my chest. "Come on, Mom."

She looks over my shoulder at the door and then lowers her voice. "He is a very respectful man and very caring. I saw how he opened the car door for you, how he carried your suitcase into the house, and when you went out to get money, he helped me cut all the onions and his eyes did not even water once."

I smile and lean against the kitchen counter. "Mom, you need to taste his *egusi* soup. It's so delicious."

"*Ehe eh*?" Mom twists her mouth and kisses her teeth. "Sweeter than mine, *abi*?"

I laugh. "Mom, nobody's food is sweeter than yours."

"It better not be." She smiles. "*Oya*, come let us go and serve your future husband."

Wait, did she just call him my future husband? Yaaas Jesus.

When Mom leaves the kitchen, I squeal internally before breaking out into the famous "*Sekem*" dance Ray has been teaching me.

"*Adamma*, are you coming?" Mom calls out, and I stop my dance charade immediately.

"Yes, Ma, I'm coming." I grab the last bowl of fried rice and join her to set up the table.

"I told you this would happen." Ray points at the scene on the TV of a middle-aged woman walking in on a man and woman making out in the kitchen.

"Okay, that's enough." Mom seizes the remote from Dad's hand and pauses the movie. "Food is ready."

In less than a minute, we settle at the table, Mom and Dad sitting opposite Ray and me. Closing our eyes, we link hands and Dad prays over the food. Ray and Mom opt for the pounded yam and *ofe oziza* or white soup, while Dad and I go for the jollof rice and chicken—we've always had a similar strategy of starting small before going large. Ray asks Mom for her *ofe oziza* recipe and when she starts explaining it to him, my heart rejoices at how much they're getting along.

"It will be really good to meet your mother, my son." Dad says and Ray turns to him.

"Yes, Daddy. I've already told her about you all and she can't wait. Before we leave tomorrow, I can arrange a video call with my mother and even my Uncle Seun and his wife who live in Arizona."

"That will be very good," Mom says. "I would like to meet the woman who brought up a wonderful young man like you." A genuine smile flashes across Mom's face and my cheeks warm up, as if the comments are for me.

The excitement building up inside of me is so uncontainable I can't stop myself from smiling. Ray squeezes my hand under the table and when I glance at him, we smile at each other.

Half an hour later, when we finish eating, Mom and Dad move back to the living room, leaving Ray and I to clear the table. When we get to the kitchen and place the plates in the sink, Ray wraps his arms around my waist and lifts me off my feet in a hug as I suppress my squeal.

"I'm so happy they love you," I whisper when he puts me down again.

"Baby girl, when God is in something, He always makes a way."

I finally told Ray about Mom's initial dislike of Yoruba men, but now that Mom has agreed to keep an open mind, there'll be no need to worry. Whenever I think about the miracle God has worked on Mom's heart, I feel like breaking out into a dance.

Ray's hands slide to my shoulders, and he gently massages them. "You okay?"

"Yeah. Are *you* okay?" I search his eyes, and run my hands over his firm biceps.

"Yes, I am." He responds and leans closer as I inhale all the protective godly man goodness he is exuding. I still can't believe I get to call him *my man.*

"Ray?"

"Yes, my love." He tucks a strand of *Frolita* behind my ear.

"Please speak to me in Yoruba."

"*Arike.*" A smile tugs at his lips. "*Olori mi.*" He kisses my forehead. "*Ife mi.*" He kisses my nose. "*Iyawo mi.*" He kisses my lips.

I frown and tilt my head. "What does the last one mean?"

His eyes sparkle. "You'll find out soon."

My gaze drops to his mouth, and when I bite my bottom lip, he takes the hint and kisses me softly. His arms find my waist again as he pulls me close, but when I lean back against the kitchen counter, an empty pot falls off the edge and it sends a clanging sound across the whole house.

"*Ah ah*, Amarachukwu, do you want to break all my pots?" Mom shouts from the living room.

We both suppress a laugh before Ray responds. "No, Ma, we are sorry, Ma. I mean, Mommy."

When we finally stop laughing, I turn the faucet on and Ray starts washing the dishes while I dry them. I turn on some afrobeat music in the background and Ray teaches me more dance moves while stealing a kiss from me every minute.

EPILOGUE

Six Months Later

I ain't gonna lie, nothing beats a Nigerian wedding—especially when it comes to my best friend's wedding. Yeah, I know Teeyana is *technically* not Nigerian, but she knows me, so that's the end of the story.

With the experience gained from all the weddings my mom has dragged me to, I take Ray's hand and we push open the double doors into the reception room when the master of ceremony announces us.

As the song *"Sekem"* blasts through the speakers, we burst out into the routine Ray choreographed for the whole squad. This was our surprise for Teeyana and Jayden, which Ray suggested since they both love afrobeats. I still don't know how Ray taught this routine to Heather, Warryn, and I in one week, but judging from their gaping mouths and wide eyes, I can safely say that the bride and groom are pleasantly surprised.

Ray and I lead the squad into the room packed with approximately fifty people spread out in tables of five. Chandeliers hang from the ceiling and coloured lights swing from side to side, highlighting the purple and white centerpieces.

When we get to the dance floor across from Teeyana and Jayden's table, we slide across the smooth tiles and into our formations, still moving our bodies to the rhythm of the music. Ray dances beside me with the tenacity and energy of a lifelong professional. Honestly, I'm sure I look like a clown next to him compared to the mastery moves he is pulling off. He looks so good in his navy blue suit, I literally have to tear my gaze away from him to stop myself from drooling. I wave at Teeyana's parents, and also at her little brother Danny, when I dance past their table.

To complete our routine, we break into the famous Nigerian dance moves; the *shoki*, the *zanku*, the *azonto*, and then finally the famous *sekem* dance move. When we finish our routine, claps, whistles and cheers erupt from the crowd as everyone rises to their feet.

Teeyana runs across the room, holding up the brush train of her ivory mermaid reception dress. Her natural hairstyle consists of flat twists on the side, a top bun, and also a side bun held together by floral hair pins. Teeyana lunges at me and squeezes me in a tight hug before she turns to hug Ray, Heather, and Warryn.

When the crowd settles down again, we clear the dance floor as the MC announces Teeyana and Jayden's first dance. Ray holds my hand as we walk to our table. He plants a kiss on my cheek before pulling out a chair for me. My insides melt at the brush of his lips on my skin. I love how affectionate he is and I always miss his touch when he's not with me.

Heather settles across the table as we watch the couple dance to *"From This Moment"* by Shania Twain. "They're so cute." Heather places both hands on her chest. The purple floor-length bridesmaid dress looks so good on her. It goes well with her auburn hair, which is now styled in an up-do, held together by a bling floral hair pin.

"Yes, they are," I respond. "Can you believe we were there when this all started and now they're finally married?"

"I know right." Heather adjusts her bangs. "Time really flies by." She drops her gaze to her red varnished fingernails, her wrist tattoo coming into full view.

"How have you been, by the way?" I ask. "We haven't spoken much since we got our dresses. How is your business coming along?"

Heather sighs and brings her head up. "It's...a lot harder than I thought."

"Aww, really? What happened?" I lean forward, hoping she'll explain a bit more, but she shakes her head.

"I'll tell you about it some other time. Today is about Teeyana and Jayden." A smile breaks through, and I reach for her hand and squeeze it.

"Okay, but no matter what it is, remember that you have worked hard for this and God sees your efforts. It'll pay off, I'm sure." I smile at her. "Do your best and then trust God to handle the rest." I add, and she smiles back at me, her green eyes misting.

"Thank you, Amara," she responds before the MC's loud voice breaks our conversation when he announces that it's time for the bride to throw her bouquet.

Heather and I and some other girls from the crowd huddle up a few meters behind Teeyana as the DJ plays the *"Sekem" song* again. Teeyana turns her back to us and tries to imitate our dance moves. After two false alarms, Teeyana finally throws the bouquet and as it flies through the air, I follow its trajectory toward me.

When I'm confident of its direction, I launch and catch it just above Heather's head. Heather claps and hugs me, whispering congratulations before stepping away. "Thank you."

Jayden has his hands wrapped around Teeyana and both of them are cheering from their table. Then, the lights dim and then the spotlight lands on me.

Another spotlight appears and roams over the crowd before landing on Ray. I lock eyes with him—the love of my life. He winks at me before making a dramatic skip in my direction.

I don't know what the boy is up to, but I'm ready. I might have wavered before, but not anymore. I'm ready to walk through the mountains and valleys with him. I can't believe I almost lost him because of my selfishness and pride.

I now know that relationships aren't about me. I choose to love Ray every day while trusting God to keep us and transform us to be more like Him. I'm not good enough, but God is, and He'll always love me.

I used to think I needed a man who loves me the way Jayden loves Teeyana, but God has sent me a man who strives to love me like Jesus loves the church. That's all I want and that's all I need.

Ray tucks his right hand behind him as he walks toward me, a smile snagging at his lips. He trains his dark gaze on me as the crowd's hollering gets louder. When he is a few inches away, he takes my hand and drops to one knee.

My stomach somersaults and I bite my bottom lip, the answer burning the tip of my tongue before he even opens his mouth to pop the question. This girl is about to become a wife. It's officially my turn to be taken off the market. *Yaas, Jesus!!!*

THE END

A PLEA

Thank you so much for reading this book. I would be very grateful if you could please leave a review online. Reviews are very important because they help the book become more visible to others so they can be blessed by it too. Thank you again and God bless you.

GLOSSARY

Adamma- My beautiful daughter

Oko mi- It literally means "my husband" but can also be used as a term of endearment for a child

Saw it with my own koro-koro eyes- Saw it with my own eyes/ experienced it myself.

Chai- Wow

How body, nau?- How are you?

Who beauty epp, sef?- Beauty is not everything

Hmm, bros, body no fine o- Hmm, my brother I'm not fine.

Issa lie- It's a lie

O boi- My guy

***Wetin?*-** What?

***Agege* bread-** A soft but dense sweet white bread made from a rich, low-yeast dough

***Suya*-** Spicy meat skewer

***Akara*-** Black-eyed peas fritters or bean fritters

***Abeg, who soccer epp?*-** Please, how is soccer going to help me?

***Wawu*-** Wow

***Ashia*-** It means "sorry" in Cameroonian pidgin

***Abeg*-** Please

***Abi o*-** I know right

***Make we dey go*-** Let's go

***Yeye*-** Not serious

***Eyaa*-** It's like saying "aww" with a sad tone of voice

***Chukwu, daalu o*-** God, thank you

***Nna m*-** My father

***Biko, obi m*-** Please, my heart

***Chop knuckle*-** Fist bump

Ah, see me see trouble o- Come and see trouble

Ah see me this guy o- Look at this guy

Oga- Boss

Abi?- Right?

E be like say Pastor Adekunle know my story o- It seems like Pastor Adekunle knows my story

See as you don baff up- Look at how you are dressed nicely

E don do- That's enough

Oya- Come on

Hmm, na wah o- Wow

Ah ah, weti dey do this one?- What's wrong with this one?

Hia, see me this girl o. Na me she dey do shakara for?- Look at this girl o. Is she playing hard to get?

Jollof rice- Spicy rice dish made with tomatoes, vegetables and meat in a single pot.

Puff-puff- Deep fried dough balls

Okra soup- Okra vegetables mixed with oil, meat/fish and spices.

Eba- Staple West African food made from dried grated cassava flour.

Pounded yam- Staple West African food made from pounding and kneading of boiled yams. Although the same texture can be gotten by mixing yam flour with boiled water.

Gbas gbos- In context in which it's used, it means the food is delicious

I no dey there- I'm not involved

Omoge- A slang used to refer to a pretty lady/woman

Chai, this girl go make me catch cold o- This girl will make me catch a cold / turn me into a lover boy

Jesu ese oh- Thank You Jesus

E ma binu- Don't be angry

This girl wey don make you kolo- This girl has made you crazy in love

This your babe na fire o- This your girl is very beautiful and friendly

Americanah- Someone who has been to the U.S

Ah ah, before nko?- Why not?

Wahala- Trouble

O boi, wet day worry you?- What is wrong with you?

Kampe- Well/healthy/strong

Nwanyi oma- Beautiful woman

Omalicha- Beauty

Chineke dalu- Thank you Lord

Oluwa e se- Thank you Lord

Ah egbami o- Rescue me

Oha soup- Traditional soup native to southeastern Nigeria made from ora leaves

Ugwu leaves- Pumpkin leaves

Oyinbo- Nigerian slang generally used to refer to Caucasians.

Loruko Jesu. Amin o- In the name of Jesus. Amen.

Who roses epp, sef?- How will roses help?

Arewa- Beautiful

Ommugwo-An Igbo which refers to the time after birth where a nursing mother and her baby is being taken care of by a close family member.

Eforiro soup- Traditional Yoruba soup made with vegetables, stock fish, palm oil, meat and other ingredients.

Ofe oziza- Traditional Igbo soup made with uziza leaves

Yoruba demon- A slang typically used for a young man of Yoruba descent who is a smooth talker, and who can make ladies fall for him easily. The slang initially started as a social media joke but is now widely used as an ethnic slur or insult.

E kaaro- Good morning

Mba- No

Nne- Mother

Olori mi- My queen

Ife mi- My love

Iyawo mi- My wife

AUTHOR'S NOTE

The inspiration for this story came to me in the summer of 2020. I was scrolling through Amazon and reading sample chapters of a recently released contemporary romance novel written by a fellow Nigerian author. The cover of the book was absolutely stunning, and the blurb was very interesting, so I decided to check it out. Unfortunately, after reading the sample chapters, I was disappointed with the direction the story was going in and how relationships were portrayed in it. So I wondered what it would be like to write a story following two people who learn about the true foundation of a Christ-centered relationship.

During the last two weeks of October 2020, I outlined the entire novel and when National Novel Writing Month (NaNoWriMo) came around; I was ready to start drafting. I cranked out 50,000 words of the first draft in November 2020 and finally finished the first draft in January 2021. While drafting, the words came to me so easily and I learnt a lot about the characters, their past hurts and how their experiences narrowed their view of the world.

One of my love languages is words of affirmation and I love encouraging others the same way I love to be encouraged. In this book, I wanted to highlight the power and effect that words can have over someone. We saw this in Amara's character arc and how she constantly battled the dark voice in her head, which was essentially the voice of her high school bully—Olivia Hastings.

For many years, Amara let those words make a home in her thoughts and then they took over her life and made her doubt her God-given abilities. I hope this story encourages you to be kind to others because the Bible says in Proverbs 15:4 that *kind words are like honey–sweet to the soul and healthy for the body.* Our words are powerful and we never know how much they can make or break someone. Kindness is a choice, so please, **always choose kind words.**

Just like the first book in the series where Teeyana learnt she wasn't self-sufficient and needed God to achieve her goals, I wanted to tackle a similar idea in this book by focusing on Amara's insecurities. We all have insecurities and God knows about all of them. But what the enemy loves to do is point out those insecurities and try to make us believe God won't use us because we are flawed. That is very far from the truth because contrary to what the world tries to preach to us, our security and confidence will never come from looking within ourselves.

The whole point of the gospel and us needing a Saviour is to show us that **we are not enough.** On our own, we will never be enough and that's why **we need Jesus** because He is more than enough for us. So when the devil tries to use your inadequacies against you, I pray you won't let it weigh you down, but that you'll always turn to God, depend on Him, and let Him show you He is the one empowering you every day to live the life He has called you to live.

Another thing I'd like to say is that contrary to what our society teaches us, **singleness is not a curse** and being single doesn't always mean you are under bondage. Being married and having children has never been a requirement to enter the kingdom of God. They are not measures of spiritual prosperity and if they were, then our Lord Jesus Christ—who lived a perfect and fulfilling life—would have gotten married and had children. Of course this is not to say that one shouldn't get married because I believe marriage is a blessing and if it is your desire, then I pray that God grants you that desire according to His will.

But as the church (the body of Christ), we need to be encouraged to move away from the toxic culture of bashing singles and making them believe they have a problem. Instead of making young men and women become so desperate that they settle for less and make wrong choices, we should instead channel our energy into encouraging each other to walk in the purpose God has called us into. Seeking God and doing His will should be our goal as Christ Himself is our reward—not a wife or husband, not a child, not money, and not even cars or houses. Christ alone is our reward and when we seek Him first, then all other things we need will be added unto us.

The foundation of the gospel is love and the Bible teaches us about unity within the body of Christ—a kind of unity which traverses skin colour, age, gender, countries, languages and ethnic groups. The only requirement we see in the Bible for a Godly marriage is that both spouses should love the LORD. But unfortunately, past experiences have clouded our judgement and caused hatred to be passed down many generations. We are all children of God, part of the same body and we have been called to follow Christ's example to love each other (John 15:12-13). Tribalism is certainly not a way to show love to our brothers and sisters. As Amara put it fairly, our actions are not because of our tribe, our actions are products of the state of our hearts. So my plea is that we encourage each other to get our priorities straight and to pray for one another, so that our hearts will learn to love and live at peace with each other, no matter what tribe or country we come from.

I had a lot of fun writing Ray's character and even though he was inspired by a very special person in my life, Ray's character is still entirely fictional. I loved writing about his quirks, his dance moves, his caring, loving nature, and how he could get back up after facing rejection. I wanted to depict resilience in his character and show that sometimes storms don't come to shake us, but to clear our path and make way for what God has prepared for us. I hope that Ray's story inspired you to stay hopeful amid rejection and failure because God is always working for us–even when it hurts.

The central Bible verse for this book was inspired by Amara and Raymond's faith journeys. Sometimes we know what the right thing to do is, but still disobey God by holding on to our own desires and wishes. We saw this with Amara's list ranking, even though she knew she had to go to God first. We also saw this when Ray held on to his goal of being married before turning thirty, even though he knew he had to wait for God's timing.

Their stories show us that even when we are unfaithful, God will always remain faithful. He died for us while we were still sinners, which was a magnificent way for Him to show His love for us. I pray that just as God revealed His loving character to

Ray and Amara, He will reveal Himself to you too and you will never, for a second, doubt God's sovereign love for you.

Finally, if you're reading this and you're yet to surrender your life to Jesus Christ as your Lord and Saviour, here's an open invitation to do so today. It is not too late. The Lord's open arms are waiting, and He is calling you to come home. There's no pain He can't heal. Jesus has already paid the price for you. He wants you to abandon your pride today and run to Him. He has loved you from the beginning of time and He always will. If you want to take that bold step today, please say this prayer with me;

Dear Jesus, I come before you today with thanksgiving in my heart. I accept that you are God and I am not. I am a sinner, but You alone are the Forgiver of sins. Please come into my heart today. I surrender my all to you as my Lord and Saviour. Make me clean and teach me how to love and obey you. In Jesus' name I've prayed. Amen.

If you've prayed this prayer of faith and are willing to walk into your new life with Jesus, congratulations. Welcome to God's family. Please get plugged into a local church if you haven't already done so. Commit to studying the Bible with fellow believers and find a spiritual mentor you trust who will help you along the journey. If you would like to share a testimony with me, please reach out to me on social media or using the contact form found on my website: www.joanembola.co.uk.

Until the next book,
    Lots of love,
    Joan.

BOOK THREE

IS GOD SOVEREIGN OVER MISTAKES AND FAILURES?

Heather Osborne's past consisted of partying, drugs, and thriving on the attention of men...until her cycle of pain and rejection brought her to the feet of Jesus. For four years, she has been struggling to shake off her demons, and when her business fails, she returns home to start a marketing internship. But Heather gets more than she bargained for when she is assigned to work with the handsome son of the CEO.

Emmanuel Madu, the managing director of Madu Health, is not sold on his father's plan for him to take over the family business. When he is coerced to supervise the new marketing intern, he accepts it for fear of disappointing his father. But when the red-haired, green-eyed intern walks into his life and challenges his cowardice, their budding friendship forces Emmanuel to reassess his values and convictions.

When Heather starts developing feelings for Emmanuel, she finds herself torn between returning to her old habits and fighting to embrace her new life of faith in God. And with time running out for Emmanuel, he must decide whether to continue living in his father's shadow or break up his family by walking away.

The One Who Sees Me, book three in the Sovereign Love series, is an uplifting standalone novel about forgiveness and learning to take comfort in the sovereign goodness of a loving God who sees all our struggles.

Coming June 6th 2023
Preorder here

FREE SHORT STORY

Subscribe to my free monthly newsletter to stay up to date with book news and to also get a free short story called *A Promise To Keep*, which follows a Nigerian couple —Dayo and Dara as they navigate the challenges of life while learning about endurance and what it means to experience the goodness of God.

ACKNOWLEDGMENTS

Drafting this book was easy but editing it was very hard for me and I would never have done it without my Heavenly Father. Thank You Lord for Your inspiration and for helping me finish this story. It was all You and I'll forever be grateful.

To my parents and brothers, thank you for always believing in me, trusting the abilities God has given me and supporting me all the way. I have so much love for you all.

To my love and biggest supporter, Oladunni. I have the confidence to write love stories because of the love you show me every day. Thank you for always being there for me and never letting me give up. Even when you don't fully understand what my 'writer's brain' is thinking, you always listen to my jumbled thoughts and cheer me on. I appreciate and love you so much.

To my spiritual mentors, Michael Okubote and his wife Tolu Okubote. Thank you for constantly encouraging me and holding me up when I've felt like giving up. I appreciate you.

To my beta readers, Olayide, Tope, Nicole and Toyin. I remember how scared I was to share this story. But you gave me amazing feedback which made the story so much better. Thank you for your tremendous help.

To my editor, Michaela Bush, thank you so much for your patience and your incredibly good eye for detail. This story wouldn't be where it is today without you. Thank you Abigayle Claire for helping me polish the blurb.

To my cover designer, Elle Maxwell, you know how much I loved the first cover. This one is even more beautiful. Thank you for using your incredible talent to bring my vision to life.

To all my author and bookish friends who have helped me on this journey. Thank you for your constant encouragement. I appreciate you.

To you reading this book, thank you for giving it a chance. I hope it has brought you hope and reminded you of the Father's sovereign love for you.

Finally, I'll have to go back to my Heavenly Father—the One who loves me. My Lord, I started this journey with You and I'm finishing it with You. To You be all the glory, honour and praise forever and ever. Amen.

ABOUT THE AUTHOR

 Joan Embola is a UK-based Cameroonian-Nigerian Christian author who aims to share God's love one word at a time. She writes books about diverse characters whose hope-filled stories point to the love and goodness of God in our broken world. She is a qualified Physician Associate and also the founder of Love Qualified, a ministry dedicated to encouraging others to experience the sovereign love of the one true God who has qualified us to be His beloved ones. She is a passionate lover and teacher of God's Word, as shared on her YouTube channel, blog, and podcast. When she's not writing or curled up with a book, you'll find her watching movies, YouTube videos, or making memories with her family and friends.

You can connect with her at www.joanembola.co.uk and on Instagram, YouTube and her podcast. Subscribe to her newsletter to stay up to date with book news, cover reveals, how to sign up for advanced reader copies, and fun giveaways. You will also get access to free books, short stories, deleted scenes from her published books and free writer resources.

DISCUSSION QUESTIONS

1. At the start of the book, Amara was in a place where she was constantly reminded of hurtful words from her past. How did she respond in this situation? Did this response help or harm her? Have you ever found yourself in a situation where you let other people's words cause you to doubt God's love for you?

2. Describe the relationships between Amara and Teeyana. How did Teeyana support Amara throughout the book and did this help Amara get to where she needed to be?

3. Describe the relationship between Amara and her parents. What role did they both play in Amara's life and what kind of influence did they have on her faith journey?

4. At the start of the book, Raymond faced repeated rejection. How did he respond after Kate dumped him? Did his response help or harm him? Have you ever found yourself in a situation where you let rejection cause you to doubt God's love for you?

5. Describe the relationship between Raymond and his mom, and also Raymond and Joe. In what ways did they support him and what kind of influence did they have on his faith journey?

6. Describe the relationship between Amara and Raymond. Did they have a good foundation for their friendship and how did their bond grow stronger over time?

7. Which characters acted as mentors in Raymond's life and how did they help him on his faith journey?

8. What lesson did Amara and Raymond have to learn to get to where God needed them to be?

9. What do you think are the important foundations of a Christ-centered relationship/ friendship?

10. Does the title of the book make sense to you? Do you get the overall theme that the author was trying to portray?

Printed in Poland
by Amazon Fulfillment
Poland Sp. z o.o., Wrocław

24659574R00197